Chapter 1.

Hi. My name is Sam Winter. I'm a part-time author, and when I'm not writing, I can be found working in the second-hand bookshop that is the family business. We're located on the south side of Mendocino, California.

OK, this is my story; every word of it is true. His name was Tomislav Petrović. We had been pen pals for a few years. He lived in Croatia in the former Yugoslavia, and had invited me out for a short vacation. He had just started teaching at a local university when we met in person.

One day while out sightseeing, we thought we'd drop into a small restaurant to have a refreshment. We sat at a table outside close to the street. Tom leaned across the table and whispered in my ear. He had overheard a conversation from the next table where a group of six men were discussing a proposed bank robbery. He said large sums of money were involved. As the group got up and began to disperse, one of them dropped a sheet of paper from his pocket. I guess the brisk breeze caught it, but the guy appeared unaware that he had lost it. I managed to trap it with my foot as it was about to pass my seat. I picked it up and handed it to Tom.

It was a detailed account of what they intended to do and the plan of a bank building with exit points and security cameras plus the position of the main safe. We decided to take our evidence to the police, and as a result, foiled a bank robbery. Arrests were made and we were called as witnesses later, so I had a slightly longer vacation than I had originally planned. No matter, it was nice to be spending it with Tom. He was on vacation too, this being the summer and the schools closed.

I wasn't really much of a witness as I had been sitting with my back to the gang and therefore couldn't identify any of them. Only Tom could do that as he saw some of their faces. I was the one who picked up the incriminating evidence and brought it to Tom's attention. As a result of the arrests and the trial, Tom began to receive threatening phone calls and from then on we had to be on our guard. We had to be careful where we went during the day; only parked the car in main streets with plenty of people about and not go out at night. I felt sorry for him as he was now saddled with the threat of retaliation hanging over his head, and I felt guilty and that it was my fault that he was in this position.

It was just two days before I was due to fly home to California. Tom had been having trouble with his car and he fancied himself as a DIY car mechanic. Some of his 'projects' or 'inventions' didn't always turn out as expected, like the car alarm system that he fitted himself went off in the middle of the night without anyone being near it, and wakening some of the neighbourhood in the process.

He been tinkering with the electrics and as a result, caused something to malfunction. He said it was just a blown fuse, and that he would have to get another one. To do this, we took a bus ride to the nearest town and did some shopping around until we found a replacement.

The following night, he fitted the new fuse in place. Now we were ready to go. We'd take off down the Magistrala – the coastal road on the Adriatic and find some of those hidden coves and go for a swim, then we'd find a secluded spot and just chill out.

In the morning, we put a packed lunch together; ham sandwiches and a bottle of wine. It was after I had settled myself in the passenger seat that I saw it; a blue insulated wire hanging from under the steering column. I didn't remember seeing it the last time we were here. I had a bad feeling about this. Maybe I've been watching too many movies, but I'm suspicious. 'Tom, that wire? It wasn't there before.' I pointed to it.

He ignored me and said, 'Come on Sam. Let's go.' His hand went to the ignition key.

I shouted, 'No! Don't touch that!'

'What the hell's wrong with you all of a sudden!' he yelled back.

He was just about to turn it, when I put my hand on the door handle preparing to open it. *I'll jump if I have to,'* I thought quickly.

He turned the ignition key to the first auxiliary position, and that's when I opened the door and threw myself out of the car, and immediately went into a roll, but I wasn't quite quick enough. The force of the explosion slammed me into something solid and that's all I remember.

I awoke in a hospital bed with multiple fractures; broken left arm and two fingers on the same hand; right leg below the knee, and two fractured ribs. I was in a coma for about a week, and spent two weeks in hospital altogether. I was taken by air ambulance to New York, then transferred to hospital in San Francisco. After a short spell there, mom took me home to Mendocino. I learned later that Tom had been trapped in the burning car. It took me a long time to get over the shock of it all, and the police never did discover who had planted the bomb.

I could only manage light tasks in the shop, but I made out OK. A lot of time was spent in the wheelchair at my desk on the laptop, working on my latest story, and typing with one hand.

Well that was three years ago now. I've just turned 21 and have no current boyfriend.

One night I got a call from my girlfriend Josie Moore. She's 18 and about my height. I've known her for about three years. I was lying in bed on my front, unable to sleep for some reason, when my cellphone went off sounding its musical tone. I grabbed it and stabbed at the answer button. 'Yeah?'

'Hi Sam. It's me Josie.' She sounded bright for this time of night.

'You in bed too, or are you at some nightclub?'

'No, I'm at home. Listen Sam. Just got some great news tonight,' she said excitedly.

'It's late Josie....' I trailed off with a sigh.

'Yeah I know, but I just have to tell you this. I've just been given a couple of return airline tickets to Croatia for my 18th birthday. How does that sound?'

'It sounds great Josie but....'

She cut me off with, 'I'd like you to come along Sam. My mom asked me to ask you to come along because you've been there before.'

I hesitated before answering her. 'Josie.....' I trailed off not knowing what to say to her. She doesn't know about my brush with death in Tomislav's car, but I did tell her before about the planned bank robbery being foiled.

'Look, you'd love it. Just the two of us. Hire a car and just take off. What do you say?'

'Couldn't you find somebody else?' I'm looking at my watch. It read one o'clock.

'No.... all my mates are too young to hire a car, and, well you can and you've been there too. We wouldn't get lost.' She giggled.

That's what I thought of telling her; to 'get lost', then, 'OK Josie, you've twisted my arm.'

I heard loud squeals from her. 'Thank you Sam.' She hesitated. 'What about accommodation?'

'We don't have to book anything; just turn up and leave again when we want to. Just look for the sign marked 'zimmer' and we should be OK for a place to stay.' It was my turn to hesitate. 'Em.... when do we leave Josie?'

'Saturday. New York then London, England, then Pula.'

I was silent for a few seconds as this brought back visions of meeting Tomislav, then of him dying in the explosion. Do I really want to go back there after what happened the last time? I said finally, 'OK Josie, but I'll have to speak to mom and dad first. The shop, you know?'

'Yeah I know. Can you see them right away? Tomorrow I mean?'

'Sure Josie. That's not a problem.' Actually it could be a problem if they couldn't find someone to cover for me in the shop. It was usually OK though. They'd find somebody. What I do there isn't exactly rocket science; like a library with a sales department?

So, that Saturday, we were off; backpacks on our backs and looking forward to our trip. As it turned out, Josie's parents had conspired with mom and dad and had plotted this one together. I only discovered this when I asked mom about Josie's proposed trip. Josie had wanted to go on a backpacking trip to Europe, but her parents didn't want her to go there on her own, as none of her friends could drive. It would mean hitching and that wasn't really an option, at least not a sensible one. Well that left only me, as I could drive, and now at 21, was eligible to hire a car too, and had been to Europe before. I had the experience after all.

I had originally planned on a trip to Italy when I turned 21, as I would now be eligible to rent a car as I mentioned earlier, and so I studied Italian. I speak it quite fluently now. I have a neighbour in Mendocino who's Italian, so I've had plenty of practice. Then I had to resit my driving test in a manual shift to enable me to drive in Europe. So I've been a busy girl over the past few years.

We arrived at Pula around 9 o'clock in the morning. I wore my brown shoulder-length hair in its usual ponytail; my white low-cut jeans that hang just below my hips and show off my California tan and my navel. Then, about three inches above the bellybutton, my white cropped top and a lot of cleavage. Josie, her long blond hair in a ponytail too. She wore cream-coloured low-cut jeans and light-blue cropped top. She had a small gold chain in her navel – ouch – and a small artificial diamond hanging there. On her back, a small Celtic knot tattoo about three inches across just above her waist. This is how we entered the office of the Avis Car Rental. We came away with a gorgeous ruby-coloured Renault Clio Sports convertible. I'm the driver here, or at least, the legal driver. As we drove out of the airport complex, the rain came pelting down on us. It bounced off the road surface and ran along the gutters. Yep, the top was still down! Trust us to hire a convertible.

We thought it was about time we found ourselves accommodation for the night, so one of the first places that we hit was Rijeka; a coastal town. Having found the Tourist Information Office, we were given the address of a house situated on a hill and close to the harbour.

Almost all of the buildings that we had seen so far in this country, were made of the local grey-white stone and had orange-red tiled roofs. This one that we were going to stay at was no exception. Houses around here were all built in a similar style; individual dwellings joined together, with some taller than their neighbours. It reminded me of pictures I had seen of Italy when I was planning my vacation to that country about a year ago.

We were able to find the street without too much difficulty and parked the car directly in front of the house in the street. The door was opened by a large elderly woman with a big smile, and dressed in a black skirt and dark blue cardigan. She wore her grey hair pulled back into a bun and fastened with a hair net. After a brief exchange of introductions, she invited us inside.

Anna and Gregori Kovačević were both Italian speakers. That was fine with me, but poor Josie would feel out of things not being able to understand anything.

We sat around a table in the family room that was a little too cluttered for my taste. A pile of newspapers stacked on an upright chair in one corner; the family washing still lying in a basket on the floor next the TV; an old-fashioned record player on a coffee table opposite one of the two windows in the room. These homes are not really designed for B&B accommodation. You are offered a bed for the night, but you have to find your own breakfast in the morning. That's not a problem for us though.

Gregori was grey haired and older than his wife and was balding on top. He wore a blue and white cardigan and black pants. Every now and then he would light up a pipe that appeared to require lighting periodically.

I sat between Gregori on my right and Josie.

'Ha assaggiato caffè turco?' *'Have you tasted Turkish coffee?'* Gregori asked Josie in Italian.

Josie shrugged.

'Josie non parla italiano.' *'Josie doesn't speak Italian,'* I said. I asked her if she had tasted it. No, was the reply. I relayed this to Gregori. I said I hadn't either.

Anna placed two white mugs in front of us and Gregori poured the coffee from what looked to me like a teapot with a spout on the side rather than at one end.

Josie grinned at me. 'Do we drink it sideways too?' She giggled.

'It wouldn't look out of place at the Mad Hatter's Tea Party though. The teapot I mean,' I laughed.

'Do you think there's a dormouse in there?' She laughed. I did too.

Gregori wondered what we were laughing at. I told him.

'Ah. Io ho letto quell'uno. È una storia molto divertente.' *'Ah. I have read that one. It's a very amusing story.'*

Anna told us to help ourselves to the sugar. Gregori said that Turkish coffee had lots of sugar in there and it was drunk black.

Josie and I put in our sugars and stirred vigorously. I tasted it. I liked it.

'Good huh?' I asked.

She nodded.

'Dove viene da?' *'Where do you come from?'* Anna asked Josie, since she sat nearest to her.

Josie just grinned and shrugged.

I said, 'Noi siamo ambo della California. Una piccola città chiamata Mendocino.' *'We're both from California. It's a small town called Mendocino.'*

Gregori said, 'È un luogo in Italia anche. Probabilmente da dove viene il nome.' *'It's a place in Italy too. Probably where the name comes from.'*

And so the conversation went. We learned a lot from these nice people, but we were grateful to get to our room at last and sleep.

Our room had a balcony with a flower box, but I couldn't see what colour the flowers were due to the dark. The shuttered windows were closed, but I had opened the door to allow some air in as we were feeling too hot in here.

Josie sat on the edge of the bed as she undressed; her bare feet on the varnished wood flooring. I joined her there and removed my sneakers and socks.

She said, 'I've never shared a bed before. How about you?'

I shook my head. 'No, I haven't either,' I said pulling on my nightie.

Josie crossed to the sink on the wall opposite our bed and began washing herself. I meantime, was sitting on the edge of the bed looking in my backpack for my soap and toothpaste, when I spotted out of the corner of my eye, something moving along the skirting board towards our bed, but before I could turn and get a better look at it, something flew in through the door from the balcony. It made a loud buzzing sound unlike any bee I had ever heard.

Josie heard it too and ducked as it flew directly over her head. 'What the hell was that?' she asked.

'God knows,' I said as I watched it fly around the main light. Then, horror of horrors, it landed on my lap. I screamed a short scream, then, 'Get it off me!' I don't like bugs on me.

Josie was in the process of drying her hands on a towel, when the bug landed on me. By the time she had finished, it had taken flight again and resumed its tour around the light.

I said, as I kept an eye on it, 'I have an idea.' I turned on the bedside lamp. I said to Josie, 'Put out the main light. Might be able to attract it to this one.'

She put out the light and came back to the bed and sat between me and the bedside lamp. The bug lost interest in the main light now and focussed its attention on this new light source. It buzzed around the lamp and even disappeared under the shade for a while.

'What is it Josie?'

'Don't know yet, but if it lands some place, I could catch it and put it outside.'

Eventually it appeared from under the shade and flew around it a few times before dropping on my pillow with a plopping sound. It was a beetle of the most gorgeous colour of iridescent green that I have ever seen. It had folded its wings across its back and seemed as though it had settled in for the night.

I thought determinedly, *Not on my pillow you don't.*

Josie grinned at me. 'Seems to like your pillow Sam.'

I said, 'Well he can find a sleeping partner some place else. Get it out of here Josie.'

She cupped her hands over the critter and carried it to the door then let it go. It flew into the night to find one of its own kind. She closed the door then returned to the bed and sat beside me again.

I said, 'Well that's enough excitement for one night.'

I had no sooner uttered those words, when Josie asked, 'Did you touch my foot.....?'

'No...' I looked down at our feet.

Josie had an ant on her bare foot.

'Ah! That's sore!' she cried. 'Something's just bit me on the foot.'

I screamed again. 'Josie, there are ants in here.' I climbed on the bed to escape from them.

She said hurriedly, 'Look, there are hundreds of them down there.' She pointed down at the skirting board. A long string of black ants was making its way towards us, then they seemed to disappear out of sight. Josie got down on her knees and looked under the bed. 'They're going into the wall. There must be a nest in there Sam.'

'Well as long as they stay in there and don't come out and…. ah! I don't even want to think about it,' I said as I got under the bedclothes.

Josie followed and lay on my left. I turned out the light and that's all I remember till the morning light came streaming in through the shutters.

We packed up our things and went down to the car to stow our packs away in the trunk. That done, we returned to the house to say our goodbyes. Anna and Gregori came out to see us off. Whilst we hugged one another, Anna said we'd be welcome back any time to their house. If we were back in Rijeka at the end of our vacation, they would like to see us again. We went back to the car and waved goodbye to them as we drove off.

First stop was a café to find our breakfast. We sat at a table outside in the warm sun waiting on someone to come and take our order.

Josie said, 'God, I'm starved.'

'Yeah me too. Not sure what they serve up for breakfast in this country. I stayed with Tomislav in his house and just ate what he ate.'

'So what was he like? What did you two get up to?' She was grinning.

'Nothing much. We went out a lot visiting a lot of the sights, then….' I was interrupted by the waitress arriving at our table. She had brought a menu with her which she handed to Josie, since she already had her hand out to take it. The waitress departed again.

Josie breathed a big sigh of contentment before she said, 'Choices, choices. You just wouldn't believe what stuff they have here. Whoa, is that fattening or what?'

I said, 'You'd better watch that figure girl or you might end up regretting it.'

All I could see were those gorgeous blue eyes looking at me over the top of the menu. She said, 'Pardon?'

'Your figure. You don't want to spoil it do you?'

She smiled. 'I don't have to worry about it.' Those blue eyes were still watching me.

'Maybe not now, but later on you might put it on,' I said. 'So what are you having?'

'Hmm. I think I'll settle for a cheese omelette.' She nodded and handed me the menu.

Before I could make up my mind, the waitress had arrived back at our table.

I said quickly, 'Cheese omelette twice and coffee please.'

Josie grinned across at me, 'Copycat.'

The waitress went off to fetch the food.

We must have been at least an hour in there, but I had fully satisfied my appetite and I'm sure Josie had too.

We had only been on the road again for about ten minutes, when I spotted a police patrol car parked on the right. A policeman stepped out from behind a small parked van and waved his arms in the air. This was a signal for us to stop. I pulled up alongside him.

He said in English, 'Can you step out of the car Miss please?'

I just stared at him, then at Josie who stared back at me.

'Sure.' I got out. Why were we being stopped? Was I speeding? No, I was within the 50 kph speed limit so it couldn't be that.

He said, 'Passports?'

I said, indicating the rear of the car with my thumb, 'They're in the trunk in our packs.'

He nodded.

We went to the trunk and I had to do some rummaging around in there to find it. Josie came to join me. She got her own out without too much trouble and handed it to the policeman. I handed mine over too.

He took them and studied us both before saying, 'On holiday here?'

We both nodded. I noticed Josie's face was flushed and she had a worried look.

He started searching our packs now. Mine first. Almost everything came out including my underwear and bikini and my camera gear. He went into everything. His hand touched a small box that he removed and opened. It was the perfume that mom had given me in a little bottle. He smiled and nodded when he smelled it, then he resumed his searching.

'What the hell's he looking for?' I wondered.

After another minute of searching he said I could put it back, then he moved onto Josie's pack. This time he told her to remove the items herself. As she pulled out her garments and personal things, she looked at me with that worried look again. I wondered what was wrong with her. Satisfied that we didn't pose a terrorist threat to the Republic of Croatia, we were allowed to put everything back in our packs and close the trunk.

'You may proceed on your way,' he said standing back for me to get into the car.

Back in the driving seat I asked out of curiosity, 'What were you looking for?' I heard Josie come in and close the door.

'Some people are using this route south for transporting drugs. We have to spot check vehicles. Enjoy your stay.' He saluted us and I thanked him.

'Have a nice day.' I don't know why I said that. I guess it was just something to say in the heat of the moment. He returned to his car.

Josie said as she fastened her belt, 'Well, was that scary or what?'

I fastened mine too as I said, 'Yeah. I thought.... oh I don't know what I thought. You hear of police in some countries planting drugs on unsuspecting travellers and they end up being charged with carrying illegal substances.' I started the car and we moved off once again.

Some time passed and we were on our way to the Adriatic proper, cruising down the Magistrala, the main route south. Josie pointed out a viewpoint on the right. We could stop here and take some photos she said, so we did. I got out my camera from my pack and so did she. Mine was an SLR complete with a selection of lenses and gadgets. Josie's was a simpler model.

As she stood with her back to me photographing something out towards the ocean, I snapped her back view. I wanted to take that cute little tattoo there.

She turned her head to me briefly with a smile and asked, 'What did you take?'

'Oh, nothing, just….' I deliberately didn't finish the sentence.

She turned to me now and leaned on the safety rail at her back. This was a signal for me to take her picture. She looked gorgeous standing there in her cream-coloured, low-cut jeans that hung just below her hips, and a white t-shirt that stopped just short of her bellybutton where her California tan was on show. Her blue eyes sparkled as did the diamond in her navel, and she brushed several strands of her beautiful blond hair from her eyes. She just stood there with that cute little smile on her lips, her two hands now in her back pockets and her legs crossed. She was every guy's dream girlfriend to die for. I snapped her, then I took several more. I crossed to her and stood in the same spot where she snapped me.

A car pulled up now and the male driver got out. He appeared to be on his own. Another visitor I think. He was, probably, twenty-something and wore a white and green striped shirt and white pants. He was intent on photographing the Adriatic too.

Josie was standing off to my right. She pointed to her camera, then to the guy at the rail. She pointed to herself and then to me. She wanted him to take us two together.

I nodded with a grin.

She approached him standing there. 'Excuse me? Could you take us together please?'

He had to agree. What guy could resist those blue eyes and that cute smile. He took her camera from her and the two of us stood back against the rail, our cutest smiles plastered on. I flicked a few strands of hair from my eyes as did she. He snapped us, then he took another one, this time holding the camera vertically.

'That was nice of him,' I thought smiling at him.

Josie, with cute smile still fixed in place, took the camera from him and, in a real sexy voice that was almost a whisper, she said, 'Thank you.'

He blushed a little and took several steps back, almost colliding with his own car. He said quickly, 'You're welcome.' He got back in and drove off heading south.

We grinned at one another and got back in the car.

We were passing through a quaint little village when Josie shouted, 'Look Sam. A castle!'

I brought the car to a sudden halt and looked to where she was pointing. There, up on a hill on the left not far from the road, and standing alongside other stone buildings, was a neat castle. It was built of the local stone – limestone I think, and mostly in ruin, at least the part that we could see from the road.

'Cool,' I said as I turned to her. 'We have to move Josie if we want to find our accommodation today, and it could take a while.'

'Pity,' she sighed. 'Hey, we could come back here tomorrow couldn't we?'

'Sure.' I nodded and we moved off again.

We found our accommodation off the right-hand side of the road after having passed through at least three road tunnels. It was an open-air café situated some distance from the road. I stopped outside on the road.

'Looks like a cool place Josie,' I said as I jumped out of the driving seat.

'Yep, sure does.'

I was thinking I'd found a place at last, but unfortunately they didn't have any vacancies. Back in the car I said, 'No vacancies.'

She shrugged.

About five minutes later, I pulled the car into the forecourt of another outdoor café, this time on the left. The sign, printed in German said there were rooms here. I understand a little German. I didn't see what the name of the place was because a large truck was partially blocking it. I could just make out the letter 'S'.

We went into the building and approached the reception just inside the door. A middle-aged guy in a red chequered shirt sat behind the desk.

I asked, 'Haben Sie zu Mietfrist einen Zimmer für zwei Leute?' *Do you have a room to let for two people?'* I'm hoping this is correct. It was.

'Ja.'

'Nur eine Nacht bitte.' *'One night only please.'*

He took a key from a hook and placed it on the counter top. Before I could pick it up, he had snatched it up himself.

I shrugged. *'Yeah. Whatever,'* I thought. I turned to Josie who was standing behind me.

She said in a whisper, 'Think it's for truckers.' She was referring to the café.

The guy said, as he came around the counter, 'Folgen Sie mir.' *Follow me.'* He led us out of the front door and round the side of the building, then it was up a flight of concrete steps. When he had reached the top he opened a door and we stepped inside. We walked along a short corridor and stopped just outside a door marked '2'.

'Dieser ist für Sie.' *'This one is for you,'* he said as he put the key into the lock.

We both nodded smiling. I don't know why Josie nodded; she doesn't understand German.

He opened the door and handed me the key.

Indicating a rather dirty-looking nylon curtain in the corner on the right, he said, 'Dusche in dort.' *'Shower in there.'*

'Sprechen Sie Italienisch? Es ist für mich leichter.' *'Do you speak Italian? It's easier for me,'* I said.

'Sì.' *'Yes,'* he said. He indicated the shower curtain again. 'Il lavandino è in qui anche.' *'The sink is in here too.'*

I nodded then turned to Josie. She just shrugged. She didn't understand.

The guy said, 'Se Lei vuole una doccia, c'è acqua calda disponibile.' *'If you want a shower, there is hot water available.'* He added, 'Ragazze, goda.' *'Girls, enjoy.'*

'Grazie.' *'Thanks,'* I said.

He left the room and we just stood there smiling at one another.

Josie said, 'So what did he say?'

'Said there's hot water for the shower if we want it.'

'OK,' she said quickly as she pulled off her top. 'I'm first.' She disappeared behind the curtain and pulled it closed.

I went to the window and opened the door that led onto the balcony. It was very warm out here with the concrete flooring, in fact it was baking hot. My watch records the temperature too. It read 102 degrees!

There were two sun loungers here. I had only just sat on the nearest one when I heard the screams. I ran back to the shower curtain. 'Josie? You OK?'

More screams.

I pulled the curtain open. Josie stood there in her birthday suit with her back to me, and trying to protect herself from the water pouring down in a solid lump from the shower head. It splashed out in all directions as it hit the floor. Where had the spray head gone? Then I saw it lying on the floor under the torrent. I laughed, in fact I couldn't stop.

She said annoyed, 'Don't just stand there Sam; do something! It's freezing!'

'Try turning on the hot.' I laughed again.

'There's no hot regulator.'

I said stepping inside, 'Sure there is. Just turn the regulator the other way.' I didn't want to get soaked myself so I made sure I didn't get too close to the water.

She was just about to reach out and adjust the water, when I noticed steam rising from the torrent. She did too and screamed again as she felt the water touch her feet.

I shouted, 'Look out Josie! It's hot!' I grasped her quickly around the waist and pulled her away from the water.

She said in exasperation, 'What's wrong with it?'

'It's an old system. Nowadays the shower would be electric,' I said with a sigh, then stepped outside the curtain.

I heard her say, 'Where.... where's the towel Sam?'

I looked around the room. There didn't appear to be any. 'None out here.'

'I never heard of a motel that didn't provide you with towels.'

'This isn't a motel Josie.' I laughed.

'Yeah, whatever.' She put her head through the curtain and framed her head with it. With a wide grin on her face she said, 'Think you could find me a towel Sam? Oh, and get us something cold to drink too?'

'Sure. I'll complain about the water and the state of the shower too. Have fun.' I laughed as I made for the door, then disappeared outside.

As I closed it I heard her say half to herself, 'I know how to warm up, and dry off at the same time.'

I thought, *'What's she talking about?'*

When I went down to the outdoor café, I was just about to go through the door, when a hand touched my arm. I turned to see a young male in a green chequered shirt and jeans standing there. He was quite a hunk with tattoos on his arms. He held a beer bottle in his hand. He said something in Croatian to me, but I didn't understand. I just shrugged and smiled.

He said, 'Parla italiano?' *'Do you speak Italian?'*

I nodded. I had to let go of the door as someone was coming out.

'Signorina. Come una bibita con me?' *'Miss. A drink with me?'*

I just smiled again at him and turned away. I thought as I pushed through the door, *'Daddy told me not to talk to strange men, especially ones holding beer bottles.'* I almost giggled out loud.

I found the same guy that I had spoken to earlier. Maybe he owned the place. No matter. He was the one who was going to provide me with an explanation. He was serving drinks at the bar when I came in. I said in Italian, 'La doccia è difettosa nella nostra stanza. Può ripararlo per favore?' *'The shower in our room is faulty. Can you fix it please?'*

He just nodded.

I said, 'Oh, e l'acqua calda ha troppo calda e Lei non può alterare la temperatura.' *'Oh, the hot water is too hot and you can't adjust the temperature.'*

'Sì Signorina. Io avrò presto un'occhiata alla doccia. Spiacente per l'inconvenienza.' *'Yes Miss. I'll have a look at the shower soon. Sorry about the inconvenience.'*

I nodded and smiled. 'Oh, e noi non abbiamo asciugamani di bagno. Lei non li lasciò.' *'Oh, and we don't have bath towels. You didn't leave them.'*

He nodded again as he dried a glass.

'Potremmo avere per favore bibite fredde? Birra sarebbe buona.' *'Could we please have cold drinks? Beer would be good.'*

He said nodding, 'Sì Signorina. E se gli piace, io posso portare le bibite alla Sua stanza?' *'Yes Miss. I can bring it to your room if you like?'*

'Sta bene grazie. Io ora li prenderò.' *'It's fine thank you. I'll take them now.'*

He turned and took a couple of bottles of beer from under the counter and handed them to me.

'Grazie.' *'Thanks,'* I said. 'Quanto?' *'How much?'*

'Sta bene. Io l'includerò col Suo conto.' *'It's fine. I'll include it with your bill.'*

I nodded. 'Em.... non ha un registro per ospiti?' *'Em... don't you have a register for guests?'*

He shook his head. 'Noi non abbiamo uno. Io ora prenderò i Suoi nomi. È in stanza numero due?' *'We don't have one. I'll take your names now. You're in room number two?'*

I nodded. 'Sam Winter e Josie Moore. Noi siamo venuti dalla California.' *'Sam Winter and Josie Moore. We've come from California.'* I turned away with my beer and made for the door. The guy who had spoken to me as I entered, opened the door for me. I just smiled at him and walked on. I could hear his footsteps behind me as I turned to ascend the steps.

'Signorina.....?' *'Miss.....?'* He trailed off. Was he asking my name, or about to ask a question?

I didn't turn, but trotted quickly up the steps.

Back in our room I couldn't see any signs of Josie. Where had she got to? I pulled open the shower curtain, but she wasn't there. I could see the door to the balcony was open, so I went there. I stopped dead in my tracks when I saw her lying on her front on a sun lounger, her long golden hair flowing over her shoulders and wearing nothing but a pair of cool shades. She didn't hear me approach, so I touched her on the back just below her tattoo with one of the ice-cold bottles.

She jumped and screamed. 'Ah! What the hell....!' Then she saw it was me. 'Jesus, Sam. I thought.......!'

'You want to be seen here? How did you get here without being seen from below?' I said as I handed her the beer. I sat down on the other lounger on her right.

'Crawled here. How do you think?' She laughed, then turned over onto her back and smiled cutely back at me.

'OK.' I nodded. 'Listen Josie. You're not on some nudist beach back home in California. They have different rules here for God's sake! Some of them are Muslims too.'

She just nodded.

I stood up again. 'That guy I spoke to will be up here soon. He's having a look at the shower, so get something on.' I added, 'Can't take you *anywhere.*' I hesitated. 'Em.... how did you turn off the shower anyway?'

She smiled. 'I'm a smart girl.'

As I turned to go I said, 'Not smart enough.' I left her that one to chew over as I headed for the door.

'What? What did you say?'

'You forgot to lock the door. Smart girls lock their bedroom doors, especially in hotels,' I said as I locked it.

There was silence from the balcony.

I went in behind the curtain intending to have a pee. The cistern was high on the wall, again indicating that this was an old place. Even the sink was ancient-looking.

When I had finished with my toilet, I reached up and pulled on the chain that would flush the toilet, but nothing happened. The water that was supposed to come down and flush it just didn't happen.

'What the hell now?' I said in exasperation. I pulled on the chain again but still nothing. I turned to the sink and turned on the hot water. Well it should have been the hot, but nothing came. I turned on the other one, then realised that there was no soap.

'Shit,' I said. 'What's with this place?' I turned off the water, went to my pack that was lying next the bed and found my soap. Always good for emergencies. Back at the sink, I turned on the water again and put in the plug and began to wash my hands. That done, I pulled the plug out and let the water flow away. It was then that I felt something wet on my feet. I thought at first I had dripped water onto the floor, but on looking down at my feet, I could see that the pipe that came down from the sink wasn't connected to anything at all, and the water just poured into a bucket. *'Oh God,'* I thought, *'what else can go wrong?'*

I went to the bed and picked up Josie's clothes where she had dropped them and took them to her. I dropped them on her still lying there sunning herself. 'Get them on Josie. He'll be up soon.'

He was too. In a few minutes there was a knock on the door. I answered it.

He said, as he came into the room, 'Il Signorina Winter....' He handed me the bath towels.

I cut him off with, 'La toletta ed il lavandino anche.' *The toilet and the sink too.'* I smiled. I know that he understood because he just nodded. Probably knew all along about the problem too.

He took a brief look at the shower and the sink, then the toilet. He nodded then said, 'C'è un'altra toletta lungo il corridoio con bagno ed un la vandino. Lei può usare quello.' *'There's another toilet along the corridor with a bath and a sink. You can use that.'*

'Quello sta bene.' *'That's fine,'* I said with a smile.

He nodded and left the room again, closing the door behind him.

Josie came through from the balcony fully dressed. 'Hey, what's up Doc?'

'We're not paying for a room with shower and toilet that doesn't work Josie. He can forget about that.' I noticed that she carried her empty beer bottle.

She said, 'Of course not.' As she continued across the room towards the door she said, 'I'll get us some more beer.'

I was just about to mention about a meal, when she disappeared out of the room and closed the door. *'Well that takes care of that then,'* I thought as I made my way to the balcony. *'It seems the meal can wait.'*

I was just about to sit on my lounger when I spotted Josie trotting down the last few steps of the staircase, her hands in her front pockets. She's got a smile plastered on and she's looking across at someone. It's that guy who spoke to me. She won't get far with him seeing she doesn't speak any German or

Italian. I promised Josie's mom that I'd look after her and that is what I intend to do even if it kills me in the process. She's never been out of the States before so everywhere and everyone is new to her.

I watched her disappear under the balcony then I sat down on the lounger and started on my beer. I thought about the castle that we saw earlier, and the meal that we should be having now. At least the meal should be soon if we're to see the castle in daylight. I had an idea. I'll give Josie a call on my cellphone. That'll get her attention all right. I went to my pack and dug out my phone, then went back to the balcony to get a better signal. I dialled her number, then I could hear a phone ring a musical tone, but it seemed very close. Yep, it was too. As I walked into the bedroom again, I heard it coming, it seemed, from Josie's pack. I thought, *'Damn, I'll have to go down there and find her.'*

I went down to the café and approached the bar. The same guy I spoke to earlier was there again polishing the glasses. He saw me approach. I said, 'Ha visto Josie il mio amico? La ragazza?' *'Have you seen Josie my friend? The girl?'*

He pointed across the room to where Josie sat at a table at the window with two guys. The three of them were laughing at something. The one who sat opposite her was probably thirty-something and wore a white shirt and had long black hair to his shoulders. The other one was about twenty five and had on a blue chequered shirt and had short brown hair. They were trying their best to communicate with her, but Josie doesn't speak anything but English and a little Spanish. She was gesturing with sign language and throwing in a few Spanish words no doubt.

I crossed to their table. 'Josie, come on, let's go,' I said.

The two guys looked up and smiled. I just smiled back.

Josie just stared at me. She looked annoyed. She said to the guy opposite in Spanish, 'Excúseme. Yo tendré que ir.' *'Excuse me. I'll have to go.'*

I thought, *'Josie, they don't do Spanish here!'* I said, 'Josie, we've got a meal to catch.'

'Hey, you're not my mom,' she replied.

The guy in the chequered shirt who was closest to me got up from his seat to let her out.

'If I were your mom, I'd put you over my knee and spank your little bottom for you,' I joked.

As she came to me she said in a low voice, *'Excuse* me? Don't treat me like a kid.'

'Stop acting like one then. Next thing I'll be changing your diaper.'

She made a face and put out her tongue then marched off in the direction of the exit.

I hurried after her, and when I had caught her up outside, I took her by the arm and said, 'Meal. This way.' I led her to an empty table and said, 'Sit.'

She did, albeit reluctantly.

I sat down opposite. 'Look Josie. I promised your mom that I'd look after you.'

'Yeah, but does that include wiping my nose too?' She looked away, avoiding my gaze.

Just before I could answer, our friend the barman/owner approached our table. He said, 'Gradirebbe un pasto o una bibita?' *'Would you like a meal or a drink?'*

Josie just stared at me with a question mark.

I said, 'Per favore gradiremmo un pasto.' *'We would like a meal please.'*

'È la zuppa del giorno e manzo e spaghetti con sugo.' *'It's soup of the day and beef and spaghetti with gravy.'*

I relayed this information to Josie. She just shrugged and looked away.

'I take that as a yes,' I thought. I nodded. 'Che genere di zuppa è?' *'What kind of soup is it?'*

'Manzo.' *'Beef.'*

I nodded. I relayed this too.

She shrugged and looked away again.

'Qualche cosa per bere?' *'Anything to drink?'* he asked.

'Josie? To drink?'

She shrugged, and yep, she looked away again. I guess she's in a huff. Now where did that idea come from?

'Due birre. Grazie.' *'Two beers. Thanks.'*

He nodded and turned away.

Nothing at all was said over the soup. Then came the beef and spaghetti. She hardly used her knife at all, preferring to use the fork. She grinned at me over a forkful of beef and spaghetti. 'Looking forward to the castle Sam. Really.' She put her left hand on mine.

I said, 'It's OK Josie.'

Chapter 2.

Back upstairs, we took turns using the bathroom down the corridor to freshen up before going out.

This castle, as I remembered, wasn't far from our accommodation. We had only planned going out for a drive to see it and didn't intend to stay long. About an hour would do it. Well, that was the plan anyway.

As we made our way downstairs, Josie ahead of me, I asked with a smirk, 'What happened to the cold drinks that you went to fetch?'

She turned to me grinning. 'It was just an excuse to see the guys.'

'I see. OK,' said smiling. 'Any ones in particular?'

As we reached the foot of the stairs she said, 'No, just any cute guy.' She walked ahead with her hands in her front pockets.

The strange man I had met with the beer bottle approached now. He had another bottle in his hand, or was that the same one? He had a smile on too.

Josie kept looking at him, then she stopped in her tracks. I almost collided with her. 'Josie, come on,' I said as I grasped her hand.

As we walked to the car I looked back over my shoulder and could see him watching us. I had left the top down as I didn't want an overheated car. I got into the driver's seat and looked back. He was still standing there watching us, or was it Josie he was watching? She was watching him too. She sighed a big sigh of contentment and turned to the front. With a big grin plastered on she said, 'Quite a hunk huh?'

I just nodded and started the car. I turned left as I drove out of the forecourt into the road then we were on our way.

About twenty minutes into the journey I turned to her. 'Did that guy say anything to you earlier?'

She replied with a smirk as she looked out of her window, 'Oh yeah.'

'So, what did he say?' I'm curious, seeing she doesn't speak his language.

'Oh, nothing really,' she said, her smirk still in place. 'Just the usual things, you know?'

'Like what?'

'Well, he said I had nice breasts, hips and a figure to die for.'

'Yeah, sure Josie,' I said trying not to laugh. 'All that with only sign language?'

'Yep. I'm a smart girl you know.' She said that with a smirk too.

I laughed. 'Not smart enough. I spoke to him first.'

She said surprised, 'What did you say to him?'

'Oh, nothing.' I still had my smirk on.

'Oh I get it. You used sign language?'

'No I didn't. Italian.' I said smugly. I continued, nodding, 'See, I'm a smart girl too.' I laughed.

She laughed too. 'I speak a language too remember. I told you I was a smart girl.'

'OK smart ass. See if you can figure this one out. Where are we? Go on, take a stab at it.' I've just realised something – we're lost!

'Em…. Croatia?' She laughed again.

I said, giving up, 'I meant, where are we? Town?'

She just looked at me curiously and shrugged.

'OK, we're lost.' Well I just had to say it.

'You mean *you're* lost.' She laughed. 'So you're a smart girl then huh? That wasn't very smart was it?' She laughed again.

'No. You're here too so you're lost as well. That's how it goes.' I laughed.

'So, when did you discover that you were lost?'

'Three tunnels we passed through earlier. I only counted two this time, and I didn't recognise any of the landmarks,' I said.

It was starting to get dark now, at least the sun was going down, the sky was clouding over and it looked like it might rain. I pushed the control on the dash that would raise the top back over our heads. As we waited for this task to be completed she said, 'So what do we do now Mr Holmes?'

'Elementary my dear Watson, you get your map out,' I replied smugly.

'Pardon?'

'Your map?'

'Em…. that could be a problem,' she said looking at me.

'Why?'

'It's not here.'

'What? But I thought you had it with you?' I don't believe this girl.

'Didn't think we'd need it. After all, you're the smart girl who knows where she's going, right?'

'Josie? Shut up.' I said annoyed. I was also trying to think how we were going to solve this little problem, then I knew. Well I thought I did.

My thoughts were interrupted when Josie asked, 'We're not going to see the castle are we?'

'No, well not tonight anyway.' I flicked on the sidelights as it had gotten darker.

'So we just retrace our steps and bingo, we're home and dry, right?' she asked.

I nodded. 'Yeah, something like that.'

It had started raining a little now. I flicked on the wipers. The sun had disappeared completely and had been replaced by dark forbidding clouds. In a few more minutes, it was dark enough for dipped lights, so I flicked them on too.

'Gonna have to look for a place to turn Josie, then we can head back.'

She pointed out a side street on the right. I turned into it and after a few clever manoeuvres, I had turned the car around. We had to wait a few minutes for a gap in the traffic, then I hit the gas and we were heading for home. Well I thought we were, until I detected another problem; I couldn't see the beams from my dipped lights. I said, 'Josie? Can you see my lights?'

She looked into my face grinning. 'Yep, sure can. They're wide open girl.'

I pulled into the side of the road and stopped. 'Josie. Get serious.'

'What? Why are you stopped?'

'Get out,' I said, 'and look at the lights for me?'

'Pardon?' She just stared at me.

'Just do it!' I was beginning to lose my cool now.

She got out and just stood there staring at me again.

'What is it now? Lights are that way stupid.' I pointed forward at the hood.

She shrugged and said, 'OK OK.' She went to the front of the car and just stood there again. She shrugged again. 'What am I looking for?'

'Like lights? As in dipped?' I'm getting annoyed with this girl.

'You have to turn them on first don't you?' She turned her palms towards the lights, but I couldn't see any beam there. Maybe I got the wrong switch. I tried again. Yes I had the right one, but I couldn't see any lights this time either.

Josie came back in. 'Looks like you don't have any dipped. Try full beam.'

I did and they were OK. This is going to be tricky.

By now it was really quite dark as the time was fast approaching 9 o'clock. Driving on full beam in traffic got us honking from other drivers especially when we hit dense traffic in dark areas.

After some minutes driving slowly on sidelights because of the danger of dazzling other road users, I thought we might ask for help. We were lost after all, and we could make at least some progress if we knew which way we had to go to reach home.

Josie spotted an hotel off to the right behind some trees. The sign was lit up and read, Hotel Buna. We drove right up to the door and got out.

I said to her, 'Well, here goes nothing.'

We went through the door and bypassed the reception desk because it wasn't manned. We stopped dead in our tracks and pondered our next move.

There was an elderly couple sitting at a large coffee table straight ahead at the far wall.

I turned to Josie. She nodded and we approached the two sitting there. I said, 'Hi. Do you speak English?'

The guy replied smiling, 'Yes.'

'We're lost,' I said. That's it. Nothing more than that.

Josie just nodded.

The guy's wife said, 'We're from Germany. We've been here many times. We know the area quite well.'

'Cool,' Josie said. 'So you can help us then?'

'We'll try,' the guy said smiling. 'So where are you staying if anywhere?'

I turned to Josie who had just seated herself on the seat beside the guy. She just looked back with a shrug.

I said, not believing this girl again, 'Didn't you catch the name of the café?' She shook her head. 'No, I thought you did.'

'So you don't know where you're staying?' the guy asked.

'No,' I replied.

The wife asked, 'Have you got a map and maybe you can point out the area where you....'

'No,' Josie interrupted. 'Left it back in the accommodation.'

'Sorry we can't help you then,' the guy said.

'Yes sorry. Hope you can find your way back OK. Best of luck,' said his wife.

We thanked them then retraced our steps back to the car and drove off once more into the night. The temperature had dropped too which didn't help matters as our warmer clothes were back in the accommodation, and we were both feeling the cold. I did have the heating on in the car too.

Try as I might, I just couldn't find the route back to our accommodation. I would recognise it if only we could find those damned tunnels, and the slow progress that we were making didn't help either; switching on and off the full beam lights, and the occasional use of sidelights only, were less than useless, but necessary at the same time because without those, no-one would ever see us at all and it would be totally illegal. I'm sure driving with no dipped ones was probably illegal too.

Around 11 o'clock, I was getting really concerned about the possibility that we may not be able to find our way back to our accommodation at all. We had made so far, almost no useful progress in our attempt to find a way out of this mess. Were we just going around in circles or what? Why hadn't we found those tunnels? Maybe if we could find a police station, that might help.

I was beginning to think that I was dreaming all this, when Josie pointed something out. 'Sam. Look.'

She was pointing to a house where several people were standing around talking aimlessly. A light from the kitchen was illuminating their faces. One had a cup of something in his hand.

I was getting tired and was apprehensive about having an accident in the dark. I thought quickly and in desperation, *'Thanks Josie. Maybe they might be able to help.'* I don't know why I thought these people could help any more than the two at the hotel could. I stopped the car outside the house anyway and got out.

Josie said concerned, 'What are you going to do Sam?'

I said, 'Oh I don't know Josie. Guess I'll think of something.' I almost ran to the house, but just as I reached it, the occupants had gone inside and closed the door. I banged it twice and I could hear voices from inside. I've no idea what they said. It was probably Croatian. The door opened and someone came out. It was an elderly male figure, but impossible to see his face properly because he was against the light of the interior.

I said in a panic, 'Please, we're lost. Can you help?'

The guy just stood there and stared at me, then I heard someone behind me. It was Josie. She said, 'Can you help us please?'

The guy retreated back into the warmth of the house and another came out. He uttered something in Croatian I think and shook his head then shrugged. I tried Italian then German but on this occasion neither language was spoken by these people. I turned and walked away, Josie at my back.

I said, 'Let's get back Josie and try to figure something out.'

We got back into the car and moved off again, then, after about another thirty minutes, Josie pointed at something. 'Look Sam. Isn't that the hotel that we were at already?'

I looked to where she was pointing. 'Yeah, but there's no point in going back there is there. We got nowhere the last time.'

I was about to drive past it when Josie put her hand on my arm. 'Got a feeling about this Sam. Let's give this one more try. It's better than doing nothing and going around in circles like this.'

'OK,' I agreed, albeit reluctantly.

I pulled up outside the Hotel Buna and we went in. This time the little lounge straight ahead was deserted, so no-one to ask there, then I spotted a middle-aged guy in a grey cardigan behind the reception desk; the only life left alive on this part of the planet Buna? I almost giggled out loud, although I wasn't really in the mood for laughing right now.

'Hi,' Josie said. 'Can you help us? We're lost.'

He obviously didn't have any English because he just shrugged.

I said in Italian, 'Noi siamo persi. Può aiutarci?' *'We are lost. Can you help us?'*

He shrugged again.

I tried German but I got nowhere there either.

I saw Josie looking at the wall on our left, then she pointed something out. A poster; it had three pictures depicting a police car, flames and a red cross symbol - Police, Fire, Ambulance. She pointed to 'police' and the guy suddenly sat up straight. Did he understand? Yep, it sure looked like it. He picked up the phone and dialled, then after a few seconds, he spoke to someone.

I just looked at Josie. She had a big smile on her face that said, 'At last we're getting somewhere now'.

I had one plastered on too, when the guy handed me the phone. 'Hello?' I said brightly.

A male voice said, 'I've been told that you're lost?'

I said excitedly, 'Oh, yes! Can you help? Em.... who am I speaking to?'

He said, 'It's the local police station.'

'Thank God for that,' I said with relief. 'I don't know how we got lost in the first place.'

'OK, let's see if I can help. Where are you staying?'

I thought for a second before answering. 'I've no idea. I mean I don't know what the name of the village is.'

'OK. Do you know the name of the accommodation?'

'No. Oh, wait a minute. Yes I think so. I think it started with an "s", oh, and it was an outdoor café with rooms. A trucker's place by the looks of it.' My excitement was mounting.

'Any more details you can give me?'

'We passed through at least three road tunnels to get there. Does that sound familiar?' I asked hopefully.

'Yes. I think you're staying at a café called "Sunce".'

I shouted, 'Yes! That's it! Thank you!'

'OK. Glad to be of help. Bye.' He hung up.

I turned to Josie. She came and flung her arms around me. I pulled away and turned to the guy behind the desk. I just smiled at him since I couldn't say thanks. On second thoughts, maybe he would understand some German. I said, 'Danke schön.' *Thank you very much.*

Josie just nodded to him and we went back to the car. Within about thirty minutes, we were pulling into the courtyard of the Café Sunce. It was in complete darkness. All the lights had been turned out. No wonder, it was after midnight! I parked the car as close to the stairway as possible, but we would still have about a hundred yards to walk to reach it.

After turning out the lights and locking the car, I put my hand around Josie's waist and we groped our way to the stairway. I had already noted that there were no obstacles that we could trip over on our way there. When we had reached the foot of the stairs, I found the handrail and we both felt our way up to the door.

In the morning, after breakfast, we set out for the castle. The time was around 10 o'clock, the sun hot and we were eager to see this historic building.

I wore the same clothes as yesterday, but Josie had a change for her top half; a white sleeveless top that didn't show off too much. It sure showed off her California tan all right.

We arrived there at 10:30. Of course the castle was at the top of our list of places to see. It was built on the side of a hill with later buildings alongside.

There were lots of houses in the village and all built using the same local grey-white stone.

I didn't park opposite the building, but someways up the road where I had spotted a restaurant. It was on the same side of the road as the castle. On the opposite side, where we were, was a river valley. It was very green down there and also very peaceful-looking.

As we alighted from the car, I said, 'Maybe we can go there later and relax.' I pointed to the river.

'Sure looks like a cool place to chill out,' she said.

We crossed the road, then it was a steep climb up a cobbled lane to reach the castle, but what a fantastic view when we had gotten to the top. You could see for miles and miles. I had my Canon digital SLR with me and Josie her digital snap-shooter. Hers does the job very well, but I like the extra control that these cameras give.

Well we must have spent at least an hour up there taking photographs of the cool landscapes and ourselves goofing around. My stomach was complaining and crying out for food. I suggested to Josie that we go up to the restaurant and have ourselves a good meal, then we could come back here, or even just chill out down at the river. She agreed and so that is where we headed first.

It was quite a climb to the top of the steps that led to the restaurant. I had promised myself that I would count the steps, but about halfway to the top I lost count. That was due to Josie stopping and uttering a loud whooping sound, then she said, 'Gosh! That's one cool view!'

She was standing admiring it when I took her by the arm. 'This way.'

When we had reached the top, I said pushing through the door, 'We can sit by the window and admire the views from there.'

We stepped into a very Olde Worlde interior with oak-panelled walls and wooden beams at the ceiling. We chose a table at the window.

The menu was already on the table. I chose a fish soup for the first course. Josie had something with prawns in it.

'So what do you think of the vacation so far?' I grinned at her.

She smiled and said, 'Cool, so far. Let you know later.'

The waiter arrived now and took our order. He understood English thank goodness. Minutes later, he was back with my soup and Josie's prawn thing.

There was a bar across the room. Several males were seated there on stools, knocking back the booze.

I sat with my back to the door so I couldn't see who was coming in. I saw Josie's eyes light up just after I heard the door open. A young guy – twenty-something and a bit of a hunk, wearing a blue short-sleeved shirt and jeans passed our table. Josie's eyes followed him all the way to the bar where he sat himself on a stool. He didn't converse with the other guys there at the bar, so maybe he was a visitor like us.

Josie's eyes were still fixed on the guy at the bar, then she turned to me with a sigh of contentment. 'Yep, I like it here Sam. Nice scenery too.' She grinned. Was she referring to the clientèle or the landscape?

We both finished eating around the same time, then, as I sat there studying the menu for the next course, I heard Josie start to giggle, then she laughed out loud.

I looked at her over the menu. 'What?'

She giggled again and said, 'Always wanted to do this.'

'Do what?' I had a smile on.

'Tell you in a minute.' She was watching the waiter across the room.

'*What*?' I asked again.

She still didn't say anything, then the waiter returned to take our plates away. Just as he turned to leave, she asked, lifting the menu and pointing to an item there, 'Em… do you by any chance have duck's legs?' She spluttered then laughed.

He just smiled and turned away again.

She said with a giggle, 'I guess not.'

I started laughing too. 'Is that really on there?'

'No.' She laughed.

'You're mad.' I laughed again.

She just nodded as she couldn't speak for laughing.

Minutes later, the waiter returned and I settled on fried squid. This was one of my favourite dishes that I enjoyed the last time I was here. Josie had the same. Well everything was new to her here anyway, and she was willing to experiment. The waiter took our order then departed.

As we waited for the second course to arrive, Josie kept looking round at the bar, or the hunk that was seated there. She said grinning at me, 'Fancy a cold beer? I'll get them.'

'*Sure you will. Any excuse to get to the bar,*' I thought. I nodded and played with my napkin, folding and unfolding it, and threatening to turn it into a paper airplane.

She got up and went over to the bar and leaned her arms on the counter. Then something of a conversation began between herself and the hunk. She paid for the beers, but stayed at the bar for a few more minutes, before turning away again and coming back to our table, clutching four bottles close to her chest. She had a large grin plastered on as she sat down. 'Ah, that's cold!' she exclaimed as one of the bottles touched her skin.

I grinned back. 'You got a date or something?'

'No. What makes you say that?'

Before I could answer her, the waiter arrived back with our order.

I tucked in immediately and so did she. We enjoyed our meal and the view outside of the window. Josie seemed to enjoy the view inside the room more than the one outside of it.

When we had finished our meal and consumed one beer each, she insisted on paying the bill, if I went on ahead. I wonder why? I agreed and suggested that I go and move the car down the road closer to the castle, as we were going back there anyway. I wanted to be closer to my camera gear too. I left her there and went back to the car with the two remaining beers. I put them into a storage compartment between the two front seats, and just behind the parking brake. I turned the key in the ignition and nothing happened. I turned it again, and with the same response.

'Oh *God!* What next!' I said. 'First the lights, and now the bloody thing won't start.'

Josie still hadn't appeared.

I looked in the glove compartment for the car rental papers. I knew there'd be an emergency number there to phone. I got out my cellphone and turned it on only to discover that the battery was flat. '*Shit!*'

I got out of the car and tried to decide what I could do about finding a telephone. I stuffed the rental papers into my back pocket and crossed the road to a house on the hill. More climbing of steps, but this time I wasn't in the mood for counting.

On knocking the door, I was greeted by a large elderly woman who had no English nor anything else I could understand, but she did direct me to the Tourist Bureau in another castle just down the road a little ways from here. She also indicated with sign language that she didn't have a phone. I thanked her and went back to the road.

I walked hurriedly down the road and found the other castle building, or what was left of it. It looked like it had been a ruin at one time, but was now the Tourist Bureau. I went in through the open door and approached a woman sitting behind a desk. She wore a floral dress of blue and yellow. I'm not sure if this was national costume or not. She looked up smiling as I came in.

'Yes? Can I help you?'

I thought with relief, '*Thank God. English at last.*' I said, 'Our car is broken down.'

'Where is it?'

I said pointing up the road, 'Just up there.' I continued, 'I have the phone number here for emergencies.'

She shook her head. 'It's OK. I know someone nearby who can help. He fixes cars.'

'Oh, right. Thanks.'

She said, 'If you want to sit there and wait, I'll just make a quick call.'

I nodded and sat on a chair on my right. I wondered who she was going to get to help. I thought, '*Is it far from here? I hope not. And where's Josie got to anyway?*'

She picked up the phone and dialled, then within seconds she was speaking to someone. She asked me the make of car and the model.

I told her.

She got up from her desk and came around to where I sat. 'There'll be someone here in a few minutes and they'll sort it out.' She disappeared outside.

I thought with relief, *'Well, at least something is being done.'* I removed my hair clasp and was just about to re-attach it, when with peripheral vision, I saw something emerge through the doorway on my left. I recognised it immediately as belonging to Josie. It was her most prominent feature – her bust. That's it. Nothing more, then seconds later, her head appeared. There was no mistaking those vivid blue eyes and little cute smile. She had her hands on either side of the doorway and was leaning herself into the room.

'Hi,' she said brightly. 'Thought I'd find you here.'

'Really?' I mocked. 'How could you know I was broken down though? I thought you'd be too preoccupied to notice.'

She sat down beside me with straight back and her chest out. 'I told you; I'm a smart girl. I can do more than one thing at a time you know.'

'Yeah. So how could you ever take your attention off of that hunk?' I teased.

'Well admittedly it was difficult especially when we started taking our clothes off, and he's such a cool kisser, you wouldn't believe.' She gave a big sigh of contentment and tried to stifle a giggle, but it came out as a splutter instead. She put her hand to her mouth. She continued, 'I saw you in the car and that you were having problems getting it started, then standing there with the rental papers in your hand, and I reckoned you were wondering where you were going to get help. You'd have to phone somebody, and that's when I left the restaurant.

'Then when I was going down all those steps to the road, I saw you coming down the steps of a house and I reckoned that you didn't have any luck there because you weren't there long enough to make a call, and so I followed you down the street. I didn't know where you'd gone for help, but the next logical place would be the Tourist Bureau. Elementary my dear Watson.'

I turned to her with a smirk. 'That's very good Josie. Good to see you're paying attention anyway.'

She was just about to say something when the woman from the Bureau came back. 'Someone to see you now,' she said. 'Oh. You pay the bill yourselves, then when you get the receipt from the guy who's going to fix the car, you'll show it to the car rental company and you'll be reimbursed, OK?'

We both nodded and stood up, although Josie didn't have much idea what this was all about.

I thanked her and we moved to the door, Josie ahead of me. She almost bumped – literally, into another hunk – late twenties I think, wearing a white t-shirt and jeans. He had muscles on his tattooed arms and who knows what else under that shirt.

Just outside the door in the street was a VW saloon with three guys in it; two in the front and one in the back, and, from what I could see through the windows, all hunks. Were we spoilt for choice or what?

The woman from the Bureau came out again. 'You get into the car with these guys and they'll take you back to your car.'

I thought with some amusement, *'How many Irishmen does it take to turn a light bulb?'*

The guy said something to us, but not anything that either of us could understand. Josie and I just stood there. She shrugged and turned to me for assistance. I shrugged too and shook my head. A big smile appeared on her face. She thinks all her birthdays have arrived at once. The guy opened the rear door for us and Josie got in first. I followed, then the hunk with the tattooed arms got in. Gosh he was hot, and sexy and….. My dreaming was interrupted as Josie attempted to converse with the guy next to her. He wore a light-blue t-shirt with wording across the front that said something in Croatian.

'Hi. I'm Josie.'

I thought, *'No Josie. You're wasting your time with these guys.'*

He responded with, 'Hallo Mädchen. Ich bin Dimitri.' *'Hello girls. I'm Dimitri.'* He put out his hand for Josie to shake.

She took it as the car moved off then turned left into the main road. Josie was speechless. Unlike her to be lost for words. She had a question mark over her head as she turned to me.

'He just says "hello girls".' I shook his hand too. 'Sam,' I said smiling.

Josie just sat there. 'Oh,' is all she said.

I laughed.

We pulled up just behind our car. How did they know which one was ours? Because it was the only one parked there. We all got out and the guys had a look at our car. One got into the driving seat and turned the key. I had left it in the ignition and the doors unlocked. Well, just shows how desperate I was. The engine made an attempt to start then died. He tried a second time but with the same result, then he popped the hood. One of the other guys, the one with the tattoos, opened the hood and leaned in. He was joined by another. There was some brief conversation then Josie stepped up to the front.

She leaned in beside them, then she straightened up and turned to me. 'It's the battery.'

I said to Josie, 'I wonder where the guy who fixes the cars….' I was interrupted by someone speaking to me in German. It was the guy who had been with us in the back seat.

'Wir nehmen jetzt das Auto zum Mechaniker, damit er es für Sie reparieren kann.' *'We take the car to the mechanic now so he can repair it for you.'*

I nodded and said, 'Ja. Danke.' *'Yes. Thanks.'*

He had a brief exchange of words with the others and they got to work immediately. One was already in the driving seat, so the other three began to push the car. They turned it around and pushed it down the hill. Josie and I followed them, not too sure what was coming next. They stopped the car just outside of the driveway of a house on the hill. A guy in blue coveralls came down from the house and greeted us at the car. One of the guys explained what the problem was and the mechanic nodded, then they went about their business, waving to us as they returned to their own car.

Josie and I waved back then turned to the guy in coveralls. He said something in Croatian to us but of course we didn't understand. He didn't have any German or Italian, however he indicated with sign language that the car would be ready in about an hour. He held up one finger.

I pointed out the faulty lights to him. I think he understood, because he went into the driver's seat and turned on the lights, then discovered the fault.

'Josie, you got your phone?' I asked.

'Yeah.' She took it out of her front pocket.

I indicated the phone to the guy.

He understood. He wrote his number in a notebook that he took from a pocket in his coveralls and handed it to Josie.

She nodded and slipped it into her pocket. She said, pointing to herself, 'Josie.'

He nodded.

We decided to go down to the river and relax, but first I rescued our cameras from the car.

An hour later and Josie gave the mechanic a call. It was answered almost immediately, 'Hello?'

'Josie,' is all she said.

'OK,' he replied. 'Car OK.'

She hesitated, not sure what to say next, 'Thanks.'

We returned to the driveway and the mechanic who was waiting for us by the car. He had a receipt for us to be presented to the car rental company. We had to pay him of course, but we split the total down the middle.

We thanked him and left satisfied. We found our way back to Café Sunce without any hitches this time.

That night I couldn't sleep. I was too hot and I kept tossing and turning. I guess I kept Josie awake too, but I couldn't help it. Even with the balcony door open it was still too warm. I had elected to wear my nightie but without any underwear. It's cooler.

I made up my mind eventually, that I was going to cool off on the balcony. Maybe I'd be able to sleep on the lounger instead. I got up without putting the light on, not wanting to disturb Josie, and lightly stepped across to the balcony. I just stood there at the door, breathing in the night air and the light breeze lifting my nightie now and then.

I heard Josie say in a low voice, 'Sam?'

I didn't turn. 'Yeah?' I whispered.

'You OK?'

'Too hot Josie. I'm cooling off. I might sleep out here on the lounger instead.'

In seconds she was behind me. 'Me too.'

I turned to her. I could just make out in this semi-darkness, her standing there in her birthday suit.

I said, 'Josie....'

She cut me off with, 'I'll get us a sheet off the bed.' She went to fetch it. Back on the balcony and clutching the topmost sheet from the bed, she said, 'Well maybe now we'll get a decent night's sleep.'

I moved my lounger closer to Josie's so that we could share the sheet, then sat down on mine.

She said, looking down on me, 'Who said we were sharing?'

'Josie, come on. It's big enough for two.' I stripped off my nightie and covered myself with my end of the sheet.

She lay down on her front and rested her head on her arms. 'Cover me?'

I drew her side of the sheet up over her back.

This time we slept, that is, until I felt a colder than usual breeze on my front. I woke up and realised that my end of the sheet was only partially covering me. I looked across at her and could see that she had more than her fair share of it. I tugged on it gently, trying not to waken her, but I guess she must have been lying on it. She wakened, at least she tried pulling on it, but I held on tight to my side.

'Sam? What are you doing?'

'Rule number one when sleeping with me is you don't steal the bedclothes,' I said sounding annoyed, and I was too.

'I'm not. Go to sleep.' She turned onto her back and now I was completely uncovered.

'Rule number two, you don't snore.' I'm winding her up now.

'I don't snore,' she said sounding sleepy.

'You do too,' I insisted.

'Bullshit. Go to sleep.'

'I need that sheet Josie otherwise....' I trailed off.

She got up and unwrapped herself, then lay down again on her front. 'Satisfied?' she asked sounding irritated.

I covered myself again with the sheet but didn't reply.

Chapter 3.

In the morning we made our way down to the café and went into pay the bill. We'd find our own breakfast someplace on the road later. I'm determined that we're not going to pay for this crap plumbing. Josie stood behind me dressed again in her white t-shirt as we waited at the reception desk for the owner/barman to make up our bill. When he had this done, I could see just over his shoulder and pinned to the wall, the actual prices of the rooms. He was charging us for the room with shower.

I thought, *'No you don't. I'm not paying for that.'* I tore up the bill and said, 'Noi non stiamo pagando per quella stanza con la piombatura rotta. Lei può fare su un altro conto.' *'We're not paying for that room with the broken plumbing. You can make up another bill.'*

He was furious. He said, 'Sta rifiutando pagare il conto?' *'Are you refusing to pay the bill?'*

I nodded. I said, 'Io pagherò il prezzo di una stanza senza doccia, ma quello è tutto.' *'I will pay the price of a room without shower but that is all.'*

'Io posso chiamare la polizia.' *'I can call the police,'* then he shrugged resignedly. He nodded, and began to make up another bill.

I already knew what the price was, so I slapped the money down on the desk and turned to Josie with a smile. I said, 'That sorted him out.'

Once he had the bill written out, I snatched it up and we left to find our breakfast elsewhere without saying goodbye.

Out of the forecourt we headed back in the direction of town to find a restaurant. We parked the car in a parking lot close to the town centre, then went to find an eating place. Now that I could see this town in daylight, it looked vaguely familiar. I was sure this is where Tomislav and I sat in a restaurant. It wasn't till we had been walking for about five minutes that I recognised the restaurant across the road. Yes I was sure this was the one where the gang were discussing their plan, and Tom overheard the conversation, and the guy dropped the sheet of paper and…..

My thoughts were interrupted by Josie pointing across the road. 'Let's go there,' she said taking my hand and pulling me across the road to the restaurant. I didn't have much choice.

We found a table and sat down, Josie on my left. I felt I needed a pee, so I excused myself and headed off to find the loo.

When I got back to our table, the waiter was hovering around awaiting the order.

'Cool place,' she said looking around.

'Yeah,' I replied absently as I sat down, my thoughts going back to that day, when we sat at a table here and I laughing at Tomislav's jokes and enjoying his company. I didn't hear what the waiter was asking me. Josie kicked my ankle and brought me down to Earth again. 'Oh, sorry. I was miles away,' I said to him blushing.

'You were way the other side of the universe there girl.' She laughed.

I said to her, 'You going to order something?'

'I have,' she said with a grin.

I had a quick look at the menu. 'Em…. mushroom omelette, oh, and coffee please?'

Josie said, 'Done that.' She grinned.

'Yeah, OK Josie,' I said annoyed and replaced the menu.

The waiter asked, 'Would you like a drink first?'

I shook my head. 'No thank you.'

He picked up the menu and retreated back inside the restaurant.

I began to recall some unpleasant thoughts about my time together with Tomislav, when Josie saw my depressed look. With a hand on my arm she asked, 'You OK?'

I could feel a tear forming. I tried to wipe it away with my fingers before Josie spotted it, but too late; she had seen it.

'Sam?'

'It's OK,' I told her, but of course we both knew it wasn't.

'Is it something I did?'

'Oh God no Josie. It's not you. Just something that happened when I was here last.' I could feel another tear forming. If I get any more depressed, I'll start to lose control.

Josie is such a nice and caring girl; always putting others before herself. I knew she was genuinely concerned. I might have to tell her the truth about what happened here. She got up and moved her seat closer to me and when she sat down again, she put her arm around my shoulders. 'Tell me about it?'

I shook my head. I was starting to sniffle now. This was only making me feel more sorry for myself.

'It's better if you talk about it Sam. You'll get it out of your system quicker, whatever it is.' She squeezed my hand.

I took a deep breath. 'Thanks,' I said, then I broke down. I had just lost control. Tears rolled down my cheeks when I began to tell her about the explosion and Tomislav dying in the burning car.

When I was done, and had calmed down a bit, she said, 'Why didn't you tell me this before? We could have stayed at home and forgotten about this trip…'

I cut her off. 'Oh no Josie, I couldn't do that. You were so looking forward to it, I didn't want to spoil it for you.'

Tears were still running down. She brushed some hair from my face. Some of them had stuck to my cheeks with the tears.

The waiter arrived now. He wasn't too sure where to put the plates since Josie had moved her seat.

He saw the tears too and asked, 'You OK? Can I get you something?'

I shook my head. 'I'll be OK thanks.' I took a Kleenex from my pocket and started on my breakfast.

There were four other tables occupied; two on either side of us. I had noticed a guy reading a newspaper at the farthest one from us. He looked to be late twenties or early thirties, with short black hair, dark glasses and small moustache. He appeared to have ordered only a coffee. Every now and then he would take a glance in our direction. Was he concerned about me or just curious. Maybe he was a psychiatrist, doctor? He certainly couldn't hear our conversation as he was too far from us for that, and then there was the street noise. I turned from his gaze and concentrated on my food instead.

Josie moved her chair back to her own position and started on her food. She had smoked fish. I had my mushroom omelette, although I hardly tasted it. I had just spoilt my meal by being upset.

As Josie poured coffee for us, she asked, 'Who do you think planted the bomb in your friend's car?'

I shook my head. 'I don't know Josie. One suggestion I heard it was the local Mafia out for revenge for putting some of them away.'

'Oh God Sam.'

'Yeah, well, that was three years ago now. It's all in the past.' I stirred my coffee and tried to concentrate on something less painful. I'm determined not to come back to this restaurant again. Too many bad memories.

When we had finished our breakfast, I paid the bill and we continued on our way. Anywhere was our destination. It didn't matter. We're on vacation and we can go anywhere we please, can't we?

Back on the road again and we headed south on the Magistrala. We thought we'd go to Zadar. It's a port where we thought we'd catch a ferry to one of the islands, but we'd have to find accommodation first.

We parked the car in a parking lot in the centre of Zadar and close to the local Tourism Bureau. We had a look around the Bureau and tried to decide what type of accommodation we would like to try this time. I went to the desk where a young woman sat in national costume. Well that's what it looked like to me anyway.

'Hi,' I said brightly. 'Can I see a list of accommodation that you have? We're thinking of housekeeping or self catering on one of the islands.'

She opened a book and had a quick flick through the pages, then after a moment she looked up and said, 'I'll just make a quick call.' She picked up the phone and dialled, and in seconds, was speaking to someone.

I turned to Josie and smiled.

As she returned it she said, 'Love to just chill out on a beach in some secluded cove.'

I nodded. 'Yeah. That would be so cool.'

The woman said finally as she put down the phone, 'There's a self catering house on the Island of Ugljan. The car ferry leaves in about thirty minutes, and the owner is on his way here.'

'Thank you. That would be ideal,' I said. This news had lifted my spirits. Now things would start to improve.

We decided we'd sit and wait for the guy to turn up. I had only just sat myself on a chair, when he pushed through the door and approached us. The woman behind the desk must have mentioned about two girls looking for a house, and we were the only girls here so.....

Josie didn't get the chance to sit down, so she was the first to get his attention. He put out his hand and introduced himself as Branimir Držislav. He was forty-something with dark wavy hair and moustache and quite tall at around six feet.

Introductions out of the way, he said, 'I'll take you to the cottage now.'

I said, 'We have our own transport, thank you.'

'OK, that's good,' he said. He quoted a price for the cottage and it seemed reasonable to us.

Outside, we went straight back to our car. Držislav leaned on the door and said to me, 'My car is that red one. We pay on the ferry.'

I just nodded and smiled back.

On the ferry, we sat in the car for a while just enjoying the coolness of the sea air. We both removed our hair clasps and let the strong breeze do its work. Once my hair was thoroughly messed up, Josie went into her pack and took out her camera and began snapping me from outside of the passenger side. She came around to my side and showed me the result. She had used a distortion mode to mutilate my features. I had a long nose and chin and it made my hair look ten times worse.

I said, 'Josie.... that's horrible,' then I started laughing. 'I'll get my own back.'

Držislav threaded his way through the cars on the deck till he reached ours. He said, 'Don't bother paying the fare girls. I'll add it onto your bill at the end of your stay. My mother lives in the next house to where you'll be staying and you can pay the bill to her. I'm away a lot on business and I may not see you when you leave.'

Josie said brightly, 'Sure.'

I nodded.

He went back to his own car that was parked two spaces in front of ours close to the front of the ferry and beside the left-hand rail, as we were some of the first to get on. I watched him pour something from a flask into a cup. Probably his lunch.

As I still held Josie's camera, I thought I'd get my own back now. I got out of the car. She had her back to me as she leaned over the rail.

I said, 'Josie! Say cheese.'

She said as she turned, 'What?'

Then with a grin plastered on her face, I snapped her. Yes! I looked at the result. Her arms, hands and fingers were elongated, and her face and chin and nose and…. I laughed and laughed.

She snatched the camera from my grasp and looked at the result. She made a face.

I said laughing, 'Now we're even.'

When the ferry docked, we were some of the first off. We followed Držislav to his cottage and parked the car outside. He showed us around the accommodation. The bathroom, two bedrooms, kitchen and living room. We'll be happy here, we said. We also asked him if there were any secluded coves or islands where we could be alone, and he told us where they were located. We said our goodbyes and he departed for the mainland again.

The time was fast approaching midday and I wanted to go shopping at a supermarket that Držislav told us about. There was only one in the area, about a ten minute walk from the cottage. We had the car, so why should we walk when we'd be carrying lots of groceries?

Just before we left for the grocery shopping, Josie said she wanted to show me something. She disappeared into her bedroom – we had one each this time – and re-emerged less than a minute later wearing….? I just stood there not believing my eyes.

She twirled on the spot with her arms outstretched on either side of her. 'Tar-rah!'

It was the most skimpy bikini that I had ever seen. The top part was all connected by thin white strings. Two narrow pieces of the same string fabric barely covered her nipples, and the bottom front, also connected in the same manner, wasn't much better. The rear? I won't even go into *that*!

'Josie. What the hell's that?'

She stopped her twirling on the spot and her almost constant smile vanished. 'Pardon?'

'What is that you're wearing? Or should I say, not wearing?'

'What does it look like?'

'Look Josie. You might get away with wearing that on a beach in California, but here….' I trailed off not believing this girl. I continued, 'And put something on. We're off to a supermarket now.'

'OK!' she exclaimed angrily, then she disappeared back into the bedroom and re-emerged seconds later wearing a white t-shirt and jeans. 'Satisfied?'

I didn't say anything, but marched out to the car, Josie in pursuit.

No words were spoken on the way to the supermarket at all.

Josie opened her door and slammed it shut behind her, then marched ahead of me into the building. She took a shopping trolley after inserting a coin and marched to the first aisle. She was picking stuff up and just throwing it into the trolley. How could she know what she was buying? All the items were printed in Croatian. She didn't have a shopping list so everything was from memory.

I was determined to put a stop to this now. We needed butcher meat, so I went to the cool cabinet where the fresh meat was kept. I took an armful of meat chosen mainly at random and turned to find Josie. Where was she? I went to the next aisle. She wasn't there, but I did find her in the next one again. She had stopped to select a bag of coffee when I stood in front of the trolley and dropped the meat into it. She tried to push the trolley forward but I stood my ground.

She had a look on her face that said, 'If you don't get out of my way, I'll run you down!'.

I had a look on that said, 'I dare you!' I said to her, 'This is going to stop right now or we're taking the first flight home, and I mean it.'

She said with venom, 'Go to hell!'

That's when I lost it. I slapped her across the face.

She screamed at me. 'You bitch!'

Two middle-aged women pushed past us and one of them gave me a look that said, 'Leave her alone.'

I gave her one back that said, 'Mind your own business.' I snatched the trolley off Josie and headed for the checkouts. As far as I was concerned, this was the end of our grocery shopping expedition. I paid with a credit card and we went back to the car.

Back at the house I made for the kitchen and emptied the grocery bags. Everything went into it's rightful place and then I began to prepare our lunch. I wasn't too sure what to make. I just wanted something that wasn't going to take too long to prepare. I settled on scrambled egg on toast. I had already made the toast, then I broke the eggs and beat them. In no time I had it ready including the coffee bubbling in the pot.

Josie came into the kitchen and just stood there watching me. The look on her face was that of total disinterest, then she turned to go.

I said, 'Lunch is ready if you are.' I don't know why I bothered saying anything at all.

She turned back to me, spitting out the words, 'You can shove it!'

'What? If you don't eat this, it's going in the trash!' I shouted as she re-treated from the kitchen.

She went into the living room and I heard her bedroom door slam shut.

'Right that does it,' I said as I scraped half the scrambled egg onto my own plate and the rest into the trash can.

As I sat at the kitchen table eating my lunch, I made up my mind that I was going to call home and tell mom what had happened, and that we would be home on the first available flight, so when I had finished my lunch, I went to fetch my cellphone, but the battery required charging. I dug out my charger and plugged in the phone. I dialled mom's number but it was engaged. Damn! To hell with it. I was going to spend the rest of the afternoon on the beach – alone.

Chapter 4.

That night, I couldn't sleep at first. Maybe something to do with my sparring with Josie, but eventually I did drift off.

We had decided to change into our bikinis as we were intending to play beach volleyball on the sand and the sun was very hot. Her outfit was very very skimpy, the front parts of which only just managed to cover her nipples. Mine was skimpy too and consisted of two small white triangles connected by string. The lower half was a small wedge at the front and a narrow strip at the rear connected by string too. We giggled and joked about what the guys might think when they saw us dressed like this, or should that be undressed like this?

When we left our accommodation, the two guys that we had met earlier in the bar were waiting for us by the net. We ran up to them and we each got a kiss on the cheek. The game got under way. I don't know how Josie's breasts stayed put inside her skimpy garment, because every jump for the ball that she made, they threatened to come out and cause an embarrassment.

Our game went on for about an hour. I was sweating profusely and could have killed for a swim in the sea, but we were beating those guys and it would be a shame to have to call a halt to the game at this stage.

There was a high stone wall about 100 feet from us on our left and beyond that, a major highway with fast-moving traffic. I hit the ball with both fists over the net and one of the guys responded by hitting it back to us. Josie knocked it back to them again, but on attempting to return it to us, one of the guys somehow managed to hit it right over the wall.

Josie ran after it. The only way out was through a gate and so this is where she went. I went after her because I was concerned for her safety. By the time I had reached the gate myself, Josie had made a dive into the road, thinking that she had time to retrieve the ball before it had disappeared under the wheels of some of the enormous trucks that thundered by now and then.

The ball rolled into the centre of the road and she went after it. At this point the road was clear, but just as she was about to snatch the ball up, I saw a semi-trailer truck approach at high speed. At the rate he was travelling, there was no possibility of stopping in time. If Josie didn't get out of there in the next few seconds, she would be killed for sure.

I screamed at her to get out of the way. She didn't hear me and wouldn't realise that there was a truck heading straight for her. I screamed and screamed at her just as she reached the ball, then the truck was on her, and, as she straightened up, she turned and spotted me, then everything seemed to happen in slow motion. The truck struck Josie full in the chest, knocking her up and into the air like a rag doll. She was catapulted backwards over the cab and landed between the cab itself and its trailer. At this point, the driver had hit the brakes and the vehicle jack-knifed. Josie's legs were trailing on the road and she was hanging onto the fuel tank, she was screaming for help. There wasn't anything I could do to help her now.

An oncoming fuel tanker coming from the other direction, tried to swerve out of the path of the jack-knifed trailer but instead, slammed into the truck's fuel tank and crushed Josie's legs. I heard her scream out for help just before the truck's tank exploded engulfing her in burning gasoline. I threw myself flat on the ground as I suspected another explosion. I heard her screams just before the two vehicles came to a sudden halt, then the tanker exploded. Something black and still burning with fuel flew towards me. It resembled an arm with the hand still attached. I threw up, then I screamed and screamed.

I think that's when I woke up! I screamed again and broke down. I cried and cried then made for the bathroom where I threw up into the lavatory bowl. I stripped off my soaking wet nightie and stepped into the shower. I just stayed there for the next ten minutes not wanting to come out.

I wondered why Josie didn't hear me scream. Well maybe she was still in her huff and wasn't interested. *'Well,'* I thought, *'suit yourself Josie.'*

I thought of going for a swim before breakfast, but first I wanted to call home to tell mom about our early return. I'd also have to buy new tickets. I unplugged my cellphone from is charger and switched it on. It takes a few seconds to come onto the main menu. I would have to call up mom's number first. All this takes time, and in the meantime, I was opening Josie's door. When I went in, she wasn't there. Her bed had been slept in though. I went up to it and felt the place where she had lain. It was cold, so it had been some time since she had left it. *'She's gone for a swim I'll bet,'* I thought.

I decided to put the call off for the moment, and it's too early anyway; 8:30. I'll have my swim first. I donned my bikini, grabbed a bath towel and ran outside, then it was down to the beach. It was rocky here with not a trace of sand to be seen anywhere. When I looked back at our cottage, I could see what looked like an hotel in the trees and several guests were playing a game of bowls.

I spread my towel on some rocks and dived into the crystal clear water of the Adriatic. There was no tide here that I could detect. If there was, it was very slow in rising.

I don't know how long I stayed there for, but I kept wondering where Josie had got to. If she was still in a huff, maybe she went out to one of the secluded spots that the owner had mentioned.

I was returning to the house, when the owner's mother appeared at her gate. She called me over. 'Hello,' she said smiling. 'I thought you might like these.' She held a large transparent plastic bag filled with what looked like cherries out to me.

I said brightly, 'Oh, thank you. That's very kind.'

'I was picking them in the garden.'

I asked her if she had seen Josie this morning. She hadn't, then she hesitated, 'What was she wearing?'

'Oh, I don't know. Maybe a bikini? She has blond hair and about my height?'

'Yes I remember someone fitting that description. She was wearing white shorts and a white t-shirt.'

'Thank you,' I said absently. *Josie, where the hell have you got to?'* I thought as I went back to the cottage. I went straight to the kitchen and washed the cherries. I'm thinking of stewing them and we can use the juice from the fridge for drinks later.

I went to my room and changed into a pair of white shorts and light-blue t-shirt, then it was back to the kitchen. I made some toast and fried a few rashers of bacon, then put on the coffee pot. As I ate my breakfast of bacon on toast, I tried to think of where Josie had got to. Had she gone for a swim or a walk, or both?

I had just put the fruit into a pan of warm water from the kettle, when I heard the front door open. My heart was in my mouth as I anticipated another confrontation, because I was all prepared to give her a lecture about going off on her own again. Well what did I have to lose now. We would be flying home soon anyway so it didn't matter.

Josie came into the kitchen. She was crying, her t-shirt was dirty at the front and her knees and legs were dirty too. Her hair was dishevelled and her hair clasp was missing.

I just stood there wondering what had happened to her. 'Josie, where have you been to get in a mess like that?'

She ran to me and flung her arms around my neck and just broke down.

'What the hell Josie? What's happened?' I led her to a chair at the table, then I sat down beside her and put my arm round her shoulders.

She calmed down a bit. 'I was stalked then I started running and I fell down a few times.'

'Let's go back to the beginning.'

She took a deep breath then she started. 'I forgot to get something at the supermarket yesterday, so I thought I'd take a walk there, but I didn't know when it opened. I had to hang around outside and that's when I spotted someone watching me.

'In the shop I saw the same guy looking at me, and when I was walking back here, I turned and he was following me. He started to increase his speed and that's when I started running. I tripped and fell on the ground and I thought I was going to be attacked.'

I'm thinking I could teach her self defence; at least some of the basic moves anyway. I put it to her.

She brightened then. 'Could you really? That would be so cool Sam.' She sniffled and wiped her nose with a Kleenex.

'I can teach you some of the basic moves and you'll have that anyway.'

'Where did you learn? You didn't tell me about this before,' she said with that incredulous look of hers. I could see a tear on her left cheek. I wiped it away with my finger.

I said, 'I was bullied at school and a friend suggested learning to defend myself.' I told her about my dad having been a gymnast at one time, and teaching me from an early age, some of those moves. Also about the handgun self defence training that I underwent and that it has come in useful in the past too.

She stood up and said brightly, her smile returning, 'When can we start?'

'Today, any time really. You should wear a pair of jeans.'

'Pardon? What's wrong with this?' she said pointing to her clothes.

'I'll show you later.'

I was looking in a cupboard above one of the worktops when I found a tin of cat meat. I thought, *Did I put that there? Well I certainly didn't buy it anyway. Josie.....?* I said, 'Where did you find the kitty cat?'

'Pardon?' She came round the table to where I stood. Her vivid blue eyes were fixed on the tin and her smile had vanished temporarily.

I held it up for her to see.

'Oh,' is all she said. 'Did I buy that? Sorry.' She reddened.

'That's OK. You can have it for your breakfast.... on toast of course.' I laughed. 'And you didn't buy it, I did. Well I paid for it anyway.'

'Oh. I must have picked it up thinking it was milk. Got it from the "reduced items" basket.' Just before she turned away, she said, 'I only have two pairs of cream-coloured jeans with me and I don't want to get them dirty when we have our fight.'

'I do. They'll fit you too. They're lying over the back of a chair in my room.'

She went off to fetch them.

The cherries had reached the boil now, so I turned down the heat and put the lid on the pan.

Josie arrived back in a few minutes. She wore a short white t-shirt that stopped just short of her bellybutton, and my faded blue jeans. She fitted into them like a glove. She came over to the cooker and sniffed her nose in the air. 'What you cooking?'

'Cherries,' I said as I stood at the window looking out.

'Don't remember you buying them.'

'Got them from next door. Maybe she had a surplus or something,' I said. 'We can have them with ice cream. I'll put the juice into the fridge for cold drinks later.' I turned off the heat for the moment and turned to her.

She said brightly, 'Cool. Sounds good to me. So, can we go out now and you can show me some tricks?' She ran out of the kitchen and I heard the front door open.

I ran after her and caught her up. There was a lawn here, just big enough for us to 'play' on.

As she approached me slowly standing there on the lawn, I said, 'This self defence depends on the element of surprise, so...' I trailed off then kicked out quickly with my right foot towards her groin area. She caught it in both hands just in time. Of course I had no intention of hitting her. That could have done her some serious damage.

She said, 'That's it?' She grinned.

I said quickly, pointing behind her, 'Look Josie!'

She turned quickly to see where I was pointing, and that's when I grabbed her around the waist with one hand and the other I clamped over her mouth. I was able to lift her off her feet.

I said, 'Struggle to get free. Your life could depend on it.'

She tried struggling and appeared to be putting all her strength into it, but my left hand was groping for her jeans' stud. In seconds, I had it loosened and then came the zipper. She was still struggling and trying to pull out of my grasp, when I pulled the zipper right down, then I let go and grabbed her legs instead and pulled them from under her. She fell on her front, then I grasped her jeans around the waist and began to pull them down her thighs.

'Sam! What....?' She was really struggling at this point and tried wriggling out of the jeans, no doubt trying to escape from me, but I simply grasped her around the waist again and pulled her up towards me. Then I let her go.

She pulled the jeans up and stood up to face me. Her face was red and she was sweating profusely. Well we both were.

'Josie, never turn your back on your attacker.' I gasped, as I tried to get my breath back. 'If I was a guy, you would have been raped. See how quickly I got your jeans off? It only took seconds.'

She nodded.

We went back inside to have lunch. Later we resumed our 'play'. Josie was a quick learner and soon had me on my back. She really surprised me when she performed a couple of cartwheels across the lawn, then several backward somersaults.

'That's impressive Josie. Where did you learn to do that?'

'Oh just something that I liked to do as a young kid. Hey how about going for a swim?' she said brightly. 'Secret coves?'

I went back in and changed into my red bikini again. I pulled my white t-shirt on top; Josie a light-blue one that stopped just short of her bellybutton. We kicked off our sneakers and took off our socks, then made off in the direction of the place where Držislav had indicated.

We followed a dirt track until we reached the sea. Yeah, this place sure did look secluded, but there probably were even better ones than this. When we had reached it, again there was no sand, only flat rocks.

We sat with our feet dangling in the crystal-clear water. As we pulled off our shirts, I could see little fishes swimming about close to where we sat. They came right up to us, then darted away quickly again.

I was intrigued by them and so was Josie, that is until.... 'Ah!' I exclaimed as something bit my toe. Well it felt like a bite to me anyway. 'Josie?' I said turning to her. 'Hey! That one bit my toe!'

'What?' she replied looking at me inquisitively.

I looked down at my feet there in the water and could see one of the fish making a dive for Josie's left foot. It's mouth made contact with one of her toes.

'Ah!' she shouted. 'That's sore!'

I said, 'It's those fish Josie.'

We both pulled our feet out of the water in a hurry. It was then that it happened; something flew around our heads with a loud buzzing sound, then disappeared back into the trees behind us.

'What was that?' Josie asked with that inquisitive look of hers again.

I shrugged. 'They went that-away.' I pointed back into the trees with my thumb.

A few seconds later and I heard buzzing again, this time there was more than one of them. Two of the bugs flew around our heads and then back into the trees again before I could get a proper look at them.

'What the hell are they? Bees?' I asked her.

She shrugged.

I said, 'Big enough for bumble bees but black and grey stripes.' I added, 'Don't know any bees like that.' I was looking back into the trees for any sign of them.

Within minutes, they were back. They flew round our heads again, and their antics were beginning to piss me off. I shouted, as I picked up my t-shirt, 'Get out of here!' I swung the shirt at them.

'Not a good idea to attack the enemy until you've got a clear idea of their numbers and strategy.' She giggled.

The bugs flew off back into the trees.

'You got a better idea?' I said annoyed.

'You didn't hit them did you? So for all we know, they could be about to return with the rest of the squadron.' She giggled again.

I heard them again, but this time I saw them approach too. I stood up to confront them. Just before I ducked, Josie asked giggling, 'Are they flying in formation or is it "shoot at will when they see the whites of our eyes"?'

I said annoyed as I dipped my shirt in the sea, 'Shut up Josie.'

My intention was to add some weight to the shirt in the hope that I could knock them out of the air. Unfortunately my plan failed, as the two bees merely flew around our heads faster this time, then escaped back into the trees again before I could hit them.

'Shit!' I said under my breath. 'Better not come back here guys, 'cause I'm ready for you next time.'

They did, but thankfully without reinforcements. As they arrived, closer together than last time, I ducked again, but this time I swung the shirt round my head and knocked one of them to the ground just beside Josie. She stood up quickly to get out of the way and jumped back.

I brought the shirt down on top of the bug and began hitting it as it lay there. I've just lost it for sure. I kept on hitting it, over and over until it had lost several of its legs and both wings, then something completely weird happened. Hundreds of ants appeared out of nowhere and began to carry off the body parts.

'Hurray, the cavalry's arrived!' Josie exclaimed excitedly, clasping her hands together. 'You're my heroes for sure.'

'I wouldn't get too carried away Josie. He's probably gone for the rest of the guys!'

'Well, you'll be able to deal with them won't you?' she said sarcastically. 'I'll just jump into the sea and escape and leave you to handle it, OK?'

'Yeah Josie. Whatever you say.'

It was sunbathe time. She sat on a rock and I applied sunblock to her back as she sat between my open legs, then she did it for me too. As soon as she had finished with my back, she jumped into the water. I did likewise.

I followed her again and we went down deep. We stayed down there for a while until my lungs were aching, then I felt I had to get some air, but Josie stayed down there. It didn't seem to bother her at all. How she was able to hold her breath for so long I don't know. She resurfaced finally and came up beside me. We were well away from the shore now. We spotted what we thought was a cave so we decided to swim out to it. I was out of the water first and just stood there looking at what indeed turned out to be a cave. I guess the action of the waves had removed the far end of it, and it was now completely open, and sunlight poured in there. There was a lot of shadow here at this end though, but I sat on the flat rocks in the sun. As Josie stepped out of the water, she had removed her bikini top and dropped it on a rock.

'Just as well we're in a secluded spot here,' I said as I turned onto my front and loosened my bikini top too. I don't want any pale bits.

I don't know what Josie did next as I had drifted off to sleep, but in what I thought was only seconds later, I heard a loud splash and I was suddenly drenched in water. I awoke immediately, turned onto my back and propping myself on my elbows. I looked to where I thought Josie would be but she wasn't there, then I sat up and clipped on my bikini top.

'Josie?' Then I saw her in the water. She was shushing me to silence with her fingers at her lips.

She reached out and picked up her bikini top from the rock where she had dropped it and began to put it on.

I jumped in beside her. 'Josie? What's up?'

'There's some bastard over there snapping us.'

'It's you he's interested in Josie, I would think,' I said.

'Yeah, maybe. Let's get back to the house.'

After some minutes, we had made it back to the shore. I was out of the water first. We pulled our t-shirts on and made our way back to the road that we had originally come down. The road surface was hot on our bare feet as we headed back to the cottage.

As we approached the cottage door, I noticed that it was open. 'Josie, we closed the door didn't we?'

'Yeah, you did. Maybe next door was in?' she suggested.

'Yeah, maybe,' I said as I stepped over the threshold. Then I thought, *'No, I do remember closing it.'* I said, looking around, 'Someone *has* been in here Josie.'

'I hope it was next door. I'm scared Sam.' She had her hand at her mouth.

'Yeah let's hope so. Check your pack. See if there's anything missing.' I went into my room and checked for my credit card wallet and currency, but everything appeared to be untouched. I remembered exactly where I'd put them. I went into Josie's room. She was satisfied too that nothing had been taken, and her money was where she had left it.

'Well,' I said, with hands on hips. 'Where do we go from here?'

'Next door. Ask her if she was in. Maybe she was cleaning the place.'

'And if it wasn't her?' I don't want to think about that.

She struggled into her jeans.

I went back to my room and pulled on my jeans too. As I returned to Josie I said, 'Come on, we'll go next door and get this cleared up.'

I took her by the hand and we ran out of the cottage. We put our legs over the fence and approached the door. I hammered on it and waited. No reply. I turned to her with a frown. 'If she's there she's not answering.'

'Maybe she's deaf and didn't hear the door.' She hammered the door with her two fists.

We waited and waited, then I said finally, 'Go round the back and have a look in the windows. She could be lying injured.'

As Josie disappeared around the side of the building, I had a look through the two front windows. I had to cup my hands on the glass in order to see in, the sunlight was so bright, but there didn't seem to be anything unusual here. Maybe she was lying on the floor out of sight.

Josie appeared again beside me. She shrugged. 'Can't see anything Sam. At least nothing out of the ordinary.'

'OK, I got an idea,' I said as I took Josie's hand again. We ran next door to the hotel, if indeed that is what it was. The door was open and we went inside. Reception desk was our first stop and our best bet. A guy in his thirties with a black moustache and wearing a blue uniform shirt sat there looking bored.

I said hurriedly, 'We're trying to contact the lady next door, Mrs Držislav?'

Josie said, 'She's not answering the door.'

He said, 'Maybe she's sleeping. Siesta time you know?'

Josie nodded, then she turned to me.

I shrugged. 'Yeah, OK, thanks anyway.'

He nodded and we left the hotel again.

Back in the house Josie said, 'I guess we're both getting paranoid Sam.'

'Yeah, well....' I trailed off as I went to the kitchen to turn the heat back on under the cherries.

That night we sat down to a chicken curry that Josie had picked up at the supermarket yesterday. I sat on the opposite side of the table from her in the living room. As she opened the wine and poured our drinks into crystal glasses, she said, 'I'm loving it.'

I said, 'Yeah. Sure is tasty.'

'No, here. The vacation. Glad I came.' She shovelled in a forkful of chicken.

I nodded as I took a gulp of wine. 'Yeah, so am I. Nice island, well, what we've seen of it so far.'

'We should go for a drive and take in some of the sights.' More shovelling.

'Where?' I shovelled too.

She shrugged. 'Anywhere. Does it matter?'

'Guess not.'

Neither one of us spoke for the next few minutes, but I could see Josie's brain was working on something. I know this because when those blue eyes start wandering, there's only one thing on this girl's mind. I was right.

She said dreamily, 'Know what we need right now? A couple of hunks to share this with.'

'Yeah,' I said absently as I scooped up the remaining rice on my plate. I went into the kitchen with my plate and to fetch the next course. I stopped at the window and looked out at the house next door. I wondered if Mrs Držislav had really been in here earlier, or had something more sinister been going on? I got the ice cream and the cherries from the fridge and brought them into the living room. The bowls were already on the table.

Chapter 5.

We decided not to explore the island immediately, but leave that till later. The mainland was more important. So, back on the mainland we headed into the mountains to see if we could find anything historical to photograph. We encountered a winding road that snaked down the mountainside, with a shear drop on the left-hand side into a very deep gorge and no barrier to protect you. Once the road had levelled out, we could see a castle on the opposite side of the gorge.

'Look! Over there!' Josie pointed it out.

I could see a place to pull in here on the left, so I did. I turned off the engine and we just sat there admiring the view.

'Cool,' she said excitedly and jumped out of the car with her camera.

There were four enormous boulders there at the edge to prevent vehicles from going over into the ravine. Josie selected one of them and disappeared down behind it. I grabbed my camera too and joined her there.

Around noon, Josie rescued our packed lunch from the car; a basket of sandwiches and a bottle of wine from the fridge wrapped in newspaper to keep it cool.

We had been there about thirty minutes snapping away and enjoying the sun, when Josie said, 'You hear something?'

I listened carefully but I could only hear the strong breeze and birds in my ears.

'No. What?' I was concentrating on composing my next shot.

'Listen. Does that sound to you like something metallic being dragged down the road?'

I listened carefully again and this time I did hear something. Like tin cans tied to a wedding car? 'Somebody just married?' I suggested.

I took picture of a bird of prey that I could see hovering there in the sky seeking out its quarry.

'You think they'd have the same custom here?' she asked.

I shrugged. 'Don't know much about the local customs.' I composed another shot and snapped the castle again.

The noise was much louder now. Whatever it was, it was coming our way and from the left. I decided to investigate, so I stood up and looked around, back the way we had just come. I could see a long line of traffic snaking its way very slowly down the side of the mountain, and what was responsible for the racket, appeared from around the bend and led by a police car with flashing lights. It was a large field gun on a transporter. This was quickly followed by a small armoured car with caterpillar tracks on another transporter. A young soldier stood on the footplate scanning the landscape with binoculars for any signs of the 'enemy'. I think the entire Croatian Army had turned out to greet us?

I thought with some amusement, *'Well guys. You didn't have to go to these lengths. I know Croatian hospitality is amongst the best I've known, but gee....'*

The equipment appeared to be pretty ancient-looking.

By this time Josie had stood up too. 'Wouldn't like to have to rely on this lot for defence.' She giggled.

As another armoured vehicle passed us by, two soldiers saluted us. Josie stood to attention, clicked her heels together and returned the salute, a large grin on her face. The line of vehicles moved slowly on, then a truck with about seven soldiers on board approached us. As we stood there shielding our eyes from the bright sunlight, two of the soldiers waved at us. Josie started waving back. I waved too just as one or two wolf whistles went up. The others started waving too now, then they passed us by.

Josie had a disappointed look, then she turned to me with a grin. 'Oh I'd love to date a soldier Sam,' she said with a big sigh.

I said as I looked back up the road to this seemingly endless line of vehicles, 'Get real Josie. We're not here to date soldiers. Anyway, we have to get back to the cottage. We don't want to be out all night. The ferry times you know?'

'Yeah. OK,' she sighed.

I sat on one of the rocks. It was tiring standing there in the hot sun. Josie joined me. I said, 'We'll have to wait for the end of the line, then give them time to get well ahead and we can get on our way. You can't overtake this lot.'

She said dreamily, 'Who'd want to with all those guys to choose from.' She giggled.

Thirty minutes had gone and I felt that we had waited long enough, then, at last, the end of the line. We waited another twenty minutes to give them plenty of time to get well ahead.

I said as I slid into the driving seat, 'Let's get moving Josie. We can take our time. No hurry.'

In only ten minutes, yep, you guessed it, we had caught them up! The vehicle directly in front was a truck with soldiers, and as we drew closer I could see that they were probably late teens or early twenties. Raw recruits?

Josie was beside herself with excitement. She had a wide grin plastered on, then she waved at them. This got their attention all right. They started waving back, then she loosened her belt and stood up, waving with one hand and the other grasping the windshield.

I waved too, just before I said, 'Josie, sit down.' I grasped her jeans at the back and pulled her down into the seat.

She protested, then reluctantly fastened her belt again. Her smile returned when one of the guys leaned over the tailgate and blew a kiss. Naturally Josie returned it, then waved and giggled. I waved too, but I could see that the attention was mostly on her, and she was loving it.

'I'll snap her out of her reverie,' I thought as I could see a town coming up now.

In a few more minutes, I saw a signpost pointing right. I didn't tell Josie what I was about to do, then, just as we arrived at the road, I signalled right and swung the wheel.

Josie's smile just vanished. 'Aw Sam!'

'We have to move Josie. We don't want to be on the road for the rest of the afternoon.'

'Yeah,' she replied in a disappointed tone.

Minutes later we were heading out into the countryside again. I was tired and just wanted to get back to the cottage as soon as possible. We were going to have to burn some rubber if we were to get to the ferry in time. I wasn't sure when the last one sailed. We passed farms and green fields; now and then cattle on the road. A few of the farms had stalls outside on the roadside where they sold fruit and vegetables. We stopped at one and bought some fresh fruit and a few vegetables that we were short on.

Farther on, I could see a cart pulled by a horse in front of us. He was moving too slow for me, so I decided on overtaking him. This was at the approach to a hill, but I signalled left and took a chance anyway. Unfortunately I had misjudged and realised my mistake when a Mercedes saloon came charging down on us from over the hill, and we were heading straight for it. I panicked and swung the wheel quickly to the left trying to avoid a collision, and narrowly missing the oncoming car.

'My God Sam! What are you doing!' Josie screamed, covering her face with her arm.

Just then, the other driver slammed on his brakes, and it's just as well too as we ended up on the grass verge, then he shot off down the road at great speed.

I just sat there trembling.

'You nearly killed us,' she said close to tears.

I turned to her. 'I'm sorry. Guess I'm tired, and I'm concerned about not reaching the ferry in time.'

'If you drive like that again we won't see it at all!'

As it turned out, we did make it back to the ferry in time with just an hour to spare. I needn't have worried, but I wondered if staying on an island was maybe not such a good idea after all.

That night after we ate supper, we settled down to play a game of scrabble that Josie had found in a drawer with other board games. We sat cross-legged on the floor, a glass of ice-cold beer in our hands. We had only just started playing the game when Josie's phone went off. She snapped it on and said brightly, 'Hi!' She mouthed 'mom' across at me.

I nodded and smiled back and wondered if mom or dad would be in touch too. I heard her say, 'It's cool mom. The weather's just right for us so far. Done some swimming and seen some sights.'

I looked through my letter tiles and found a word to place in the centre of the board; 'dazzle'. When I had totalled it up I had gained 35 points. 'Yes!' I exclaimed.

Josie had a frown on for a second as she looked at me, then, 'We're staying on an island. It's awesome! You wouldn't believe the secluded spots we've found. Yeah, we've got the place to ourselves all right.'

I thought as I looked at the board, *'You haven't got a chance against me Josie.'* Relieved that I was on a winning streak, I got up from my position on the floor and went to the kitchen to get us some more ice for our drinks. I heard Josie say, 'Bye mom. Talk to you again soon.'

I returned to the living room with ice in an ice bucket. I placed it beside us on the floor as I sat down again with my right leg tucked under me. 'Everything fine back home Josie?'

She smiled. 'Yeah. Mom's got a slight cold otherwise....' She hesitated as her eyes took in the tiles that I had placed in the centre of the board. 'Hey, what's that you've got there?' She laughed as she pointed to the tiles.

I laughed too. 'May as well give up now Josie. I got you beat.'

She started looking through her own tiles. 'Ha!' she exclaimed triumphantly and giggled as she began to place her own tiles on the board. The word 'dozey' materialised there, then she sat back to examine my expression with a wide grin plastered on.

I was mentally totalling her score when her cellphone rang its musical tone again.

She frowned as she said, 'Maybe mom again.' She snapped it on. 'Hi, mom?' She hesitated, then, 'Hello? Is someone there? Hello?' She shrugged as she closed the phone.

'Wrong number?' I asked as I fidgeted with my tiles on the floor.

'Dunno,' she said frowning. 'Guess so.' She sighed as she threw the phone onto the couch then returned her attention to the game.

We had only been playing for about thirty minutes when my cellphone went off this time. 'Yeah?'

A male voice with a thick east European accent said, 'You don't know me, but I was a friend of your friend, Tomislav Petrović?'

My heart missed a beat. 'OK,' I said wondering what this was all about.

Josie played with her tiles on the floor; arranging and rearranging them.

'He and I shared some good times, and photos were taken of us together. I was wondering if you had any idea where they might be?'

'How would I know? I don't know what you look like?'

Josie was studying my face with a question mark above her head.

He said, 'Yes, well that was going to be my next question. Can we meet somewhere and maybe when you see me it could jog a memory? He must have shown you photos at some point, yes?'

I thought for a few seconds. 'Yes, he did, and you're right, I might recognise you.'

Josie had stopped trying to form words for the moment, her attention fully on my face.

'So, can we meet in Restoran National?'

'I've honestly no idea where that is.'

'You were there already with your young friend a few days ago.'

'Oh, OK....' I broke off wondering how he knew, then, 'Were you the guy behind the newspaper?' I gave a short laugh.

He laughed too as he said, 'That was me. I recognised you from the newspaper photograph after the bomb blast. I kept the photograph after Tomislav was killed.'

'Oh, yes, of course. I'd forgotten about that.'

The police had suggested putting my picture in the newspaper after Tomislav's car blew up, and claiming that I had been killed in the explosion to avoid any possible reprisals. They knew, or suspected, that there were some members of the gang (some of the ringleaders presumably) still at large, and that they could have escaped across the border into one of the neighbouring states where there was no extradition agreement. I mentioned this to him.

'When I saw you in the restaurant I was certain I'd seen you before. I've a good memory for faces.' He laughed.

I joined in.

He continued, 'Maybe we can go to his house and see if we can find those pictures?'

'Where would you start looking?' I asked finding myself becoming interested.

'Well they could be on a disc like a CD or maybe his PC's hard drive? Could take a while.'

'Oh, what did you say your name was, and how did you get my cellphone number?'

'It's Milos Dragović, and I got your number from one of his diaries.'

My heart missed another beat. 'You've been at his house then?'

'Yes. His mother still lives there.'

'I know. Why didn't you just ask her for whatever you were looking for?' I fiddled with my tiles.

Josie's looking at me in curiosity again.

He laughed. 'She wouldn't give them to me.'

I laughed too. 'Neither would I.'

'She said she wouldn't give any of his things to a stranger, and she wouldn't let me get near the PC.'

'Sensible woman. I'd do the same.' I laughed. 'Ah!' I exclaimed as I found a word to put on the board.

'What did you say?' he asked.

'Oh, nothing. Just......' I trailed off as I mentally worked on my score. *'Twenty six for "jockey",'* I thought as I placed the tiles on the board.

'So, I'll meet you at the restaurant at say......12 noon tomorrow?' He hesitated, then added, 'I'll buy you lunch.'

'OK Mr Dragović, I accept. I'll meet you at the restaurant at noon.'

I was about to switch off my phone when he said, 'Call me Milos, Sam.'

I laughed. 'OK, Milos, bye,' I said as I turned off the phone.

As Josie placed her contribution on the board she said, 'Looks like you got a date?'

I smiled but didn't say anything. I found another word and placed it.

She said with a smirk, 'Looks like I'll have this place to myself tomorrow then.'

'Oh no you don't Josie. You're coming along with me, but you'll sit in the car and wait for me.' I'm playing it safe here until I can trust this guy. I want her out of harm's way as well for the moment.

'What? But you're having lunch with him. What about my lunch?' she asked sounding annoyed.

'Bring sandwiches and a drink.'

She sighed. 'Yeah, OK,' she agreed reluctantly.

Next morning around half eleven, we headed off to that restarant with all the bad memories. I parked the car along the street facing the restaurant and within sight of it, then I told Josie to sit there and wait for me to give her a signal, namely, when I stand up from the table. I may need her to come rescue me.

As I stepped out of the car onto the sidewalk I turned to her. 'Remember what I said.'

Josie just nodded and looked away. She's not happy about this; maybe even jealous. Well, I can't say I blame her. I think I would be too.

As I drew near to the restaurant, I looked back to the car and gave her a little wave. She returned it, albeit, reluctantly. When I reached the restaurant, it was deserted; unusual for lunchtime, but more importantly, where was he? I sat down at the nearest table with my back to the street, and one that gave me a clear view of our car. I wanted Josie to see me should I require her assistance.

As I turned my attention back to the matter in hand, I spotted Milos inside the restaurant. Well I thought it was him anyway. If it was, he had lost the moustache and put away his dark glasses for the moment. He wore a bright orange Hawaiian shirt and white pants. He was speaking to someone, then he came outside. Gosh he was handsome. He spotted me sitting there on my own. He approached the table and I almost stood up, but I caught myself in time.

'Sam, at last. It's a pleasure to meet you.'

As he took my hand to kiss it, I blushed and said, 'I'd stand up only my foot is sore.' I smiled and nodded.

After he kissed it he said surprised, 'Oh? I have some medical knowledge.'

He was just about to bend to examine it when I said quickly, 'No, it's OK, I'll survive, thanks.' I glanced quickly down the street towards our car. Josie was sitting behind the wheel. *Hope she doesn't have any ideas about taking off in the car. She's under-age,'* I thought.

He saw my look. 'Your friend?'

I nodded. 'Oh, she's shopping.' I reddened. 'Keeps her out of mischief you know?' I laughed.

He sat down.

I said, leaning across the table to him, 'A little quiet for this time in the day isn't it?'

He nodded. 'That'll change shortly.' He smiled.

I wondered what he meant by that. Was he psychic as well as good-looking? I almost giggled out loud. I stole another glance down the street. Josie was engaged in conversation with a guy leaning on the door. Was he chatting her up or asking directions, or was it the other way round? No, Josie wouldn't ask directions.

Just before I turned back to Milos, I had caught with peripheral vision, a middle-aged guy in a yellow shirt and blue pants come out of the restaurant interior. *'Clientèle at last?'* I thought. No. Diners don't carry mandolins under their arms. He was quickly followed by another around the same age in identical clothes and carrying an acoustic guitar, then another figure, and yes, you guessed right, wearing the same uniform, but somewhat younger, and carrying a double-bass. He joined his comrades close to our table. They stood a little off to my left. They didn't make any attempt to play anything, but appeared to be awaiting instructions.

My heart was doing a marathon. *'Does he do this for every girl he meets?'* I thought smiling to myself.

He smiled and said, 'I thought we might do this properly.'

I just nodded and smiled, oh, and blushed too.

'Would you like to request something?'

I said blushing again, 'Oh, em, really Milos.....' I thought happily with a contented sigh, *'Gosh this is so romantic, but why is he doing this?'*

He interrupted with, 'It's OK, I'll choose then.' He said something in Croatian I think, to one of the musicians, and they started playing something resembling a Greek number. Well that's how it sounded to me anyway. It was slow and very nice, oh, and romantic, then one of them began to sing.

I looked quickly down the street again and could see Josie standing up in the driver's side. She's heard the music. Hope she doesn't think of joining us.

He said as he pushed his chair back preparing to stand, 'Do you dance?'

I blushed again. 'I can't Milos.' I pointed to my foot. 'My foot?'

He stood up and said smiling, 'That's OK. You can put your weight on the other one. I'll hold you.'

I was just about to say something when my life was saved by the waiter arriving at our table. He just stood there, pen poised over notebook. He looked at us both in turn.

Milos sat down again.

'Ah,' I said and gave a silent sigh of relief. 'Em.… I haven't really had time to study the menu.' It had been propped against a sauce bottle in the centre of the table. I picked it up and began to scan down the list of lunch items.

'I'll choose if you like?' Milos said.

'Pardon?' I looked at him over the menu.

He laughed. 'I can choose if you can't decide.'

I looked at him over the menu again. 'Oh, no, it's OK.' I turned to the waiter. 'Cheese and tomato omelette?' Well I think that's what it said, but then I could have been mistaken. Some kind of omelette anyway. It was printed in Croatian.

He wore a blank expression.

I said quickly in Italian, 'Un'omelette di formaggio e pomodoro?' *'Cheese and tomato omelette?'*

He nodded and wrote it down.

The band began to play a fast number. I found my feet tapping to the rhythm.

Milos nodded to the waiter. 'Schinken und Pilzomelette für mich, ach und Kaffee, danke.' *'Ham and mushroom omelette for me, oh and coffee please,'* he said in German.

I placed the menu back in the centre of the table and asked, 'Milos, why did you go to all this trouble for me? I thought it was the photographs that you wanted?' I thought suddenly, *'No silly. It's you he wants.'*

He reached out and took my right hand in his two. 'When I saw your picture in the newspaper, I realised there was a chemistry between us. I just had to meet you in person.'

'Listen Milos. I don't think I have seen you in any photograph. It's been three years now since the bomb blast, but I think I would have remembered you.'

'We all forget things with time. When we get to the house, if any photographs exist, we'll find them.' He nodded.

'Seems a lot of trouble to go to just for some pictures,' I said as he returned my hand.

'Believe me, it's important. They mean a lot to me.'

The waiter arrived with our meal and placed the plates in front of us. We tucked in immediately. I was starved. I think Milos was too the way he attacked that omelette.

I said through a mouthful of food, 'Could take a while to find them, especially if he had a large collection of photos.'

'Yes. Well, that's where you come in. Mrs Petrović, as I told you, didn't want to give anything to me, but she might give you access to his things.' He elected to be mom and poured the coffee for us.

'Thanks,' I said in response to the coffee. 'Maybe Josie can help us too,' I suggested. Do I want her in on this? I can't decide right now.

His eyebrows went up just then. 'Josie?'

'My friend?'

'Oh, yes, well, why not. Wouldn't do any harm.' He smiled.

'And after we find whatever it is you're looking for?' I produced one of my broadest smiles.

He laid his hand on mine. 'Maybe we can get to know one another better too.'

I thought, smiling to myself, *'Hmm. I think I like this guy. He sure is handsome but I think I like him better with the moustache.'* I wondered if he used the photos as an excuse to meet me, or was he using me as a means to get to the photos, in which case they must be very important?

The next few minutes passed without any conversation, then I asked, 'What do you do for a living Milos?' I drank down some coffee.

'Bank. I handle money. Big responsibility you know, and you?'

I told him about the second-hand bookshop and my writing. He seemed interested and asked a few questions, then I felt I needed a pee and that's when I blew it.

'You didn't happen to notice where the restroom was? The Ladies' I mean?' I laughed as I pushed my chair back and stood up. 'I need a.... shit!' I said under my breath when I suddenly realised my mistake.

'Pardon?' he said.

With my face reddening, I said hurriedly, 'The bathroom. Have to go.'

As I marched off to find it, I heard him say to my back, 'It's just off....' I couldn't hear the rest over the street noise.

I found the restroom on the left. I thought just as I pushed through the door, *Jesus. Josie will be here soon. Have to make this quick.'*

As I came out of the restroom, I spotted Josie walking up to the table closest to the street, where she sat down. She's enjoying this. I could tell by the way she smiled that little cute smile and her gemstone in her navel glinting in the sunlight, and her California tan on show.

Milos stared straight ahead. His attention seemed to be fixed on Josie, or was that just my impression? I noticed also that the musicians had gone.

I thought, *'No you don't Josie. This is my show.'* I marched up to our table and said as I looked down on him, 'Hi. I'm back.'

Did he even notice me? If he did, he didn't react. *'I'll get his attention all right,'* I thought as I sat down in my place and hopefully blocking his view of Josie.

Yep, it worked. He snapped out of his trance and began to focus his attention on me once more, well, that is, until I heard Josie push her chair back and, in seconds, was standing by our table. She just stood there with her hands in her back pockets and chest thrust out. A lot of cleavage on show here. Did she dress like that on purpose today? She put out her hand for him to shake, 'Hi, I'm Josie.'

Milos stood up and kissed her hand. 'So you're Josie?' He leaned toward her and kissed her on the left cheek. 'Milos Dragović. Pleased to meet you Josie.'

She reddened and looked round for a chair to sit down. Milos found one for her and she sat between the two of us on my right, her arms resting on the table.

As he sat down again he said, 'I'll ask the waiter to get us a drink. Are you hungry?'

She shook her head, her smile still in place. 'It's OK, and I've eaten, thanks.'

He said, 'We could do with some extra help Josie.'

She looked at me for an explanation.

I forgot that she didn't know what this was all about. 'He thinks my friend Tomislav had photos of the two of them together. Personal stuff you know? He'd like to have them.' I told her about Tomislav's mom not wanting to give him his things etc.

She turned back to Milos. 'Must be important to you?'

He nodded. 'Very.'

I had just finished off my omelette. He hadn't quite finished his but he pushed his plate away anyway and dabbed at his lips with his napkin. He said, 'There may be other mementoes as well as the photos, but they can come later.'

I had just finished off my coffee. I poured another cup and offered it to Josie. She shook her head.

Chapter 6.

Before we set off for Tomislav's house, Milos suggested that we travel in his car, but I insisted on Josie and I following him in his. Just playing it safe.

We headed out into the countryside with green fields and farms. I couldn't remember precisely where Tom's house was located, but Milos seemed to know, and it wasn't long before we were pulling up outside it. It was situated at the end of a row of five almost identical cottages, built of the local grey stone and with red tiled roofs.

I knocked the heavy wooden door. It was opened by a short elderly woman about my height with a very wrinkled face, and wearing a long black dress with bright red flowers. I had met Tomislav's mom three years ago when I was here last, and she recognised me immediately. Mrs Petrović shook my hand and threw her arms around me and kissed me warmly on both cheeks, then shook Josie's hand too.

She smiled when she saw Josie and I standing there, but her hand went to her throat and her smile vanished when her eyes took in Milos who was standing just off to the right at Josie's back.

Josie and I exchanged glances. I said in Italian, because I knew she had no English, 'Cosa è la questione? C'è qualche cosa sbagliato?' *'What's the matter? Is there something wrong?'*

There was alarm in her voice as she said in a whisper, 'È quell'uomo.' *'It's that man.'*

I said reassuringly as I patted her arm, 'È OK. Lui è il mio amico. Oh, e questo è il mio amico Josie Moore.' *'It's OK. He's my friend. Oh, and this is my friend Josie Moore.'*

'Oh mio caro. Lei sia nella macchina quando la bomba esplose. Loro dissero che Lei era stato ucciso nell'esplosione. La Sua salute è meglio? Per favore entri.' *'Oh my dear. You were in the car when the bomb exploded. They said that you had been killed in the explosion. Is your health better? Please come in.'* I told her about the newspaper photograph and the plan to get the remaining gang members off my back.

She nodded her understanding.

We stepped into the living room, but as Milos stepped over the threshold, she turned her face away from him and beckoned Josie and I to sit down. Milos wasn't even invited.

'È meraviglioso per vederLa di nuovo. Lei non cambiò siccome io La vidi prima.' *'It's wonderful to see you again. You haven't changed since I saw you before.'*

Josie wasn't getting any of this of course. I said, 'Josie non capisce italiano.' *'Josie doesn't understand Italian.'*

She nodded and said, 'Può tradurre per lei?' *'You can translate for her?'*

I nodded.

She asked, 'Josie è dell'America anche?' *'Is Josie from America too?'*

I nodded. 'Sì.' *'Yes.'*

'Quindi quello che La porta di nuovo qui mio caro?' *'What brings you here again my dear?'* she asked.

'È delle fotografie e cose alle quali Tomislav ed io abbiamo guardato quando io lo visitai. Stavo chiedendomi se Lei potesse permettermi di avere le fotografie?' *'It was some photographs and things that Tomislav and I looked at when I visited him. I was wondering if you could let me have the photos?'* I relayed this to Josie.

'Io non sono sicuro che io dovrei fare questo. Io non voglio dare via qualsiasi cosa.' *'I'm not sure that I should do this. I don't want to give away anything.'* She looked anxious. 'È l'unico modo che io posso ricordarlo.' *'It's the only way that I can remember him,'* she continued. She was close to tears.

I translated for Josie again.

I patted her arm reassuringly. 'È del tutto corretto. Noi possiamo fare una copia delle fotografie e Lei può tenere l'originale.' *'That's all right. We can make a copy and you keep the original.'* I said to Josie, 'We can make a copy.'

She nodded. 'Yeah.'

Mrs Petrović nodded and seemed satisfied with that, then added, 'Posso parlare con Lei Sam? È importante.' *'Can I speak with you Sam? It's important.'*

I looked at Josie. 'Back in a minute.' My heart was racing. What was wrong with her? Before I could ask, she took me by the arm and led me into the kitchen. She said hurriedly as she closed the door, 'Non mi piace quell'uomo.' *'I don't like that man.'* She started to shed a tear.

My heart was doing a marathon now. I thought, *'Milos? She doesn't like him?'* 'Cosa disse?' *'What did you say?'* I asked.

'Mi piacerebbe se lui andrebbe e mi lascerebbe in pace.' *'I would like it if he would go and leave me in peace.'*

I said, trying to reassure her, 'Non preoccupi. Noi saremo andati al più presto possibile.' *'Don't worry. We'll be gone as soon as possible.'*

'Quell'uomo che Milos ritornava qui un tempo. Lui disse lui era un amico di Tomislav e che lui volle fotografie che mio figlio aveva preso di ambo di loro. Io rifiutai di darglieli. Io gli dissi di andare via e non infastidirmi di nuovo.'

'That man Milos was here a while back. He said he was a friend of Tomislav and that he wanted photographs that my son had taken of both of them. I refused to give them to him. I told him to go away and not bother me again.' She continued as she clasped her hands together in front of her, 'Prima che Tomislav fosse ucciso, lui mi disse che lui era stato minacciato da alcuni dei membri di banda che non erano stati arrestati.' *'Before Tomislav was killed, he told me that he had been threatened by some of the gang members who had not been arrested.'*

I nodded. 'Sì, io so. Lui mi disse anche.' *'Yes, I know. He told me too.'*

I opened the kitchen door and called Josie in. She and Milos had been on Tom's PC searching discs. She came into the kitchen and I told her what Mrs Petrović had just told me. She said, a little shocked, 'Maybe Tomislav deleted them when he was threatened, because we're not any closer to finding anything that has Milos in it.'

I relayed this to Tom's mom.

'No, lui non farebbe quello. Gli piacque molto Lei Sam. Forse lui dimenticò che lui aveva le fotografie.' *'No, he wouldn't do that. He liked you a lot Sam. Maybe he forgot that he had the photos.'*

'Forse.' *'Maybe,'* I said lost in thought. I relayed this to Josie. 'Le fotografie di me non avevano valore. Io stavo ponendo facce sciocche quando lui prese la mia fotografia, così ancora è possibile che lui faceva li cancellati.' *'The photos of me had no value. I was making silly faces when he took my photograph, so it's still possible that he did delete them.'*

I translated for Josie. She said, 'I'd better get back to Milos and see if we can find those pictures, if they exist.'

'I'll join you shortly Josie,' I said.

Mrs Petrović told me to go back to Josie and the computer and she would bring us in coffee. I did and found Milos looking in drawers in the computer desk. I started doing the same with another drawer on the right-hand side of the desk, while Josie busied herself on the PC searching the hard drive and CDs.

Mrs Petrović brought in three mugs of coffee and some chocolate cake for us. The coffee was welcome. I think that omelette was a little salty.

Milos was looking through some DVDs in a large cardboard box on a tabletop for anything labelled 'photos'.

I was on my knees searching the bottom drawer in the desk when Josie squeezed my arm. I looked up at her. She put a finger to her lips hushing me to silence. I thought, my heart racing, *'God. She's found something.'* I looked at the screen. She had typed into 'search', the word 'restaurant' and the system came up with six pictures. They were only thumbnails but I could just make out myself sitting there making silly faces into the camera. There were other people there in the background but I couldn't make them out properly due to the small size of the pictures. I turned to Milos who was too preoccupied to notice what we had found, and I wasn't about to tell him.

Without saying a word to me, Josie enlarged one of the pictures on the screen and there was no doubt about it; this was the photo that the gang were looking for. I was sitting facing the camera with my back to them and…. no, I don't believe it – Milos was seated with them facing the camera.

'Shit,' I heard Josie say under her breath. She chose 'select all' from a pull-down menu which highlighted all six photos, then hit 'delete'. They vanished from the screen and would be transferred to the 'trashcan', then it's just a matter of retrieving them from there. This was so Milos wouldn't see them.

I turned to Milos who was still searching through CDs that he found on a shelf. 'We're going to search the trashcan now. See if they're there.'

He said, straightening up, 'Off to find the bathroom.' He went into the kitchen and closed the door.

My heart was racing now for sure. I said to Josie, 'That dirty, rotten…..' I was fuming. I have to keep my cool. Everything has to seem normal to Milos when he gets back here. We don't want him to get suspicious. I rummaged in the bottom drawer again where I had previously seen a blue flash memory stick. I found it and handed it to Josie.

As she double-clicked the trashcan icon on the desktop, she said in a low voice, 'Sure had you fooled there didn't he? Falling for his charms. Believing it all…..' She trailed off.

'I did not. I had this feeling about him. Uncomfortable feeling, you know?'

'Yeah sure you did,' she teased. Now she had the trashcan open. She put the flash memory into a USB socket and in seconds, had it's contents displayed there on the screen. None of them meant anything to us. Resizing both windows (making them smaller on the screen), all she had to do now was 'drag' the deleted pictures across from the trashcan and 'drop' them into the flash memory window; here they would be saved. This only took seconds to do. Now we have evidence for the police.

I'm just remembering something. Milos had told me that he found my cell number in one of Tomislav's diaries. That was a lie because I didn't give him my number. If we wanted to communicate quickly we did it by e-mail. The reason why he was in the cottage was to get my number so he could phone me and pretend he was Tomislav's friend.

As Josie turned off the PC, I could hear the toilet being flushed. He'll be here in a minute. I put an arm around Josie's shoulder and kissed her on the left cheek. I said, 'Got you now Mister Casanova.'

Just then, the kitchen door opened and Milos came in. 'Find anything?' he asked as his eyes took in the blank monitor.

I turned. 'Oh, no. Well not what you were looking for anyway.' I looked at Josie. She pursed her lips and stared straight ahead.

'Well that's very disappointing,' he said rubbing his chin in thought.

I said, 'Yeah, well, Tomislav has obviously deleted them.'

He shook his head. 'No, he wouldn't do that. He was my friend re-member?'

I thought, *'Liar.'*

Josie said as she slid herself out of the computer chair, 'We'll have to be going now. Got a ferry to catch.' She put out her hand to him. He shook it but didn't say anything.

I said as I put out my hand to him too, 'Well it was nice meeting you Milos. Thanks for the lunch, oh and the music.' I blushed, then I stood up on tiptoes and kissed him on the left cheek. I felt my face burn.

He just stood there looking at both of us in turn, then he smiled. 'Yes it was a pleasure meeting you both. Perhaps we'll meet again at a later date.'

'Not if I can help it,' I thought quickly, then turned to go. 'We'll go into town and catch a few sights before heading off home.' I took Josie's hand as we headed for the front door. I shouted to Mrs Petrović, 'Ciao a Lei la Sigra Petrović! Noi ora stiamo andando via!' *'Goodbye Mrs Petrović! We are just leaving!'*

The kitchen door opened and she came through. We said our goodbyes and there were tears all round, well, with the exception of Milos. He had already opened the door and was stepping out of the house.

As we returned to our car, I turned to see Milos heading off in the opposite direction from town. I jumped into the driving seat and immediately had flashbacks to that awful day when Tomislav was killed. I said, 'Sure you got the flash memory?'

She nodded smiling and patting her front pocket.

I smiled too and started the engine.

Back in town, I parked in the town square, then we headed straight for the Police Station in an adjoining street. This is the same place where Tom and I had taken our evidence that day. Well that was our intended destination anyway. I could see it across the busy main street, so it was just a matter of crossing and...... my cellphone went off. As I reached for the phone in my front pocket, I was slightly irritated at having to answer it in the street. I usually find it difficult to hear what the caller is saying for all the street noise. 'Hi.' I stopped just before I reached the curb. I covered my other ear with my hand in order to hear better.

'Don't..... the street!' a male voice said.

I couldn't make out what he was saying. 'Sorry? What......? Who's calling?' There was no number displayed.

'Just do as I say. Don't step off.....' A heavy truck thundered by.

'I'm sorry. I can't....' I just missed that one too.

'There's a high-powered rifle aimed at you.....!' Some honking of vehicle horns.

'What!' My heart was thumping hard.

Josie had just stepped off the sidewalk. I panicked and screamed at her to get back. She turned to me with a look of alarm.

The voice shouted, 'Don't go to the police..... photographs.....' More loud noise.

I grabbed Josie's hand and pulled her down behind a parked car with me. I was now sitting on the ground with Josie on top of my right leg.

She asked concerned, 'What's wrong Sam? What are you doing'?'

She made a move to rise, and I pulled her down toward me. This time she fell on top of me. I was lying on my back now.

'What are you *doing*?' she asked again; a tremble in her voice.

'There's a guy somewhere nearby threatening to shoot us with a high-powered rifle if we try to go to the police with the photos.....' I trailed off wondering what our next move should be.

'*What*! I don't believe it. Is this anything to do with that guy Milos?'

'I don't know Josie. Probably.'

The voice spoke again, and this time there was no mistaking what he said, 'I will be in touch again, and we will agree to a rendezvous point where you will hand over the photos. Is that clear?'

I shouted back in defiance, 'You can go to hell!' Well maybe that wasn't the most intelligent thing to say right then, but I had just lost my cool and....

Josie cut into my thoughts, 'Sam? What the hell have you got us into?' She was on the verge of tears.

I asked, not believing this girl, '*I* got us into?'

'Well, if it hadn't been for you...' She interrupted herself, 'What did they say right then?'

I told her about the rendezvous point.

She shook her head. 'We can't Sam. How do we know they won't just shoot us? We can identify Milos.'

I nodded. 'There won't be a rendezvous point, or if there is, it'll be on our terms Josie.'

I could tell by her expression that she wasn't believing this. I was right. 'Yeah, right,' she said standing up. 'They're not going to shoot us now are they?' she said looking around apprehensively. 'They need those pictures.'

I got up too and grasped her hand quickly. I said as I began to pull her with me, 'Get back to the car. We'll sort this out later.'

When we got back to the town square, and the parked car, I said, 'Check the car Josie.'

She suddenly let go of my hand and just stood there staring at me with that incredulous look of hers. 'What?'

'Josie, we have to check the car.'

She said, hands on hips, 'What are you talking about?'

I said hurriedly, 'You check the front, I'll take the rear.' I was about to turn away, but Josie continued to stand and stare at me with a confused look.

'*What*?' I asked.

'Sam, could you tell me what we're looking for, and where do I look?'

'Under the front? Like a small black ball with a fuse sticking out of the top?' I turned away from her and got down on the ground to have a look. I'm not too sure what I'm looking for either.

I heard Josie shout, 'This is no time for jokes.....!'

I cut in with, 'I ain't joking. Do I look as though I'm laughing?' Well at least this end was clear of anything suspicious.

I went back to Josie. She was just getting up as I approached. She had a smile on. 'OK this end too,' she proclaimed.

I suddenly had a thought. We haven't checked under the hood. I told Josie to pop the hood, then I had a look inside. I'm not familiar with this make of car so I don't know my way around the engine compartment. I checked anyway but didn't find anything suspicious, thank God.

'Let's get moving,' I said jumping into the driving seat. 'If we take the freeway heading south we'll be in plenty of time for the 5 pm ferry.'

I knew there was a freeway running almost parallel with the Magistrala, and would be a whole lot quicker route to Zadar. We found it without too much hassle and now we were well on our way to the ferry and home. Everything was going well; we had not a care in the world, that is, so long as this gang kept off our backs, and we didn't go to the police. The freeway was busy with the usual daredevil kamikaze brigade zigzagging in and out of and between vehicles, but we weren't in any particular hurry.

At a certain point on the journey, we had noticed that it had become un-usually quiet, with very little traffic now. No-one passed us at all; no-one tried to overtake, and we didn't meet any other vehicles approaching on the oppo-site carriageway. Very strange. I voiced my thoughts to Josie. She agreed.

I had the radio volume turned up high; Elvis was belting out of the speakers and Josie was singing at the top of her lungs and trying to do Elvis impersonations from her seat. She loosened her belt, stood up and pretended to play a guitar.

As we sped along the highway at around 60 mph, I took my hands off the wheel to clap her performance, then, as we were fast approaching a bend, I took control again. I said laughing, 'Better get down Josie. Don't want the cops stopping us.'

She was just about to sit when she suddenly let out a loud scream, 'Sam! Slow down! Now!'

I couldn't hear her properly for the loud music and the wind in my ears. 'What! What's wrong Josie!'

She sat down quickly and fastened her belt. 'Hit the brake quick!'

'Pardon?' I stabbed at the radio 'off' button.

'Hit the brake damn it!' she screamed.

I did and the car slew across the road and came to a sudden halt. I un-buckled my belt and stood up quickly. The pavement had just given way to gravel, and the drop was around two feet! We could have been killed if the car had gone off here!

'Sam? How did we get here?' She was standing too at this point.

We couldn't believe our eyes. I just shook my head. I was close to tears and trembling. I think we both were.

'We didn't go through any barriers did we? We just shouldn't be here at all,' she said sitting down again.

I shook my head again. 'I don't know Josie. It doesn't make any sense.' I sat down and put the car into gear.

'Do you think it could have been anything to do with them?'

As I turned the car around I said, 'Maybe, or maybe just someone's stupid mistake.'

I hit the gas hard and we shot off to find an exit ramp.

That night we had beef lasagne, and over dinner, Josie brought up the subject of our dilemma. 'Sam. Maybe we should tell the police.'

I said, not believing my ears, 'Are you crazy? They'll probably kill us.'

'How are they going to know?'

'Quite simple. Police get onto them and try to make some arrests. OK, they will have the photo of Milos, but the others, if there are any others, may be more difficult to catch, and that's when we become targets.' I poured myself some more wine.

'But we can't just sit around doing nothing can we?' She poured herself a glassful.

'That's exactly what we do – nothing. Let them make all the moves. They need the pictures, so, let then come and get them.' I had a smug look in place.

'Just like that huh?'

I took a gulp of my drink. 'Yep. Just like that.'

'O-K,' she said slowly, then, 'You really are mad aren't you?' She laughed.

'Listen Josie. I don't believe in playing games by other people's rules. We wait till they tell us what their rendezvous plans are, then promptly refuse to have anything to do with them. Simple.'

Josie was speechless. She had a forkful of lasagne halfway to her mouth when I made that last statement. 'But.....'

I cut in with, 'Josie, you worry too much.' I reached over and poured her glass to the top. 'We're leaving here tomorrow. Pack your things.'

She almost choked on her lasagne. 'What? But I thought you liked it here?'

'Yeah I do, but they know where we are. It's not safe here Josie. How do you think Milos got my number? Someone was in here the other day.'

She nodded.

'OK, so the sooner we get out of here the better. I'm going next door to tell Mrs Držislav that we're moving on.' So that's what I did. We just had three nights to pay for.

Next morning we were off to Zadar and there we deposited the car. That's all the driving that I intended to do for the moment. Milos and Co know our car and will no doubt be looking out for it. Maybe now we can relax a little and get on with our vacation. The plan was to set out from Zadar by bus and travel to the Plitviče Lakes National Park where we hoped to view wildlife and the gorgeous lakes there. The Tourism Bureau recommended it. It's a UNESCO World Heritage site too so it should be interesting.

We stepped off the bus two hours later, just before the park entrance, then hiked back the way we had just come. That's because I had spotted a house offering rooms. The door was answered by an overweight elderly woman wearing a dark blue dress and cardigan to match. She had a big friendly smiling face and lots of motherly love to heap on us. She introduced herself as Ana Lenković.

'Pozdravi.' *'Greetings,'* she said as she shook our hands warmly.

We didn't say anything at all at first, then I thought I'd try German, but she didn't understand, so I tried Italian, again with the same result. What I was trying to say was 'hello', so I did, 'Hello.'

She nodded and smiled then she stepped aside to let us into the hallway. She was so nice to us despite her almost total lack of English. No sooner had we stepped into the living room, and she produced a lovely spread of home baking and all the Turkish coffee we could drink.

She invited us to sit down. We nodded our thanks and sat on a beautiful red satin couch. The food was set on a long coffee table. Ana left us to it as she disappeared into the kitchen.

'This is nice. I like it,' I said nodding.

'Yeah, sure is.' Josie was pouring the coffee for us into orange mugs.

I was tucking into a piece of fruit cake as I said, 'I'd like to get my hands on a Croatian phrasebook, or just anything that will translate for us.'

Once we had drunk enough coffee and eaten our fill of the baking, I said, 'If I eat any more I won't have room for lunch.' I looked at my watch and it was fast approaching 11 o'clock.

Josie stood up and started making her way to the living room door. She said turning, 'I'm off to the bathroom to have a shower,' then she hesitated. 'Going to have to ask Ana. What is the Croatian for bathroom anyway?'

I shrugged and shook my head. I joined her there at the door.

Just then, the door opened and Ana came in. She still had that big friendly smile on her face.

I said, 'Bathroom?'

Josie nodded.

Ana had a blank stare.

I said, 'Toilet?'

Another blank stare and this time a shrug.

Josie said, 'Ladies?'

More shrugs from Ana, then, at last, she stepped back into the hallway and made for a door on the right. She pointed to it and we followed her there. Sure enough it was the bathroom. She pointed to it again and said, 'Kupaonica.'

Josie tried pronouncing it. It sounded very close to how Ana had pronounced it.

I smiled at Josie and attempted it myself.

Ana nodded and smiled. 'Vrlo dobro.'

We both smiled back and shrugged. Ana just laughed and turned to the kitchen. We went to the bathroom to freshen up.

I said, as I stood at the sink about to wash my face, 'Next stop's the park Josie. We can find lunch there too.'

Josie was stripping off her clothes preparing to shower. 'Maybe we can find a shop selling phrase books?'

'Yeah. Might be a fun language to learn. Maybe I'll get one of those home study language courses when we get back.'

She stepped into the shower and I heard the water being turned on. 'Or we could do it together? Like going to a class together if they have them locally?'

'Yeah. I'll have to look into that when we get back. Would be fun to come back here and just mix with the locals and not have any language problems.'

I finished with my washing and reattached my hair clasp, then turned to the shower cubicle at my back. I pulled the curtain aside quickly.

Josie had a surprised look on her face as she sprayed her front with the water. 'What?'

'Nothing.....' I was cut off by Josie directing the water onto me. 'Hey!' I laughed.

I stepped into the shower briefly and snatched the shower head out of her grasp, then turned the water temperature to cold! Yep, all the way, then directed the spray onto her.

She screamed and screamed at me and giggled at the same time, then turned her back to the spray. 'Stop it! It's freezing!'

I turned the temperature up again and stepped out of the cubicle.

As I drew the curtain closed again, I heard her say, 'I'll get you back when you least expect it.' She laughed.

Josie joined me back in the hallway just outside the bathroom. We met Ana there. She said, 'Idemo?' She indicated that we follow her. She opened a bedroom door on the left just beyond the kitchen.

We both stood at the doorway and looked into the room. Looked nice and clean and tidy. Well it's only for sleeping in after all. I went in and looked around. No bathroom here. I joined them again at the door. I said, 'Money? How much?'

Ana shrugged with a blank look.

I found some coins in my pocket. I jiggled them together without taking them out. She got the message. She told us the price and we both nodded.

Chapter 7.

We carried our cameras; mine slung around my neck and Josie's tucked into her front pocket. We walked arm-in-arm down the road towards the park entrance. There was no gate here, just a sign over the road indicating the name of the park. A road branched off to the right and we could see several cars parked beside a wooden building. I could see, or thought I could, flames now and then coming from somewhere close to this structure. I'm curious. I turned to Josie. I think she read my thoughts. We quickened our steps and in seconds, had reached what turned out to be three buildings. The first appeared to be a gift shop and the next was circular, or more precisely, hexagonal, and was a completely open structure without walls; just a shelter. Here barbecued food was being prepared. Three girls dressed in black vests and pants appeared to be responsible for the cooking. The third building was a small supermarket.

There were several other people, visitors I think, having something prepared on this enormous barbecue. No gas bottles here that I could see, then I spotted a guy bringing wood in from someplace.

Josie turned to me. 'Oh God Sam. Doesn't that smell good?'

'You still hungry after all that coffee and.....' I trailed off as Josie approached the barbecue. I followed on and almost collided with her when she stopped abruptly.

She turned to me. 'Yeah. I think I will have something.' She nodded.

I shrugged. I watched as the other people here were being handed enormous buns with a large slab of meat on there. They must have been all of nine inches across! Well, maybe not quite as big, but big enough. Too much for me especially after all that wonderful home baking. I said, 'You're not serious Josie?'

She nodded. 'Just a small one for now. We can come back here later for lunch.'

I said, 'If you eat one of those now you won't need lunch.' I almost laughed.

One of the girls wearing a blue-striped apron asked Josie in English what she wanted.

'Do you have smaller buns?' Josie asked. They did. She was handed a more sensible sized one and Josie bit into it. Her eyebrows went up just then.

'Good?' I asked.

She nodded. 'Best hamburger I've had in years. You should taste it.'

I shook my head. 'I don't know where you're putting it.'

She turned with a large grin and patting her stomach.

I said, taking her by the arm, 'Let's go before you eat yourself to death.'

After about a half hour walking, we found another road branching off to the left. We took that, then another thirty minutes walking took us into an area of more dense forest along a narrow road. I had picked up a tourist leaflet from just inside Ana's front door. It showed walking trails through the forest and indicated the many waterfalls and lakes there. No traffic so far and the temperature on my watch reading 32 degrees.

Some minutes later, Josie stopped suddenly in her tracks. As I had been walking behind, I almost collided with her. 'What is it?'

She was looking down at the ground just off the road. She pointed down. 'Look.'

I was looking over her shoulder, then I spotted a tangle of snakes. A gaggle of geese? A herd of cows? Well, they were there anyway. They looked as though they were tied together in a hopeless knot. As we watched, they were very quickly disentangling themselves.

Josie had her hand at her mouth. 'Never seen that done before.'

She pointed her camera at them and snapped them. I rested mine on her shoulder briefly and snapped them too. They quickly disappeared into the undergrowth. We walked on.

Minutes later, she stopped again, but just before she could say anything, I had spotted it too; a shiny black, lizard-like critter with bright yellow spots, like somebody had daubed him with a paintbrush? He was about a foot long from nose to tail, and he was moving very sluggishly on the edge of the pavement.

Josie didn't say anything, but slowly readied her camera for a shot. Well, he wasn't exactly breaking any speed records here, except perhaps for the slowest critter on the planet. She said finally, 'What is it?'

I snapped him too. 'Salamander. Yellow is a warning to back off.'

'Hmm,' she said and walked on.

I watched him for a few seconds as he ambled off into the undergrowth, then followed after her.

After a while, Josie stopped walking and turned to me. 'What time is it?' She doesn't wear a watch.

'About noon.'

'Let's get back for lunch. We can come back here later. I'm starved.' She started walking back the way we had just come on the left-hand side.

'Starved?' I said. 'After all you ate?' I said shaking my head as I followed her.

In a short while, we were back onto the main road once again. The traffic here was heavier than earlier. As we rounded a left-hand bend, I thought I could see something on the road next the grass verge. Another animal?

Josie reached it first as she was ahead of me anyway. She picked it up then held it up for me to see without turning. 'Brick,' she said.

A brick? I thought. It was too.

She threw it into the grass and walked on.

As we continued round the bend, more of them were scattered over the road on our side.

'Look, more of them!' she shouted and began to pick them up. She threw them onto the grass and I gave her a hand. There must have been at least thirty of them there.

'Doesn't nobody think to clear them away?' I said as I threw the last of them into the grass.

We continued on our way, then, in another few minutes, we saw the road on the left where the small cluster of buildings that we had encountered earlier were. Josie stopped in her tracks and started sniffing the air. Yep, I smelled it too; barbecued food. Gosh I was hungry. I could have eaten a horse right there had there been one at hand.

Josie saw my look and was just about to head off to the first of the buildings, when she heard me shout, 'Josie!' She turned and retraced her steps back to the main road.

I just found the most beautiful snail in its shell about to make a kamikaze 'dash' across the road. He was already about two feet from the grass verge. I felt sorry for the poor little guy, just about to be crushed to death under the wheels of something. He was cream-coloured and his shell was brown and cream spirals too. Then I spotted more of them, in fact there were hundreds of them, all about to make a headlong dash across the highway. Not if I can help it. I can't stand to see any living thing killed when help is at hand.

I said, 'Come on Josie. Give me a hand.' I began to pick some of the snails off the road and throw them across to the other side. Well that's where they wanted to go wasn't it?

She just stood there staring at me.

'What?' I asked as I picked up another one.

She said, 'Sam, the birds will get them. Leave them.'

I replied in an incredulous tone, 'Josie, I don't believe you could be so cruel.'

She just stood there with her arms folded and shrugged. 'Come on, let's go and eat,' she said and turned to go.

I said, 'Josie, give me a hand with this? It'll only take a few seconds.' I was still picking them up and throwing them across the road, then I stopped what I was doing as I realised that she had no intention of helping me. She just stood and watched me standing there looking at her.

'Well,' I said, 'are you going to help me or not?'

'You're interfering with nature Sam. These guys don't even have any sense of self awareness for God's sake, so why are you wasting your time with them?' She turned to go again.

Just then, I heard what I thought was a heavy truck approaching from around the bend. I thought I'd just pick up a few more of those guys from the road before I stepped back onto the grass verge out of the way. Yep, just another two should do it. I didn't see what happened next, but I did hear it though; the roaring truck I failed to notice approaching at speed, and I was in its path. It happened so quick that I didn't have time to react. I felt someone grasp me around the waist quickly and I was pulled backwards off my feet. I landed on my back on the grass verge with Josie under me. 'Oh my God!' I exclaimed as the truck thundered past us.

'Ah!' she exclaimed.

I suddenly realised that I had elbowed her in the stomach. 'Sorry.'

Several minutes passed as we lay there trying to recover from the shock, then I stood up and helped her to her feet. I threw my arms around her and we just held onto each other. I could feel tears forming, and I could hear Josie sniffle too, then I pulled away again.

'Sam, you can be so crazy at times. Don't give me any more frights please.'

I pulled a Kleenex from my pocket and dried my tear-filled eyes and cheeks. I turned away from her and said, taking her by the hand, 'Let's go and eat.'

Back at the barbecue stand, we ordered a large hamburger each. I asked the girl about drinks. She said, 'Beer, fruit juice, mineral water......' She broke off smiling.

'Beer, thanks,' I said and turned to Josie.

She nodded her approval.

'Do you want to sit in the shade at a table over there?' the girl said pointing over to the left and close to the barbecue stand. 'I'll bring it to you there.'

I said smiling, 'Oh, thank you.'

'Shouldn't take long,' she said and busied herself with the food.

We chose a table farthest from the barbecue and sat opposite one another. I was still shaking after my ordeal. I said, as I put my hand on Josie's, 'Thanks Josie, for back there.'

She put her right hand on mine and squeezed it without saying anything. I could see tears forming in her eyes, then she looked quickly away towards the barbecue stand. As she turned back to me, a smile appeared on her lips, then she sniffled and tucked a few strands of that lovely golden hair behind her right ear. She said, 'Looks like it's me who's looking out for you.' She gave a short laugh and sniffled again.

At that moment, the girl from the barbecue arrived at our table with the beers, two glasses and the most enormous hamburgers I've ever seen on napkins. Josie's eyes nearly popped out when she saw them.

I said, teasing her, 'You're not going to eat all that are you, considering what you've already put away?'

She just grinned back.

The girl put our food in front of us and was just about to depart when Josie asked, 'Does the gift shop sell phrase books and dictionaries?'

'Yes...'

I interrupted with, 'Is there an eating place around here like a restaurant? Like for evening meals?'

'Yes. Where are you staying?'

I told her about Ana's house.

'If you keep walking past that house, there's a road on the left, then you walk another ten minutes and you'll see a small restaurant there on the right. They have live entertainment too.'

'Oh, really?' Josie said brightly.

I nodded. 'OK, thanks. Sounds like a nice place to go.'

The girl left and returned to the barbecue stand.

After our delicious meal, I went to the barbecue stand and paid the bill, then we paid a visit to the gift shop. I was able to find an interesting Croatian phrasebook and English-Croatian dictionary. As I flicked through the pages, Josie found something on a shelf, which she held up for me to see.

I went over to her. 'What you got?' I whispered.

'Textbook. "Jeste li nosio donje rublje?". Don't know if that's correct or not.'

I turned to her with a question mark.

She said in a normal voice and trying to stifle a giggle, 'Are you wearing underwear?'

Did I hear right? 'Pardon?'

She giggled. Then she started again. 'Jeste li nosio grudnjak?'

I laughed. 'What did you say?'

She replied, again in a normal voice, 'Are you wearing a bra?' She giggled again.

I whispered and blushed as I looked around the shop, 'Josie. Stop it! You'll get us thrown out.' I giggled too.

'Oh what fun we could have with this,' she said as she turned the page.

'You're easily amused I see,' I said and giggled again.

As I flicked through the pages of the dictionary, an elderly female shop assistant with her glasses halfway down her nose, pushed in front of us, intending to put several books on the shelf. She asked, 'Zabavu?' She wasn't smiling.

I turned to her. 'I beg your pardon?'

She repeated what she had said.

It was pure guesswork on my part, but I thought I'd take a stab at it anyway. Isn't this how you learn? I found it in the dictionary. 'Having fun?' it said.

The woman stepped back and out of the way, then retreated back to her position behind the counter.

Josie whispered, 'What did she say?'

I told her.

She whispered again, 'Cheeky old bat. I'll fix her good.' She began to search the book for something suitable to say.

'No Josie. It's OK,' I said, but of course I knew it wasn't. Josie wouldn't be satisfied until she had gotten her own back.

A few more minutes passed then she said finally, 'Ready to go?'

I nodded. 'Think this'll do.' I turned to the counter with my purchases and paid for them. Josie stood beside me after having placed her book on the counter, and, with chest thrust out and her hands in her front pockets, and with that cute little smile fixed firmly in place, she glanced at me and back to the assistant. God, I could tell that she had something devious in mind.

Once she had been handed her change, she said to the old bat, 'Jeste li nosi gaćice? Have a nice day.' She laughed. I joined in. We both turned to go, but just before we made our getaway, I heard the old bat utter something. I didn't catch what it was, and I didn't really care.

I was curious as to what Josie had said. 'What did you say to her?' I was laughing.

'"Are you wearing panties?"' She laughed as we pushed through the door to the outside. 'Looks like I pronounced it OK too.' We both giggled.

As we left the building, we had to pass the barbecue stand. The girl who served us, waved. We returned it and made our way back to Ana's house. As we entered through the garden gate, I spotted the house name on a post. I had seen it earlier, but now I could translate it. It read 'Mir i Tišina'; 'Peace and Quiet'. We let ourselves in with the key that Ana had given us.

In our bedroom, we unwrapped our purchases. This should be fun to learn. Well, at least we can make ourselves understood now. Well, that was the plan anyway.

Josie sat cross-legged on her bed close to the window and flicked through the pages of the textbook. 'Oh God,' she said laughing. 'You wouldn't believe some of the stuff that's in here.'

I said, 'Did you see the look on the face of the old bat in the shop?' I said laughing.

'No, but I remember the look on your face when you met Milos that day.' She laughed. 'He really had you fooled, didn't he?'

I got up from my bed and paced the room with arms folded and getting annoyed. 'Don't be ridiculous Josie. He did not.'

'He did too. And when that music started playing...... How could you not see through....?'

I said, beginning to lose my cool, 'Josie, drop it!'

She retreated behind her book again but didn't say anything.

I said finally, 'OK, I admit I was taken in by it at the start, but....'

She interrupted, 'Yeah you sure were. It was so transparent, I don't know how you could have fallen for his charms?' She laughed as she looked at me over her book.

I said, ignoring her last remark, 'Come on. Let's get back to the park and do some exploring.' I suddenly remembered the tourist literature that I had picked up at the tourist office. I went into my pack to fetch it, then I began to read the front of the four-page guide. There were lovely photographs on the outside and even better ones inside. 'Says here that there are sixteen lakes covering an area of about 2 km² or 0.7 miles².' I sat on my bed with my legs tucked under me, then continued, 'It says, "The lakes are separated by natural dams of travertine". What's that?'

'Pardon?' Her blue eyes looked at me over her book.

I sighed. 'Oh nothing.' I continued, '"Algae, moss and bacteria accumulate on top of one another forming travertine barriers that grow at a rate of about 1 cm or 0.39 inches per year. The lakes all have distinctive colours." Good for pictures huh?'

'Pardon?'

Is she doing this deliberately? 'I don't know why I say anything at all to you.'

'Hmm.'

'Yeah, OK.' I continued, 'And "ranging from azure to green, grey or blue" and the colours are changing constantly, "depending on the content of minerals or organisms in the water and the angle of the sun". Fascinating don't you think?'

'Hmm.'

'"The lakes are divided into twelve Upper Lakes - Gornja jezera, and four Lower Lakes - Donja jezera". Hmm. Interesting.'

There was silence from the other bed.

'The deepest lake is Prošćansko jezero 37 m or 121 ft. Oh, no. There's an even deeper one than that; Kozjak at 47 m or 154 ft.' I continued despite Josie's apparent disinterest, 'Just learned a word; jezero means lake and jezera is plural.'

'Really? OK. I'll remember it.'

'Now I've got her attention at last,' I thought as I continued to read. '"Trees consist of beech, spruce and firs and is heavily forested. Mixture of Mediterranean and Alpine vegetation. Fauna consists of European brown bear, lynx, wild cat, eagles, wolves, 126 species of birds...."' I trailed off. 'Wonder if we'll get to see any of them.'

She said putting down her book, 'We might want to go for a swim. I'm changing into my bikini anyway.'

'I thought I read somewhere that swimming wasn't allowed in this area,' I said as I dug out my swimwear from my pack.

'Didn't see any signs, did you?' she giggled. 'No signs up, so they can't do anything to us right?'

I said as I pulled on my bikini top, 'Well, if it turns out that it is illegal, and we get caught at it, I'll just say it was your idea, OK?' I laughed.

She made a face and put out her tongue. She had her bikini on now, but it was so skimpy, I don't know why she bothered wearing anything at all. Anyway, I've already described it earlier; pieces of string tied together and only just managing to…. oh, what the hell?

We took the same route through the park as we did earlier. I'm looking forward to seeing some of the wildlife here. Maybe we'll get lucky.

After a while, we could hear the delicious sound of running water. We headed straight for it. In no time at all, we could see what appeared to be a large waterfall tumbling into a beautiful emerald green pool. Actually the pool was really quite small, but it appeared to be deep enough though. There was a dirt track here leading down to it.

Josie had a large grin plastered on, as did I. She said, 'Let's do it.'

We lost no time in getting down to the waterfall. Josie got there first and began stripping off her jeans and t-shirt. The vegetation was quite thick here, so we'd have some privacy at least. I caught her up and began to snap her with my camera. Oh, she looked gorgeous standing there, her lightly bronzed skin contrasting with the white of her string bikini. I stripped off too and joined her at the edge of the pool. We held hands, preparing to jump in feet-first.

I said, 'OK, after three…. one, two, three!'

We both jumped together, hitting the water at the same time and uttering a loud scream. God, it was deliciously cool in there, and the deeper we dived, the cooler it got.

Josie swam ahead of me and making for the waterfall. By the time I had caught her up, she had pulled herself out of the water and had disappeared out of sight. I got out too and had to scramble over a few rocks to get behind the cascade. There she was, standing knee-deep in a pool under a secondary cascade. As I joined her there, I looked back to the main cascade, but couldn't see anything through it.

I said to her, and hoping she would hear me over the roar of the water, 'Josie?'

Her eyes were closed, and I don't think she heard me because she didn't respond. The water was pouring down on top of her head, and her hands were smoothing her hair down at the back when I touched her left arm.

She screamed and jumped with her hand at her breast. 'Oh my God! What…..!' Her eyes snapped open.

I said quickly, 'Sorry!'

'Sam. What the hell…..?' She broke off. 'I didn't hear you. Don't give me any more frights please!'

'You're helluva jumpy all of a sudden?' I said laughing.

She didn't say anything.

'Josie, what did you do with the flash memory?' I said as I stood under the torrent and let the water pour onto my back, then I turned my face up towards it.

'In my pack, why?' She sat on a rock and turned to me.

I sat beside her. 'Just wondering.'

'It's in a safe place. Don't worry.'

I nodded. 'OK.'

We stayed under the waterfall for ages just enjoying the coolness.

After a while, I said, 'How's about we move on? Maybe we'll get lucky and see some wildlife.'

'OK. Race you back?' she said quickly, then dived into the pool. I followed.

She beat me back to our clothes lying there on the banks of the pool. Before moving on, we lay in the hot sun to dry off before redressing.

Back on the road, we headed south once more. Only one vehicle passed us; a small truck, then, another track on the left. We left the road and decided to follow it. Again, it wasn't marked as a trail, but what the heck; we're here to explore and we can't really get lost here, can we?

About fifteen minutes walking through the trees and vegetation, and Josie, who was ahead of me, stopped abruptly.

I almost collided with her. 'What is it?' I couldn't see what she was seeing.

She pointed to the ground just off to our left. 'There. Snake. Don't move.'

Then I saw it slithering towards the track about three feet ahead. I had to look again. Snake she said? No, wait. This isn't a snake because snakes don't have eyelids. This one was blinking! 'Not a snake Josie.'

'What do you mean? Course it is.' She laughed. 'What else could it be? If it acts like a snake, looks like a snake, then as sure as hell it's a snake, OK?'

I said a little annoyed, 'You can be so....' I broke off as I stepped around her. By this time the critter had crossed in front of us and was heading for the vegetation on the other side of the track.

She screamed, 'No Sam! Don't go near it! Suppose it bites?' She grasped my arm tightly.

Of course I had no intention of touching it. I said, pulling out of her grasp, 'Josie, stop it. I know what I'm doing. I've read about these critters. I think they call it a slow worm. It's a legless lizard. The eyelids? Snakes don't have them. Didn't you see it blink?'

She went quiet now, then that little cute smile appeared again. 'Whatever you say Mr Darwin.' She giggled.

I turned from her and marched off, taking up the lead this time.

Sometime in the late afternoon, we found ourselves walking along the banks of a river. Big boulders lay at the water's edge, and another waterfall up ahead. We thought we'd take a rest here. Anyway, I was anxious to learn something of this strange language, and this seemed like an opportune moment to do it. With the phrasebook came a quick reference guide that listed common phrases and told how to pronounce them. It only consisted of about twenty pages so could easily slide into a pocket. I took it from my back pocket and sat on a large rock, my bare feet in the water. Josie had rolled up her jeans to paddle in the river. The roar from the waterfall was loud and Josie had difficulty hearing me as I read some of the phrases out to her.

I think it was while I was onto the third page, that it happened; I thought I detected with peripheral vision, movement on the pebbles about four feet to the left of where I sat. When I looked up quickly from my reading, I could see that Josie had spotted it too.

She screamed. 'Sam! Snake!' She pointed to the critter that was slithering away from me.

Where the hell had it come from? Was I sitting on its nest? If I sit still maybe it won't know that I'm here. Well, that's wishful thinking on my part of course, and there's no way that he couldn't know I was here. He would smell me somewhere nearby, so it's just a matter of time before my precise location would be known, then if he was the biting sort....! I'm not waiting around to find out, so I thought it was time for me to make a quick departure. Well that was the plan anyway. Josie stood in the middle of the river, her hand at her mouth and probably in a state of shock too. I thought I'd stand up quickly and make my escape before he turned and saw me, so I did. Was that a mistake or what? I had only just managed to stand up, when he turned his head in my direction and in a flash, had given a whole new meaning to the term 'greased lightening'! Before I could do anything else, he had made a dash? A lunge? A dive? Oh, what the hell.... he was at my rock anyway before I could give it up. I heard Josie scream and that's when I made a run away from the rock, then I turned and looked back.

'Where did he go Josie? Did you see?' I was walking cautiously back to the rock and bending to see under it. I had left my camera lying beside the rock, but no way was I going to pick it up whilst this critter was within biting distance of me.

Josie was still in a state of shock I think, because she didn't say anything. She just stood there knee-deep in the water with both hands at her mouth. She must have stepped back into the deeper part, but she didn't appear to notice or care.

I got closer to the rock and just kept bending to have a look under there, then I spotted him. I grabbed my camera and took a shot of him as he curled up at the rear of his hiding place, then I left him alone. We decided to make ourselves scarce at this point and head back to our accommodation and Ana's house.

Back at the house, we changed our clothes. Josie wore her cream-coloured, low-cut jeans and light-blue short top that showed off a lot of cleavage and California tan. I wore my white low-cut jeans and white short top.

We collected our money as we intended to have a meal at the restaurant, then it was a ten-minute walk along the road that the girl at the barbecue stand had mentioned. The restaurant itself was lovely inside, with green and cream-coloured wallpaper. This was not an expensive or posh place, just a country restaurant for locals and tourists alike.

We sat at a window table with a view to the lakes. Josie sat opposite me. I noticed a guy in his fifties with what looked to me like a piano-accordion. It was plugged into a bank of electronics where he manipulated the controls and made the music happen. The music started. It sounded to me like a Greek number, and it could have been too, but it was beautiful anyway.

I looked at the menu and after some deliberation, I chose steak, potatoes and veg. She chose mushroom pizza with side salad. We'd wash it down with a bottle of wine.

Well the first course arrived about fifteen minutes after the order was placed with the waitress. The steak was beautiful; very tasty and tender too, and I relayed this fact to Josie.

She opened the wine and filled our glasses. 'Looks good too,' she said making eyes at my steak.

I had already cut several pieces of it, when Josie stabbed her fork into one of them, then dipped it in the gravy.

'Hey,' I said laughing. I stabbed part of her pizza with my fork.

She said, licking her lips, 'Hmm, now that's delicious. Wish I had ordered the steak now.'

'Nice pizza too,' I said as I washed it down with the wine.

OK, first course over with, and the music tempo increased, we're both feeling a little light-headed with the wine. Well, we were now well into our second bottle. The waitress came to take our plates away.

I ordered a chocolate ice cream. I asked Josie, 'What you having?'

She looked hurriedly at the menu, running her finger down it. 'Oh, I think I'll have a chocolate ice cream sundae.' She smiled at the waitress, then grinned across at me.

I said with a straight face, 'What? On a Saturday?' I just managed to stifle a giggle.

Her eyebrows went up, then she gave a short laugh. 'What....?'

I said, just before I burst into state of giggles, 'Sundae?'

She joined me in a fit of laughter that had several of the clientèle's heads turn in our direction.

I poured more wine into our glasses. Just as well neither of us was driving. My head was swimming.

The musician was playing a waltz now. It was very nice and slow and oh-so romantic. I downed my wine quickly 'cos I just had a really cool idea. I'd like to dance. I don't suppose I'll get a guy to dance with, so Josie will have to substitute. Some people were getting up to dance anyway.

I leaned across to Josie who was just finishing off her ice cream sundae, 'Fancy a dance?'

She nodded and grinned, then stood up. 'Em.... I haven't danced before, well not like that anyway.' She pointed to where the dancers were.

I stood up too. 'It's easy. I'll show you how. It's a waltz. Just hold onto each other and go for it.' I took Josie by the hand and began to make my way forward to where couples were already forming or dancing.

Once we began to 'mingle' with the others, Josie just stood there looking at me obviously awaiting instructions. She said, 'I've seen it done but....'

I cut her off with, 'Look, like this.' I put one hand behind her butt and pulled her close, then, with the other one I clasped her free hand in the air. I said laughing, 'Me Tarzan, you Jane.'

She just stared at me with that look of curiosity again on her face.

'What?' I asked.

'That one's lost on me. Don't know that expression, or was it a joke?' she giggled then hiccuped.

I shook my head. 'You wanna get out more girl.' I laughed too.

So, I was the guy and she the girl. Round and round we went. The music was so captivating, I failed to notice this guy heading on a collision course with us. He was, I think, twenty-something and with a short brown haircut. He wore a light-blue sleeveless shirt and black pants and was dancing with a black-haired girl in a red dress when he collided with me.

I turned and smiled. 'Oops, sorry!' I shouted and laughed, then we resumed our dancing.

'*Gosh,*' I thought for one fleeting moment. '*I'm in love.... with Josie!*' No. That's silly. Must be the wine. I giggled.

She asked, 'What?'

I just smiled back but didn't say anything.

After a while, the music stopped and he began another waltz, but his time it was slower. That was followed by a fast one. All the couples – we just copied what the others were doing – were forming rings of six people holding hands, then they danced in a circle. It was very fast, and yes, you guessed it; I collided with the same guy again. I think he's doing this deliberately. I giggled again, and turned to see him but we had drifted too far apart for me to say anything, and we were moving too fast anyway.

After the music had stopped and the musician had broken off for a break, I suggested to Josie that she go back to our table and I would get us a couple of cold beers. I made my way to the bar and had to wait for the bar girl to come as she was not available right now. Presently, I was aware of someone at my back. I turned to see this same guy standing there, a big smile on his face. He must have been about six feet tall, as he was towering above me.

'Hi,' I said brightly.

'Hi there.' His accent was British. 'We meet again.'

By this time, the girl had arrived back at the bar. 'Two beers, thank you,' I said.

She placed two bottles and two glasses on there.

I fished in my pocket for the currency and handed it over, then, as I picked up the bottles and glasses from the bar, he said smiling, 'You always deliberately bump into people or was that just coincidence back there?'

I smiled but didn't say anything, then I started making my way back to our table. He bought something himself and followed me back to Josie. She had her back to me when I arrived at her left side, so she wasn't immediately aware of the guy who appeared on her right. She looked up at him. 'Oh!' she said surprised. 'Hi there.'

No, Josie.' I thought. *'This one is mine. Your turn will come later.'* I placed the bottle in front of her, and she looked up at me with another surprised expression.

The guy arrived by my side now. Gosh he was hot and a bit of a hunk now that I could see him properly and up close. Oh, those muscles on his arms and the tattoos there too. He said smiling, 'So, you didn't answer my question.'

I still didn't say anything, but sat down opposite Josie, who by now had taken an interest in our conversation. I said as I removed the bottle top and prepared to pour my beer into the glass, 'Which one?' I teased.

'The one about bumping into people deliberately?'

'Maybe. But it wasn't deliberate. You bumped into me remember?' I smiled as I poured the beer.

He pulled up another chair and sat beside me. He put out his hand. 'I'm Bob.'

I shook it. 'Sam,' I said, 'and this is Josie.'

'Hi,' she said brightly as she opened her bottle.

He nodded. 'So where are you from? You guys together right?' he said looking at Josie and back to me.

I nodded.

Josie said, 'California.'

I said, 'You on your own?'

He nodded. 'Well actually I was hitching and met this guy Gorge. He's from Croatia. We were both going the same way and decided to team up.'

'Is he here too?' I asked looking around.

'He was. Drinks too much and I think he's on something too.'

Josie asked, 'Like what? Drugs?'

He shrugged. 'Who knows.'

I asked him where he was from. Near London, England he said, and was studying to be a lawyer. When his family moved to Canada, he moved into a flat with his girlfriend. He had taken himself off on this trip when he split with her. I liked Bob. He was nice, and I'd like to get to know him better. It was too bad that for our own safety, we'd have to move on. Maybe we'll meet again sometime on our travels.

He stood up suddenly and made a signal to somebody across the room. Was that Gorge? I could see a guy dressed in faded blue jeans and green chequered shirt standing at a table and looking a little lost, then he saw Bob waving. He came over to our table and just hovered. He's looking for an introduction I think. Bob obliged, then he stood up just as Gorge was sitting down next to Josie on her right. Not my type at all; black close-cropped hair and an unshaven chin as though he was trying to grow a beard. There was just something about him that I didn't feel comfortable with. Was it the body language? The way he looked at her? Oh, I don't know; just a feeling. He couldn't keep his eyes off of her anyway. Josie's vivid blue eyes lit up and that cute little smile appeared on her lips that no guy could resist. Her golden hair pulled back into a ponytail and her navel with the diamond hanging from its chain. Yes, she was every guy's dream girlfriend to die for.

Bob had gone off to fetch more drinks for us. I played with my glass of beer. It was halfway down. The more I watched this guy and his interest in Josie, the more I disliked him. He gave me the creeps. Well, just not my type anyway.

Presently, Bob returned with the drinks. Beers all round in bottles and straight from the fridge.

'Thank you,' I said as he placed mine on the tabletop in front of me.

We chatted for almost an hour. I felt I'd known him for years. He reminded me of somebody I used to know from high school.

The music was playing fast now and we got up to join the others on the floor. Gorge and Josie, me and Bob having a good time. The music stopped and a waltz began. Josie and Gorge were well into one another by now. Well so was I with Bob. I couldn't resist touching his muscled arms and running my fingers through the fur. It sent a tingle up my spine.

Later, I think it was around 8 pm, I noticed it was getting dark outside. I'm concerned about walking back to Ana's house in the dark, so back at our table and after Gorge had excused himself to find the restroom, I said in a low voice to Bob, 'We'll have to go now. I don't like the idea of walking back in the dark.'

He said, 'Yeah, OK.' He added, 'Enjoyed your company. Maybe we can do this again sometime?' He stood up and pushed his seat under the table preparing to leave.

'Me too,' I said, then I stood up on tiptoes and kissed him on the left cheek, my hand touching his arm and briefly stroking the fur there, then quickly withdrawing it. 'Thanks for a good time, oh, and the drinks.' I smiled and blushed and hiccuped and giggled and…. Well I had been giggly all night so what's new? Josie doesn't drink much so she was completely sober. She hardly touched her beer all night. She likes to keep alert especially when around guys she doesn't know. Maybe she didn't trust Gorge fully. I certainly didn't.

I paid the bill and we left the restaurant. We started making our way back to Ana's place. It was much darker now. The sky was a royal blue colour and some stars could be seen, oh, and a crescent Moon was shining too.

As we quickened our pace, a loud hooting sound could be heard from an owl. As I had my arm around Josie's shoulders, I felt her jump. 'God, it's spooky here.' She shivered.

'Well you're easily spooked anyway,' I teased.

We reached the house in only five minutes, that's because we ran, or rather jogged part of the way, well, most of the way actually. Yep, she got spooked again, but not by an owl this time. We both heard it; footsteps behind us, and when we quickened our pace, they speeded up too. Yeah, OK, I was spooked too. Anyone would be. When we reached the house, I couldn't get the key into the lock quick enough. Oh, what a relief!

We went straight to our room. Once the door was closed she asked, 'Do you think that was actually footsteps behind us, or is that just us getting paranoid?' she laughed.

I shrugged and began to strip off my clothes. I'm intending to take a hot shower, then I'm going to try a little language learning. 'Dunno. Maybe.'

'What? Maybe we're getting paranoid or it *was* footsteps?' She giggled as she sat on her bed.

I said as I opened a closet, 'Doesn't matter now, does it? We made it back safely before the bogeyman caught us.' I laughed. I found a couple of white bathrobes. I threw her one.

We showered separately then collected our language books from the bedroom. I sat on the couch cross-legged facing Josie with the textbook in my hands.

She asked in curiosity, and with a short laugh, 'What are you doing? Yoga?'
I shook my head.

She shrugged and grinned back. 'So what's....?'

I cut in with, 'Josie, this is how I learn. Well it works for me anyway.' I grinned back. I said, 'Come on. Let's do it. Join me?'

She didn't argue. She sat cross-legged on the couch too and facing me. That grin still in place she said, 'You're crazy.'

'OK, let's hold hands.' I held out both hands to her.

'You *are* crazy,' she said laughing.

We held hands. I said, 'Close your eyes and concentrate.' I closed my eyes, then I opened them again. Hers were still open. 'What?' I asked.

'What are we concentrating on?'

'Josie, I'm just coming to that,' I said impatiently. 'Close your eyes.'
She did.

I said, 'OK, what was the word the old bat,' I giggled, 'used today? Think.'

There was silence from her. I could hear the wheels turning. She said finally, 'Zab-something, I think.'

'Zab.....,' I trailed off, 'what?'

'Zabavu?'

'Hey, you got it!' I exclaimed. I pulled her close and gave her a big hug, then I detected something off of her, or I thought I did. That smelled like Mom's perfume. I pulled away and said, 'Josie what's that you're wearing?'

She looked down and plucked at her robe. She said, with her little cute smile in place, 'Bathrobe?' She laughed.

I said getting irritated, 'Yeah I know. I meant what's that perfume you're wearing?'

'Oh, just....' She gave a little giggle.

I cut her off. I wasn't laughing. I was serious. I said, 'Josie, have you been into my pack?'

'Pardon?' Her smile was almost gone.

'My pack? Were you.....?'

She broke in, 'Well, so what? It's only perfume.'

'What? Josie that's expensive stuff.' I'm beginning to lose my cool here.

'Go on,' she said laughing. 'You buying expensive perfume? Yeah right.'

'OK, I didn't buy it. Mom gave it to me. Does it matter? You were into my pack.' I said mockingly, 'So what else did you take from it?'

'Nothing, well, a pack of Kleenex?'

'Oh, really?' I mocked. 'Maybe you'd like my pin number and my bank card too?' I said trying to stifle a giggle, 'Maybe clean out my bank account while you're at it huh?'

She nodded. 'You would do that Sam, for me?' she laughed. 'You would really do that? Gosh, is there no limit to how far our friendship can go?' She sighed in contentment then giggled.

I laughed too, then, 'Let's get serious.' I cleared my throat then continued, 'Kako se zoveš? What is your name?'

A question mark, then, 'Pardon?' She said, 'Is that how you pronounce it?'

I said annoyed, 'Josie, give me a break? Of course it is. I've got it right here.'

'OK,' she said brightly. 'Shoot.'

We held hands again and closed our eyes. I whispered, 'Concentrate. Zabavu?'

'Having fun?'

I was just about to say something when I heard the living room door handle being turned. When I opened my eyes, Ana had come into the room. She said, 'Čaj?'

I glanced quickly at my watch. It was almost 9 pm. Josie still had her eyes closed.

Ana took a pen and notepad from her apron pocket and wrote down the word, then handed it to me.

I looked it up in my dictionary: 'tea' it said. I nodded to Ana then looked at Josie. 'You can come back down from whichever planet you're.....'

She said, opening her eyes, 'Oh. OK, what did you say?' She smiled at Ana.

'She said "tea" Josie.'

She nodded. 'Oh, yeah sure,' she said to Ana, then turned to me again. 'How did you know that?' she asked curiously.

Ana retreated from the room to fetch the tea.

'Because,' I said teasing her, 'I'm a very smart girl.' I smiled.

'Yeah, right. You looked it up in the dictionary.'

'Josie, sometimes your unusual high level of intelligence astounds me and I have to pinch myself to make sure that I'm not dreaming.' I smiled as I turned the pages of the dictionary.

She made a face and put out her tongue.

Ana arrived now with a jug of hot water for the tea, that big smile on her face once more, then she left the room again. My phone rang its musical tone. I jumped. I forgot I'd left it switched on. I had to go into my pack to fetch it. Josie whispered to me that she was going off to help Ana, then she left the room closing the door behind her.

Whoever it was, they were withholding their number. 'Hello?' *Jesus'*, I thought quickly. *'This could be them about to arrange their rendezvous. The bastards.'*

'Miss Sam Winter. So good to speak with you.' It was a male voice and probably about late fifties. It was east European. How did he know my last name?

'Who is this? Do I know you?'

'No, but you will in time. Now let me get to the point. It's about those pictures that you took from your friend's PC.' I heard a cough, then he continued, 'You do know what I'm talking about don't you?'

I was silent.

Another cough. Sounded like a smoker. I hope he chokes on it. 'We know where you are and it's just a matter of finding your exact location.'

'Pardon?' I swallowed hard. I'm not taking this in properly. They know where we are? How is that possible? We didn't tell Milos where we were going. 'How......?'

He interrupted. 'You were seen boarding a bus bound for the lakes. So you see, there's no place for you to hide. We can come for you any time we like.' He laughed.

I didn't say anything.

'OK. You will meet our contact at a certain hotel and hand over the pictures that we want.' He waited for my reaction.

He got it. 'What pictures?'

'Come come Miss Winter. You and I both know that your friend Tomislav took pictures of some of us that day.'

I was silent.

He continued, 'He threatened to take them to the police just like you were trying to do, so we had to kill him.'

I screamed into the phone, 'You bastard! You murdered an innocent.....!' I was almost in tears now. 'And you could have killed me too.....!'

He interrupted, 'Now that would have been unfortunate wouldn't it?' He laughed.

I screamed again, 'We don't have your damn pictures, OK! Leave us alone!' I was in tears now.

He said, 'OK, we're going to hunt you down, and your young friend there might be kidnapped. You can't watch her all the time can you?' He laughed.

'Shut up!' I screamed again. 'You leave her alone!' I screamed. 'She's got nothing to do with this!'

'When we get her, she'll talk. They always do. Women are so much easier to break, and so much more fun too.' He laughed almost hysterically.

I shouted into the phone, 'Shut up, shut up!' I'm losing control. I can feel it.

He ignored me. 'Do you know what Boris – that's not his real name of course – does to them before he resorts to torture?'

I cut him off with, 'You dirty, slimy…… I'll never give you any pictures even if I had them! I'll see you in hell first!'

'Now now, that's no way for a lady to talk. Now, do you know where Josie is at this moment? We could be watching you right now, just waiting to take her.'

I thought, *What the hell's he talking about?*

'Josie…. let me see, yes….. Moore isn't it? Do you know where she is now?'

'What the hell are you talking about!' I screamed then I lost it! I panicked big-time! 'Josie? Josie!' I shouted then I screamed and dropped the phone as I ran for the living room door. I threw it open quickly and ran straight into Ana who had just come out of the kitchen with our tea! She screamed and stumbled backwards. The tray she'd been carrying flew up into the air along with the home baking, plates, mugs, and teapot, then she lost her balance and struck the back of her head on the wall opposite and slid down it onto the floor, the food and plates landing on her lap. The scalding hot tea poured from the broken teapot on the floor and onto her right hand.

I'm in a real panic now. I was crying and crying and wasn't sure what to do next, then I ran into the kitchen and grabbed a tea towel from a worktop and soaked in tap water, then returned to Ana. She was still lying there on the floor. She seemed to be out cold. I wrapped her hand in the towel then I felt for a pulse. She was OK, at least for now. I stood up quickly and shouted for Josie! There was no reply!

'Josie, for God's sake answer me!' I ran into our bedroom. Nothing! I ran to the bathroom door. I hammered on it and shouted, 'Are you in there Josie!'

She answered back, 'Sam, what's wrong!'

I hammered on the door again.

The door opened quickly. She just stood there with a worried expression. 'What's wrong?'

'Josie, you're safe. Thank God.' I was crying.

'Sam, what are you talking about?'

I'm still crying. 'Josie, there's been an accident. We'll have to get an ambulance.'

'Accident? But....' She moved to the sink and began to wash her hands.

I joined her at the sink. 'It's Ana.' I told her what happened.

'Oh God,' she said and ran out of the bathroom with me in pursuit. She went straight to Ana's side. She was still lying on the floor, her head resting on the wall behind.

'Josie is she OK?' I'm shaking and I'm feeling sick.

She pulled Ana's head forward and her hand came away with blood on it. 'Jesus,' she said. 'Get an ambulance quick!'

I ran into the living room and looked up the word 'ambulance' in the dictionary. OK, I've got the word, now what do I do with it. Jesus I can't think straight. I'm still in a panic. I'm feeling ill. My thoughts were interrupted by the front door being opened.

'Josie!' I cried running into the hallway and was just in time to see Josie run out of the front door! It's dark out there! 'Josie!' I screamed. 'Come back!' If these bastards are around, they could get her. I can't let that happen. I ran outside too and caught her up. I grasped her arm tightly and pulled her around to face me. 'Josie what the hell are you doing!'

She yelled back, 'I'm trying to get help Sam!'

We both heard a vehicle approach. Josie suddenly pulled out of my grasp and ran into the roadway. She began to wave frantically at it, jumping up and down. It turned out to be a red car with a couple in their fifties. He was driving. Josie went round to the driver's side and tried to tell him what the problem was, but unfortunately they didn't have any English. I ran over to the car. His wife put the window down.

I said in Italian, 'Potrebbe telefonare per ed ambulanza per noi per favore?' *'Could you phone for an ambulance for us please?'*

The woman got out of the car and was quickly joined by her husband.

I said as I led them to the house, 'C'è stato un incidente e noi non sappiamo come usare il telefono.' *'There's been an accident and we don't know how to use the telephone.'*

Within minutes, they had an ambulance on its way to the house. The woman said her name was Gerda and on vacation from Switzerland. She said that she was a nurse and that she'd go with Ana to the hospital. She assured us Ana would be OK. We both sighed a big sigh of relief when we heard the ambulance doors close.

We cleaned up the mess of broken crockery and spoilt home baking, and Josie mopped the floor of tea, then I headed for the shower. As I stood under the hot water, I was still shaking after this terrible ordeal. Poor Ana, I hope she's OK. It's my fault she's gone to hospital. I had only just started lathering myself when I heard the door being opened. I jumped. With a sharp intake of breath I said, 'Jesus!' Of course it was Josie. Who else would it be?

'You finished yet?'

'Yeah, em....' I trailed off as I could feel the tears coming. I'm losing it again.

Josie sniffled before she said, 'What did that guy on the phone say?'

I had a large lump in my throat that was in danger of choking me to death. I could hardly speak. 'Josie, he knows your last name.....' I trailed off wondering how could that be.

She sniffled. 'I don't know how. I didn't tell Milos my last name.'

I suddenly had a thought. 'When Milos was in the cottage on the island he looked into our things, that's how he got my number. Josie, they'll know all about us then. Our home addresses, mom.....' I trailed off. The implications.....!

'Credit cards? We'll have to cancel them just in case.'

'Identity theft. Oh Jesus!' I broke off again sniffling. 'I'll phone my bank and cancel immediately.'

'That soap smells nice,' she said. 'Hmm, the guys won't be able to tell us apart. We'll both smell the same.' She giggled.

'Smells like apples,' I said as I smelled the gel just before I replaced the cap on the bottle.

Out of the shower, we got on our phones and cancelled our cards. We arranged to pick up our new ones at a certain bank in Sarajevo since we would be heading there anyway.

Later, in bed, I had a bad dream. Josie had been snatched from her bed and I was tied to mine with thick ropes minus my nightie or any underwear. I struggled and fought to free myself, but the ropes held me tight. Each of my hands were tied to the two posts at the top of the bed, and my feet tied together. I heard Josie scream for help but I couldn't do anything to help her. Then, somehow, I was able to free my left hand and began to untie my other one, then I started on my feet. I heard something outside the bedroom door. I crossed to it and threw it open. Josie was lying there on her back minus her nightie and covered in blood; a vicious-looking knife stuck in her chest between the breasts. I screamed and screamed. Suddenly my world was flooded by light. I felt something heavy land beside me in the bed. I snapped open my eyes instinctively and turned to see Josie there.

'You've had a nightmare Sam,' she said concerned and looking into my eyes.

'Josie, did you lock the doors?'

'Well, no. I didn't.....'

I said frantically, 'Go check the doors?'

She got out of the bed and padded across to the bedroom door. I noticed that she wore only a long grey nightshirt. She turned to me as she opened the door. 'Sam....?'

'What?' I asked.

She hesitated, then, in an abject tone she replied, 'Nothing.' She padded out of the room and made for the front door.

I thought I'd head for the bathroom and have a shower. My nightie was soaking and I didn't have a replacement. I had only just reached the bathroom when Josie passed me on her way to the kitchen to check the back door. Once in, I turned on the shower, pulled off my nightie and prepared to step in. It was then that I heard it; the back door being opened. 'Josie!' I shouted. I can't let her go out there! She was only supposed to check if it was locked. I grabbed a bath towel and wrapped it quickly, then headed for the kitchen.

Josie was just turning from the back door, when I entered. She was cradling something in her arms and talking to it. It was a small grey cat with a fluffy coat. The door was still open.

I thought quickly, *'What's wrong with that girl!'* I screamed, 'Josie, close the door!'

She jumped and looked up startled. 'What....?' She kicked it closed with her heel, then looked at me again with a surprised look.

'What are you doing with that kitty cat?'

She sighed. 'What does it look like? He's hungry, aren't you?' She put her face close to the cat's head and kissed it there.

My eyes shot heavenwards. 'Jesus,' I muttered under my breath and locked the door, then I removed the key and dropped it onto the worktop. 'Josie, you shouldn't be taking in stray cats. This isn't your house.'

She cuddled the cat and said to it, 'You're not a stray kitty cat are you? No, of course you're not. Just ignore her.'

'Come on Josie, stop it,' I said annoyed.

She snapped back. 'Sam, you stop it!' She kissed the cat again. 'How would you like it if somebody threw you outside in the cold night, when you were hungry and only looking for love and....'

I interrupted with, 'Oh for God's sake Josie; it's only a cat. And it's *not* cold outside.'

I was about to return to the bathroom when Josie laid her head on top of the cat's and looked at me. 'See, gorgeous blue eyes, just like mine.' She fluttered her eyelids, and that cute little smile appeared again. Well, that's enough about the cat!

'OK,' I said finally as I stood with hands on hips. 'Let's see if we can find any cat food, and if we can't, he goes straight back out, OK?'

She didn't say anything.

'Cat got you're tongue?' I almost laughed at my own joke.

Josie put out her tongue to me and made a face.

'Obviously not,' I said smiling. I turned to one of the cupboards above the worktop closest to the door and began searching.

'There.' She pointed to a small tin at the back of the cupboard. She said to the cat, 'Now you can eat. You won't go hungry now will you?'

I opened the tin with a wall can opener and scraped the contents onto a plate on the floor. Josie put the cat on the floor and he started wolfing down the food.

I said, as I made my way to the door, 'I'm off to the shower.'

'Yeah, I'm off to bed in a minute.' She bent to pet the cat.

I stepped out of the shower about ten minutes later and started to dry off, then I heard the screams and hysterical laughter coming from the bedroom. 'What's she laughing at?' I wondered. I threw on a bathrobe from a closet and went into the bedroom.

Josie was lying on her back in my bed! She was wearing her nightshirt with the sheet below her navel. Every now and then, something would move under the sheet just below her waist, and she would laugh and giggle and..... Then I suddenly realised what was going on. I said, 'Josie, get that cat out of my bed now.'

She didn't hear me as I approached the bed from my side. 'Jesus! Stop it! Hey not there. Ah! Oh God! Hey! What......?' She laughed. 'That's ticklish, ah! Stop it! Hmm. That tongue; it's like sandpaper. Ah!'

I took off the bathrobe and threw it over a chair back, pulled on my nightie, then got into the bed and sat up. By this time, the cat had worked its way under her shirt and was crawling upwards towards her chest, then it poked its head out of the top of her shirt. She laughed and kissed it again.

I wasn't in a mood for arguing and I'm not sleeping with a cat in my bed. I said, 'Josie. Not in my bed thank you. He goes now!' I meant it too.

She looked at me curiously. 'You're jealous aren't you? Come on, admit it?'

I'm just about to lose my cool here. 'Josie. Maybe you're not too particular about your choice of sleeping partners, but I am, so if you don't mind, I'd rather you put that cat out or sleep in your own bed, OK?' I added, 'And I'm not jealous.'

She teased, 'You are too. You're just jealous that this poor little kitty cat has taking a liking to me and adopted me.'

'Oh for God's sake Josie, grow up. You're acting like a kid again.'

She said annoyed, 'And you're sounding like mom again.'

I joked, 'If I were your mom, I'd.....'

She interrupted with a sigh, 'Yeah, I know. You'd put me over your knee and spank my little bottom for me.' She got out of the bed and went into her own.

'Good to see you're paying attention.' I laughed and lay on my back, then I turned onto my right side. 'Goodnight.'

She was silent.

I awoke with a start. Something hairy had touched my left cheek. I turned onto my left side and found my face being licked with a rough tongue. My eyes were open and the cat was smiling at me. 'You'll be looking for breakfast now no doubt, huh?' I said to him with a sigh and a yawn. God, I didn't feel like getting up at all. I could lie here forever.

Josie stirred and stretched then turned onto her right side, her cute little smile appearing again. 'Hi,' she said brightly. She yawned. 'How's our guest?'

'As perky as ever,' I said as I stroked his little head. I added, 'And we're the guests not him. Maybe he should be throwing us out.' I laughed.

She propped herself on her elbow. 'What do you fancy doing today?'

I sat up. I shrugged. 'Dunno. Try to keep a low profile I guess.' I laughed.

Josie sat up too and swung her legs out of the bed, then she came over to mine and sat herself beside me. I hadn't noticed where the cat had gone, then I knew. I felt his rough tongue licking my stomach. 'Hey, get out of there!' I shouted. 'Ah! Stop it!' I almost laughed. It was ticklish. I pulled him out from under the sheet.

Josie laughed. 'How about breakfast?'

I said, 'We could go back to the restaurant, couldn't we?' I got out of the bed and began to dress. It's a blue jeans day. For my top half, a white sleeveless top that just makes it to the top of my jeans.

Josie got out of the bed and began to dress. 'How's about the barbecue place?'

'OK, the barbecue joint it is.' I smiled.

She struggled into her jeans. These were regular cut and hung on her hips, but you could still see her cute little Celtic tattoo on her lower back, then she pulled on a tight-fitting, light-blue sleeveless top that I hadn't seen before. It stopped just short of her navel, and, well, you know the rest.

Out of the front door, we headed for the park and the barbecue place. It didn't take us long to reach it. There were a few cars parked beside the small supermarket. One, a black sedan with darkened windows, was parked a few yards from the tables close to the barbecue stand. Two young guys wearing shades – late teens I think, dressed in matching black sleeveless shirts and jeans, sat at one of the farthest tables from us. They were drinking from beer bottles. That was the only table occupied.

'What you having Josie?' I asked. I'm looking to see what else they have on offer. So far I've only seen hamburgers.

'Oh.....' She trailed off shaking her head.

A voice from over on our left shouted, 'Bok!' It was Croatian. We should have learned more.

We both turned at the same time. It was one of the guys in black.

I turned back to the barbecue stand. I was just about to ask one of the girls there, what else was on offer, but I'd have to attract her attention first. She was tending to something on one of the barbecue grills.

A wolf whistle sounded. We didn't respond to it. I smiled at Josie and said, 'Sausages sound good to you?'

She nodded. 'Hmm.'

'Doäi ovamo beba!' someone shouted and then laughter from the two of them.

We still didn't turn.

One of the girls approached now. She asked Josie what she wanted. Josie said, 'Sausages?'

'We have different flavours; smoked.....'

Josie interrupted, 'Yeah I'll have that, thanks.'

I nodded. 'Same.'

The girl turned away to prepare our food.

I saw Josie turn to someone approaching from our left. Yep, it was one of the guys, then I noticed that the other one was missing from the table too, then I jumped as he suddenly appeared at my right side.

'Kako ste?' he said leaning against the wall. They were both taller than us.

What do they want? I wondered.

He spotted my question mark. 'Maybe you understand English?'

I nodded, but I didn't look at him. I fixed my gaze on the girl preparing our food. The other one leaned his elbow on the counter and looked Josie up and down. He had a grin plastered on, and his eyes kept flicking from Josie to his mate. I have an uncomfortable feeling about this. He said to Josie, 'Do you like spiders?'

'Pardon?' Josie's startled expression was almost comical as she turned to him. Her smile had vanished for an instant. 'What did you say?'

I was wishing the girl would hurry with our food, then we could move on.

The guy straightened up and moved to Josie's side. 'I said, do you like spiders?' His hand touched the top of her left shoulder.

Josie stepped closer to me out of the way but didn't say anything.

He said, sounding annoyed, 'I asked you a question babe?'

Josie put her arm around my waist. She's getting bad vibes too.

The girl at the barbecue said, 'Leave them alone.' She had just arrived with our sausages inside circular buns; more sensible sized ones this time. She placed them on the counter on paper plates.

My guy said to her, 'Shut up.'

She turned away.

I was about to pick up one of the plates, when my guy moved round to my back, then, as he passed Josie, he touched the top of her left arm with his finger. She flinched and tried to step closer to me. I handed her her plate and we started on our food immediately.

I said to her, 'Let's go Josie.' She had a look of alarm on her face, and her almost constant smile had long-since vanished.

The other guy moved farther down the counter and ordered four beers, then he brought them back to us. He handed two bottles to his mate and the remainder to Josie. She didn't make any attempt to take them from him. He shrugged and that grin or what passed for a smile, had just gone. He's not happy. He looked us both up and down one last time, then turned on his heel and headed back to their car.

The girl returned and I paid for our food.

'Come on. I think we have to go now,' I said taking Josie's hand and pulling her with me. I had my bun in my other hand. I was walking back the way we had just come; back towards Ana's house. My intention was to finish our breakfast in the restaurant where we had been last night. At least we'd be in safe company there.

I heard a car engine start and rev hard, then then the sound of screeching tyres. The sound receded and Josie read my thoughts again. Well, hopefully these guys have taken off back to their cave and won't annoy us again. We finished off our food, then we broke into a jog and in no time, had reached the road where we had gone down last night to reach the restaurant. It'd take us only ten minutes walking, but we decided to jog this one too.

Several cars had passed us on the road and we had to slow down and step onto the grass verge out of the way. I had been talking to Josie when I heard the sound of an engine revving hard, and it was heading in our direction, but not at speed. It sounded like the same car that we heard coming from the barbecue stand. We exchanged glances, and Josie had that worried look again, and again, I think she read my thoughts. I knew even before I turned, that it was those guys again. Yep, it was too. They speeded up now but didn't overtake us. A sudden thought passed through my mind that these guys might have something to do with the gang that were after us, then, almost immediately, I had dismissed that theory. It's just two guys with too much to drink having what they call 'fun'. Well, not with us they're not. We just kept up our same jogging pace and ignored them. The engine began to rev hard again and this time they were a lot closer to us. We didn't stop or turn.

The restaurant was now within sight, but not close enough for us though. Josie was about to say something to me when she stopped abruptly. I turned and saw that the car was now so close to us, that it was in danger of hitting Josie. She turned in alarm to see the car immediately behind her and if she had sat down, she would have been sitting on its hood. There were yells of laughter from the car despite the roaring of the engine as it was revved over and over.

We jogged on and again they followed us, and just getting close enough but not coming in contact. Then they drew up alongside us. The guy in the passenger seat, I noticed, had his window right down; his arm outstretched towards Josie. He touched her on the thigh and she stopped in her tracks immediately.

I heard her say something under her breath, but didn't catch it, then the car stopped and the guy opened his door and stood up. Josie kicked the door hard and the edge of it caught the guy in the crotch. It was a really sore one if the way he doubled up was anything to go by, then he sat down again in the car and groaned. By this time, the other one had got out too.

He started to come around to where Josie stood. 'Hey, you just assaulted my friend. Why did you do that?'

Josie turned to me for some kind of assistance.

I said to the guy, 'Leave her alone!'

He turned to me. 'Keep out of this.' He began to approach Josie slowly standing there by the side of the road.

The injured one stood up and leaned on the door. I don't know what their intentions were, but I wasn't about to let them harm Josie. I suddenly had a plan. I ran around to the driver's side and switched off the motor. That got their attention all right.

The driver shouted turning to me, 'Hey, what do you think you're doing!'

I pulled the key out of the ignition, and threw it as hard and as far as I could over the top of the nearest hedge.

They couldn't believe what they were seeing. 'What the hell did you do that for?' the other one shouted.

I ran back to Josie and pulled her by the hand. 'Come on, let's get out of here.' As I walked backwards away from them, I said smiling, 'Have a nice day guys.'

The driver went right up to the hedge and began to look for a way to get into the field. He'd have to find a gate to do that, and we hadn't passed any so far.

We jogged down the road at a leisurely pace, safe in the knowledge that we weren't going to be followed, well at least not by them. We laughed and giggled all the way to the restaurant. We're not about to be bullied by anyone.

No sooner had we entered the premises and I spotted Bob sitting at a table across the room on his own. There was no sign of Gorge. We found a table close to the window again. We just wanted our own company for a while.

I said to Josie, 'What you did back there? That wasn't a clever thing to do.'

Josie just stared at me. Her expression asked 'why?'

'For all you knew, he could have pulled a knife on you.'

'Yeah, I thought about that, but how would you have handled it?'

'Josie, we weren't attacked and there wasn't anything to suggest that we would be. That back there was fuelled by booze, and they thought they'd have a bit of fun with us.'

I looked across the room and could see Bob rising from his seat, then he spotted us. He waved. I returned it with a smile.

I continued, 'And, I think you should have accepted the beer too.'

'What? Come on Sam. You played your part pretty well too; throwing the car keys into that field.' She laughed.

'I could see a problem arising out of your actions, that's why I thought it was time to do something about it. Just wanted to make sure that they couldn't follow us.'

She laughed again. 'Probably still looking for them.'

'They're still kids. That'll teach them to mess with the girls.' I laughed.

Bob arrived at our table. 'Hi,' he said looking at us both in turn. 'Can I join you?'

'Sure,' I said brightly.

As he pulled out a chair to sit down, he asked, 'What brings you here? I thought you'd go to the barbecue place because it's closer?'

'Yeah, we were there but a couple of kids were annoying us so we moved on,' I said looking at Josie. She had a smirk on her face as she looked back.

'Ah,' he said nodding. 'So are you going to order now?'

I nodded.

Josie snatched up the menu before I did and began to scrutinise it.

I said teasing her, 'Three-courser is it then?'

All I could see were those gorgeous blue eyes looking at me over the menu. She made a face, and although I couldn't see her expression, her eyes said it all.

Bob said to me, 'We're looking for two, err… opponents to play beach volleyball? Thought you might be interested.'

My heart skipped a beat. I'm remembering that nightmare I had; Josie getting killed on the road? With my hand at my throat, I said, 'Beach volleyball and no beach?' I almost laughed.

He nodded. 'Yeah. We're staying at a hotel not far from here. There's an area beside a swimming pool with a net for playing the game.'

Josie said seriously, 'We've got a little problem with hotels right now.'

'Really? Can't afford them?' He laughed.

My smile just vanished. I said, 'It's more serious than that.'

He frowned. 'Serious? There's some kind of trouble?' He said shaking his head, 'Sorry. None of my business.'

I said, 'No it's OK. But yes it is serious. Police-type serious. Oh it's a long story.' I grabbed the menu that Josie had just propped against a sauce bottle. I'm hoping he'll drop the subject.

He didn't. 'Someone been hurt?' he asked concerned.

Just before I answered, the waitress arrived at our table. I had to scan the menu quickly, then I spotted Josie trying to catch my eye.

She mouthed 'omelette'.

I nodded and smiled over the menu. Thanks Josie. Saves me having to search. I ordered a cheese one. Bob ordered the same.

I said to Bob, shaking my head, 'It's nothing like that.'

Josie said, 'We have to watch our backs. Just be careful where we go.'

He said to me with that concerned look again, 'OK. You want to tell me what's going on?'

I said, touching his arm, 'Don't want you getting involved. You could get hurt.' I nodded.

He said incredulously, '*What*? I could get hurt? What about you two? So who's doing this Sam?'

I told him the whole story, starting from Tomislav overhearing the plans for the bank robbery and him being killed in the explosion, and finishing up with our present predicament.

He just sat there not believing his ears. 'How many of these guys are in the photos?'

Josie said, 'Three of them are facing the camera. Only one we know, and we don't know which ones have already been caught.'

He sighed. 'This is a real mess.'

'Yeah, tell me about it,' I said with a sigh too.

The waitress arrived back with our breakfast.

As I poured the coffee for us, I said, 'This was supposed to be a peaceful vacation, and now look at us?' I sighed again as I placed the coffee pot back in the centre of the table. 'I'm only sorry that I got Josie mixed up in this too.'

'Have you phoned home?' he asked.

'Yeah, but not recently. I might be tempted to tell mom the truth, but that would only worry her and dad. Better not to say anything for now.'

'So you're not going to turn up at any rendezvous point?' he asked.

'No,' I said as I started on my omelette.

He said, 'If they have to come to you, there's no guarantee you won't be harmed.' He leaned closer. 'I have a plan. You don't have to go along with it. That's up to you.'

'OK, I'm listening,' I said, my fork halfway to my mouth.

'Give them the photos. Give them what they want.' He waited for my reaction, and he got it too.

'Bob, are you mad? What about.....?'

He cut me off with, 'Make a copy of the photos onto some storage device, then put the original into an envelope and open a PO box where they can come and collect it, that way you are in the clear. You give them what they want, and you have your copy to give to the police.'

Josie said, 'And make sure we give the police the photos after we've left the country, or just before we leave. Simple, isn't it?'

I said, frowning, 'Yeah, sounds a little too easy though.'

Bob said, 'What other choice do you have Sam?'

'OK,' I said at last. 'Josie, what do you say? We go for Bob's plan?'

She nodded. 'Sure. Do we have any other choice? Not that I can see.'

I finished off my omelette. 'More coffee guys?' The two of them nodded. I paid for Josie and I.

Chapter 8.

Josie and I agreed to play volleyball at the hotel where Bob and Gorge were staying. Bob had hired a car locally and he took us back to Ana's house to change into our bikinis. We wore our clothes on top.

Back at the hotel, we sat at a table in the hot sun, all three of us, then, a while later, Gorge joined us for drinks.

There was no-one using our pool, at least for the moment, so we took this opportunity to start playing our game, but first we had to change. The guys stripped down to their trunks at the poolside. We stood back out of the way and out of their direct gaze as we stripped off our clothes. I guess we're a little shy, well Josie was anyway. That very skimpy string bikini of hers she hadn't worn in public before. As the guys stood at the poolside discussing something, she sprinted passed them and dived headlong into the water. The two heads turned simultaneously towards the pool. They couldn't take their eyes off of her. I followed her seconds later.

The volleyball court – well there wasn't one, just a net and sand to play on. We're not at the seaside here, but there is the pool where we can cool off. We started the game; the guys on one side of the net, and us on the other. There was a wall about six feet high with the road on the other side of it. This was reminiscent of the nightmare that I had that time in the cottage.

We were now well into the game, and we were beating the guys here. Every now and then, the ball would end up in the pool and one of us – usually Josie, would dive in after it. This time however, Gorge dived in beside her and once she had retrieved the ball, he carried her to the poolside with her giggling all the while.

She said to me, when we had got back into the game, 'Quite a hunk huh?'

I didn't say anything. I don't like him.

At one point, Gorge managed to hit the ball right over the wall. It was bound to go there eventually, since it was being hit very hard and fast by all four of us. Josie went to fetch it. I managed to grasp her arm just before she made for the door in the wall.

She said to me with a surprised look, 'What…..?'

I shouted, 'Don't go out there Josie!'

She pulled free and was outside the open door before I could stop her. I ran after her and caught her up just before a familiar vehicle pulled up at the curb. It was the black sedan with the two guys!

I thought, *'Obviously I didn't throw the keys far enough.'* I was now beside Josie who was standing with her arms folded and the ball in the road. A car sped passed but thankfully, it didn't run the ball over.

The driver's door opened and one of the guys got out. He closed it slowly then leaned casually against it and studied the two of us for a moment. The passenger door opened and the other one got out.

The driver said, 'Hello. We meet again.' He was smiling.

I wasn't as I said, 'What the hell do you want?'

The other one picked up the ball.

Josie made a move towards the road, probably intending to take the ball from him. I held her back. 'Get back inside Josie!'

The driver said, 'I think you know what we're here for. The photographs?'

Startled, I turned back to the driver who was now moving towards us. 'I beg your pardon?' I said backing away from him and with a lump in my throat. *'Is this part of the gang who were after us?'* I thought quickly. *'No, they're too young. They would have been kids when the gang were planning their robbery.'* Sons of one of the gang members maybe?'

I turned quickly to Josie again who was, I noticed, standing behind me, then she turned on her heel and ran inside.

The other guy started moving towards me now.

I was aware of someone at my back.

A voice said, 'These guys giving you trouble Sam?' then I felt something being thrust into my hand. It was a baseball bat. The voice was Gorge's, but why was he leaving me on my own with those guys? Shouldn't he be wading in there and….. oh what the hell! As usual, a guy leaving the woman to do all the work. I whispered back, 'Thanks.' Well that's the only sensible thing I could think of to say in the heat of the moment. I heard him retreat away from me.

Something flashed in the sunlight and the guy closest to me made a lunge at me, a sharp-pointed knife in his hand. It took me completely by surprise, so I didn't realise what his intentions were. Now it's war! I've just lost it for sure! I swung the bat upwards aiming for the knife hand and heard it make contact with his wrist. He screamed out just as his companion came at me with a knife too. I made as if to strike his hand too, then turned quickly to the injured one and thrust my weapon home into his crotch. He doubled up, stumbled backwards and collided with the car then slid down it onto the ground. His companion was on me now. He got me in a neck hold from behind with his left arm. I felt I was choking to death; I could hardly breathe, then he thrust the knife up between my breasts with the other hand, and the sharp pointy end digging into my chest.

He said, 'Now drop the bat. You don't make me angry or I'll cut you up! Where are the photographs?'

My heart just missed a beat. My left hand was trying to remove his arm from around my neck, and my right was pinned to my side and still holding the bat. I couldn't move it. I could see Josie standing just inside the doorway, Bob and Gorge behind her. I guess they thought I might get hurt if they intervened. Complying with the first request was probably the wisest move I'd make all day, but instead of dropping the baseball bat, I threw it towards Josie. She didn't make any move to retrieve it.

He said, 'Not a good move.' He tightened his grip. Now I really am choking! 'Photographs!' He demanded.

I'm not sure how to answer. What should I say? I said finally, 'They're in my pack.' Well I had to say something!

I shouted to Josie to bring the pictures. Josie hesitated, then on a nod from me, she darted back into the complex. When she came out again less than a minute later, she had pulled on her blue t-shirt and jeans again. She approached us slowly then just stood there awaiting instructions.

He said, 'OK, get them out and hand them to me slowly.' The knife-point was still on my chest.

Josie had an expression plastered on that I simply couldn't read, but I guessed she had a plan either about to execute or having already done so. I'm hoping and praying that she hasn't done anything stupid. She slipped her hand inside her front pocket and produced a red flash memory stick.

'Holy shit,' I thought. *'The flash memory card was blue! I'm sure it was. Josie, what have you done?'*

She handed it to him but he told her to slip it into his front pocket, which she did, then he released me. Josie and I backed away towards the open door in the wall. His companion stood up from his position on the ground. He had sat there all the time that the knife was held at me. I guess I must have hurt him bad. Tough! He deserved it! We went in and closed the door. Josie found me my shirt and I pulled it on.

The guys suggested that we stay around longer, so we did. We'd stay for lunch, then we'd be heading out for another adventure in the park, well that was the plan anyway. The guys had gone to the bar first; they'd catch us up later they said.

The restaurant was self-service with few clientèle. I was quite hungry, in fact we both were. We stood in line waiting for our turn to choose. Josie was in front of me. I don't know what she chose for sandwiches, but when she picked a pastry thing from under the glass, I just had to try it. Maybe I'd like one myself too. I thought I'd try it for taste first, so I did. She had no sooner placed the item on her plate when I snatched it up and...

'Hey!' she shouted turning to me with a grin.

Oh gosh, it was oh-so delicious-looking, my mouth was watering even before it had reached my lips. I took a bite. Pastry filled with dairy cream and apple I think. Yummy! Well it was only supposed to be a bite, but then I just had to have another, and this led to..... well you get the idea? I couldn't return what was left of it to her plate, there was so little of it, so I finished it off!

'The nerve,' she said and chose another one of the same. 'You'll have to pay for that now.' She laughed.

'Yeah,' I sighed. I said to one of the girls behind the counter, 'Do you have any ham sandwiches without anything on, like no sauces or salad cream?' I could have gone through a whole list of condiments that I don't like on sandwiches, but there wasn't time to mention them all right now.

She nodded. 'I'll have it brought to your table when it's ready.'

'Thank you,' I said.

She went of to fetch it as Josie paid for her food. I stood behind her and chose another identical pastry thing. I paid for mine and the one that I had already eaten, then followed Josie to a table close to the centre of the room. This was where the coffee station was; just help yourself to the coffee at no extra charge, and as much as you can drink. We filled china mugs with coffee and helped ourselves to the sugar and cream, then we chose a table at a window where we could look out over the countryside.

As we sat down opposite one another, I asked, 'About the flash memory Josie?'

'Yeah? What about it?' she asked as she stirred her coffee.

'It was red. The one that you saved the photos on was blue. Yes?' I stirred my coffee too. I was eyeing up her pastry thing lying on her plate.

She saw me look. 'You're not getting it. You've got your own there anyway.' She laughed as she picked up her bread roll sandwich.

I nodded. 'I will,' I teased as I took a sip of my coffee.

As she bit into her sandwich, some of the sauce – God, it was pink-coloured - ran down her chin.

As she attempted to wipe it away with her napkin, I said, 'Josie, I don't know how you can eat that. What is that stuff anyway?'

She shrugged as she took another bite.

I said, 'So, about the flash memory?'

She didn't reply. Instead, she took another bite, then a drink of her coffee.

I said getting annoyed, 'Josie come on. Where did you get that flash memory?'

She sighed. 'Kinda borrowed it?' She grinned.

'Josie, they don't have those photos do they? You didn't have time to copy them onto that flash, so all they have is a blank one, or something belonging to the office, the front desk, reception or....'

She cut me off with, 'Sam. You're too....'

I cut in with, 'Josie our lives could depend on those pictures reaching them, and now you've gone and....'

I was interrupted by a girl approaching our table with my food. Even before she had it on the table, I could smell it; that vinegary odour that I detest. Nothing with vinegar in it for me, thank you very much!

I said to the girl, 'Could you take that back please? I said I didn't want anything on it, like sauce or ketchup or mayonnaise?' I thought feeling irritated, *Jesus. Do they never listen?'*

She shrugged and took it back with her to the counter.

As Josie finished off her sandwich, she said, 'Sam you're too particular. Just eat the food and enjoy it.' She swallowed a mouthful of coffee.

I said getting irritated, 'You eat your food and I'll eat mine, OK? I don't happen to like the taste of vinegar so I don't want it in my food. It tastes like something gone bad. It dominates all the other flavours. I want to taste the food, not the vinegar, thank you.' Well that's told her!

She sighed and shrugged. 'Yeah OK.' She stood up. 'Want more coffee?'

I nodded. Mine was getting cold, so I drank the remainder and handed her my cup. 'Yeah, sure, thanks.'

I looked out of the window. The sky was beginning to cloud over now. Well that would put paid to any more sunbathing and a walk in the park.

Josie arrived back with our coffee, then, seconds later, the girl arrived at our table with my food. I decided to inspect it before she placed it in front of me, so I did. Yep, it was satisfactory; strips of fried bacon with nothing on.

She said, 'We didn't have any more ham, but I thought you might like the bacon?'

I nodded and smiled. 'Thank you.'

She departed and I turned to Josie. 'Weather's turning.'

'Where did the guys get to? I thought they were joining us?' she asked.

I shook my head.

She put a hand on my arm. 'Look Sam, I'm sorry about the flash memory but I didn't know what to do. Your life was in danger and I had to think fast.'

I looked out of the window. 'Yeah, you sure did that all right,' I said annoyed. 'Without thinking ahead?' I paused as I turned to her. 'Why Josie? We already had a plan that would ensure that we....' Oh what's the use of talking to her?

'Sam. You said yourself that we needed the photos to give to the police, and there just wasn't time to copy them, so what would you have done? This way we still have them.'

'Yes OK Josie, I'm sorry.' I looked out of the window.

She brightened. 'Let's go find the guys huh?'

'Yeah. When I'm finished this Josie. You go on ahead. They said they'd be in the bar.' She got up and made for it.

In the evening around 6, we headed back into the restaurant and had ourselves a scrumptious meal. Well I did anyway. I can't speak for the others though. Josie had a rosy complexion and was giggling a lot. Yeah, that was the wine.

After the meal, we headed back into the bar and spent at least the next couple of hours there just chatting. At one point I left Josie with Gorge and Bob at our table while I went off to find the restroom. I was delayed getting back to the bar because all the cubicles were occupied. I stood at one of the sinks and fixed my hair in the mirror while I waited, then, at last, one of the doors opened and an elderly lady emerged. I went in and closed the door. I was in there much longer than I had planned, and, as a result, when I got back to the bar, Gorge, Bob and Josie had gone. Gone where? I had to find her. I don't feel comfortable when she disappears on her own like that. Or was she alone? We're supposed to be sticking together; staying close as much as possible and looking out for each other.

I went to the bar and tried to attract the bartender's attention. He was attending to an elderly male customer in a blue chequered shirt, then, as he turned in my direction, I waved to him. He came over to me. His expression said, 'What can I do for you?'

'Have you seen my friend the blond girl? Maybe you don't remember?'

He said nodding, 'You were sitting with a blond girl; yes I remember.'

'Did she leave or is she still here? Did you see where she went?' I said feeling myself begin to panic.

'She left with those two men you had been with earlier.' He began to polish some glasses. He added, 'I think she was drunk. They carried her between them.'

I thought panicking, *'What? Josie drunk? No way.'* She doesn't drink that much to get drunk. I asked hurriedly, 'Left? Where did they go? Did you see?'

'I think they said something about going upstairs?'

I didn't wait to hear the rest. I headed straight for Reception in a run where I had seen a flight of stairs earlier. What the hell did she think she was doing? This is not like Josie. Did they put something in her drink?

The young woman at the desk wore a light blue dress. She looked up quickly as I materialised in front of her. She smiled, then frowned. She was about to say something, but I got in first. 'Did you see two guys carrying a blond girl upstairs?'

She hesitated, then, 'Yes....'

I interrupted, 'What room are they in?'

She hesitated again. 'Em.....' She turned to the keys hanging on hooks on the wall behind her.

I grabbed the guest book and turned it around quickly, running my finger down the page. 'When did they check in?'

She turned back to the desk and pointed to the entry. 'They're not in the same room, and they didn't check-in together.'

I looked for 'Bob' and 'Gorge'. I found them in rooms '5' and '8' respectively. I said hurriedly; it was almost a shout, 'Keys for those rooms please!'

'Pardon?'

'Just do it for God's sake. This could be very important!' Now I was shouting.

She said, 'I don't think I can do that Miss......'

'If you don't give me the keys I'm calling the police!' I was just about to loose my cool completely. I wasn't bluffing either. Well, maybe just a little.

She turned reluctantly on her swivel chair and took the relevant keys off their hooks and threw them onto the desk with a look of annoyance. I snatched them up quickly and made for the stairs. I could have taken the lift, but I had visions of me standing there waiting forever for it to come down. I ran up the stairs taking them two at a time, then down the hallway until I reached number '5'. I knocked then listened with my ear pressed against the door. No answer nor any sounds from the room. I knocked again. Time for action. I fumbled with the key as I tried to insert it into the lock. I turned it counter-clockwise, and.... it was already open! I knocked. I waited. More silence.

I'm thinking, 'I'm going in anyway and I don't care if he is in a state of un-dress; it's nothing I haven't seen before.'

I opened the door and stepped into the room. There was no-one here, at least not in the bedroom, then I heard the shower. I made straight for it. I could see him through the frosted glass showering himself. *What I'd give to be in there with him,'* I thought smiling to myself.

He must have seen me through the glass because he shouted, 'Who's there?'

'Sam!' I shouted back. 'What have you done with Josie?'

There was hesitation. 'What?'

I repeated what I had just said.

'Nothing..... em.... she's in number "8".'

'Thank you,' I said and turned to go, then I hesitated. As I turned back to him, I asked, 'Why is she in number "8"?'

'Sam, can you get me a towel?'

'After you answer my question.' I stood my ground; hands on hips.

'She was drunk and....'

I interrupted, 'No she wasn't. She doesn't drink like that. What did you give her?'

'Nothing. Gorge suggested she be put in his room.'

'Oh really? And you just went along with it huh!' I screamed. I grabbed a bath towel from a towel rail and threw it over the partition. 'What were you thinking?' I screamed again.

He shrugged. Well I could see that much through the frosted glass, and a few other things besides.

I'm concerned for Josie's safety. If she was given a drug to knock her out, why? That one doesn't bear thinking about.

I said hurriedly as I made for the bedroom door, 'I'm going to number "8", and if he's so much as laid a finger on her, I'll kill him.'

I flung open the bedroom door and was just about to make for room '8', when I stopped myself. I'm going to require assistance if Josie is incapacitated and that guy Gorge has to be tackled. There could be some serious trouble ahead.

I put my head around the door and shouted, 'Are you coming? May need your help!'

As I sprinted down the corridor to room '8', I could hear him stumbling and cursing as he pulled on his pants presumably, then he joined me in the hallway. We both arrived outside the room simultaneously, him at my back. He wasn't wearing a shirt, and had evidently not had time to dry off sufficiently, as some foam still clung to his furry chest. He reached out and tried the handle. It was locked. We both exchanged glances and read one another's thoughts; well at least I thought I did, until he made a move to kick the door in, and that's when I stopped him.

'What is it?' he asked looking at me in curiosity.

I produced the key from my pocket and held it up for him to see without saying a word.

He nodded.

I fumbled with this one too, then, at last, I had it in the lock. I flung open the door and we both practically ran into the room. There were two double beds here. The farthest one from us on the right was occupied! *Josie?'* I thought quickly. Alarm bells are ringing in my head.

It was then that we heard it; a shower being used. It was coming from behind the door on our left. Bob and I exchanged glances again, but this time there was genuine anxiety on his face. God knows how mine looked.

As I crossed to the bed, I realised it was her. She was lying on her front and covered by the sheet, but her shoulders were bare! As I sat on the edge of the bed, the sheet slid down her back a little. She was naked, at least on her top half! I touched her on the back. She stirred a little and moaned then gave a soft sigh.

I said softly, 'Josie? Can you hear me?'

Bob arrived at my side. 'What the hell did he think he was doing?' he said angrily. 'I'll kill the bastard!'

He crossed the room to the bathroom door. He tried the handle; it was locked.

Josie turned onto her back and sat up suddenly and her vivid blue eyes snapped open. Her sheet fell down and onto her lap. I pulled it up to cover her, then she realised her predicament.

'Sam, how did I get here? Who took my clothes off?' There was panic in her voice. 'Was it Gorge? Did he do this?'

'Let's get you dressed first,' I said as I began to look around for her clothes. I found them lying on the floor on the opposite side of the bed. Jeans and top were there, but there was no sign of her bikini top. I placed the top and jeans beside her.

I said, 'Bikini top not here Josie.' She found it herself lying beside her under the sheet. As she put it on I said, 'Gorge did this Josie. He put you here.'

She had a totally shocked expression on her face, but otherwise remained silent. I could see tears forming, then she got out of the bed and stood up.

'When he comes out of the shower, I'm calling the police, or else I'll just kill him with my bare hands.' I was furious. I'm losing my cool.

As the tears gathered momentum, she said, 'Don't do that Sam.'

'What? Don't call the police or don't kill him with my bare hands?' I gave a short laugh.

She flung her arms around my neck and just whimpered. I rubbed her back, trying my best to console her.

'I trusted him Sam. I thought he liked me. I thought I was in love,' she said through her tears.

As she pulled on her top I said, 'He took advantage of you Josie. He was all ready to start and would have too if we hadn't walked in on it.' I heard the shower being turned off.

Bob was pacing the floor. He was very angry. Maybe I won't have to kill him after all. He opened a closet then stood behind the door and waited. He didn't have long to wait though. The bathroom door opened and Gorge came in, a towel wrapped around his middle. He stopped abruptly just inside the door, and had a surprised, or should that be shocked expression on his face when he spotted Josie and I standing by the bed, her head buried in my chest.

Bob shouted, as he came out from behind the closet door in a fit of rage, 'You dirty....!' He threw a punch at Gorge that caught him full in the mouth. 'That's for Josie!' The punch knocked him off balance and he stumbled backwards and crashed onto the floor holding his face. There was blood on his lip.

'What's going on?' he asked. 'Why did you do that?' He started to get up, then Bob hit him again.

'You,' Bob said fuming and pointing an accusing finger, 'took advantage of Josie and thought you could get away with it!'

'She asked for it,' he pleaded. 'She woke up and said she wanted to have sex. I just thought.....'

Josie cut him off. 'You lying....,' she screamed as she pulled away from me and would have crossed the room to kill Gorge if I hadn't intervened by grasping her arm.

'No Josie. I'll deal with this,' I said, and crossed the room to kill him myself.

I was all ready to start but Bob got in there first. 'You have just two minutes to get dressed and be out of here, or we're calling the police!' he shouted.

Gorge wasted no time in picking himself up off the floor and made straight for the bathroom where he locked himself in. Wise move in the circumstances. In seconds, the bathroom door opened again and Gorge ran from the room clutching his clothes. Had the bedroom door not been left open, I'm sure he'd have gone straight through it! All he wore were his underpants! We all laughed, then Bob came over to me and hugged me tight. Josie joined us and we all hugged each other. Josie was crying, I was too.

'Where will you go now?' he asked pulling away.

I was wiping my eyes with a Kleenex as I replied, 'We'll head for Sarajevo in Bosnia-Herzegovina.' I sniffled and wiped my nose. 'It's a different country these days. Might have to go to Zadar first though.'

Josie nodded.

I said, half joking, 'You and Gorge still travelling together?'

He said seriously, 'Never again. We're finished.' He continued, 'I don't have any set destination, so who knows where I'll end up. Hope to bump into you two again at some point. Maybe I will.'

I flung my arms around his neck and kissed him on the cheek. I said in his ear, 'Thanks. That would be nice. I'd like to see you again Bob.' As I pulled away, I felt myself sniffle again.

It was Josie's turn now. She hugged him and kissed him on the cheek, then whispered something in his ear. I didn't catch it.

I suddenly had an idea. Why doesn't he come with us if he has no destination? It would be nice to have him along for company, so I asked him.

He shook his head. 'I'm sorry. I can't…. I've someone to see.'

I said surprised, 'Oh? I thought you said you had….?'

He broke in with, 'I got a phone call from a friend. We've never met. It's my only chance to see her.' He smiled.

'Oh? Girlfriend?'

'Em….. no. We've been writing for a few years.'

My heart missed a beat as visions of Tomislav came back to me.

'We didn't plan to meet up at all.'

I thought, *'Yeah, bet you didn't.'*

Josie broke into my thoughts with, 'Hey, look,' she said pointing out of the window, 'it's getting dark out there. About time we were getting back.'

I looked at my watch: time was about 8.30. I said, 'Yeah, time we were going.'

Bob suggested that he take us back to Ana's house in his car. Well he surely didn't think that we'd want to walk back in the dark? We'd had quite enough drama for one night!

The house was dark and spooky-looking after the lights of Bob's car had gone. It was really quite dark here. We couldn't even see where we were putting our feet. We had our arms around each other's waists as we picked our way carefully along the gravel path to the house. Had there been a huge hole there in front of us, we'd walk right into it and disappear forever. I shivered as I fumbled for the key, and was just about to put it into the lock when something walked over my right foot. I jumped. 'What the hell!'

Josie jumped too. 'What is it?' she whispered.

Before I could answer, we heard a soft meowing sound coming from down on the ground. I felt Josie bend then she straightened up again beside me. I felt something warm and furry placed against my left cheek!

'Shit!' I said suddenly and almost dropped the key on the step in fright. *'Josie!* What the hell are you doing?' I shivered again.

'It's the little kitty cat again,' she replied. I heard her kiss it. I hope she kissed the right end!

Without any light at all, I was having great difficulty in locating the exact position of the lock.

I said, 'Don't let that cat into the bedroom, thanks.'

She didn't reply.

I found the lock at last and inserted the key, then we stepped inside. Josie snapped on the hall light. I was just in time to see the cat disappear into a room. Kitchen? I wasn't sure. Well he can stay in there if he wants. I just don't want him in *my* bed.

As Josie went off to the bathroom, I busied myself in the kitchen with making the tea. We both felt we needed a nightcap. Something rubbed itself against my legs and I almost tripped. Of course it was the cat.

I said to him, 'You're going outside.'

I almost had a change of heart, then I picked him up and carried him to the back door intending to put him out, when Josie appeared. She had that cute little smile on her lips when she entered, but now it had gone.

She said, crossing to the back door, 'What are you doing?'

I said feeling a little annoyed having to explain the obvious, 'What does it look like? He's better off outside where he can hunt and....'

She cut in with, 'Sam, you are so cruel. Give me the kitty cat. He's adopted me anyway.' Her smile appeared again as she cocked her head to one side.

'Oh, what the hell.' I handed the cat to her. I give up!

I made the tea while Josie talked to the cat wrapped in her arms.

Josie sat at the table opposite me, the cat clutched to her chest with one hand, and the other her tea. As she raised the mug to her lips I said, 'You had a lucky escape there. If I hadn't come....'

She cut in shaking her head, 'I don't want to talk about it. I just want to get to bed.'

I said sympathetically, 'Sure, OK.' I decided on a change of subject. 'Tomorrow we're out of here fast. We don't want these bastards catching us up.'

'No, but where do we go?'

'Head for Zadar again. Maybe we can catch a bus to Sarajevo from there.'

She nodded.

When we had finished our tea, we headed off to bed. I was hoping that Josie wouldn't take the cat into the bed with her, because it was only a matter of time before it ended up in mine. She was in first and lay on her back with the cat on her chest, then she pulled up the sheet and covered his back with it. The two of them dozed off in that position. I turned over onto my right side and put out the light. Well, if they're happy in each other's company......

Chapter 9.

In the morning around 9 o'clock, we left a note for Ana thanking her for her hospitality and I apologising for her being in the hospital, and wishing she'd get well soon. She wouldn't be able to read our letter as she didn't have any English, but I'm sure she'd find someone who could read it to her. We left the money for our stay including a generous tip. This was to cover the damage for broken crockery. I locked the door on our way out and slipped the key under a plant pot. Isn't that what you do? Well, where else could I put it? Hopefully she'd find it there.

We went out to the roadside hoping to catch a bus to Zadar. We had been standing there for about twenty minutes then, at last, a red and cream-coloured bus arrived. The destination board read 'Split', but was it going to Zadar? We took a chance anyway. There were two doors here. One was halfway up the bus, and the other in the usual place at the front. We happened to be closest to the halfway one, so we went on and found seats together. Our packs were too big to go on the luggage racks, so we sat with them on our laps.

There was a conductor here. He was at the back of the bus when we got on, then he began to move down towards us checking tickets as he went. Eventually he reached our seat. I was seated at the aisle. I said, 'Zadar?'

He shook his head. 'Not Zadar. Wrong bus. You missed earlier.'

I said, my heart racing, 'Where can we get a bus to Zadar?'

'You get off at next stop? Yes? I show you.'

We both nodded.

'I won't charge you for short trip.' He went to the front of the bus and spoke to the driver.

Well our little problem had just been solved. All we had to do now was catch another bus from this next stop and we'd be on our way to Zadar. Simple.

Another ten minutes I think, and the bus began to slow. Josie pointed through the window. 'Look. Across there. Buses.' Yep, there sure were buses there behind a cluster of buildings.

The conductor came back. He pointed to the buildings across the road. 'Camp-site. You get bus there for Zadar. OK?'

We both nodded. 'Thank you,' Josie said.

The bus stopped and we got off. There were two barriers at the entrance to the camp-site. We ducked under one of them and walked past the little kiosk where two girls sat at opposite windows. There were trailer homes here, or what the British call caravans; several rows of them, then just beyond those, sites for pitching your tent. We made for the buses immediately. Would we be in time to catch ours? There were two here; one behind the other. The one at the front was being loaded with luggage, in fact they both were. We couldn't decide who the drivers were as no-one was wearing a uniform. I asked a middle-aged guy with a beard and a red striped shirt if this bus was going to Zadar. He said it wasn't. He thought we had missed it and maybe we'd better ask inside. By that he meant inside the building where we had seen other people come out. We pushed through the door and made for an information window straight ahead. As it turned out, the guy was right; we had missed the bus to Zadar, and the next one wasn't till tomorrow around 9 o'clock! I turned to Josie and gave her the bad news.

'So what now? We've nowhere to stay,' she said frustratedly.

'Ask at the kiosk? Why not?'

She nodded. 'Yeah, OK.' She didn't sound too enthusiastic.

We walked arm-in-arm back to the entrance and the kiosk. I asked the girl if there was accommodation somewhere close by. 'There are guest houses near the park, or you can pitch your tent here. The price is...'

I cut in with, 'We don't have a tent.'

She turned and pointed through the window. 'Caravan?'

I turned to Josie. 'Trailer?'

She nodded. 'Sure,' she said brightly.

The girl quoted a price. We both nodded. Well we didn't have any other choice did we?

'Number "2", there?' She pointed out of the window again. She handed me the key and we headed off to the trailer.

Once inside I began to open the windows as the temperature was rising. It was already 26 degrees and it wasn't even noon yet! Meanwhile, Josie was looking in cupboards, then she turned her attention to the sink.

'Sam, there's no gas here. We can't make anything without gas.'

'Ask at the kiosk,' I said, then looked into the cupboard under the sink only to find the plastic water container empty. Well it would be wouldn't it? Josie went off to ask at the kiosk, whilst I took out the container and tried to decide where to find the water. It would have to be suitable for drinking and cooking. First though, I felt although the windows at the front were open, it was beginning to feel too hot and stuffy in here, so I decided to open the large window at the rear. I pulled the handle up and attempted to push the window outwards, and that's when I heard a thud and suddenly realised that the glass had come out of its frame and was in danger of falling onto the ground. I had to push it back up somehow! I need help to do this, then I can close it.

Josie wasn't coming back. Well she hadn't been away very long. I said, 'Come on Josie, hurry up. You're only asking about gas.' Another few minutes – it seemed like eternity, and Josie still hadn't arrived. I let go of the glass and it slipped a little then stopped. My heart was in my mouth. I took a chance and made a dash out of the door and round to the rear. I was just in time to catch the glass as it dropped some more. I had difficultly pushing it up again, but I did manage it in the end, then it was just a matter of pushing the window closed, or was it? I pushed it up but it wouldn't stay put. 'Damn,' I said under my breath. I tried pushing it up again, this time it jammed. 'Come on Josie. Where the hell are you?' I said as I tried pushing it up again, but it still wasn't staying put. *'How the hell did it come out in the first place?'* I thought in frustration.

Josie arrived at my side now with a plastic carrier bag. She had a large grin on her face.

'Where have you been?' I asked feeling annoyed.

She didn't answer directly. 'What you doing?' she asked, that little cute smile appearing on her lips and her head cocked to one side.

'Oh, just rearranging the window glass. What does it look like?' I wasn't laughing. 'So where have you been?'

Her smile vanished for a second. 'Asking about the gas? I was told that there's no point buying gas if we're only here for a day. Too expensive you know?'

I said, 'When we get back inside, don't go opening this window please. The glass isn't secure.'

'OK,' she said brightly.

'So what have you been buying? Hey, I thought you said you went to ask about the gas?' Now I really was feeling annoyed.

'I did, but then I got to thinking about something to eat. There's a mini-mart along there. We shan't go hungry.'

'I wasn't planning to.' I went around to the door and stepped in. I turned to Josie. 'See if you can find us some water? We'll need drinking water....' Then I remembered. 'No, we won't. We've no gas for making coffee or tea. Damn!'

'Well we've got plenty to eat here anyway, and drink.' She started to empty the contents of her bag onto the table at the rear opposite the sink. First out, a bottle of red wine and from California no less. Even better. A wedge of cheese was next, then two bottles of mineral water, boiled ham and a lovely torpedo-shaped crusty loaf. That'll do for sandwiches.

As she took a carton of milk out of the bag, she said, 'I was just thinking, maybe these guys who tried to get the photos from us were paid to do it? Not part of the gang I mean.'

I nodded. 'Yeah, good thinking Josie. Hadn't thought of that one.'

'And the gang won't know where we are now. They couldn't know where we were staying either.' Out came a bag of potato chips – a big one.

I said, 'They probably think we're on our way to Zadar, so they'll be looking out for us there today. They will be disappointed. It'll get them off our backs for a while anyway.'

Now that she had all the contents of the bag emptied onto the table she said, 'I'll go find us the water now.' Then she stepped outside.

I suddenly realised that she'd left without the plastic water container. I shouted her back. I had to unscrew it from the plastic tube under the sink and gave it to her.

In no time at all, Josie was back with the container filled to the top with fresh water. Yes it was drinking water, but we'd be using it for washing too.

Around 1.30, we had a meal at a small restaurant that Josie had seen when she had visited the mini-mart. I started with vegetable soup, whilst Josie had something with crab in it. I finished up with fried squid, my favourite meal in this country. She had boiled ham and potato with salad. Yuck!

In the evening, back in the trailer, we ate the boiled ham and cheese washed down with the wine. I was ready for a sleep and looking forward to getting out of here in the morning.

Next morning we were off to find a bus that will take us to Sarajevo in Bosnia-Herzegovina. We wanted to try to throw the gang off the scent. They'll find out soon enough that they've been stymied. We found a bus that was going our way and now we can relax, at least for now. We boarded the bus at the front this time. I asked the driver if we would be going to Zadar. Yes was the reply, but we'd have to change buses! I don't like the sound of this.

About two hours later, the bus pulled into the bus station at Zadar. We changed to the Sarajevo one now. We sat waiting for the bus to be loaded with luggage and passengers, and kept looking around to see if we were being watched. Any unusual attention being paid to us. Yeah, I think we were getting paranoid all right. The gang can't know we're here though. We didn't know we'd be here either until yesterday.

I said to Josie, 'Pity we couldn't disguise ourselves.' The reason why I mentioned this was because there were a few Muslim women on board wearing head scarves. If only we could find clothing like this. I'll file that one away for later.

'Yeah,' she whispered. 'We could always mug a couple of women.' She giggled.

The bus was almost full now, and as far as I could see, with every seat taken. The driver started the engine and we were on our way once more. First stop was the city of Split, right on the coast, then we were off again. Cityscape soon gave way to countryside once more, and the usual grey-white stone and red tiled roofed farmhouses could be seen along the route, green fields and cattle and some horses; really peaceful-looking.

After about an hour I think, we could see a barrier across the road and a cluster of buildings. This was the customs border crossing into Bosnia-Herzegovina. An elderly guy dressed in what I took to be grey army uniform came on and spoke to the driver. The driver stood up and made an announcement. Unfortunately this was in Croatian and of course we couldn't understand. The passengers started getting off one by one with their possessions. I heard a baby start to cry, which set off another two. They were still crying as their mothers took them off the bus. Some young kids passed us as well.

Josie turned to me with a look of concern. She hadn't made a move to stand but I did.

'What's happening Sam? Everyone have to get off here?' she asked, then she stood up too.

'Looks like it,' I said as I reached up to the overhead luggage rack for my pack. I took Josie's down too and handed it to her, then we made our way forward and stepped off the bus.

Once the bus had been emptied of passengers, a second guy in uniform came forward and opened the trunk. All the baggage had to come out, then we all had to open our luggage and the uniform began to inspect the contents. The first uniform was taking the contents out and just putting them onto the road surface. I thought, *'He'd better not do that with mine or....'*

My thoughts were cut short as Josie tugged on my arm. She was trying to attract my attention. The second uniform approached us from behind. I turned to him.

He said, unsmiling, something in Bosnian? Well what else would it be? I shook my head and shrugged. I said in Italian, 'Parla italiano?' *'Do you speak Italian?'*

He just nodded. 'Il Suo passaporto?' *'Your passport?'*

I went down on my knees and opened my pack and handed it to him without standing up again.

'Ah. Americano?' he said as he looked at the front of the passport.

I nodded.

'Potrebbe rimuovere per favore i contenuti del Suo zaino?' *'Could you please take out the contents of your backpack?'*

I nodded and began to take out some of my clothing. Josie came forward to take them from me, but the uniform stopped her. 'Potrebbe rimuovere per favore anche i contenuti del Suo zaino?' *'Could you please remove the contents of your backpack too?'*

Josie just stood there shrugging and looking to me for assistance. I said to her, 'Empty your pack.'

She looked shocked, then she bent to take out the contents of her own pack.

I hesitated before I removed anything else as I didn't want to dirty my white jeans by putting them onto the ground.

He said angrily, 'Fretta. Noi non abbiamo molta volta.' *'Hurry. We don't have a lot of time.'* He bent and began to pull my clothes out of my pack in an aggressive manner and dropping them onto the ground.

I turned to him angrily and pulled my jeans and other clothing out of his grasp. 'Ehi, non faccia quello!' *'Hey, don't do that!'*

Oops! Did I miscalculate or what? He stood up quickly and I could tell that his hackles were up now, as his hand moved swiftly to his handgun strapped to his right hip! Was it something I said? I stood up in alarm, my face flushed. I thought quickly, *'Oh God! What's he going to do with that?'*

By this time, the other passengers were taking an interest in us. They appeared to have had most of their luggage already checked. There weren't many bags to check anyway. Many people had a look of fear on their faces. God knows how mine looked. I glanced at Josie who had a look of concern on hers.

The uniform was joined now by his companion. The other one said, 'Bene. Vuole giocarlo renda ruvido?' *'OK. You want to play it rough?'* He pushed me violently against the bus.

I responded with, 'Ora fermi questo!' *'Stop this now!'*

He ignored me. He said, 'Mani sull'autobus.' *'Hands on the bus.'*

I didn't have much choice. I turned and placed both hands on the bus, then he said, 'Per favore apra le Sue gambe.' *'Please open your legs.'*

I did and he began to frisk me, starting from my ankles. He was taking his time doing it too. I stole a glance over my right shoulder. Josie was being frisked where she stood by the other uniform too. She wore a worried expression.

'What the hell are they looking for? We're not armed,' I thought as I felt myself begin to panic.

'My' uniform had only gotten as far as my waist when an army car drew up. Someone in a green uniform and cap and obviously in charge stepped out. He was about forty-something with a small moustache. He said, 'Svatko natrag na autobus!' People started collecting their belongings and boarding the bus again.

I turned to Josie as 'my' uniform had stopped his frisking. She still wore a worried expression.

The guy in charge approached 'my' uniform now. He demanded, 'Što radiš?'

'My' uniform replied, pointing to me and Josie in turn, 'Ta dva sudavanja problema gospodine.'

When I heard that word 'problem' I responded immediately. 'Excuse me? Am I causing a problem?'

The guy in charge smiled at me. 'Oh. You're British?' English at last!

I said annoyed, 'No. American.'

'OK,' he said. 'Were you causing trouble?' He still had his smile in place as he looked to Josie and back to me.

I shook my head. 'No.'

He said, 'Passport please?'

I said meekly, 'One of them has it.'

'Tko je passport?' One of the uniforms handed it to him. He looked at it briefly then returned it to me with a smile. He barked an order to the other two and they walked off towards one of the buildings.

'Thank you,' I said as I bent to put my passport into my pack.

'Sorry about all this. This isn't our normal procedure. Some of those guys are jumpy after the war you know.' He looked across at Josie, then back to me. 'We don't empty the bus like this. They've overstepped their authority. It won't happen again. You can go now.' At that, he took a few steps back and saluted us.

I just smiled back. I said, 'Come on Josie, let's go.' We went back onto the bus.

He headed off to one of the buildings.

As the bus sped through the countryside, we began to see houses in ruin by the side of the road. Many were little more than burnt-out shells, sometimes with what looked like bullet holes in the walls.

Josie had the window seat on my left. She said, her hand at her mouth, 'Oh my gosh. Did we do that?'

'We?' I asked turning to her.

'Who did this?' Her hand was still at her mouth.

'The Bosnian War. Not sure who did this though.'

There was no sign of life here at all. Did people not return to their land after the war was over? Did nobody even bother to rebuild? I guess not.

Josie said, 'What happened to them? Did they just get up and leave?'

'Don't you read the newspapers or watch TV?'

'Yeah, but I don't remember a lot about it. I guess I was just a kid then.' She turned from the window.

'I don't know who was doing it, but people were being rounded up and then the males, with the exception of the elderly, were separated out and shot. The women, children and old people were sent off in buses to God-knows-where.'

Josie just gasped, then she said in a low voice, 'Ethnic cleansing?'

I nodded.

She said, disgustedly, 'I don't want to see any more.' She turned from the window and looked straight ahead instead.

In a few minutes we could see signs of habitation; a small town ahead. A road sign said something that I didn't catch, then before we knew it, we were passing a hotel and some shops and a supermarket. Well it appears that some people returned anyway, thank goodness. The bus slowed now and turned into a large parking lot.

'What now?' Josie asked.

I looked at my watch; it was almost noon. I smiled and turned to Josie. 'Think it's lunchtime.'

'We should have brought something to eat,' she said.

'I did.'

'Didn't see you wrap anything,' she grinned.

'Remember the crusty loaf, and the ham and cheese as well?'

She nodded.

I brought my pack down from the overhead luggage rack and sat down again. '*We* don't have to worry about food anyway.'

With my pack on my lap, I began to remove the contents. Everything was well wrapped in tin foil that I found in a cupboard above the sink.

Josie spotted the large bag of potato chips. 'That's mine.' She made as if to snatch it out of the pack, when I slapped her hand.

'Like hell it is,' I teased. 'We're sharing.' I laughed.

People were getting up from their seats and getting off the bus without taking their belongings, so I guess I was right about the lunch stop. Then some kid started screeching; it was ear-piercing. Just as I was trying to decide how to put this little terror out of our misery – slow strangulation came to mind - the noise stopped suddenly. Someone read my thoughts? We started on our lunch, washing it down with the wine that Josie bought yesterday.

We both slept for most of this 5 ½ hour journey, lying on our backs on the seat with our legs drawn up to our chests and using Josie's backpack as an improvised pillow.

I was first to waken as I heard the driver change down through the gears and begin to make a left-hand turn. We had entered Sarajevo, capital of Bosnia-Herzegovina. The driver had just pulled into a bus station and we came to a sudden stop.

I had to shake Josie to waken her. Her blue eyes snapped open. She said with a yawn and a stretch, 'Here already?'

As I stood up for my pack in the overhead rack I said, 'Yeah, and first stop's the tourist bureau.'

Well, we found ourselves a lovely bed and breakfast in a block of flats in an old part of town. It had one double bed, remote control TV, fridge and even a washing machine. The price quoted was just right for us too. Next stop was a car rental office where we came away with a bright yellow Volkswagen convertible. Yep, another manual shift. We took it back to the street where our accommodation was located and parked it in the courtyard beside all the others already there. We weren't in the mood for looking around the town or browsing in the bazaars; that could wait till tomorrow. The time was fast approaching five o'clock and we decided on a meal at an outdoor café.

That night we were so exhausted after our journey, we just lay on the bed and watched a movie on TV, and munching our way through the half bag of potato chips that was left over from lunch.

Chapter 10.

Josie was up and about before I was and had showered too, in fact this is what wakened me. We had opted last night to have our breakfast brought to our room instead of having it in the dining room. I was still in bed when Josie answered a knock at our door. Sure enough, this was our breakfast. God I was starved. She brought the tray to the bed and we sat there together watching TV. Most of this we didn't understand, but I found a Western movie on one of the other channels.

Breakfast consisted of a fry-up with coffee and toast. We used some of our crusty loaf, cheese and finished off the remainder of the ham. Well I had satisfied my hunger anyway. As I drank down the last of my coffee, I noticed that Josie was buttering another slice of our wonderful crusty loaf. I just had to join her.

Josie got up and took the tray over to the coffee table by the window. As she straightened up she said, 'Our car is blocked in Sam.'

I got out of the bed as I was intending to shower anyway. As I passed the window I could see that we were indeed blocked in. I think most of the owners worked in nearby shops and offices. But that didn't matter for today as we wanted to look around the city on foot anyway.

As I made my way to the bathroom I said 'We can deal with that problem tomorrow if it exists. Time to see some of the sights.'

'Yeah sure. Cool,' she said brightly turning from the window. 'Buy some souvenirs too,' she said.

We had to pick up our new bank cards, so, out on the street we started looking for the bank. We were in the old quarter of the city as it turned out, and perhaps we weren't in the right area for banks. I thought we'd ask someone outside a block of residential flats. He was a middle-aged guy with receding hairline and was about to get into his car that was parked at the curb.

I asked in Italian where the bank was. He said he knew where it was. Good. He got into his car and indicated that we do the same. Josie and I exchanged glances.

She shrugged. 'Cool.'

'OK, let's go,' I said finally.

I got in the front and she the rear. He took us to the downtown part of the city, and parked the car at the curb outside a bank. We thanked him and pushed through the door. There was no-one standing in line here at all. I was just about to approach one of the clerks, when I was aware of the door opening behind us. The guy who had given us the ride passed us and made for one of the clerks. He spoke to a young woman behind the glass and indicated the two of us standing there.

We're not not believing this. I exchanged glances with Josie again. She had a smirk on. 'Friendly people in this country huh?' she said.

I said in a low voice; it was almost a whisper, 'Yeah. That would never do back home would it?' I laughed.

The guy stood back from the window and the clerk beckoned us to come forward, then he left the bank. The transaction was all over in about five minutes, then it was Josie's turn. She had to change her currency too. This took longer.

I turned to Josie. 'Guess we find our own way back now huh?'

She shrugged. 'Maybe he's waiting for us Sam.'

'Yeah. You think?'

Yep, he was too. As we pushed through the door, he was sitting in the driving seat waiting for us. I got in beside him and Josie the back, and we headed for the old quarter again. About fifteen minutes later we were pulling up at the curb outside the block of flats where we had started. I turned to him with a smile, 'Grazie. Lei non doveva fare questo Lei sa?' *Thank you. You didn't have to do this you know?'*

'Non è un problema.' *It's not a problem,'* he said getting out of the car.

We got out too and I thanked him again. Josie just nodded, then we continued our exploring. We'd stop here and there taking photos of the centuries-old buildings, at least those that were still standing after the Bosnian War. Some had holes in them that had been filled in later. There were also large gaps between others that was obviously the result of bomb or rocket attack. Then we found ourselves in the bazaar area of the city; it wasn't far from where we were staying. We spent the next few hours walking around the stalls and I bought some souvenirs as did Josie. We now carried a plastic carrier bag each. We'd put them in our pockets before we left the flat because we knew we'd be buying stuff.

It was when we were standing at one particular stall that was selling footwear, that Josie put her hand on my arm. 'Sam. There's a guy over there taking photographs of us.' She didn't point him out.

I said in alarm, 'Where?' Jesus, did they finally catch us up?

She whispered, 'In the doorway over there on the left.' Again, she didn't point.

I picked up a soft leather shoe from the display and pretended to examine it. Yep, sure enough, there was a guy standing in the doorway of a building taking pictures, but it could also be quite innocent. He was, I think, thirty-something and about 5 foot 8 with short black hair and wearing a blue short-sleeved shirt and brown pants.

I turned to Josie. 'Let's move and see if we're followed.'

We went onto the next stall. Pottery vessels were on sale here. We pretended to be interested in them. I even asked the male stall-holder – in Italian – how much they were. Josie kept watch, and before I could even finish my conversation with the guy, Josie had tugged on my arm again.

She whispered, 'He *is* following us. Camera's pointing our way again.'

'OK. Plan of action,' I said picking up an earthenware pot and pretending to examine it. Only one way to find out for sure; leave the area. I remembered seeing street cars in a nearby street. Maybe we could board one. I voiced my plan to Josie.

'Which street?' she asked.

I said taking her by the hand, 'This way.'

We walked briskly along a main and busy thoroughfare until I spotted a shopping mall. I said, 'Quick, in here.' I pulled her in with me. We were momentarily 'lost' in a crowd of shoppers.

Josie said, 'Sam!' She pulled me into a department store.

As it turned out, there was a window looking out onto the street that we had just come from. There were female manikins in wedding dresses there in the window. I pretended to examine them carefully, but my attention was really on the world outside of the window. So far I didn't see the guy and neither did Josie.

An elderly assistant approached now. She said something in Bosnian. I didn't understand of course, and even our pathetic attempt at learning Croatian would have been of no use here either. Again I tried German and Italian but she just shrugged and smiled then walked away again.

I turned to Josie who was staring through the window to the street beyond. I said, 'See him?'

'No.' She gave a big sigh. 'But that doesn't mean that he's not out there waiting for us.'

I suddenly had an idea; change our appearance. 'Josie? Ever had a makeover?'

She just stood there and stared. 'Pardon?'

'Oh God,' I sighed. 'Let's buy some clothes.'

She was still staring at me with a question mark. 'Don't need them. Wasn't planning on buying any.'

I said, getting annoyed, 'Look Josie. We need to change our appearance so we can walk down the street without being seen by this guy, so come on.'

I removed my hair clasp and let my hair fall. 'Well it's a start anyway,' I said taking her by the hand again.

She started to protest, 'But….'

I interrupted, 'Josie come on!' I'm looking for the cosmetics department now, then I spotted it on the left of the elevator in the corner.

'Where are we going?' She asked.

'Watch,' I said getting more annoyed.

When we had reached an aisle with lipstick I said turning to her, 'OK, let's see.' I chose a lipstick at random; a nice shade of red. I opened the top.

'Sam, I don't wear lipstick on my lips.'

'Where do you normally wear it then?' I said sarcastically as I pulled her by the hand again, this time to a mirror on the wall. I thrust the lipstick into her hand. 'Now, put it on.'

She protested, 'Sam….'

I cut her off. 'Shut up and listen.' I was beginning to lose my cool. 'Put it on.'

'But….'

'Look….. *Jesus!*' I took it off her again and began to put it on my own lips. I don't wear it either and haven't done this since I was a young kid of about 8 years old.

Slowly, a grin appeared on her face and she took the lipstick from me. As she began to apply it to her own lips, I reached around to her back and removed her hair clasp, then put it into her front pocket. She didn't protest.

We went to the counter and paid for the lipstick, then I took her by the hand again and we began to look for the denim department. OK, we found it without too much trouble, but Josie's wearing cream-coloured jeans. Would we be able to find her a matching jacket? Yep, there was one hanging there. I took it off its hanger and she tried it on. It was satisfactory. Cool. I found one for myself easily enough since I was wearing blue jeans anyway.

OK, that out of the way, I said, 'Let's swap tops.' I was wearing a white one; her her blue.

Again, she didn't protest. We found a changing booth in a corner. She took her top off and we swapped. After paying for the jackets, we went to the place where they sold cool shades. I bought rose coloured ones; she dark brown. We paid for them, then I took her by the hand again and we left the store. We stopped short of the entrance and looked out. We both looked up and down the street, but there were so many people about, he could be anywhere. Anyway, if he was here, the advance of modern technology meant that he could have already taken the photos on a digital camera, downloaded them either to a laptop or cellphone and sent them via e-mail or a text message. Our presence here would already be known. I relayed my thoughts to Josie just before we stepped out of the entrance. But what I didn't want was him following us back to our flat, so I suggested to Josie that we take a street car or tram as they're called here, directly to our flat; it was close to the tourist bureau. I remembered seeing tram lines there, so we may be able to do this, and without being followed. We found a tourist information kiosk on the street and asked there about the trams here and if we could get one to our accommodation. Yes was the reply. We were told that we could buy tickets at a cigarette kiosk, so we did. This one was close to the tram stop, then we stood in line at the stop sign and waited for a number 4. Luckily, we were close to the front of the line. We stood there looking around apprehensively. Would we be recognised despite our 'disguise'?

We must have stood there waiting for at least five minutes, then, at last, we could see a number 4 turning the corner into our street some distance off. It was followed by a number 6.

Josie said, without pointing, 'Look Sam. Over there by the church.'

Sure enough, as I looked across the street, he was standing there watching us, or was it someone else he was watching? And he must have seen us looking at him too! He won't recognise us now will he? There must be a million other girls looking just like us. The tram arrived and we got on. We watched and copied what the other passengers were doing; stamping their tickets in a little metal stamp fixed to one of the vertical poles. Above that was an emergency button. Hopefully we won't have to use that.

We found seats together at a window where we could see the church. Josie had a look of concern on her face when she said, 'He's gone! Where did he go to? Did you see?'

'What?' My heart was in my mouth. I didn't notice that he had gone. 'I hope he didn't get on here.' I was referring to our tram.

I looked around at all the faces. They were mostly women but there were a few males too, but no-one fitting this guy's description. I turned my attention to the world outside once more. Josie was still looking around through the window, in fact all the windows, at least the ones that we could see out of. Our tram had begun to move now. We would be home soon.

I asked, 'See anything?'

She shook her head. 'No,' she said looking around the passengers. 'Hope he doesn't follow us back to the flat.'

Minutes later our tram was turning the corner into our street, and I recognised the courtyard where our car was parked. We got off here and ran across the street. We didn't stop running till we had reached the top of the stairs and were standing outside our flat. We were totally out of breath, and my heart was still thumping hard. We both banged on the door simultaneously, then I remembered the key that Franjo had given us. I was fumbling in my front jeans' pocket when the door was flung open.

Franjo just stood there with an incredulous look on his face. 'What....?' Franjo Kovačević was a widow in his late 50's, about 5 foot 7 and balding on top.

Both of us were still trying to catch our breath so couldn't speak immediately.

He didn't recognise us right away, with our dark shades, new jackets, lipstick and our hair down. 'Sorry, no vac.....' Then, 'Sam? What....?'

'Yeah,' I said with a sigh, 'it's a long story.'

We entered the hallway and he stood aside to let us pass.

He was looking at Josie when he said with a frown, 'Something wrong?' This is because she had been wiping away a tear from her cheek with her fingers.

She covered her face with both hands and turned away. I handed her the key and she let herself into the bedroom. I said, 'We were followed.'

'Followed? Here? Did you call the police?' He went to fetch his phone; it was lying on the lounge coffee table. He picked it up.

I crossed the room quickly to him. 'No,' I pleaded. 'Please don't do that. We're in enough trouble as it is.' I took the shades off.

Now he really did look concerned. 'You have to tell the police. They'll sort it out Sam.' He still held the phone.

I said, 'No. It's a problem for the Croatian police. There's a gang after us and we have to be careful where we go and what we do. Just be on our guard.'

He put the phone back on the table. 'OK, if you're sure?'

I nodded. 'Yeah.' I added, 'This guy was taking photos of us and followed us to another street. We managed to lose him I think.' I turned to go.

'Maybe it's all quite innocent,' he said. 'Where were you when he was doing this?'

'In the bazaar quarter.'

'That's a favourite place for photographers. Our local camera club frequently showed pictures taken there.'

'Yeah, well, maybe that's all it is,' I said but I still wasn't entirely convinced. We start getting jumpy every time someone points a camera at us? I said, 'We'll go for lunch soon.' I made for the bedroom.

He said, 'I could make you up sandwiches if you like? Save you going out?'

'Oh, no thanks,' I said turning back to him, 'We don't want to feel like prisoners here. We have to get out some time.'

'Yes I know.' He sat on the couch and fumbled with the TV remote.

I headed for the bedroom. When I got in, Josie was sleeping on her front on top the duvet fully clothed. I decided not to waken her just yet. I went to the fridge and took out the wine bottle and the remainder of the cheese wedge. There was still a glassful in it. I sat on the bed beside Josie with the wine bottle and cheese, then, with the glass on the bedside table, I poured the wine to the top. I replaced the empty bottle on the table. Josie stirred now and turned to face me, but her eyes were still closed.

I pressed the TV remote and put the volume down, then flicked through the satellite channels. Josie's eyes opened. 'What you doing?' she asked sleepily, then she turned onto her back.

I took a sip of the wine and grinned back. 'What does it look like?'

Her hand went out for the glass, but I moved it away, teasing her.

She sat up now and reached for the glass again. I moved it away to the right out of her reach.

'Sam.....,' she protested, then she grasped my hand with the glass and pulled it towards her lips.

As she took a gulp of the wine, I said jokingly, 'Suppose you want a bite of my cheese as well?' I held up the wedge for her to see.

She nodded then grasped my left hand and drew it towards her mouth, then took a bite.

'Hey,' I said smiling, 'leave some for me.'

She just grinned back. 'Any food left in the fridge?'

'Nothing but a small piece of the crusty loaf, but it's probably dried up by now.'

She sighed. 'Well we'll have to find lunch somewhere outside?'

I nodded. 'Yeah. I thought of taking the cable car up Bjelašnica Mountain. There's a restaurant at the top.' I took another drink of the wine.

She pulled my hand towards her and took a gulp too. 'Where's that?'

'South west of here. Read about it before we came on vacation.'

She took a bite of the cheese. 'Sounds like a good idea.'

As I finished off the wine, I said handing her what was left of the cheese, 'OK, let's go.'

Before we left, we put on fresh lipstick and our new shades. We brought our cameras but left the backpacks behind as we went down to the courtyard to fetch the car. It wasn't until we had exited the building that Josie noticed that our car was still 'trapped' in behind a white Fiat. I had a good look round for our 'friend' the photographer, but so far at least, he wasn't in evidence. Thank goodness. We can relax at least for now.

'Well, that's all we need. That's a different car from the one that was there yesterday,' she said as we approached it.

I said frustratedly, 'So how do we get out?' I walked around the Fiat trying to think what to do.

Josie joined me. She said, 'Does nobody know how to park in this country? There must be a law against this.'

We were at a loss as to how we were going to solve this little problem, then I spotted two young hunks wearing white t-shirts and jeans coming into the courtyard. They were probably about twenty-something and they were coming our way. The two of them exchanged glances as they approached us and smiles appeared on their faces.

Josie and I exchanged glances too, and her little cute smile appeared now. She stood with her hands in her back pockets as the two hunks drew near. One was slightly taller than his companion and had a short haircut; the other's head was almost completely shaven and had a goatee beard. The taller of the two reached us first and, without hesitation, went to the rear of the Fiat and began to lift it! The muscles on his arms rippled, and no doubt under the shirt too. It sent a tingle up my spine. Josie's eyes, I could see, were fixed on him too.

I said, 'What's he.....?' I couldn't believe what I was seeing. I had a frown on.

His companion joined him immediately at the rear and between them, they moved the Fiat and unblocked our car. It only took seconds. I'd never seen that done before!

Josie's face was flushed. With her hands still in her back pockets, and that little cute sexy smile still in place, she said in what amounted to a whisper, 'Thank you.'

The two hunks just smiled back and exchanged glances again, then walked off towards the street. Probably had no English.

'Well,' I said smiling, 'that's their good deed for the day.'

As we got into the car, Josie said, 'Probably happens a lot here because there's no organised parking.'

I pressed the button that would put the top down, then started the engine. 'First stop's the ski lift.'

'Ski lift?' she asked with raised eyebrows. 'I've never skied before.'

'Cable car.' The top was now fully down.

In about thirty minutes we were pulling up outside the entrance to the ski lift and the cable car station. I parked in an almost empty parking lot – yes, a real one this time. Cars were actually parked in neat rows. I counted only ten. No wonder it was quiet; this was outside of the tourist ski season and the snow mostly gone.

As I stepped out of the car, I had a good look round to see if I could spot our stalker, and again, he was nowhere to be seen.

Josie saw me looking as she closed her door. 'Relax Sam. We've shaken him off. It worked didn't it?'

'Josie, don't be too sure. I don't know if it was much of a disguise anyway,' I said as we made our way to the short covered platform. 'Would you be fooled by it?'

One car was ready to go up the mountain, and another was just coming in. An elderly guy in a grey uniform opened the door for us and we stepped aboard.

A bell rang and our car started to move; slowly at first, then, as we were about to leave the end of the platform, it picked up speed and we were on our way. And what spectacular views. Our cameras were clicking all the way up there, and it was such a beautiful day too. Then a problem about fifteen minutes into the journey; Josie was standing facing downhill with her back to me taking pictures. I was looking in the opposite direction and facing the mountain when it happened. There was a loud metallic clanging sound and the car came to a sudden halt! Josie gave a short scream. I guess it was the mechanism above our heads that we heard.

I shouted, 'What the hell now!'

The car was swaying from side-to-side as it was buffeted by the wind. We weren't the only ones stuck up here. I could see another car further down the mountain was stopped as well. It had passed us earlier.

I said to Josie, 'Hope this is just a temporary fault. Wouldn't like to be stuck up here for the rest of the day.'

'This is scary.' She shivered, then a big gust of wind hit us and the car swung to the left suddenly, throwing us both off balance. We were flung against the right-hand wall, and we just held on tight to the handrail there in case there should be another gust. There was! We both screamed this time. I don't know why we bothered; no-one to hear us up here anyway. There was a metal ladder on the inside beside the door. When I looked up at the ceiling, there was a trapdoor there for emergencies with a window. I could see part of the mechanism there. It looked so flimsy. I took a photo of it. Another gust and this time, a loud creaking sound from the mechanism above our heads.

Jesus, it was scary! You see on the movies those nuts and bolts that hold on the mechanism for the cable car, coming out one-by-one, then the car plunging down......ugh! I shuddered at the thought. Have to stop thinking like this. Think positively girl! We're going to be OK, aren't we? I shivered.

'I hope we start soon, I'm bursting for a pee,' she said.

'No you're not. Just concentrate on something else and you won't feel so bad.'

'Thank you for your concern,' she said annoyed. 'I.....,' is all she got out before there was a loud clanking metallic sound and the car started moving again. 'At last,' she said with a sigh of relief. 'If we'd been up here any longer, I might have had to open the door and just...?' She giggled.

I interrupted, 'And give a whole new meaning to the term "pissing down"?' We both giggled. 'Thank you God,' I said half to myself.

At the top we found a gift shop and a restaurant. We'd have lunch here. We were both starved. Josie headed straight for the loo. I found us a table outside overlooking the ski lift. There were only two other tables occupied. I found myself looking around for any sign of our stalker again. Yeah, I think Josie is right; I am getting paranoid. Too much stress recently.

The menu was already on the table. Thank goodness it was printed in English. I chose prawns with side salad. The sun was hot even up here and I just fancied something cold this time. I'd finish off with a raspberry ice cream. Made my mouth water just thinking about it. The waiter arrived now and took my order. I was going to order for Josie as well, but I wasn't sure what she'd like, then I thought I'd wind her up a little. So this is what happened next. Josie came strolling in and sat herself down.

'You order yet?' she asked.

I nodded. I'm not telling her that I only ordered for me.

While waiting for the order to arrive, I thought I'd head off to the loo as well. I voiced my intentions to Josie and marched off to find it. I was delayed getting back because I was trying to perfect my camouflage. OK, I'm ready now. I headed back to Josie, and, as I made my way to our table, I almost died when I saw what had been put at my place. A large oval plate heaped with....

'What the hell's that!' I thought, then I knew. I asked for prawns but not like this; all tentacles and legs, and horror of horrors – the head still attached!

As I sat down at my place, I could see those little black beady eyes looking up at me! Ugh! No thank you! I like the flesh, but preferably without the body, thank you very much!

Josie saw my look of disgust but didn't say anything. Instead, she just sat there with a Cheshire cat-like grin, then I noticed she had the remains of a prawn, or possibly more than one if I know her on her side plate.

I said annoyed, 'Help yourself to mine why don't you?' I just sat there staring at those grotesque-looking critters on my plate. Even if I was going to eat them, it'd take me the best part of a week to get through this lot. I'd just lost my appetite anyway.

She said grinning, 'Oh, thank you. I think I will have another one.' She reached out and took another two. She broke the shell of one with ease and popped the flesh into her mouth.

I said with a smirk, 'Good huh?'

'Mm, very. You should try it.' She grinned again, then a frown appeared. 'Hey, what happened to my food?'

I shrugged.

'Sam, you said you ordered it didn't you?'

I was trying to keep a straight face. 'No. You asked me if I ordered and I said yes, OK?'

The smile still hadn't reappeared. She said, 'Pardon? You mean you ordered your own but nothing for me?'

I nodded. 'Josie. Can't you take a joke? I was winding you up.'

'So, you had me sitting here waiting for a meal that had no intentions of coming?'

I nodded again. I seem to be doing this a lot lately.

'Sam, how could you do that to a friend?' She sounded serious. Yep, I think she was too!

I said, putting a hand on her wrist. 'Josie, for God's sake. It was only a wind-up, OK?'

She didn't say anything, and her smile still hadn't reappeared.

'Look,' I said pushing those 'things' towards her, 'I'm sorry. I'll make it up to you now. You eat them. I think I've just lost my appetite anyway.'

That grin appeared again. She reached out and took another, then another. She pulled the plate towards her and started in earnest. Now she really was going for gold. She said offering me some of the meat, 'Here, try it. It's your meal anyway.'

I hesitated.

'Hey, they don't bite.' She laughed.

I took it from her and ate it. I'm feeling hungry now. I'm wishing I'd ordered something else instead though. I swear to God I'll never eat another prawn in my entire life, especially if they look like this! She began to break open more prawns and put them onto a side plate for me. I picked them up and couldn't get them into my mouth quick enough. Yep, I was hungry all right. Felt as though I hadn't eaten for a year. Like I just come out of hibernation? Now I know how bears feel.

One plate on my right contained the side salad, and another, various dips. I ignored them, as I don't eat them, but Josie didn't appear to mind, in fact she couldn't get enough of them. I ate the lettuce and cucumber but ignored the coleslaw. For me, cream is for dessert or coffee or cakes or.... Just not with the main course, thank you very much! And this was more vinegar, ugh!

Josie poured water for us into glasses. I was ready for a drink. Those prawns were salty. Well they would be wouldn't they? They came out of the sea after all! Well, we finished them off in about fifteen minutes flat.

Josie said as she dabbed her mouth with her napkin, 'Did you order anything else?' She was grinning.

I nodded.

'Like ice cream?'

'How did you know that?'

'But not for me, huh?'

I shook my head as I grinned back.

'Well we can share that too,' she said as her little cute smile appeared again.

I shook my head as I wound her up again. 'No way. It's mine. Get your own.'

'Hey I thought we were friends. Friends share you know?' she said, her smile still in place.

'I've just changed the rules,' I said as I spotted the waiter arriving with my raspberry ice cream.

She said, fluttering her eyelids at me, 'But you'd make an exception for me wouldn't you?'

I stood my ground and shook my head smiling.

The waiter put my ice cream in front of me. I nodded my thanks, then he departed with the dirty plates. Before I knew it, Josie had attacked my ice cream with a teaspoon.

'Hey!' I exclaimed laughing.

As she spooned it into her mouth, she said, 'Mmm-mm! That's good!' That shows how good it was! If it meets with Josie's approval, then it must be good. Yep, it was too. One of the best ice creams I've tasted.

In a few minutes the waiter returned to our table. He asked Josie what she wanted. She settled on a chocolate ice cream.

When I was finished mine I went off to the Ladies again and left Josie to finish hers. Again I was delayed getting back because after I had washed my hands, I found there were no towels for drying them; not even a hot air blower. I had to go ask someone in reception about it. The girl receptionist found towels for me and the problem was solved.

When I got back to the restaurant, Josie was gone. *'Oh shit! Where is she? Josie, don't do this to me,'* I thought as I began to panic.

I paid my bill, then I went to the gift shop. No luck. Well there was only one explanation; she had taken a car back to the bottom. I practically ran down the few steps to the cable car station. There was an empty car waiting at the platform, so I grabbed the attendant by the arm and said quickly, 'Have you seen a blond girl about my height, white jeans and jacket and white top go down recently?'

'Yes. She's just gone in that last car.' He held the door open for me.

I went inside but I couldn't sit down. The car began to move and I began to pace up and down. I'm cursing the snail-pace of this vehicle. What was she thinking? She shouldn't be going off on her own like that. My heart was in my mouth all the way to the foot of the mountain. The attendant at the station pulled open the door and I just ran out without thanking him. I ran down a flight of steps, then I spotted her standing there with her back to me and looking out over the countryside. I went straight up to her and took her by the arm.

'Josie, what do you think you're doing?'

She turned to me. The face was wrinkled and ancient-looking. It wasn't her. 'I beg your pardon?' She had a British accent.

My face turned scarlet. 'I'm sorry,' I apologised and turned away quickly.

I ran outside and into the parking lot, then I spotted her sitting in our car. What's she done to her hair? It was back in it's usual ponytail!

I marched up to her. 'Josie. What the hell....?' I broke off as she turned to me. Her lipstick had gone and the new shades too; she was back to her old ones! She just sat there looking at me with that cute smile. I slid into the driving seat. 'Well?' I said looking into her face.

'What's up?' Her smile was beginning to melt.

'What do you mean what's up? Look at you.'

'Sam, I think you're too uptight. Relax.'

'What? Relax? Uptight? Like I had a high-powered rifle aimed at me and I'm supposed to relax?'

'We don't know if he had a rifle or not. Could have been bluffing.'

'Oh yeah? I call their bluff and you get shot? Get real Josie. You'd just stepped off the sidewalk. You were probably the target!'

She said, 'But we don't need the disguise now do we? We fooled him didn't we?' She laughed. 'Wasn't much of a disguise anyway. You said so your-self.'

I'm feeling annoyed again. 'Well that was a stupid thing you did removing your lipstick and putting your hair back, not to mention the shades. It's my life on the line as well as yours you know.'

'What the hell's wrong with you? Every little thing that happens, you have to go over the top with it; seeing evil round every corner.'

I said, beginning to lose my cool, 'Josie, just drop it.' I turned away from her. I'm looking up and down the parking lot for any signs of our stalker, but I guess he could have changed his appearance too by now. Maybe our disguise worked after all.

'Where to now?' she asked sounding a little brighter.

'Back to town? Have a look around the old quarter?'

So that's what we did. We found a parking lot and headed off to find something historical to photograph.

Chapter 11.

We found the most lovely old church. It was still being used for services, but what interested us most was the steeple. We could see visitors up there admiring the views so we decided to join them. There was a small entrance fee to be paid, then we climbed the eighty-four steps to the top. How do I know how many steps there were? I counted them. Took so long to reach the top, our muscles were aching by the time we got there, and the stairway was so narrow that we had to stand with our backs pressed against the wall to let other people pass us on their way down. You just don't wanna be claustrophobic going up there!

When we had gotten to the top, we had the place to ourselves. Josie stood beside a square pillar with her back to the parapet while I snapped her against the city backdrop. It was while I was composing my next shot of her, that I thought I recognised someone on the street below. He wore a brown coat and white pants. Was that Bob? Was he here? I did mention to him that we'd be here. I felt my heartbeat quicken at the thought of us bumping into one another again. Maybe I'd get to kiss him properly this time. Yeah, well, I can dream can't I? I need something to take my mind off of our present situation.

Josie must have seen my expression. She asked, 'What is it?' She had a smirk on.

I said smiling with my face reddening, 'Oh, nothing.' With that I stepped around her and took up position facing her, waiting for her to snap me.

She took a few shots, then I turned and looked down on the street, but I couldn't find him again. Oh well, maybe I was mistaken; just someone who looked like him I guess. Feeling disappointed I turned again to Josie. 'Let's go.'

We returned to the street and the parking lot. As we got into the car, I was going over in my mind, the image of the guy I had seen on the street.

Josie looks at me with that 'knowing' look of hers. 'You've got that faraway look again,' she said with a smirk. She's seen it before and knows what it means.

'It's nothing, just.....' I trailed off dreaming.

'Yeah I know.' She laughed. 'You seen a hunk or something.' Again that 'knowing' look.

I gave in. 'Think I spotted Bob in the street. I don't know. Can't be sure.' I looked away to the left across the parking lot.

'I thought as much.' She laughed again.

I thought I'd make a quick call home. Mom and dad would be wondering about us. I had no sooner turned on my cell, when I noticed that I had voice-mail. I thought quickly, *It's them again.*' Then I dismissed that idea when I accessed the message and saw the number on my screen. They wouldn't leave one to be traced later, so who could it be? I didn't recognise it. I pressed 'call' and heard it ring.

A male voice said something in Bosnian. I said, 'Who's that?' I had to cover my other ear in order to hear better.

'Franjo from the flat?' he said. 'I tried to call you.'

'Oh! Hi!' I remembered giving him my number in case he had to get in touch with us when we were out.

'I have....' Traffic noise. 'Idea for....' Signal breakup? 'You for disguise.'

'Really? I can't hear you very well. What kind of disguise?' What did he mean by that?

He said, 'I had a.....' More traffic sounds. 'With one.... my neighbours... a Muslim.'

Oops! I thought I knew what was coming. 'And?'

'She says.....' The signal just broke up again! 'Have....' Street noise, a car honking, tram. 'Her clothes to wear.'

Did I hear right? Clothes? Was that what he said? I said, 'Sorry? What did you say? Bad signal here I think.'

Josie's got a question mark there.

I just smiled back.

She mouthed, 'What?'

Franjo said, 'Can you...... hear....?'

'Sorry? We'll come back to the flat, OK? See you soon.' I switched off the phone and turned to Josie.

'Who was that?' she asked smiling.

'Josie. If I heard him right, he's got the perfect disguise for us.'

'Pardon? Who?' her smile just vanished.

'Our host, Franjo.' I started the engine.

'What kind of disguise? We don't need one now anyway Sam.' She said smugly.

I said as I backed out of the parking lot, 'Josie, this'll work. Trust me.'

'What kind of disguise?' she repeated as we headed back to the flat.

I turned to her. 'Wait and see.'

Back at the flat, Franjo was waiting for us at the door. He must have seen our car come into the parking lot. He said, as he stood aside to let us in, 'Sonja will show you how to put the clothes on.'

Sonja? A young woman – all smiles - appeared from the living room wearing a blue floral dress and a white top. She was taller than us and about twenty five, with long black hair flowing to her shoulders. Franjo explained that she had no English.

I turned to Josie smiling, just as Sonja approached us and took her by the arm.

Josie just stared back with that question mark again. She whispered to me, 'I don't want to do this.'

I whispered back through clenched teeth, 'Of course you do. You were the one who suggested mugging a couple of Muslim women remember?' I almost laughed.

Sonja turned to one of the armchairs and picked up a length of dark brown cloth off of it, then she held it out to Josie.

She took it from her albeit reluctantly then turned to me. 'Sam. We'll be roasted alive inside these together with our own clothes. It's hot enough as it is out there.'

I nodded. I had to agree with her. She had a point.

Franjo said, 'You would have to wear underwear; not your outdoor clothes.'

Josie said, 'No. I still don't like it.'

I said, feeling frustrated, 'Josie you can wear your bikini under it.'

She made a face. 'OK OK,' she said holding up her hands in submission, 'I give up.'

Sonja spent the next ten minutes showing us how to put these garments on. She'll want these clothes back at some point. I asked Franjo about this. He spoke to Sonja but she shook her head. No. We could keep them if we wanted. It wasn't important. Franjo had told her about our predicament of course.

Well it did feel strange to be wearing these clothes, especially over our own. At least now we can go out and about without fear of being spotted. We'd also have our faces covered by a veil. Yep, I think this will work.

'Thank you Sonja.' I looked to Franjo to translate.

He did, then it was Josie's turn to thank her.

We went to our bedroom and just sat on the bed. After a moment's thought, I began to remove the Muslim clothes. We don't need them right away.

'What are you doing?' she asked looking at me curiously.

'Get them off Josie. There'll be time for those later.'

'I thought you....' she broke off, then she too began to take off hers.

That afternoon we didn't go out anywhere because we wanted to move on. We thought we'd go find the railroad station later. I thought maybe Zagreb. Just places that I had read about in the tourist literature. Josie suggested that we take the night sleeper train and I agreed. Neither of us had been on one of those before, so now was the time.

Josie had gone for forty winks on her front beside me on the bed, whilst I had elected to watch something on TV. I had only just started watching a movie when my cellphone rang its musical tone. No caller ID again. My heart missed a few beats as I thought it might be our adversaries.

It was, but before I could say anything he said, 'There is no hiding place for you. We know where you are....' It was the same voice as before.

I interrupted; it was almost a shout, 'Go to hell!' I didn't want to waken Josie.

He said, 'I suggest that you have the photographs ready to hand over to our contact, otherwise your friend....'

I interrupted again, 'Shut up!' This time it was a shout, then I switched off. 'Bastard!' I shouted out loud.

Josie woke up with a start. 'Sam, what's going on?' She sat up and stared at me.

My hand was at my breast as I tried to recover from the shock of it all. 'Just got a call from.... 'them'. They know where we are Josie and they want us to hand over the photos to their contact.'

'And, are you?'

I shook my head. 'Nope.' I had a smug look on.

She sighed and shook her head too. 'You're going to get us killed yet. I can feel it.'

'Josie, shut up. I'm trying to think what to do.' I got up and began to pace the floor.

'I know what to do; hand them over and let's get this nightmare over with.' She got up too and just stood there awaiting my response. She got it too.

'Josie, I'm not in the mood for arguing. Now if we're going to move on, they don't know that we have an almost foolproof disguise this time, so we dress in these clothes that Sonja gave us and go look for the railroad station to book our cabin, OK?'

She shrugged. 'Guess so.'

We took off our clothes down to underwear, then we helped each other put on the Muslim clothing. The only thing we couldn't change was our footwear, and Muslim women wouldn't wear sneakers. It would probably be sandals, but we don't have any with us. Maybe we could buy them. Something to think about later. I slipped some paper currency into my pocket, then we headed down to the street, veils covering our faces. We decided to walk instead. It's easier to ask directions this way.

Finding the railroad station proved more difficult than we anticipated, so we had to stop and ask people where it was. Sometimes I had to use sign language. Having found it, we headed off to the ticket office, but as luck would have it, the elderly female clerk had little English. I was trying to tell her that we wanted a double-berth cabin to ourselves. She wrote out the ticket and stamped it. At the top it read '6'. That's the cabin number. Well at least we'll know which one we'll be in.

Next stop was a café for our supper. We found a table outside on the street, and sat beside one another this time; Josie on my left. I want to get a full view of the street. I'm still nervous after that phone call. Looks as though our disguise didn't work after all, but we should be OK this time.

The waiter arrived now with the menu and handed it to Josie, then departed again. She still had her veil in place as she turned to me, 'How long do we have to wear these? You can't eat with this in place that's for sure.'

I shook my head. 'Don't know Josie. Not sure what the customs are. Just keep it in place till the food arrives.'

She began to study the menu, and it was then that I thought I spotted the guy I had seen from the church steeple. Could that have been Bob? It certainly looked like him. He wore a brown jacket and white pants. Unusual attire for someone backpacking. He disappeared momentarily in a crowd of people, then he reappeared again seconds later and leaned against a bus stop sign.

God! It has to be him. I said excitedly to Josie, 'Look!' I didn't want to point. 'Across the street there beside the bus stop.'

Josie looked up from her scrutinising of the menu. 'Pardon?'

'Across the street there?'

She looked at where I was looking. 'What did you see?'

'Not what; who. Does that look like Bob over there?'

Again she looked to where I was looking and hesitated, 'Yeah, sure looks like it Sam, unless he has a double.' She giggled.

With my excitement mounting, I was tempted to stand up and wave to attract his attention, but if those vile people were in the vicinity, that wouldn't be such a clever move. He was looking around as though searching for something or somebody. Me? Us? Should I go across there and surprise him? He'd be pleased to see me again no doubt. Oh, I can't wait to speak to him again. If I want to see him again, we're going to have to order soon. We don't need a big meal this time having eaten at lunchtime.

Josie handed me the menu but I didn't have a clue what it said as it was printed in Bosnian. I said, 'Did you choose something?'

She nodded.

'What? You can't read it.'

'Doesn't matter. Unlike you, I can eat anything,' she said smugly.

'Ooh!' I said looking down the menu.

The waiter arrived back now. I pointed out something on there to him and took a chance. I'd no idea what I ordered. Let's hope I can eat it. Josie pointed out something there too and the waiter departed.

'Well, we'll see what he brings. Maybe I won't like it.'

She removed her veil. 'You're too particular Sam. Be like me and take a chance. Be adventurous.'

I sighed feeling annoyed. 'Oh shut up.' It was then that I noticed that Bob was gone. Where did he go?

Josie saw my look. 'What's up?'

'He's gone. God, just my luck!'

The waiter arrived back with our food. It turned out that she had ordered the same as me. It consisted of little sausages; ten I think, and raw onions.... yuck! I don't like them, and a flat bread on a side plate. I tasted the bread. It was very nice. So far so good. Now for the sausages. Yummy! I'll add this one to my list of favourite foods too.

Josie saw me hesitate at the onions before starting on her own food.

'Yeah, yeah, OK.' I sighed and began to scrape mine onto her plate.

She grinned back. 'Thanks.' She started on her food.

There was water on the table in a glass jug. I poured for us. 'See if you can spot Bob anywhere.'

She looked up from her food. 'Been doing that.' She grinned. Why does she keep doing that to me? Always one step ahead. It pisses me off sometimes.

Minutes later we were finished our meal, and Bob still hadn't reappeared. Guess we've missed him. Maybe he was just waiting for a friend. Well he did say that he was seeing a girl, so that's probably what he was doing. Oh well, time to move on. I paid the waiter then we paid a visit to the loo.

Out on the street, we decided to return to the flat and spend the remainder of the afternoon inside. We'll be heading off on the night sleeper tonight to Zagreb. First though, we have to return the car to the rental office. We walked off in the direction of the flat, and that's when I thought I spotted Bob again. He was standing across the road looking in a shop window, then turned our way. We still had our veils up so he wouldn't recognise us anyway. I just stopped in my tracks. So did Josie.

Now he was looking around. Was he looking for us? Me?

Josie said, 'See what I see?'

'Do I?' I said excitedly. 'I'd know that hunk anywhere.' I laughed. I stepped into the road, pulling Josie with me.

He turned away from us again towards the shop front.

I'm thinking I'll just walk up to him, take him by the arm, pull my veil down and say 'hi!' so that's what I did.

He turned. Oh shit! It wasn't him, and he had a startled look at first, then he smiled. It wasn't friendly.

When I realised my mistake, I blushed and said, 'Oh, so sorry.' I gave a short nervous laugh. 'Thought you were someone else.' I turned to Josie who was standing at my left side intending to move on, when I felt my right wrist grasped tightly. It was hurting. I turned back to him in alarm. 'Hey! What....?'

'Hey, I know who you are!' He pulled on my arm; his grip tightening. 'You come with me now.' He had a thick east European accent.

I said, 'I beg your pardon? I will not.' I tried pulling out of his grasp but his grip was too tight. 'Let go of me or I'll scream!'

He said, 'No you won't.' His right hand moved quickly under his coat. I could just make out the black muzzle of a weapon, and it was pointed at me! Oh shit, shit, shit! I just blew our cover right out of the water!

Josie just froze to the spot.

'You both come with me. We see boss now.'

'Like hell we will,' I thought in a panic. Well, maybe I'll just file that one away for later.

He said, pushing me forward in front of him, 'You go ahead now and your friend too. If you try anything, I will shoot you dead OK?'

I nodded.

Shit! How could I not see this coming? I should have been more careful. I'm mentally kicking myself very hard now. Approaching strange men in the street? What was I thinking? Damn!

By now, other passersby were beginning to take notice. Some even avoided us by stepping out of our way. He pushed us into a narrow lane lined with shops on either side. It was cobbled with no discernible sidewalk. An old street I think.

Josie was ahead of me. She turned and smiled back. What's she smiling at? Has she a plan? I'm hoping she doesn't do anything stupid. He's still pushing me forward, and I can feel the weapon in the small of my back. He means business. Would he really pull the trigger and shoot a woman in the back? I push that idea firmly to one side.

There's an alley coming up on the right about 100 yards ahead. I can feel a plan coming on. Well, sort of, then Josie shouts back to me, or was it the gunman she was trying to warn? 'Police!'

What? Police? Where? He put his arm around my neck and I felt myself being dragged backwards, the weapon still in the small of my back. I'm choking. I just managed, 'Josie!' Then, 'This way! Come on!' I spluttered. I was being pulled through a door. *'What the hell now?'* I thought panicking.

A voice from somewhere behind me shouted something and the gunman turned in surprise towards the source. That was my opportunity for escape. I just managed to elbow him in the groin; well that's what I intended anyway. Well it seemed to work, because he let out a loud gasp and stumbled backwards falling onto his back on the floor at the same time letting go of me. I scampered out of there like a bat-out-of-hell. I almost knocked Josie down in my haste to get to freedom. We both ran down the street, not daring to look back lest it slow us down. We didn't stop until we had reached another alleyway on the left. Josie pulled me into it and we ran into a crowd of shoppers. That's when I stopped and looked back. He was nowhere to be seen, thank God, but we won't be able to relax till we're back at the flat.

I took Josie by the arm and pulled her to me. 'Police? There wasn't any was there?'

She turned to me and that little cute smile appeared again. She shook her head. 'Nope.' She turned away and walked ahead.

I shook my head too and followed her.

Back at the flat, we made straight for the parking lot to collect the car, then it was off to the car rental office.

The top was down, and, as I was about to reach for the switch to close it, Josie grasped my arm. 'Sam. It's him.'

'Who?' I looked to where she was pointing.

'Bob.'

I just saw his back as he pushed through the door. He was wearing a blue sleeveless shirt and black pants. He must be hiring a car, or maybe he was returning one.

'Oh my God!' My heart was thumping hard. I put the top up and opened the door. 'I'm going to surprise him.' I giggled as I closed the door.

Josie followed me into the office. We both had our veils in place.

He was standing at the desk with his back to us. I walked straight up to him, my sneakers making no sound on the carpeting and poked him in the ribs. 'Hi!' I said brightly.

He jumped visibly and turned to me with a puzzled expression. Yep, it was him all right this time. He doesn't know me. I pulled my veil down, then a smile appeared briefly on his lips.

'Sam?'

I nodded with a grin. 'Yes!' I put the car keys on the desk and the girl threw them across to another desk on her right where a young guy in a black suit sat. He went out to check our car.

'So what's with the dress?' he asked looking me up and down, then at Josie.

'Oh....' is all I got out.

Josie interrupted with, 'It's a long story.'

The girl behind the desk interrupted now. 'Excuse me?'

He was hiring. 'Moving on Bob?'

'Oh, yeah. Nowhere in particular. Where are you off to if anywhere?' he asked.

The girl asked again, 'Excuse me? Are you wanting to hire a car sir?'

Bob just turned and nodded.

I thought, as I smiled up at him, *'Can't you see he's busy?'* I said, 'We're taking the night sleeper tonight to Zagreb. Should be fun I think. Would be even more fun with you there though.' Oops! That sounded as though I couldn't wait to get him into bed with me. Well, I can dream can't I? But I digress!

His smile just got broader, then he pulled me close and looked into my eyes. I thought he was going to kiss me. 'Meet you there if you like?' he said smiling.

Josie cleared her throat trying to get my attention. 'Em..... Sam? We got a train to catch tonight remember?'

I said sounding annoyed, 'Josie....'

She said in a huffy tone, 'OK OK. Just reminding you is all.'

That girl, she's jealous. I heard the door open behind me and then slam shut. I turned my head quickly to the door, but she was already marching down the street.

I said, 'Josie!' I was about to turn and follow her, when Bob pulled me ever closer and that's when it happened; he bent and kissed me full on the lips!

Oh God! It was a very slow and passionate kiss that sent a tingle up my spine. I thought I was going into orbit. I haven't been kissed like that in ages. He pulled away briefly then started again.

I jumped as the desk telephone rang, bringing us both down to Earth again with a thud. Bob turned to the desk now and tried to concentrate on the paperwork that the girl had placed there in front of him. In no time, the transaction was complete and we walked out of the building towards the parking lot across the road.

He led me to a red Volkswagen convertible, but instead of opening his door to get in, he pushed me against the side of the car and kissed me on the lips again. Oh my God, I think I'm in love!

Just before I got carried away to Heaven, he said, 'Yeah. I'd love to get you onto the night sleeper too. Just think,' he said laughing, 'you on top, me on the bottom.'

What? Did I hear right? I said, as I gave a short laugh, 'Pardon?'

He laughed too. 'Your favourite position?'

I gave a short incredulous laugh. 'What?'

'Bunk beds?'

'Oh! Right.' I blushed and laughed.

He stepped over the door and into the driving seat. I joined him in the front. He asked as he put his arm across the back of my seat, 'So, about this.... clothing Sam?'

'Oh, yeah, well.' I told him the whole story from where he left us at Ana's house near the Plitvice Lakes National Park, to the clothing that Franjo's neighbour gave us oh, and the guy watching out for us, and us thinking it was himself, and the weapon pointing at me, and well, you know the rest.

He was silent all the while, then he said, 'I think you're very brave not to go to the police. So how do you expect to get the evidence to them?'

'Oh,' I sighed. 'I'll think of something – eventually.' I gave a short laugh.

'Maybe I could help out there.' He waited for my reaction.

He got it too. 'How do you mean Bob?'

'I could take it to the police for you; get those thugs off your backs?'

'What? Are you serious? No way. We're not giving the photos to "them" till we're ready, and it'll be on our terms.'

'Whoa!' he said. 'Hey, that's pretty tough talking Sam. I admire your determination even if it is crazy.'

I stared straight ahead. 'You wanna believe it. You just haven't seen me in action yet.' I nodded.

He laughed. 'So, where is it anyway?' he said looking at me intently.

'The flash memory? Josie's got it.'

'Where is she now? Back at the flat?'

'Oh my God! I forgot about..... Josie?' I forgot about me blowing our cover. God knows where she is now. Hopefully back at the flat, if not..... It didn't bear thinking about. I'll never forgive myself if anything's happened to her. I thought, *'Cellphone – where is it?'* Then I remembered I'd left it back at the flat. Didn't think I'd need it. Damn!

Bob said concerned. 'What are you going to do Sam?'

I said as I got out of the car, 'Was going to phone her but I've left my cell at the flat. I'll have to go back there and see if she's there.'

'Where is it? We can go together,' he said getting out too.

'Short distance from here. Come on.'

Chapter 12.

Back at the flat, Bob and I ran upstairs. I fumbled with the key, trying to get it into the lock. The door opened just as I turned the key. It was Franjo. He must have heard me put the key in. He just stood there with a puzzled expression. 'What's wrong?'

I said, trying to catch my breath, 'Is Josie here?'

He shook his head. 'No. Should she be?'

'Franjo, she left us at the car rental office and she's not here either. Where the hell is she?' I'm close to tears now.

'Is she in danger?' he asked concerned.

'I hope to God she isn't,' I replied feeling helpless. 'And it's partly my fault.'

Franjo just stood there with a question mark. 'How so?'

I told him about us mistaking the gunman for Bob. I said quickly, 'Oh, this is Bob… em.' I broke off because I didn't know his second name. I glanced at Bob.

'It's Patterson.' He said, 'If she's got her phone with her you can call.'

I ran to our bedroom. I'm looking around for her phone, but it's nowhere in sight. I found her backpack on the floor next the dressing table. As I began to rummage through it, Bob came into the room. 'Find it?'

'No, not yet,' I replied. Some more searching and I had decided that it wasn't there. Well, she must have it with her. There's hope yet.

Bob's eyes were fixed on me as I went around the bed to my side and picked up my phone. He didn't say anything.

I switched on the phone. Franjo came into the room and just hovered. I found her number in the directory and pushed the 'send' button. I waited and waited. Nothing! The answering service kicked in now and my heart sank.

Bob said, 'She's not answering is she?'

I shook my head. I threw the phone on the bed and, picking my blue jeans and a red top off a chair back, retreated into the en suite bathroom to change.

After I had a good cry to myself, I put my hair back in its usual ponytail. It's my fault Josie's missing. If anything's happened to her..... After a few minutes, I pulled myself together and dried my eyes on a towel, then returned to Franjo and Bob who were waiting for me.

Bob said, 'Plan of action? We go looking for her? We each go a different way and keep in touch by phone.'

I nodded. Well I just didn't have any better idea so I went along with it. We exchanged numbers. Bob wrote them on a slip of paper he took from his pocket. I did the same, then it was out of the flat and down the stairs to the street.

Franjo was the first to exit the building. He said as he took his cellphone from his pocket, 'I have an idea. I'll call Sonja and ask her if she will let us know if your friend comes back to the flat while we're out.' So that's what he did.

I had taken my shades with me. I put them on as I could feel a tear forming. *Josie, where are you?'* I thought looking up and down the street. I said, 'Remember she's still wearing the Muslim dress so may have the veil in place too.'

'Great!' Bob said unsmiling, 'So now all we have to do is walk up to any Muslim woman wearing this dress and ask them to remove their veil?'

I said with a sigh, 'We'll just have to hope that she isn't using the veil, and take it from there, OK?' I was feeling annoyed and frustrated as I turned away from them heading for the car rental office. I want to try to trace her last movements. Rather than walk there, I ran, every now and then almost colliding with other people going about their daily business and pedestrians too.

Eventually I made it to the car rental. I could see that she wasn't waiting for me inside the office as I was hoping she might be, as the front of the office was mostly glass. I decided to head off in the same direction that she took, looking for clues, like shops that she might visit or be interested in? I'm thinking that I could be wasting my time here. Maybe I'll get lucky and she'll just walk up to me. She could be in any one of the department stores here browsing the jeans section, or..... Oh God! Why did I let her go off on her own like that?

I stopped in my tracks and looked up her number on my phone. Maybe, just maybe she'd answer this time and everything will be fine. I pressed 'call' and waited, and waited. *Josie answer please!'* I thought, then the answering service kicked in again. This time I responded to it. I could hardly get the words out because a large lump was forming and threatening to choke me to death. 'Josie, where the hell are you? Come back to the flat immediately or just tell us you're somewhere safe, please?' I pleaded. I pulled a Kleenex from my pocket and blew my nose.

I continued walking, then I broke into a jog. I'm wasting time. I have to find her quick. I stopped again just inside the doorway of a department store. I called Franjo. 'Any luck Franjo?'

'Sorry. Not yet. We're looking for a needle in a haystack, as you British say.'

'Pardon?'

'Oh, sorry. I keep forgetting.' He laughed.

I didn't. 'I'll call Bob and see if he has any luck.' I hung up, then dialled Bob's number.

He answered immediately. 'Sam.....' He hesitated, 'I'm not sure, but I think I could have just missed her.'

My heart missed a beat. 'What? Where?'

'Not far from your flat. I started tailing a woman in Muslim clothing around Josie's height.'

'OK, thanks. I'm making my way there now.' I don't want to get my hopes up. Probably a false alarm. I turned off my phone. Well I didn't stop running until I had almost reached our flat.

I stood on the sidewalk and looked around hoping to spot Bob or Franjo and that's when it happened; Josie walked right up to me! 'Hi Sam!' she said brightly, just like that.

'Oh. You're OK then huh?'

She pulled her veil down and nodded. 'Why shouldn't I be?' Her smile just vanished.

'Josie, where the hell have you been?'

She shrugged. 'Around.'

'Josie, we've been worried sick about you.'

'We?' There was that incredulous look again. She started walking backwards away from me.

'Me, Bob and Franjo.' I pulled out my phone intending to call them. 'Where are you off to now?'

'Back to the flat?'

Before I could respond, she had turned on her heel and was marching into the courtyard where our car had been parked earlier. I turned my attention to the task in hand and called Bob and Franjo in turn, then I trotted after her.

Back at the flat, we made straight for our room. As Josie started taking off the Muslim dress, I said sounding annoyed, 'Josie, you really had us worried back there you know. What the hell were you thinking?'

She threw the clothing over a chair back, then headed for the bathroom. 'You are paranoid, aren't you? I was in disguise wasn't I?'

I pulled her by the arm. 'Josie, I'm only being careful. We're supposed to be sticking together and looking out for each other for God's sake. These people are very dangerous. You just don't wanna get caught by them!'

She went into the bathroom, slamming the door behind her.

I heard the flat door being opened then close again. 'They're back,' I said half to myself. Josie probably wouldn't hear me anyway as I could hear water running. She was filling the tub by the sound of it. I opened the bedroom door and went out to meet them. As I closed the door behind me, I heard Franjo and Bob talking in the lounge. I went in to see them. They were both sitting on the couch. Bob was nearest. 'Is she OK?' he asked.

I sighed, flicking strands of hair from my eyes. 'Yeah, I think so.'

Franjo asked, 'Did she say where she went?'

I shook my head. 'Don't think she wandered far, but she didn't say where.' I sat in one of the big armchairs opposite.

Bob nodded. 'Well so long as she's OK.' He stood up smiling. 'So you're off where tonight?'

I stood up too. 'Zagreb.' I smiled up at him.

He came closer. 'Maybe I'll see you there.'

'Maybe.' I moved closer. We were almost touching.

'I'll race you. I'll be there before your train pulls in.' Now we were touching. His hands were on my shoulders, then they moved to my neck.

I said, taking him by the hand, 'Come on, before Josie comes out.' Maybe I can kiss him some more. I giggled as I pulled him to the bedroom door with me. I let go of his hand, and that's when he pushed me against the door and started kissing me again, this time it was on the side of my neck above the right shoulder. I moved away from the wall and stood with my back to the door, my left hand fumbling for the doorknob. I had almost found it, when his two hands went under my top at the back. I found the doorknob eventually, turned it then stepped backwards into the room. He kicked the door closed with his heel, then he pushed me back against the wall, then his lips found the top of my left shoulder. I could hear Josie splashing in the tub. She was humming a tune to herself.

He said laughing, 'Like to get you in there. Wash your back?' He laughed again.

I giggled. 'Another time. I'll be joining her shortly, then we'll be looking for a meal before we board the train.'

Just then, the bathroom door opened and Josie put her head round the door. She had a piece of bubble bath foam hanging from the end of her nose. She said, in that soft sexy voice of hers, 'Hi guys. Hope I didn't interrupt anything.' She giggled.

I sighed and looked at Bob. 'No.'

He said, 'I'll have to go. Got a date tonight.'

'Oh, so soon?' I sighed. 'Just when I was getting into the swing of things.' I sighed again. I added, teasing him. 'This your girlfriend again or something?'

I heard Josie close the door.

He shook his head, looking a little miffed. 'It's not a girlfriend. Pen pal. We write one another. We arranged to meet tonight in a restaurant.' He put his hand on the doorknob preparing to open it.

I said, teasing again, 'Your girlfriend live in Sarajevo then? Seems to be following you around a lot.'

He opened the door and turned to me looking irritated for a second. 'She's not my girlfriend. And no, she doesn't live here.'

I moved closer to him, intending to go for his lips. 'Yeah, OK, whatever.'

He smiled, then he bent and kissed me on the lips and that's when I threw my arms around his neck, then I just couldn't stop myself. Well, I had to do it! The kissing was intense, and passionate, and ooh, so very sexy.

I heard the bathroom door open and Josie say, 'Hey Sam. Save some for me?' She giggled.

I pulled away and turned to her making a face. 'Josie, go heat the bath water for us. I'll be right there.' I thought, *Eventually,* and sighed with contentment. I continued where I had left off.

I could've gone on all night but Bob pulled away and said, 'Keep in touch Sam. You've got my number. I'll catch you up at some point.'

I sighed again as I stepped back farther into the room. 'Yeah, but don't make it too long. We might be out of the country on our way home by that time.'

We said our goodbyes and I closed the door, then headed straight for the bathroom.

When I got in, Josie was lying back in the tub smiling up at me. 'Sure took your time.' She grinned.

I pulled off my jeans. 'Josie, some things you just don't wanna rush, know what I mean?' I dropped my underwear on the floor where I stood and stepped into the tub. Gosh it was hot! Well I did say, 'Heat up the water', so.... The surface of the water was thick with foam. I was at the 'tap' end.

She said teasing, 'So, what's he like then?'

'Like?' I asked curiously.

She lowered her voice. 'Kissing?'

I gave a big sigh of contentment. 'Oh, Josie. You just wouldn't believe what it's like to be kissed by those lips.' I'm making her jealous again, I know it.

'Oh I don't know. I might get the chance to kiss him too, knowing how irresistible I am.' She spluttered and giggled. 'I'm sooo cute.' She giggled again.

My eyes shot heavenwards. 'Jesus, here we go again.' I laughed too, then I cupped my hands under the water quickly and threw some of the water and foam towards her head.

She tried to protect her face but I was too quick for her. She screamed at me and laughed at the same time, then she returned the favour.

Chapter 13.

Around 7 o'clock, we said our goodbyes to Franjo. Sonja had come in to see us off too, and we thanked her again for the Muslim clothing that she had so kindly given us. We went straight to the railroad station where we found a small restaurant and hopefully, satisfy our ravenous appetites. I didn't eat much of the prawns at lunchtime, and then I had an ice cream. It wasn't much and now I'm starved. Josie had even less to eat.

We decided on leaving our backpacks in the Left Luggage Office, then, after we boarded the train, one of us would leave again and retrieve them. It would attract too much attention if two Muslim women were seen carrying backpacks. A strange sight indeed I would think.

We found a table by a window overlooking one of the platforms. I had only just picked up the menu when I remembered that I hadn't called home for ages. Mom and dad will be worried sick about me, and what about Josie's parents? I dug out my cellphone and snapped it on.

Josie had seen me. 'Who are you calling?'

I didn't reply immediately. I dialled home and waited. Meanwhile Josie had her phone out too and was dialling.

I said finally, 'Calling home. I keep forgetting to do it.'

I heard Josie say, 'Oh, hi mom. How's things? Great ….. sure….'

I concentrated on my own call now as it was finally answered. 'Hello, that you Sam?' It was mom. 'Where have you been?'

'Yeah. Sorry. I meant to phone earlier but you know how it is when you're enjoying yourself, and the time just flies by and……?'

'You could have called earlier. Dad and me were worried about you and Josie. You've heard the stories about some of the things that can happen to people in those foreign places?'

I want to avoid telling them the truth. 'We're OK though…. really.'

She interrupted, 'Here's dad.' I'm relieved about the change of subject. If dad heard about the thugs who were after us, he would have the police onto the case immediately, and it would be in all the newspapers, and all the world would know, and then we really would be in the sugar, wouldn't we? Weren't we in enough trouble as it was?

'Hi Sam. How's the Italian coming along? Get a chance to use it yet?'

'Oh, it's been very helpful. Don't know how we'd get by without it.' I laughed.

'I knew you wouldn't have a problem with it, you were always so good with languages honey.'

I hadn't up to now, been tuned into Josie's conversation, but now something she said caught my attention. She started to sniffle, then, 'Oh, it's these people....' She hesitated just long enough for me to kick her on the ankle. She mouthed, '*What?*' to me.

I indicated with my hand that she should halt the conversation now! Again she mouthed, '*What?*' back at me.

She said finally, 'It's OK mom. I'll call you again sometime, bye.' She closed her phone.

I said, covering the phone with my hand, my anger mounting, 'Josie, what the hell are you doing?'

'What the hell's with you anyway?'

I said in a low voice, hoping dad wouldn't hear, 'Josie, we can't go telling the world about these guys who are on our backs. They'll be watching us, and you know damn well they are, and if the police get wind of this, our lives won't be worth living.'

She just sat there not saying a word.

I heard dad say, 'Everything OK there?'

'Yeah, sure.' I could feel the tears welling up, and there was a lump forming. I could hardly get the words out. I'm losing it. 'Why shouldn't it be?' I said quickly, 'Bye. Love you both.' I hung up quickly before dad heard me cry, then I broke down. I pulled a Kleenex from my pocket.

Josie put her hand on my arm, trying to comfort me. I think she was about to join me, then she caught herself in time as the waitress arrived at our table. She snatched up the menu hurriedly and pointed to several items there. The waitress made a quick note in her notepad and retreated back to the kitchen.

She said, putting her hand on my arm again, 'I ordered for us.'

I thought quickly, '*What?*' I said sniffling, 'I might not like it though.'

'Trust me. It's OK. You'll see,' she said.

I said, as I dried my eyes with the Kleenex, 'They could be watching us here too.'

Josie poured water from a jug into glasses for us. 'Here?' She pointed down at the table.

I nodded and took a drink. I said, 'These people are so ruthless that they'd most likely kill us after they got their hands on the pictures. They were planning to rob a bank that we managed to foil, then they murdered my friend

Tom, and narrowly missed killing me as well. They just don't give a shit who they kill Josie.'

She didn't say anything, then, 'Here's our food coming Sam.'

I looked over my right shoulder and sure enough, the waitress was approaching our table. I could smell something that I recognised. As she placed the plates in front of us, I squealed in delight. It was my favourite meal of fried squid.

I reached out and squeezed Josie's hand. 'Thanks.' She knows how to cheer me up, and it certainly worked this time.

We went to catch our train around 8 o'clock. It was due to leave at 8.30. We found the female toilets and went in together and noted that this time at least, there was no-one to see us. We'd have to work fast if we were going to share the same cubicle. We were planning on dressing one another, but it'd look strange if we were spotted sharing the same cubicle. We put the Muslim clothing on top of our own.

After we dressed and freshened up, we pulled our veils up to cover our faces then stood just inside the toilet entrance to survey the scene before us. I suggested to Josie that we go to the train one at a time to cut down the chances of us attracting attention, so this is what we did. She went first and then I followed her. They'd be looking out now for two girls dressed in Muslim clothing. We can't afford to take any chances as we headed for our train. It was a diesel-electric with an overhead trolley connected by wires. A guy in uniform checked our tickets before we boarded. It was a corridor train, so we had to stand aside sometimes to let other people pass as the corridor was narrow, and they had to get on their way to find their cabins as well.

Josie was well ahead of me and found our cabin without difficultly. She opened the door and stepped inside, then, almost immediately, stepped back into the corridor again and closed the door. She whispered as I drew closer, 'This our cabin? Sure you got the right one?'

I hadn't quite reached her at this point. I mouthed, 'What?'

As I reached it, I looked at the number and nodded. Yep, number "6" it said on the door. That's ours. I looked at the ticket and nodded. I whispered back frowning, 'What's wrong?'

'Occupied,' she whispered again.

I shook my head. 'No, that can't be Josie. You remember we asked for a two berth?'

She nodded.

'OK. No point debating it.' I opened the door and we went in. A woman lay fast asleep with her back to us in the lower bunk on the left. She had long black hair turning grey. There were also bunks on the right-hand side of the cabin, so we chose those; Josie in the bottom one and me on top.

I decided to do a little exploring; looking for the toilet and a place to wash. I found a door on the right just beyond our bunk beds. It was the toilet and a sink but no shower. *'Well I guess I can survive without it seeing we're only here for one night anyway,'* I thought as I stepped inside.

Josie arrived at my back and stepped in too. 'Are you going to be long?' she whispered.

I just remembered a joke I heard. I turned to her and said in a low voice, 'Want a laugh?'

She nodded smiling.

'Teacher asks class, "Where does Jesus live?" A little girl says, "Heaven".' I hesitated.

Josie's smile broadened.

'Heard it?'

'No,' she whispered, 'but I've this uncanny feeling that I'm just about to.' She giggled.

I continued, laughing myself, 'Little Robbie said, "I think Jesus lives in Heaven too", then little Jimmy says, "I think Jesus lives in our bathroom".'

Josie's eyebrows went up.

'Teacher asks, "How do you mean, Jesus lives in your bathroom?". Jimmy replies, "Because every morning my dad says, Jesus, are you still in there?".'

Josie broke up.

I could hear stirring from the occupant in the lower bunk. 'Oops,' I said laughing. I let Josie use the toilet first, then it was my turn.

Before we turned in, one of us was going to have to go get our packs from the Left Luggage Office. I elected to go.

I still wore the Muslim garments as I stepped into the corridor. I looked left and right for any sign of someone watching me, then I opened the first door that I came to and stepped onto the platform. I made straight for the LLO. The elderly male clerk had no English – so what's new? He wore a puzzled expression as he took our tickets from me and examined them. He probably couldn't work out what a Muslim woman dressed like this would want with two backpacks.

Once I had our packs in my possession, I went to the toilets, found an empty cubicle and took off the Muslim clothes. I stuffed them into my pack, then put it on my back. I shouldered Josie's and opened the door. There were two women there; one was quite young with black hair, the other middle-aged. They both stood with their backs to me at the sinks, but didn't look up at the mirrors as I exited the cubicle. Well, we were being pursued by males, so I don't know why I should have felt a little uneasy even here. Nevertheless, I tiptoed out of there as quickly and as quietly as I could, but hesitated as I was about to step outside the entrance. Looking up and down the platform, I decided that it was safe to proceed to the train. No-one watching me, thank goodness. No strange men hiding behind newspapers or...... Oh what the hell? I have to stop this paranoia.

I was almost at the train, when I was aware of a figure approaching from my right. My heart leaped into my mouth briefly, then I realised it was only the ticket inspector. He checked my ticket and in Bosnian, I think, wished me a safe journey, I think. I just nodded and smiled. Whew! No more frights, please God.

Back on the train, I lost no time on reaching our cabin and tapped softly on the door a couple of times. It was answered almost immediately, but not by Josie. 'What the hell?' I said under my breath.

It was the woman from the lower bunk. Her expression was one of annoyance. Did I disturb her sleep or something? Tough. She said, in what sounded like a French accent, 'Oui?' *'Yes?'*

'Je vis ici.' *'I live here,'* I said getting annoyed.

She didn't seem convinced and was just about to close the door in my face, when I put my foot in it. The door I mean.

'C'est ma cabane.' *'This is my cabin,'* I said, my temper beginning to fray at the edges. Then, 'Josie. Come rescue me?' I didn't want to be standing outside in the corridor engaged in an unnecessary argument that could draw unwanted attention. If these bastards are on the train…! Jesus, that one doesn't bear thinking about.

I could see Josie was now at the woman's back. She said to her, 'Mi amigo, Sam.'

Josie doesn't have any French so…. Thanks Josie! Good thinking.

The woman stepped aside immediately and I pushed the door open. 'Merci,' I said as I entered, then dropped our packs on the floor.

Josie wore her grey nightshirt. 'You OK out there Sam? Anyone see you?'

I said to her, 'Yeah, I'm OK. Let's hope no-one did.' I took my nightie from my pack. 'Let's not worry about it for now huh?' I made my way to the bathroom where I changed into my nightie, then it was off to bed and the top bunk. Josie was already settled in and lying on her back lost in thought.

I could see that the woman was sitting on the edge of her bed with a slightly worried expression. I'm thinking; she's seen us dressed in Muslim clothing, and now we've changed into Western gear. Clearly, we are not Muslims, so this is looking very odd. Maybe we're escaping from something? The police perhaps? Trying to keep a low profile? Yep, we sure are. Trying to stay alive would be more like it.

The woman eventually lay down and turned onto her left side to face the wall. I lay on my right side and tried to get some sleep, just as the train decided to move accompanied by squealing, metallic creaking and groaning sounds. I lay there for a while wondering if this woman who shared our cabin might report us to the police. Whilst that wouldn't be welcome, it was still better than those evil people finding out where we were.

I must have drifted off to sleep because I woke with a start and sat bolt upright. I couldn't think what had wakened me, but I did notice that the train had stopped and was shunting, or at least that is how it sounded to me. Perhaps we were in a siding or stopped at a junction maybe? Then I noticed that the woman had gone! I looked at my watch: 11 o'clock!

'Oh shit!' I thought suddenly. I hope she's not decided to inform on us, or am I getting paranoid again?

I heard Josie stir in the lower bunk, then, in a whisper she said, 'Sam. You awake?'

I whispered back, 'Yeah.'

'Could you sleep?' She got out of the bed and just stood there looking up at me.

'Yeah. I think I must have dozed off.' I said, pointing to the empty bunk, 'Our friend has gone.'

'Yeah. You thinking what I'm thinking?'

I don't like it when she's thinking what I'm thinking. That usually means we're both right, and in this case, it's not a good omen.

'Hope she's not gone to the police Sam.'

'It's not the police that worries me....'

Josie cut me off with, 'Look. She's taken her coat. It was hanging at the back of the door, and her bag too.' Her overnight bag had been lying by the side of her bed.

'Oh,' I said in a state of shock; I'm not entirely sure why.

As Josie looked around the cabin she said, 'She didn't stay long did she? Where could she go? We haven't stopped at any station for her to get off have we?'

'Maybe moved to another part of the train. Some of these sleepers are made up of several trains together, each with a set destination, and maybe she was not on the correct one. They have to shunt the carriages about so each train can proceed on its way. At least that's how I understand it.' Well it made sense to me anyway.

'Wonder how she got by in this country on French alone?' she said.

'She wouldn't. They don't do French here Josie. Must have Italian or German.'

I thought I heard footsteps outside in the corridor, then there was a knock on the door; two knocks in fact. I jumped down onto the floor. I'd rather be dressed if I have to answer it, so I pulled off my nightie and started on the jeans.

'What you doing?' she asked curiously.

'Getting dressed.'

'I can see that. Why?'

I explained why as I pulled on my red t-shirt. 'Josie. Take your clothes into the bathroom and get dressed.'

'Are you serious?' she asked as she reluctantly picked her jeans and blue top off of a chair back.

I didn't reply as I stepped to the door.

She said, opening the bathroom door, 'You *are* serious.'

Another three knocks. I daren't say anything in English and betray our nationality, just in case. Then I found my socks and sneakers and put them on too.

I said in my best French accent, 'Oui? Qui est là? Qu'est-ce que vous voulez?' *'Yes? Who is there? What do you want?'*

There was silence from the other side of the door.

I waited. I heard Josie close the door behind me, then appear at my back.

'Do you speak English?' a male voice asked.

'Non,' I said and almost giggled out loud.

More silence.

Why was I finding this so funny?

He said in Italian, 'Rinfresco, Signorina?' *'Refreshment, Miss?'*

'Sì,' I almost giggled out loud again. I turned to Josie.

She nodded.

I said, 'Tè o caffè. Può lasciarlo sul pavimento alla porta? Grazie.' *'Tea or coffee. Can you leave it on the floor at the door? Thank you.'*

'Sì Signorina.' *'Yes Miss.'*

I could hear clinking of crockery. I could breathe easy now. It's safe to open the door. There was a security chain on it anyway. I opened it as far as the chain would allow and looked out. Yep he was gone, and he had left the food there on a small tray on the floor as requested. I brought it into the room and placed it on a small table under the window. The refreshment consisted of two tea bags in plastic sheaths, and several cookies on a plate, together with a teapot of hot water, sugar, milk, etc.

Josie fixed the tea for us while I tried to open the window, by pushing it downwards, but I wasn't having any success; it just wouldn't budge.

As she poured the tea into the two white mugs, she said, 'You seem to be having a thing with windows lately?' She's referring to the incident at the camp site.

'Yeah, yeah, OK.' I tried once more to shift it but it just wasn't co-operating. I wanted some air badly.

The train started moving again. I decided to go out into the corridor now to feel and breathe that cool air and enjoy my tea at the same time. It felt so stuffy in the cabin. It was very dark out there. I could see trees and buildings silhouetted against the sky; now and then the odd vehicle's lights on a road. It wasn't cold tonight, so when I went to the nearest door to pull the window down, the cool air felt so refreshing. I stood there just breathing in the air, now and then taking a sip of my tea, then I detected the familiar smell of diesel. It made me feel a little nauseated.

I was feeling somewhat exhausted after everything that happened that day, and I really was wishing that I could just lie down and get myself a good night's sleep.

I was just about to push up the window again, when I thought I detected someone at my back. Of course the first person that came to mind was Josie, but the approach was all wrong. Maybe I have a sixth sense, but I began to panic, and suddenly had visions of being attacked from behind. It made the hairs on the back of my neck stand straight up!

I heard him before I saw him. He grabbed me around the waist with one hand, the other he clamped over my mouth. My mug smashed on the floor. I started to scream in my throat, then I was lifted up into the air. I struggled and fought to get free. He took his hand from my mouth briefly to open the door and that's when I screamed at the top of my lungs! The hand was clamped again. I screamed in my throat, then he tried to push me out through the open door, but I was able to prevent myself from being pushed outside by holding onto the door frame with both hands. I'm still screaming.

'Pictures!' he demanded.

He removed his hand from my mouth. He pushed me farther out still. I screamed again! I was now holding on to the door frame by my fingertips. My fingers were on fire. I couldn't hold on any longer, and I had to let go. Now the only thing preventing me from falling outside was him. I had to think of something fast.

I shouted. It was almost a scream, 'It's in my front pocket!'

He hesitated. 'If you lie, you die, OK!'

I thought I heard a door opening. I was able to turn my head briefly. It was our cabin. Josie stood in the doorway, unsure what to do. I know she'll come up with something, but it had better be quick.

She shouted, 'Sam! He's got a knife!'

I thought quickly, *'Shit! That's all I need!'*

He pulled me back inside. Back on my feet, instead of turning to him, I threw my full weight against him, knocking him off-balance. He struck the opposite wall and this winded him slightly, but he recovered quickly and made a lunge at me. I saw a knife flash in his hand. That's when Josie made her move. She caught him with a vicious kick in the small of his back that threw him towards me and the open door. I threw myself backwards out of the way and landed on my back on the floor. The result? He went sailing head-first out of the train. He screamed. I hadn't noticed the tunnel coming up. Neither would he. Blood splattered on the windows now and the train began to apply the emergency brakes, then came to a sudden halt. Now we were both on the floor. Someone must have pulled the emergency cord, but how could they know anything had happened? Most of the passengers would be asleep.

We were stopped in the tunnel and, as I picked myself up I could see cabin lights coming on, and people were running about in a panic. I could tell this by the fact that the corridor was suddenly filled with them. Most were in their nightclothes.

Josie was crying. I joined her, then lots of nice people were trying to comfort us all at the same time. It was all too overwhelming for me. I was in a daze. It all felt so unreal. This was just a bad dream, and I'll waken up soon. Some people were beginning to return to their cabins now.

Josie took my hand and we made for our cabin, then I felt myself being led by the arm down the corridor by a nice young man from the buffet car. He wore the black and blue uniform vest and pants of the train company. He sported a black close-cropped beard, dark hair and seemed to be late twenties.

He said, 'I'll get you something to drink.' He had an accent that I couldn't place immediately, then I thought it was British.

'Oh, thank you,' I said, then began to sniffle again. I pulled a Kleenex out and kept dabbing at my eyes and nose. 'How did you know I spoke English?'

As we approached the buffet car, that appeared to be an extension of the lounge, he said smiling, 'That was a very bad French accent.'

I turned to Josie who had a smirk on, then back to him. I reddened. 'I beg your pardon?' I thought I knew what was coming.

He laughed. 'I was the guy who brought the tea to your cabin?' He went around the bar and poured tea for us into blue mugs from a tea urn, then placed them on the counter.

'Oh,' I said and turned a darker shade of scarlet.

Josie was trying her best not to laugh as she wiped the last of her tears from her eyes.

He put out his hand. 'My name's Alex. I'm French, from Bordeaux.'

I said, shaking it, 'Sam. And this is Josie. We're from Mendocino, California.'

He shook Josie's too.

'Have an ear for accents,' he said as he took a bowl of sugar from under the counter.

I sniffled again and said joking, 'So what does your other ear do then?'

Josie spluttered through her tea and almost choked on it.

He laughed. 'Pardon?'

I sugared my tea and stirred. I shrugged. 'Oh, nothing.' I sniffled again.

He poured himself some tea too, then came around the counter to join us. 'We'll take it over here,' he said taking us to several armchairs grouped around a coffee table.

I sat next to Josie opposite Alex. He asked, 'So what are two nice girls from America doing in Bosnia all on their own?' He sipped his tea.

'What's a Frenchman doing in Bosnia?' I asked him smiling. I dried my nose and dabbed at a tear.

'You first,' he said smiling.

I looked at him over my mug. 'Been doing a bit of sightseeing and taking in the historical buildings. I like to take photos. It's a hobby of mine.' I nodded.

Josie said, 'Been chased around by some guys who want photos from us.' She blew her nose.

'Really? If I had the time, I'd be chasing you two around as well.' He laughed.

We didn't.

I said, 'It's not that kind of chasing. This guy tonight? The one that,' I sniffled again, 'went off the train? Wanted the photos. He was quite prepared to kill me if I didn't tell him where they were.'

'Oh?' he said surprised. 'That's scary.'

I thought, *Well, that's one way to put it.* I said, 'Tell me about it.'

'And you didn't give them to him?'

'No, I didn't. Josie's got them anyway.'

Josie said, her vivid blue eyes looking at him over her mug, 'Somewhere.' She smiled.

'Must be important to them?'

I said, 'Oh yeah.' I told him the story about why they wanted the photos so badly.

He was shocked. 'Now that is scary.' He finished his tea and put the cup down.

I wish he'd stop saying that!

Josie said, putting her cup down too, 'Just a bit.'

'You'll have to tell the police everything. They'll be here soon.'

I said, 'We were hoping that we wouldn't have to. We've been told if we go to the police, we'd be killed.'

I noticed a woman approaching us now. It was the one from the lower bunk. She wore a red two-piece suit and matching high heels. She said in French, 'Bonjour encore.' *Hello again.*

'Bonjour,' I said looking up at her. 'Est-ce que vous aimeriez nous joindre?' *'Would you like to join us?'*

She pulled up a chair and sat on my right. 'Est-ce que vous saviez qu'homme qui est tombé du train?' *'Did you know that man who fell off the train?'*

I shook my head.

Alex said, pointing at me, 'Il a essayé de tuer Sam.' *'He tried to kill Sam.'*

She was clearly shocked. 'Oh! Je me demande si c'est le même homme qui m'a parlé.' *'Oh! I wonder if it's the same man who spoke to me.'*

I had a question mark there.

She continued, 'Si c'est le même homme, il a dit qu'il était agent de police, et il m'a demandé si j'avais vu deux filles sur le train. Il m'a donné votre description.' *'If it is the same man, he said that he was a policeman, and he asked me if I had seen two girls on the train. He gave me your description.'*

I translated for Josie.

Alex nodded. 'Il m'a demandé aussi. Je pense qu'il a demandé à tout le monde sur le train.' *'He asked me too. I think he asked everyone on the train.'*

'Aucun émerveillement qu'il savait où nous trouver.' *'No wonder he knew where to find us,'* I said. I translated for Josie. She looked shocked.

'Je suis très désolé au sujet de cela. Les vêtements musulmans ont semblé soupçonneux à moi.' *'I'm very sorry about that. The Muslim clothes looked suspicious to me.'*

I just smiled and nodded.

Again I translated for Josie.

I have no intention of telling the police about these guys. I'm concerned for our safety, and getting them involved is going to expose us even more. I'll think of a plan, but I'll have to come up with something quick. They'll be here before I know it. Also I want to tell Josie about the plan to ensure that if we are interviewed separately, we come up with the same story.

The woman said, 'Si vous m'excuserez, j'ai un coup de téléphone pour faire.' *'If you will excuse me, I have a telephone call to make.'*

She left us and went off to make her call.

I said to Alex, 'I would rather if you didn't tell the cops about what I told you. We're in enough trouble as it is with these guys on our backs. All we have to say is that we were stalked by the guy and he tried to rob us at knife-point. Well it's true up to a point, isn't it?'

He said, leaning forward in his chair smiling, 'It's OK. Your secret is safe with me. I had heard screaming and wondered where it was coming from, then when I reached the corridor where you were, I couldn't intervene. I saw the knife in his hand and I saw you being attacked. That's all they have to know.'

'Thank you,' I said.

Josie just sat there without saying anything, lost in thought.

'What's up?' I asked her.

'That guy was the same one that we met on the street. I'm sure of it.'

I suddenly felt unwell. Maybe it's with the recent trauma. I'm thinking of heading back to our cabin and lie down. I need some sleep anyway.

I said, surprised at Josie's statement, 'Really? I didn't get a proper look at him. Everything was happening so quickly.' I stood up from my chair. 'So, we've just killed one of their number. It's looking bad for us Josie. All the more reason why we can't afford to let them catch us.'

She asked, standing up too, 'Where are you off to?'

'Back to our cabin. I don't feel so well. Think I'll have to lie down. See you later Alex?'

He stood up and touched my arm. 'I'll let you know when they arrive.'

'Thanks,' said as I felt a lump forming in my throat. I turned and made for our cabin.

Once in, I took off my hair clasp and kicked off my sneakers, but didn't bother to undress, then climbed up to my cosy nest. I think I was asleep before my head hit the pillow.

In what seemed like only seconds, I awoke abruptly and heard the door close. My head was still on the pillow.

Josie stood there looking up at me with a concerned look. 'You OK?'

I started feeling sorry for myself now. I could feel the tears welling up and a large lump was forming fast in my throat. Then I lost it completely. I covered my face with my hands and let the tears flow.

I heard Josie say in a concerned voice, 'Sam?' In seconds, she was in the bed beside me. As I sat up, she pulled my head towards her own and rubbed my back. 'Let it all out,' she said.

I did.

'Police will be here in a minute. They're on the train now.'

'Josie. You know that he threatened to push me out of the train. I had to hang on to the door frame to prevent myself from going through it. It was awful.'

She didn't say anything, but kept rubbing my back.

'If I ever get a gun in my hands, I'll shoot them all dead. I mean it!' I started sobbing again.

She started to cry too. 'I'll be right beside you. Don't worry. We'll take all those bastards out one by one. Jail is too good for them!'

'I know you will Josie. You're the best friend I've ever had.'

We just hung onto one another tight and let the tears flow, then I heard footsteps in the corridor. 'This'll be them now,' I said.

She nodded as she dried her eyes with a Kleenex, then she got out of the bed. She said to me, 'Ready?'

I nodded.

The door was knocked several times.

I was only halfway down the ladder, when Josie opened the door and a tall elderly gentleman wearing a black parka and a fur hat on his head stood there.

'Which one of you two ladies is Sam?'

As I stepped off the ladder I said, 'I am.'

He removed his hat, and I could see that he was balding on top. 'Stjepan Kardovic, Police Inspector, Sarajevo. Can I come in?' His English was very good.

We stood aside to let him in. He shook my hand warmly.

Josie introduced herself and shook his hand too.

I indicated the bed opposite and he sat down. 'So, you want to tell me what happened here? I've spoken to someone called Alex from France. He said you'd be in number 6?'

I nodded. I sat on the bed beside Josie.

'Says he witnessed this attack, yes?'

I nodded again and pulled a Kleenex from my pocket as I could feel a tear coming. I sniffled. 'It was horrible. He lifted me up and pushed me head-first through the open door. I didn't have a chance despite my training in self defence. It wouldn't have saved me. I guess he found my Achilles heel huh?' I gave a short nervous laugh. I'll file that one away for later too. I sniffled again and blew my nose.

'It seems that this man was posing as a policeman? Asking if you two were on the train?'

I nodded.

'Why should he do that? He must have known who you were?'

We both nodded.

'Boyfriend?'

'God no!' I exclaimed with horror. 'We met him earlier, at least I think it was the same one. Didn't get to see his face this time. Everything was happening too fast.' Oops, I think I've probably said too much already.

Kardovic remained silent.

I continued, 'We had met a guy named Bob earlier. He's from London, England, and while sitting in a restaurant, we thought we saw him across the street, but as it turned out, it wasn't him.' I brushed some strands of hair from my eyes. 'We crossed the street to meet him and that was when he pulled a gun on us.' I smiled meekly and looked away avoiding his gaze, then to Josie.

He's not believing this. He said, 'You just happened to pick someone on the street that resembled your friend Bob, and he just happened to be carrying a weapon?'

We both nodded and exchanged glances.

He thought for a moment. 'Why did he pull a weapon on you? Was he trying to rob you?'

'He wanted something from us.' I told him about us being led along the street at gunpoint and how we managed to escape.

'Was this about money?'

Josie was looking at me as she said, 'No.'

I was so tired and exhausted, I didn't care any more. I realised that we were going to have to tell the truth sooner or later. I sighed in resignation and ran my fingers through my hair before saying, 'We have photographs that they want.'

'They?' He got up and began to pace the floor. He produced a notebook and pen from his pocket and began to scribble.

I had to go back to the beginning and tell him the whole story starting with the explosion that killed Tomislav. Josie chipped in now and then.

He stopped his pacing and sat down again. 'My advice to you would be to get out of the country as fast as possible – take the next flight home, yes?'

I said, 'We'll probably head for Belgrade after Zagreb.' I turned to Josie for her approval.

I got it too. She nodded. 'We have disguise with us.' She left it hanging there.

He's standing there with a question mark.

I went into my pack and pulled out the Muslim clothing for him to see.

'Well, you're certainly well organised. Not something that I would have thought of. Impressive,' he said.

There was a knock at the door. I opened it and a middle-aged guy in a blue parka stood there. He held something wrapped in a grey cloth. Kardovic said something in Bosnian to him and the two them spoke briefly, then the guy handed him the cloth. He closed the door and turned to us. We're both wearing question marks.

Kardovic opened the cloth. There lay what I took to be a hunting knife and a handgun.

'Recognise these?' he asked.

I nodded. 'Not sure about the knife, because I only got a brief glimpse of it, but the gun, yes,' I ran my fingers through my hair, 'that was the one that was pointed at me, at least it sure looks like it.'

He wrapped the weapons again. 'All I can say is that you are two very de-termined young ladies. I think most people your age would be returning home on the first available flight.'

Josie and I exchanged glances again. 'I just don't believe in giving in to scum like that, and I don't believe in playing by other people's rules either. I have my self defence and weapons training, from around the age of twelve, and I reckon I can take care of myself. You just don't wanna get me angry.' I finished up with a smug look.

He nodded. 'Yes I believe you can too. Just be careful where you go. We'd like to have you back here again.' He stood up from the bed.

I said, 'Thank you.'

'I will leave you two young ladies to catch up on your sleep now.' He stepped to the door. 'Just don't do anything silly.'

Just as he put his hand on the door handle, I asked, 'Did you find out who he was?'

He shook his head. 'He had no ID on him. We'll find out soon enough.' He shook our hands again and departed from the room.

I said to Josie, 'I've had enough for one day. If I don't get sleep soon I'll drop with exhaustion.'

Josie lay down fully clothed and curled up facing the wall. 'Night Sam. See you in the morning.'

'Yeah,' I replied absently as images of recent events started to form in my mind.

As I began climb the ladder up to mine, the train started moving. I had to hold onto the ladder tight.

Once in, I just lay there thinking. This is usually a mistake on my part. If I start to think about something before going to sleep, I probably won't sleep, especially if something dramatic has been happening beforehand. Reading before I sleep is usually good therapy though. Well, it works for me anyway. Unfortunately I didn't have anything to read, so I just lay there feeling sorry for myself. I cried softly for a while then I think I may have drifted off, but then I heard the train stop and I was wide awake again! During the night I awoke with a start as the train appeared to be shunting again. I looked at my watch: 2 o'clock! There was a lot of clanking and squealing and the train would move then stop for a while, then start moving again. This would be repeated over and over several times throughout the night. How do they expect passengers to get a good night's sleep if they make so much noise?

As a result of all this raucous during the night, and the drama earlier, I had very little sleep. Josie, I know, got more than I did, so she should be fully awake, but she wasn't. Around 7.15, and it just getting light outside, she was still in the Land of Nod, and I was still so exhausted, I didn't want to get up at all. However I did manage to drag myself out of the bed eventually and made my way, with eyes half shut, to the bathroom and washed etc. Josie was still in bed!

As I exited the bathroom, I spotted a notice on the door that read, 'Breakfast served from 07.30 – 08.30 hours,' in Italian, German and English.

I thought, *'They'll be serving up breakfast soon.'* I want to get down to the dining car and find us a table before they're all taken.

She still wasn't up, so I grabbed her ankle and shook it gently. 'Come on, waken up.'

She moaned and groaned, then turned over to face me, but otherwise didn't respond.

I shook her arm this time. 'Josie, get up!'

She started to stir now. Her vivid blue eyes slowly flickered open.

'We don't want to miss our place in the dining car for breakfast, do we?'

'What time is it?' She sat up, stretched and yawned.

'Just after seven. Be a while before we hit Zagreb because of last night. We've been delayed a while.'

She began to get out of the bed, but it was slow.

I said frustratedly, 'Come on Josie, hurry up!' I felt like going back to mine and to hell with breakfast. I could quite happily sleep for the rest of the day, or the week!

She hurried to the bathroom and disappeared inside. I fixed my hair in it's ponytail and put some of mom's perfume around my neck.

OK, we're ready, and now it's off to the dining car.

Even here, sitting close to the window with the world speeding past me, I felt like putting my head down on the table and just sleeping off the rest of the day. I thought if I concentrated hard enough on the menu, it would come floating across to me, but I didn't even have the strength to do that. Neither did Josie by the look of it. She was resting her head on one hand and looking very sleepy.

'You OK?' I asked.

She nodded. 'Yeah. No.' She shook her head. 'Not enough sleep.' Yawn. 'The train, you know? All this starting and stopping. Remind me not to get on another,' she yawned again, 'sleeper.'

Jesus it was infectious! I started yawning too. Oh God, why did we inflict this on ourselves? Josie doesn't know that I intend to travel to Belgrade by night sleeper again tonight. The scenery on this journey south is way too boring; very flat land and vineyards as far as the eye can see. Well that's what I read anyway. Not for me, thank you!

Josie finally decided to make a move and picked the menu up. 'It's in English this time thank goodness,' she said running her finger down the list of items there.

Chapter 14.

I turned to the window lost in thought. I'm thinking we've thrown these people off our scent. Hopefully this guy that we dealt with last night was their only contact in Bosnia. Unfortunately we will be back in Croatia again soon when we hit Zagreb, then we'll have to be on our guard once more, so the sooner we get out of the country again the better. I was about to convey my thoughts to Josie when I spotted Alex arriving at our table.

'Morning, Guter Morgen, Bonjour, Buenos días or whatever your language is today.' He smiled at us both in turn.

I just smiled back.

Josie's blue eyes looked at him over the menu.

'Recovered from your ordeal yet?' he asked in a concerned tone.

I shook my head as I could feel a tear coming.

He sat in the seat opposite Josie. 'What did the policeman say? Was he satisfied with your story?'

I nodded. I took a Kleenex from my pocket and dabbed quickly at the tears that had formed in the hope that he hadn't seen them, but too late; he'd seen them. Josie put a comforting hand on my arm, as she studied the menu.

'You OK?' he asked.

I shook my head. 'No. I feel ill.' And I did too. I thought, feeling sick to my stomach, *'Oh my God, I don't know how much more I can take of this.'* I dabbed at my eyes again and blew my nose. 'Couldn't sleep last night with all the trauma earlier, and the train shunting etc., didn't help either.'

A cellphone rang a musical tone from somewhere. I jumped, but it wasn't mine this time, and not Josie's either. The ringtone was unfamiliar to me.

Alex said as he put his hand on my arm, 'Why don't you go back to your....?'

He was interrupted by another cellphone going off very close by. It was mine this time.

I jumped again. I had left it lying on the seat between the two of us. I picked it up quickly and could see the caller had withheld their number. I whispered this to Josie.

Before I could do anything, she had snatched it out of my hand and pressed the answer button. She shouted into the phone, 'Leave us alone you....!' She broke off, and her face reddening. 'Oh, sorry. It's me, Josie.'

I mouthed, 'Who is it?'

She handed me the phone and mouthed back, 'Your mom.'

I thought, *'Shit Josie. What have you done?'* I nodded and took it from her. 'Hi mom.'

'I want you to tell me what's going on there. Something bad has happened hasn't it?'

'Mom. I can't talk right now.' I sniffled, and I could feel a lump forming in my throat. If this goes on, I'll lose it for sure.

'Listen honey. Your dad and I had a talk about this and we decided that he should go out there to meet you....'

I cut in with, 'No! Don't do that please! Something might happen! Everything's under control. Honestly.'

'I can tell you're lying. Why are you doing this to us?'

'Excuse me? I'm doing?' I asked disbelievingly.

'Look, we can contact the American Embassy and....'

I cut in again, this time it was almost a scream, 'No!'

'What's wrong with you? You're obviously in danger and...'

I said with a sigh, 'The police have it sorted out, OK?' I blew my nose again and sniffled.

'Police? Sam what are you not telling us?' I heard her start to cry. 'What have you gotten yourselves into there!'

I said hurriedly, before she heard me start too, 'Have to go. Talk later.' I snapped off the phone, then I lost it.

Josie put her arm around my shoulders. 'Come on back to our cabin. I've just lost my appetite anyway.'

We both stood up preparing to leave, then Alex said, 'I'll bring breakfast to you.'

Josie shook her head. 'No it's OK. We'll find something in Zagreb.'

I just nodded my thanks as I could hardly speak through the tears. Josie led me back to our cabin.

Once in, I just sat on the edge of the bed beside Josie and cried my eyes out. Josie had her arm around my shoulders and put her head close to mine. We cried quietly together there for the next few minutes, then we were interrupted by several knocks on the door.

We exchanged glances, then Josie said standing up, 'I'll get it.'

The chain wasn't on the door I noticed. I stood up too intending to stop her, but she had it open before I could react.

Alex stood there with a big smile on his face. 'Madame. Le petit déjeuner est servi.' *'Madam. Breakfast is served.'*

I gave a short laugh then nodded. I sniffled before I said, 'Merci.'

'I thought you might like this. Ce n'est rien spécial. Bacon, saucisse, oeuf brouillé, oh, et quelque thé et toast.' *It's nothing special. Bacon, sausage, scrambled egg, oh, and some tea and toast.'*

We stood aside to let him in. He put the tray onto the table by the window. 'Well, anything else I can do for you two?'

Josie replied brightly, 'No thanks.' Then she stood up on tiptoes and kissed him on the left cheek.

He reddened at this unexpected surprise, and backed away to the door smiling. He said hurriedly, 'I'll see you later when we get to Zagreb. If you need anything, you know where I am.' With that he departed from the room.

We lost no time in tucking into the food. The bacon was delicious, just the way I like it; not overdone and the sausages were tasty too. Josie poured the tea for us.

One and a half hours later, the train pulled into Zagreb. We were relieved that this horrible ordeal was over, and now we could put it behind us. We said our goodbyes to Alex and the rest of the train crew. They had known what had happened of course and wished us a safe and pleasant journey. I never did get to ask Alex what a Frenchman was doing in Bosnia.

First stop was the booking office to reserve another night sleeper, this time to Belgrade, or Beograd as it's known to it's inhabitants. This time the male clerk had some English, thank goodness, and I was able to purchase a two-berth cabin for us this time. I couldn't wait to get into that bunk bed and sleep my worries away.

The time was 9.15 with the temperature around 25°C. We strolled out of the railroad station, backpacks on our backs and our arms around each other's waists. This was mainly for support. I just wanted to get my head down some place and sleep off this exhaustion. I wasn't caring where and neither was Josie. I could have lain down right there on the sidewalk and slept I was so tired.

We had only been walking for about ten minutes – very slowly. I was just putting one foot in front of the other and let Josie guide me along, or was that the other way round? She looked as tired as I felt. We decided on resting up in a park that she had spotted across the busy main street. We crossed and found a bench in the park in a fairly quiet spot opposite the most gorgeous flower bed. It was massive and had miniature trees in there too. The fragrance of the flowers was wonderful and I could have sat there all day just breathing it in, but we had a train to catch tonight. We sat there together, Josie's head resting against my arm, my head on hers at first, then I began to look for a more comfortable position, so we ended up lying on our backs on the bench with our knees drawn up to our chests and using our packs as improvised pillows.

I woke up suddenly with someone shaking my shoulder. It was Josie and she was in a sitting position on the bench.

I sat up too but stayed where I was. 'What?' I asked as I looked around. My watch said 2 pm! I thought, *'God, have we been asleep all this time?'*

Leaning close, she whispered, 'Think I saw Milos.'

I whispered back, 'Oh God no Josie. You sure?' Surely not here? Of course I should have known that that bastard on the train would have informed his boss about us! I voiced my thoughts to Josie. Cellphones. Too convenient sometimes.

She said in a low voice, 'It sure looked like him Sam.'

I whispered again, 'Where? Can you point him out? Is he still around?' I swung my legs round into a sitting position too, and looked around myself now into the wide open space to our left. Moms with kids in strollers, small kids playing with balls, girlfriends and boyfriends walking hand-in-hand, but I couldn't see him anywhere. Now I turned my attention to our right. Couples again, walking hand-in-hand and some of them lying on their backs on the grass soaking up the sun, others sitting on the grass under the shade of nearby trees. A few mothers with small kids playing at their feet and a small dog running around barking every now and then.

She's looking off to our left, then she points. She said in a low voice, 'He was over there just strolling about and looking around.' She shivered despite the heat.

I whispered, 'He knows we're in Zagreb Josie. The train goes no further than here, so we have to be here somewhere.'

'How did he get here so soon?'

'Maybe he was on the train with us all along?'

'Yeah, that's possible,' she sighed.

'That is, if it was him that you saw.' I smiled at her and stood up, slinging my pack up onto my shoulder. 'Come on. Let's find something to eat. I'm starved. I don't know about you.'

Josie stood up too with her backpack on her shoulder. 'I'm sure it was him.'

I said, taking her by the hand, 'Like we were both sure we saw Bob across the street?'

'Yeah, OK,' she agreed reluctantly.

We looked around for any signs of Milos or his twin brother as we made our way towards the park entrance, but thankfully, we didn't see any sign of him or notice anyone following us. We crossed the road at traffic signals and made for a 'restoran' as they are called in Croatia.

We sat inside this time for obvious reasons, but close to a window looking out on the street and opposite one another. We wanted to enjoy our meal without having to look over our shoulders all the time. The décor here was nice with red floral wallpaper and red shades on the ceiling lamps. The waiters would be rushed off their feet today as it was busy with plenty of clientèle and almost every table taken.

I studied the menu. My eye went straight to the squid; grilled this time. The price was 40 Kuna, but that's OK. To start with I'd have mushroom soup with crusty bread. I handed the menu across to Josie.

As she studied it, her eyes brightened and that cute smile appeared again. 'What?' I asked curiously.

'I know what you're having.' She laughed.

I just smiled back.

'You should be more.... adventurous. Try something different for a change. Every meal should be an experience....'

I cut her off shaking my head. 'Josie, if you say that again,' I said teasing her. 'For your information, it's grilled not fried.' I was interrupted by the waitress arriving at our table. I gave her my order.

Josie ordered soup as well followed by Croatian chicken with sour cream. The waitress asked in English if we wanted wine. We both nodded.

I said, 'Yes please.'

'Any preference? Or can I recommend Croatian wine?'

We both nodded again.

I said, 'That would be fine, thank you.'

She departed with the order.

'I thought it was fried squid that you liked huh?'

'Maybe I like to explore a little. Push the boat out?' I joked.

She gave a short laugh. 'Yeah, well, just don't push it out too far.' She wrinkled her nose. 'It might have a hole in it.' She laughed again.

Presently, the waitress brought our wine. She opened it and poured a little into each of our glasses. We sampled it. Yep, we'll take it. We both nodded our approval. The waitress departed again and in a few minutes brought our soup.

Whilst she ladled the soup into china bowls for us, I was watching the world outside the window; people going about their business and.... oh no! I thought I spotted Milos in the street. Surely not! How could he know....? Did he follow us here? Maybe Josie was right after all about seeing him.

Josie saw my look. 'What's up?'

The waitress left.

I said in a low voice, 'Think I've just seen Milos out there.'

'See, I told you it was him,' she said with a self-satisfied look. She started on her soup.

'Yeah, so you did,' I said turning to the window again. 'Let's hope he doesn't decide to come in here.' I want to enjoy my meal and not worry about him.

'That's unlikely. Just enjoy your meal. We'll cross that bridge later if we have to.'

I started on my soup. It was delicious, and the crusty bread that came with it too. There was butter on the plate as well wrapped in gold foil.

As I cut open the bread, and began to spread the butter on there, Josie said, 'Nice place huh?'

'Yeah. Let's hope we get to enjoy it.'

When we had finished our soup, the waitress came with the next course. I was looking forward to this grilled squid. Would it taste the same? Maybe I'll add it to my growing list of favourite Croatian foods.

The waitress put my plate in front of me. When I saw what was on there I thought, *'Oh no! What the hell's that?'* On one side of the plate was.... coleslaw! Yuck! How can any civilised person eat this stuff?

The waitress saw my look of disgust as she placed a server with mashed potato, carrots and peas on the table in front of me. 'Something wrong madam?'

I nodded. 'You bet there is.' I pointed to the alien life-form that had decided to invade my plate, and appeared to be consuming my food. It was certainly contaminating it!

'It's coleslaw madam,' she said.

'Yes, I know what it is. Thank you. I just don't want it contaminating my food, OK?'

She nodded and reached out to take it. 'I'll take it back to the chef and....'

I shook my head and smiled back at her. 'No. It's OK. I'll fix it thanks.' I nodded. This is because I could see Josie making eyes at it.

The waitress departed again.

'Yeah, OK Josie.' I nodded and scraped the coleslaw onto her plate.

She just grinned back and began to tuck into my coleslaw.

I was just about to spoon out the mashed potato when I spotted something sticking out of the top of it. It looked suspiciously like raw onion! I put the potato onto my plate along with the other vegetables. I'd pick out the onion as I went along. Raw onion? No way! I wondered if it was mentioned in the menu, oh, and the coleslaw too? I picked it up and... it was! How could I miss that? It should have been shouting at me from the page! Too much trauma recently. Can't concentrate. Yeah, that's it.

We really were enjoying our meal now without interruptions. We hadn't said much either throughout, then.... 'God!' I said under my breath. I thought I had seen Milos again outside walking past the window.

Josie heard me but didn't say anything; her fork halfway to her mouth. Her expression asked, 'What's up Doc?'

I'm hoping he doesn't come in here. A few more minutes passed and there was no sign of him, thank goodness.

I'm almost finished my meal now. It was delicious. I'll have that again sometime, but of course, without the offending coleslaw.

I turned from the window and looked across the room towards Reception. He was standing there beside the desk looking around!

'Oh, Jesus,' I said in a low voice and turning to the window, 'he's here. Don't look at him Josie.'

I heard her say under her breath, 'God! Here we go.'

She continued to eat her chicken, turning every now and then to look out of the the window. Within seconds, I was aware of someone standing by our table. I'm hoping it's the waitress, but of course it wasn't. I didn't look at him.

He just stood there and hovered. He's probably waiting for an invitation to sit. Well he can wait.

He didn't. 'Can I sit down? Thank you.' He sat down and leaned his arms on the table. He's looking at us both in turn, but we're refusing to acknowledge him.

'So, I finally caught you up. You know, you two are very difficult to pin down?' He laughed.

I didn't respond.

Josie had stopped eating and was playing with her food, chasing it around her plate with her fork. She's formulating a plan in her head, I can tell. Every now and then she looks at me with her vivid blue eyes, and with that little cute smile of hers in place, and tucks several strands of her beautiful golden hair behind her right ear.

'Is this the way you greet all your friends?' he asked. He's looking at me.

I still didn't respond. I stabbed several pieces of squid with my fork and was just about to raise it to my mouth, when he clamped his hand on my lower arm. It was vice-like.

Josie put down her fork and dabbed at her lips with the napkin.

I said firmly as I continued to gaze out of the window, 'Get your hand off my arm please?'

'What?' He gave a short incredulous laugh. Instead of removing it, his grip tightened, or was that just how it appeared to me?

Josie said to him as she tried to keep a straight face, 'You just don't wanna get her angry is all.' She nodded.

Another incredulous laugh. 'What?'

Josie said to no-one in particular as she stood up and dropping her napkin on the table, 'Off to the loo. See ya.'

Before he could respond, she was off.

He said earnestly, 'I'm trying to make it easy for you, that's why I'm here. My boss means business. You can save yourself a lot of trouble by giving those photos to me now.' He let go of my arm.

'Milos. Are you really as naïve as you look? We're not about to hand over any pictures to you *or* anyone else.' I said that with a smug look of defiance, and I was satisfied with it too. I thought, *Jesus, I'm playing with fire here. These people shouldn't be messed with.*' But I'm determined not to give in to them. I'm in a rebellious mood. It might get me killed though. Now that's a scary thought.

Within minutes, Josie was back. She sat down with a self-satisfied smile in place. Jesus, she does have a plan! I'm hoping it's something useful and she's not going to do something stupid, then we really will be in the sugar.

He turned to Josie now, looking into her eyes. 'You could persuade your friend to give me those photos couldn't you?'

She didn't respond but looked across at me with that cute smile still in place. What's she planning? I hope there's a Plan 'B' just in case this doesn't work whatever it is!

'This can be done the easy way or....'

I cut him off. 'Forget it Milos. You're not getting them. We're taking them to the police!' Well that's told him.

He shook his head. 'Foolish move. I thought you would have had more sense than that.' He took a cellphone from his pocket. 'I'll just give my boss a quick call and give him your answer.'

Josie said, shifting her chair back preparing to stand, 'Oops, just dropped a contact lens.' She gave a short laugh.

He looked surprised.

So was I because Josie doesn't wear contacts! This has to be part of her plan. What's she up to?

She went down on the floor and searched.

He said, 'I can help you find it?'

She said quickly, 'No it's OK. I know how to do this.' Her head appeared briefly above the level of the table. She wrinkled her nose. 'Somebody might stand on it you know?' She gave a short laugh.

He turned his attention to me again, 'Well, I can give you another chance just before I make this call, OK?'

I said defiantly, 'No chance.'

Seconds later and Josie was back in her seat, again with that little cute smile of hers in place. Jesus, what has she done?

Milos was concentrating on his phone now and preparing to dial.

Josie kicked my ankle to get my attention, then tucked another strand of her hair behind her ear. She was about to make a move. Plan 'A' was about to be executed!

I responded immediately by smiling back, but my stomach was in a knot, although I was ready for anything, well, almost anything.

She said to Milos smiling, 'I've got them here.'

That got his attention all right. 'You got what?'

He diverted his attention from the phone to stare directly at her, and that's when she made her move. She threw her wine into his face.

Some of the clientèle were becoming concerned now; heads turned in our direction.

I thought quickly, *Josie what are you doing?'* I suspected that she had a plan, but this?

He shouted, 'What the hell.... are you doing!' He pulled a green cloth handkerchief from his pocket and began to rub his eyes and dry his face.

We both stood up quickly grabbing our packs, and made a dash from our seats towards the entrance. I turned back briefly to see if he was following us. He couldn't because Josie had tied his right leg to the table leg and he had fallen to the floor. All I could hear behind us as we made for the door was cursing and swearing from him, and laughter from some of the clientèle. Time to make ourselves scarce big time! Once in the street, we both broke down in a fit of giggles. I suddenly realised something; we hadn't paid the bill! I mentioned this to Josie, but it was OK; she paid it herself when she went to the toilet.

We were both still very tired from last night, so we decided to return to the park where we had been earlier and sleep off the afternoon. Our train wasn't due to leave till 20.30 hours anyway.

Chapter 15.

We awoke around 5.30 pm and went to find a coffee house where we had sandwiches and a bowl of chicken soup. The next few hours were spent in a movie theatre. It was Star Trek complete with subtitles in Croatian, then it was off to the railroad station again to catch our train. Milos couldn't know where we were headed next as we hadn't told him, so we could relax now.

On the train, we had cabin number '8' this time. Just before we settled in for the night, Josie paid a visit to the buffet car and bought us a couple of bottles of locally brewed beer. It was ice-cold from the fridge and I was ready for it too. I had the top bunk again, and, having consumed the beer in less than a minute, I was asleep in no time, and didn't waken again until the train had begun to slow as it entered the City of Belgrade in Serbia. No breakfast this time as we had slept through it, but no matter; we'd find it elsewhere.

We found a café on a busy main street in Downtown Belgrade. We'd look for accommodation later, but first things first. We sat opposite one another at a window table. We weren't sure what to order as the menu was printed in Cyrillic script. Damn, I'd forgotten about this alphabet being used in these parts. This was going to be a problem. Having to cope with understanding the language was one thing, but learning the alphabet was quite another altogether.

'Oh Jesus Josie,' I sighed as I tried in vain to make something of this menu. 'What do we do about this?'

She shrugged. 'Didn't you learn any of this alphabet before you came?'

'Yeah, a little, but I'd kinda forgot about it, you know? Too many other things to think about and get ready for the trip.'

'OK,' she said finally. 'I'm picking something at random. I'll eat it whatever it is.' She handed the menu back to me with a grin.

I looked at it but of course it made no sense to me at all, so I simply copied Josie and picked something at random. Second item down from the top. Let's hope I can eat it!

A waitress came and took our order and within minutes, was back again with it.

'Wow, that was quick, huh? These must be popular dishes,' Josie said.

She had scrambled egg on toast. I had sausages and bacon on a bread roll.

'Yeah. That's the quickest service we've had yet anywhere,' I said as I bit into my sandwich.

The next ten minutes or so were spent eating our breakfast, but with no real conversation. I was trying to recall the Cyrillic alphabet in this country and comparing it to the Roman alphabet. I pulled a reporter's notebook from my pack. I had found a brochure at the railroad station that mentioned about the Natural History Museum. We could go there next, if we could find it.

I said, 'We can make a start with the Cyrillic alphabet now. Some letters anyway.' I wrote the Cyrillic first; 'Природњачки Музеј', then the Roman; 'Prirodnjački muzej'. I turned the notebook around for Josie to see. 'Look, "Prirodnjački muzej" is "Natural History Museum", and this is the Cyrillic. See, "П" equals "P", "р" equals "r", and so on?'

'Yeah, OK.' She nodded. 'God, it's like a coded message isn't it?'

'Sure is.' I continued, '"C" equals "s" in Roman and…..'

She cut me off grinning. 'Hey, how come you know so much about it anyway?'

'Josie, unlike you, I came prepared,' I said smugly. 'I remember some of it from high school but not much.' Actually there wasn't time to learn anything before we went on vacation, it was all so short-notice.

I began to write the Cyrillic letters down the page with the Roman equivalent opposite each one. This took me a few minutes because I wasn't familiar with the alphabet. Well it's a start anyway.

'No you didn't. You only had a few days before we left,' she said teasing.

'Well, maybe I'm a fast learner.' My smug look remained.

'Yeah, right.'

When we had finished our breakfast, we went off to find the museum. Was this difficult or what? We stopped a young couple walking hand-in-hand. They had no English; so what's new? Next up, an elderly guy dressed in a bright Hawaiian shirt. Tourist?

'Do you speak English?' Josie asked.

He nodded.

I asked, 'Natural History Museum? Do you know where it is?'

He pointed down the street. 'On this side.' He nodded.

I said, 'Oh, thank you.'

We walked down to where he indicated. It was an old stone building. The sign on the outside said something in Serbian Cyrillic. The one on the door read…. 'National History Museum'!

I said irritatedly, 'Damn. This is the wrong one! I said, "Natural History Museum" for God's sake.'

She shrugged. 'Let's go in anyway.'

We did.

On our right, the National Museum gallery, and straight ahead, a stairway and an arrow pointing up to an art gallery. We headed there instead.

As we pushed through the double glass doors, Josie, who was ahead of me, gave a loud gasp. 'Gosh, it's awesome Sam. I just love paintings.'

She strolled along the first wall on our right. I followed her. Yep, they sure were amazing all right. Some of those old paintings were so realistic, you'd think the people in them could step right out of there and shake your hand. Most were nineteenth century. One section of the gallery was devoted to contemporary art. Did I say art? No way!

Josie found it first. She just stood there and gasped at one painting in particular that was nothing more than a mass of coloured streaks; every colour you could think of. This is not art. Why do some people make such a big deal out of it?

'Isn't it awesome!' she exclaimed excitedly.

I decided to treat it with the contempt it deserved. 'If you say so.' I walked on.

None of those so-called 'works of art' meant anything at all to me. It's just colour thrown together in minutes. Hardly what you'd call art.

'Sam,' I heard her say at my back. 'You should open up your mind to….'

I turned to her quickly. 'Josie. That's not art. The definition of the word art is "skill", OK? Where's the skill in that, huh?' I walked on.

She hurried to keep up. 'You'd appreciate life a lot more if you just….'

I said in an irritated tone, 'Josie, shut up.' She was beginning to piss me off.

She stopped again to admire another painting.

I carried on walking and didn't stop until I was almost at the exit. I turned to her. 'You coming? We've got accommodation to look for.'

She was so engrossed in one particular painting that she didn't hear me.

'Josie!' I shouted. 'Is it that good!'

Out on the street again, we kept our eyes open for the Tourist Bureau, but with no luck. In the end, Josie spotted a small hotel between two shopping arcades. This would be our accommodation for tonight anyway. The price was just right for us too. We can relax now and not worry about being pursued any more.

We left our backpacks in our room while we went off to find the Natural History Museum. After much asking around, we found it. The words 'Природњачки Музеј' were displayed on the front of the building. I just kinda memorised the name as I saw it written in the brochure that I mentioned earlier. I had left it in the room. I didn't take my camera with me either. Didn't think there'd be much to photograph here, but Josie had hers with her.

As we went into the building, Josie started snapping away almost at random.

I said in a low voice, 'Don't take anything till we find out if it's OK to do it.'

She turned to me with an inquisitive look. She whispered back, 'OK to do what?'

'Can't take you anywhere,' I said mockingly as I approached the Reception desk. I asked the girl there if it was OK to take photos here and she said it was. *'Someone else who speaks English. Things are looking up,'* I thought happily.

Josie just grinned at me and walked ahead.

First up on our right was the Palaeontology section. As we strolled in, she started snapping at the enormous dinosaur skeletons here. We found T-Rex in all his splendour; so big that Josie couldn't get all of him into the frame, so she shot him in sections instead. She'd stitch the pictures together later in her PC. A useful tool if your wide-angle lens is not quite wide enough. We just had to photograph one another against this unusual backdrop. Josie was making silly faces into the camera when I snapped her.

After visiting the Ornithology section, we headed for another, but I wasn't paying attention to where we were going. Josie was leading the way, then she turned and snapped me, but continued walking backwards into the next gallery. It wasn't until we were well into the room, that I suddenly realised where we were; the bugs section! I don't like them. I was on the point of turning away again, when Josie grasped my arm and began pulling me towards a large glass table cabinet.

My expression asked, 'What?' and, 'I don't want to see it whatever it is.' A bug is a bug. You can keep them!

Josie was looking into the case. She said pointing into it, 'There's a spider in there Sam. See if you can spot it?'

'Pardon?' I held back. I don't want to see it.

'What are those?' She pointed to several large bugs about an inch and a half long with many legs that were scattered around on the sand-strewn floor of the case. There were lots of twigs and small tree branches in there too. What were these bugs, cockroaches? I wasn't sure, but then.... ugh! They were disgusting! Were they dead or what? None of them moved, or had the spider got to them earlier. Maybe they were too frightened to move lest the spider should find them. I think I'd be playing dead too if I was in there.

'Look! There on that twig!' She pointed to a twig with white bark. I was on the point of turning away, when she exclaimed, 'There it is!'

Sure enough, I could see the spider there on the twig, superbly camouflaged against the bark, with four front legs stretched out before it, and four legs behind. It gave me the goosebumps. I turned away. I'd seen enough.

I was feeling sick and made for the Ladies, Josie in pursuit, where I threw up into the sink. Then we headed straight back to the hotel, where I went for a lie down.

Later, we thought we'd take a stroll around town and take in some of the sights. My phone was out of credit, so I left it in my pack. Josie left her camera in her pack too. It was just as well that we did, because of what happened next.

As we crossed a road bridge over the Danube, the pedestrian traffic was exceptionally dense with people jostling for space to walk. Both Josie and I are only five foot tall, so it was difficult for me to see exactly where she was a lot of the time. She kept trailing behind; stopping every once in a while to admire the views, and getting further and further away from me. Every now and then, she would disappear behind a group of bodies much taller than herself. The last time I saw her, she had stopped to look over the parapet, then when I turned again, she had vanished.

'*Where the hell's she got to now?*' I thought as I tried to see round people coming and going on the sidewalk, then somebody let out a loud scream. It was a young woman, and she was looking over the parapet into the river. I looked over too and could see a female figure lying face-down in the water. She had blond hair pulled back into a ponytail, and was wearing a pair of white, low-cut jeans and a blue cropped top, and there was no mistaking that tattoo on her lower back.

I panicked now and began to cry out for Josie. I jumped up onto the parapet and would have dived into the water, but someone grasped me around the waist and tried to pull me back down. I struggled and fought them, then I lost my footing and the hands that held me had to let go. I fell head-over-heals, over and over, over and over, then I hit the water hard. I don't remember anything very clearly after that. I think I probably knocked myself out.

I opened my eyes. I was lying in a hospital bed on my back in a private room. A curtain had been pulled around the bed. 'Were they doing something to me?' I wondered about the curtain.

I wore a white cotton gown with my panties and bra. I tried to sit up. Yep, I could do that all right so no broken bones anyway thank goodness. I wore a green plastic identity tag on my left wrist. How long have I been here? Where's Josie? Is she all right? I need some answers.

The curtain was drawn aside and a young doctor in his late twenties wearing a white coat and a stethoscope around his neck entered. He had a small moustache and black wavy hair. He said, 'Oh, you're back.' His accent was American. Where am I?

'Was I unconscious? Where's Josie?' I'm worried about her.

'Em….. Josie is not available right now Miss Winter.'

'What do you mean? I have to see her.'

'All in good time.' He stepped closer. He asked, changing the subject, 'Do you mind being photographed?'

'Sorry?'

'It's for medical research. We ask patients if they mind being pho-tographed. It's voluntary of course,' he said nodding.

'Oh, no, I don't mind. Anything to help medical research.' I smiled.

'OK. I'll get a nurse in here to give you further instructions.' He turned on his heel and left through the curtain again.

'Oh, OK.' I said to his back. I'm wondering what's coming next. He didn't really tell me anything and I'm concerned about Josie.

In a few minutes I heard footsteps coming down a corridor towards my room, since the door appeared to have been left open. It was a woman's walk. The curtain was pulled aside and a young nurse appeared. She was barely out of school.

She said, 'Doctor says to take your clothes off.' She giggled. Her accent was American too. What's going on here? Am I back home?

'Pardon?'

She came closer. 'Take off all your clothes and sit here and wait for someone to come to see you.' She giggled again.

'What's so damned funny?' I asked annoyed.

'Nothing. Just the look on your face.' She turned and left the room again still giggling.

'Well, I don't know what this is all about but here goes,' I thought as I pulled off my gown, then my underwear.

I got back into the bed and covered myself with the single cotton sheet. I was still sitting up in the bed when the curtain opened and a guy in his fifties wearing a blue sleeveless shirt and black pants came in carrying a camera and tripod.

He set them up close to the foot of my bed and said, 'OK, get up and stand facing the camera.' Yep, another American accent. I must be back home, but how?

'*Excuse* me?' I said incredulously.

'Get out the bed,' he said sounding annoyed.

'I can't! I'm not dressed.' I'm panicking now.

'If you don't co-operate you can be made to obey,' he said in a threatening tone. He continued, 'Are you refusing?'

'Yes. I guess I am.' I'm standing my ground here. He can't and will not dictate to me. I stayed put in the bed.

'OK guys,' he shouted to somebody.

The curtain opened and two muscle-bound guys built like mountains came in. They were bald and unshaven. Hospital staff? Never! They approached the bed and the sheet was pulled off of me, then I was dragged out of the bed. I had no choice but to stand up.

I began to protest. 'You can't do this! I have rights you know!'

The two goons held me by the arms and I was made to stand with my arms by my sides, then the clicking started. They turned me around and my back view was photographed, then my right and left sides. The two goons let me go and left the room.

'Well, that wasn't so difficult now was it? If you'd just co-operate you'd make it a lot easier on yourself.'

'Go to hell! I yelled.

Before I could get back into the bed, the same nurse who had been in earlier, came in through the curtain. She was followed by the doctor with the moustache, then another doctor. He was taller than the first with grey hair and beard. He approached the bed and said, 'You can lie down now.'

I did and covered myself with the sheet only to have him pull it right off me again. 'What the hell!' I yelled. 'What kind of hospital is this?' I screamed at them.

They all laughed at me. I could feel the bed being pushed forward. *What the hell's going on? Where are they taking me?'* I thought in alarm.

The curtain was pulled open completely and I could see that the room was crowded with people, some of them patients wearing gowns just like me. They were laughing at me; some of them were almost hysterical. It's like an asylum for the insane.

I started to sit up but the second doctor pushed me right back down again. I refused to lie down. He slapped me across the face.

I lay down and cried, 'Why are you doing this!'

The laughter continued. I tried to sit up again but hands pushed me back down, then, as they pushed the bed towards the door, a needle was thrust into my left arm. I think it was the second doctor. My limbs were.... I couldn't move my limbs! They were totally paralysed! I started to scream, then my mouth was taped up. I screamed in my throat.

The laughter was louder now as I was pushed right out into the corridor, with people reaching out to touch me everywhere, and I couldn't stop them. It was horrible. As I was pushed along through the crowds of people, I noticed visitors coming in. They were reaching out to touch me as well. It was disgusting.

I had made up my mind that this was not a hospital at all, but some kind of madhouse. Or was it me who was mad. I didn't want to think about that.

All the while that I was being wheeled along, I could see lights in the ceiling above me, and their brightness hurt my eyes. Then, finally, I was pushed through a double door and I recognised it as an operating theatre. I screamed and screamed in my throat, and tried to shout 'no' but I couldn't form the words anyway! I was positioned under a single large light and left there for about ten minutes.

'What the hell are they going to do to me?' I still can't move. I screamed again in my throat, but no-one cared about me because my cries were not heard, or perhaps they were simply ignored. Somebody approached the bed now. He was tall with a full beard with grey hair and wearing a green surgical gown. He was accompanied by a second figure of the same age group and dressed in a similar fashion. They lifted me with their bare hands onto an operating table.

The bearded one said, 'Now this looks like a fine specimen.' He laughed almost hysterically.

'Yeah, sure does,' the other agreed.

'The last one was even better don't you think?' He laughed. He sounded drunk.

The bearded one reached somewhere behind himself and brought a bottle of scotch into my view. He took several gulps before passing it to his accomplice. The other one took a swig too, then hiccuped. The bastards were drunk or very nearly so, and what the hell were they going to do to me here with my limbs paralysed and unable to defend myself.

The bearded one said, 'I think she wants to say something.'

He pulled the tape off my mouth.

'Who were you talking about there? What have you done with Josie?'

They laughed.

I screamed, 'What have you done to her!'

The bearded one turned to his colleague. 'Such a pretty one. Blue eyes and what a cute smile.' He pointed to his accomplice. 'And he took the tattoo off her back. He collects them you know?'

The second one replied nodding, 'So young and defenceless. Once her hair was off, well she wasn't quite so pretty.' He laughed.

'Shut up!' I shouted. 'You murdered her!'

'We need fresh and living organs for transplanting into other patients,' the bearded one said, his speech getting more slurred.

'You bastards!' I shouted.

The other one took another swig of scotch. 'Where shall we start?'

'No!' I shouted. 'Leave me alone! Stop it!' I've just lost control. I screamed and cried and couldn't stop! They had no intention of anaesthetising me.

The bearded one took a knife from somewhere and placed it on my chest. It was a butcher knife. The blade was vicious-looking and sharp. He drew the point down my chest between the breasts and continued down. It drew blood. Somewhere between my chest and navel, the blade went deeper; much deeper!

I screamed and screamed. I screamed even more when the other one slipped his hand inside me just above my bellybutton and removed something red and slimy-looking, then the knife moved swiftly upwards and it was sliced through. The two of them laughed and laughed. The pain was excruciating. I blacked out.

Someone was trying to talk to me. It was Josie. My eyes snapped open. She was seated in a chair on my right. 'Sam! You're back.'

I started to cry.

She hugged me tight and broke down too. We stayed that way for a few seconds, then she pulled away with, 'It's been so long. I never thought you'd pull through, but you made it.' She wiped her tears with a Kleenex from the bedside cabinet.

What did she mean by that? Have I been in a coma or....? 'So long? How long have I been here Josie?'

She ignored me and changed the subject abruptly. 'Oh, you have to meet Rob!' she said excitedly and stood up. 'I'll just get him.'

I stopped her right there. 'Josie, what are you talking about? Who's Rob?' Doesn't she mean Bob?

'Oh, of course. You've been asleep awhile. I'm getting married Sam. Isn't that exciting?'

She was about to fetch Rob, when I stopped her again. 'Josie, you're not getting married! Stop it now!'

'What? Of course I am. Don't you remember? We met in San Francisco in 2000.'

My heart was thumping hard now. 'What the hell's going on here?'

She said turning away, 'I'll just get him.' She left me lying there wondering how long I had been asleep. This can't be happening!

My thoughts were interrupted by Josie returning a few minutes later with Rob. He was taller than her with black close-cropped hair and a ready smile, and a bit of a hunk too. My type. He wore a blue shirt and black jeans. I'm beginning to feel afraid now. If I've been in a coma for a while, where am I now?

Rob pulled up a chair and sat down facing the bed. Josie sat beside him.

I sat up. I had a confused expression on my face.

Rob offered his hand to me. 'Hi. Good to meet you Sam.'

I put out my hand and shook his, then I felt tears run down my cheeks.

Josie and Rob exchanged glances. He said, 'We wanted to wait till you regained consciousness so you could be at the wedding.'

'Oh? Where am I? Unconscious? You mean….?'

She said, 'Mendocino. Yes you've been in a coma since 2000!'

He nodded. He exchanged glances again with Josie.

More tears. I was beginning to choke on them now. 'How long….?'

She said, 'This is 2003!'

Three years I've been out of it? No, there has to be a mistake!

'Sam, there was an accident,' Rob said seriously.

'Accident?' I asked, my tears getting larger. I choked on them again and swallowed hard. I had a lump in my throat that refused to shift.

'It's your mom and dad,' Josie said as a tear ran down her left cheek.

'No! What are you saying Josie?'

She nodded. 'It's your house. There was a fire and they were both,' she paused, tears rolling down, 'trapped in the flames. It was completely gutted!'

I screamed and screamed, then I lost consciousness.

I awoke gradually with someone touching my right arm. It was the gentle caress of soft feminine fingers. Josie came to mind. I opened my eyes and, yes, it was her. As she leaned over me, I could see there were tears in her eyes. She was back in her low-cut jeans and cropped top, and her diamond sparkling in the light from the window.

'Thank God you're back Sam,' she sniffled as a tear ran down her left cheek. 'Thought I'd lost you.'

I sat up and threw both arms around her neck. We just hung onto each other and cried, then she pulled away and sat down on a chair.

When I had recovered sufficiently, I asked, 'How long was I .....?'

She interrupted with, 'About three days. Doc thought your might not make it, but here you are. You were knocked unconscious when you hit the water.'

I sniffled and reached for a Kleenex from the bedside cabinet. 'What about you Josie? Why did you jump off the bridge? Didn't you have enough swimming in the sea?' I finished off with a short laugh.

She wasn't laughing as she said, 'I didn't jump Sam. Somebody was trying to abduct me. I was grabbed from behind, and I struggled to get free.'

I just sat there not believing my ears. 'What?' OK, we have a problem here. These guys know where we are? How is that possible?

She nodded. 'Yeah. I did manage to free myself briefly, then I took this opportunity to leap up onto the parapet, then my right leg was grasped briefly and I lost my balance and toppled into the water. Doc says I knocked myself out and was lying face down.'

I nodded. 'I saw you.' I told her about me jumping into rescue her.

'A passing tugboat pulled me out. They got you seconds later.' She hugged me again and we shed a few more tears before she pulled away and wiped them with a Kleenex. She added, 'Sam, how were they able to find us anyway? We didn't tell anyone where we were going.'

I'm lost in thought now. Well there's only one explanation to all this. We've been bugged! That has to be it. So if that's true, is it a tracking device and/or a listening one too? It has to be in one of our packs or in our clothing. I can't voice my thoughts to her because they're going to know that we.... Hell, I'm tired of all this cloak and dagger crap. Some vacation this turned out to be. I'm regretting having agreed to come here again.

Josie's wondering what's wrong. She's looking concerned.

'Josie, can you get me a pen and paper?'

A question mark appeared above her head now. She hesitated for a second then nodded. She turned and disappeared from the room. I'm wondering about this bug, if there is one. Where would it be? Who'd have the chance to plant it on us?

Within minutes she was back with a pen and several sheets of A4 paper. 'There you go,' she said handing them to me.

I got out of the bed and sat on the edge of it.

Josie looked at me concerned. 'You sure you're fit enough?'

'What? Do I look ill?' I tried standing and took a few steps forward, then stumbled. My right leg wasn't quite making it.

Josie caught my arm. 'Hey, steady!'

'Thanks,' I said as I straightened up. 'I'll be OK.' I sat down again.

'Why are you sitting down if your OK?' she asked curiously.

'Trust me. I'm OK. I'm going to make a list.' I beckoned her to sit beside me, then I began to scribble.

'List?'

I nodded, all the while writing what I really wanted to say. My scrawl across the page read, 'Think we have a bug in our clothing or packs. This is how they knew where we were all the time.'

She looked shocked. She mouthed, 'Who?' She took the pen from me and wrote, 'Where? When planted?'

I shrugged, then a sudden thought occurred to me. Of course! The cottage. That's what Milos was doing there. I wrote down my thoughts.

She nodded.

So that's what that guy on the phone meant when he said, 'It's just a matter of finding your exact location.' I wrote that down as well.

She nodded again.

I turned to her. 'See if you can find the doctor who fixed me Josie. I want to get out of here.'

'That might not be a good idea....'

I cut in with, 'Josie, just do it please!'

'Sure.' She sighed. 'I'll just get him.' She got up from the bed and made for the door.

As she disappeared out of the room, I began to think again of where this bug could be hidden. It's unlikely to be in our clothing, but it's still a possibility. Most probably in one of our packs. We'll have to dispose of it somehow. I'll think of something later.

Presently, Josie arrived back with the doctor. He wore an open white coat over a grey suit, was slightly taller than me at around five foot four, elderly and with a receding hairline.

He put out his hand as he approached me smiling. 'I'm Dr. Marić.' He pronounced it 'Mar-itch'.

As I shook his hand he said smiling, 'Miss Moore here tells me you want to leave us? What, so soon?'

I sighed. 'Yeah. Have this thing about hospitals you know?'

He gave a short laugh. 'You don't like them?'

'You got it.'

'Your medical insurance forms are here. All you have to do is fill them out,' he said.

I nodded then looked to Josie for an explanation. They were in my pack. How did they get here?

'While you were out of it, I went back to the hotel and got the forms from your pack.' She nodded. Well she seemed satisfied with her answer anyway.

I stood with hands on hips and keeping a straight face. 'You were in my pack again?'

She nodded.

Marić said turning to go, 'I'll leave you to get dressed. I'll be in my office.'

I nodded again. I said as I turned to the bed, 'So what did you take this time, huh? Where are my clothes?'

'Nothing except the insurance forms. They're in the bedside cabinet. I put them there for safe keeping along with your watch etc.' She nodded.

'OK, thanks.' As I pulled the curtain around the bed I said teasing, 'Did you touch my perfume?'

'No.'

I smiled. 'Good. Just checking.' I opened the bedside cabinet and began to dress. I strapped on my watch and noted the time was 3.30. When I was ready, we went off to the doctor's office where I filled out the forms. Doc wasn't too happy about me leaving so soon, but hey, I'm standing up so....

Chapter 16.

Once in our room, I had planned to take a shower. It was only because I wanted to mask our voices from the 'bug', assuming there was one that is. Well it has to be a 'bug'; how else could they know where we were? Also, I wanted to search our clothing without making it too obvious what we were up to. The sound of the shower water should mask the searching of seams etc. This 'bug' is going to be small so could quite easily be hidden in clothing. If I can get Josie's co-operation that is.

I said to her, 'Get your clothes off.'

'I beg your pardon?' That question mark appeared again.

Feeling exasperated I said, 'Josie, just do it OK?'

'Why?'

As I pulled my top off I said, 'Come on, get them off!'

'Why?' she asked again. 'You haven't answered my question.' She still hadn't made a move to remove anything.

'Because girl, I want to see you naked!' I'm beginning to lose my cool with her.

'*What?*' She gave a short laugh. 'Why are you....?'

I cut her off with, 'Why do you *think*? Come on, let's go.' I unclipped my brassiere and dropped it onto the bed.

'I think you hit your head harder than you thought.'

I unzipped my jeans. 'So you think I'm crazy huh?'

She didn't say anything, nor did she make any attempt to take anything off.

I said finally, 'Oh, what's the use.'

I went into the bathroom with the bra, then, once I had the remainder of my clothes off, stepped into the shower, closed the curtain and turned on the water. Once I had the temperature adjusted to my satisfaction, I started with my bra. Standing under the hot water, I felt around every seam of that garment until I had satisfied myself that there was definitely nothing sinister lurking there. I was just about to start on my panties, when I had a sudden change of plan. I stepped out of the shower and grabbed a towel and wrapped it, then returned to Josie.

I whispered, 'Just had an idea.' I held my finger to my lips, shushing her to silence. I made straight for our packs lying on the floor, and emptied them onto the bed, then began a thorough search. I started with the front pockets. I had four zippers there, and each one had several items, but I didn't find anything unusual even in the corners. I'm not too sure what I'm looking for here anyway. Whatever it is, it has to be small; very small.

Josie started to search her own starting with the pockets.

I said, 'Josie? About that list?'

'Oh, yeah. I made it out.'

'Read it to me, thanks.' I started on the main compartment now. My camera and related items had been in here along with my clothes and personal effects. Nothing unusual here at all.

'Bra?' she said.

'Check.' I put my hand into the zippered pocket where I put my passport, and….. Jesus! There it was, right at the foot in the corner! It was silvery and smaller than my pinkie's fingernail and resembling a small battery. Now what? How do I get this out of my pack without making it obvious that I've found it?

'Jeans…..' She hesitated then as she realised that I had found something. I gestured to her to continue. We have to keep up the pretence. 'Check.'

'Four tops.'

'Check.' I'm still wondering what to do with this object.

'Four pairs of socks.'

'Check.' I crossed to the window.

We had a room at the back of the hotel that looked out onto a courtyard with a fire escape outside our window. I'm thinking maybe I'd throw it outside, then, just as I was about to turn away again - a kitty cat! It was a tortoiseshell, and it had just landed on the fire escape outside the window. Where the hell did it come from? I didn't say anything immediately to Josie; she'd only want to take it to bed with her. I suddenly had such a cool idea. If I could only find a way to attach this 'bug' to the cat's collar. Now that would really confuse them!

I thought, *Gum.* I turned to Josie. 'You have any gum on you?'

'Pardon?' She looked up from her pack.

'Gum,' I repeated. 'You got any?'

'No. Don't eat it.'

I said half to myself, 'What do you normally do with it then?' I can think of a few places where I'd like to put it though, but I think I'll file that one away for later. I pulled the window up to open it and the cat came right up to me. I began to sing that little song to myself; you know the one? 'I tawt I taw a puddy-tat, as….'

I broke off as Josie joined me at the window in a flash. Her face lit up. 'A kitty-cat!'

'Don't even think about it,' I said determinedly.

I had no sooner spoken, when the cat suddenly leapt through the open window and onto the floor. Josie bent to pick it up, but the cat had other ideas. It ran into the bathroom with her in pursuit.

'Oh Jesus,' I said, my eyes shooting heavenwards. 'Here we go.'

'I'll get him,' she shouted from the bathroom.

'I hope so!' I shouted at her back. Then another thought. Better than gum – Scotch tape! I don't have any with me. 'Josie? Got any Scotch tape?'

'What?' She came out cradling the cat.

'Scotch tape. Got any?'

She shook her head, then she kissed the cat on the top of the head. Why does she do that?

'Well, go down to Reception and get us some then,' I said annoyed.

'Why don't you do it?'

'Because, as soon as I turn my back, you'll have him in the bed,' I retorted. 'Or somebody's bed; probably mine.'

She put the cat on the floor.

I whispered close to her ear, 'I want to attach it to the cat's collar.'

She nodded.

Within seconds, she was out of the room. I looked out of the window again and – pigeons! Yes, of course! They would be ideal for this. Attach the 'bug' to a pigeon's leg and….. I'm going to have to attract them to our window, because at this moment, they were alighting on the fire escape; well two of them were anyway. I'm wondering where I'm going to find bread or cookies. I dressed hurriedly, oh, and in a fresh bra, then ran out of the room, forgetting to close the door behind me. As I ran down the stairs, I got a glimpse of something furry shooting past me. Of course it was the cat. I'll deny all knowledge of course. Yep, sure it was Josie! They can't prove it was me, can they? I reached the foot of the stairs and headed straight for Reception where I met Josie. She had just been handed a roll of Scotch tape by the girl. She looked at me in surprise.

I said hurriedly to the girl, 'Cookies? Bread?'

She just stared at me blankly and shrugged.

'Yeah, OK,' I said, then ran into the dining room.

Several guests were enjoying afternoon tea, as I entered. I went right up to an elderly couple sitting at the nearest table. That's because I could see cookies on a silver plate in the centre of it.

I grabbed several of them and said quickly, 'Can I borrow those? Thanks!' and dashed off again.

I heard the woman say at my back just before I exited the room, 'Well, did you see that? The nerve…..'

I snatched the roll of tape out of Josie's hand and headed for our room again. Once in, I made for the window and damn – the birds had gone! I was just about to turn away again, when one of them flew up and onto the fire escape. Yes! Now all I have to do is entice this one onto the outside windowsill and he's mine. I broke one of the cookies onto the windowsill and waited. He came closer, then, just when I thought I had him, Josie dashed into the room slamming the door behind her. The ensuing racket frightened the bird and it took off across the courtyard in a flurry of feathers.

I turned to her in annoyance. 'Josie! Couldn't you enter just a little more quietly please? No wonder the bird flew off.'

'Sorry,' she said as she approached the window. 'What are you doing anyway?'

I replied, irritatedly, 'I was trying to.....?' I was interrupted by a pigeon landing on the windowsill. I grabbed him and took him inside. Holding him with one hand close to my chest I whispered into her ear, 'A small piece of tape Josie.'

While she was busy with the tape, I went to my pack and, with a Kleenex from my pocket, lifted the 'bug' out of there very carefully and brought it back to the window. With one hand, I wrapped it in a small piece of the tissue then Josie wound the tape around this 'package' and the bird's right leg, then I let it go. It flew out of the window and alighted on a wire, then flew off again. I didn't see where it went, and I wasn't really caring so long as that 'bug' was well out of our sight.

In the evening I went down to Reception to ask if we could get a train to Podgorica. The woman behind the desk didn't know, but she did phone the local railroad station for us and, yes, there was one going about 8.30 in the morning. That suited us fine, so next morning after breakfast we made straight for the station and bought ourselves tickets. Unfortunately we had language difficulties here again.

As we boarded the train, I was looking for a non-smoking compartment, but they were all full already so we had to take a smoking one. Most of the passengers appeared to be students on some kind of trip. Many were sitting in the corridor on backpacks.

We put our packs on the overhead luggage racks. I sat at the window, my camera ready for action, with Josie on my left. An elderly gentleman balding on top and wearing a black suit, sat opposite us. He appeared to be travelling alone. On his right were two Muslim women, and in the corner nearest the corridor, a young guy about twenty-something with a full black beard and wearing jeans and a blue chequered shirt. He slept a lot, and using his rolled-up jacket as an improvised pillow. On Josie's left was a middle-aged guy with a black moustache and wearing a blue shirt and black pants. He seemed to have a fat cigar between his lips throughout the journey, regardless of whether it was lit or not. When he did light his cigar, that's when I left the compartment to stand in the corridor. Passive smoking I can do without.

I didn't sleep at all, but Josie did, in fact she slept most of the journey, with her head resting against my arm. At times when I had to leave the compartment, she lay on her back with her knees drawn up to her chest. When I suggested to her about going off to the dining car to eat, she didn't seem interested, but when I returned with hamburgers and coffee…. As I entered the compartment carrying a plastic carrier bag and two coffees in cardboard tumblers, Josie was lying on her back in her usual position with her head partially on my seat, so I had to squeeze myself into the small space that she had left me. I was starved and the smell of food was killing me. I placed the tumblers on the window table and waved one of the burgers under her nose, that's when she came to life; that little cute smile appearing once more on her lips. I handed her one of the coffees and she sat up.

The guy sitting opposite me had some English. He said his name was Petar, and he was travelling to Podgorica to visit his niece. Every now and then, he'd point out some interesting subject for me to photograph. As a result, my camera card was filling up fast. I had to go into my pack to retrieve my hard disk drive to download the pictures into. This is where I keep the photographs that I take for viewing on my PC later when I get home. Josie didn't take many photos as she was asleep most of the time.

At one point on the journey, Petar asked me to put my camera away as we were fast approaching a station and Border Guards would be boarding the train. They would be checking our tickets and probably passports too, and they didn't like cameras. O-K!

As the train pulled into the station, I took my pack down from the overhead luggage rack and put my camera away, then dug out my passport. As I sat down again, I gave Josie a nudge with my elbow to waken her.

Her eyes opened. 'We here already?'

'No. Border guards coming aboard. Get your passport out just in case.'

She got her pack down and began to look for her passport, and that's when the train came to a sudden halt. I could hear doors opening and closing. Passengers getting off and on and the platform filling with people carrying luggage and meeting friends, relatives. After about five minutes of almost complete silence, I heard a door opening somewhere down the train. Another few minutes and two policemen appeared from somewhere up the corridor. One of them opened the compartment door and began to ask for passports, documents etc. They didn't speak in English, but then they didn't have to. It was obvious what was going on. Everyone around us was looking in bags and pockets for their papers, passports or whatever ID they had with them. Josie and I handed our passports over and they were looked at briefly then handed back to us, then they continued down the train. I breathed a big sigh of relief. I'm not sure why.

Josie turned to me. 'Why were they checking our ID?'

I shrugged.

Petar said, 'It's the border crossing into Montenegro.'

'It's a wonder they didn't check all the baggage as well,' I said and gave a short laugh.

About an hour later, our train pulled into Podgorica; it said so on the station platform. It also said Подгорица. Just as well the Roman alphabet was there too otherwise we'd be lost.

With our backpacks on our shoulders, we left the compartment and strolled down the corridor towards the door. As I was ahead of Josie, I pulled down the window and stuck my head out. I'm scanning the platform for any sign of suspicious-looking characters. Well, that's probably half the population of the town. We'll hire a car here and head off to explore this country of Montenegro, but first we have to find a place to stay. As we exited the station, Josie spotted a hotel across the street. We headed there and booked a double room for two nights.

Inside our room there was a balcony and it looked out over a courtyard where the outdoor part of the restaurant was located. We were no sooner inside the door, when Josie made a beeline for the balcony. She opened the sliding glass door and dropped her backpack on the floor where she stood and gasped. 'Gosh! Look at those awesome views Sam.'

I joined her there, my pack slowly sliding off my shoulder onto the floor. I had to agree. It was a breathtaking sight; those mountains. I crossed to the balustrade and, as I looked below to the courtyard, I could see that only a few tables were occupied. I was starved, not having had a decent meal all day.

She said nodding, 'I like it here.'

'Yeah, me too,' I said. 'I can't wait to eat though.'

I turned away from the balcony and threw my pack onto the bed closest to the window, then went into the en suite bathroom to freshen up. I washed my face and fixed my hair in its usual ponytail.

Josie came in at my back. 'Glad we found that bug.'

'Yeah,' I agreed. Then something occurred to me. I don't know why I didn't think of this earlier. That bug that we found. Seemed just a little too easy to find. Maybe we were supposed to find it. Maybe there's another one to yet find. We didn't check Josie's pack thoroughly. I said, 'Something I just thought of.' I stepped aside to let her get to the sink.

As she fixed her own ponytail, she asked, 'What?'

I told her.

She shrugged. 'You found it. What more do you want?'

'Let's have a look at your pack?'

'Pardon?' She just stood there with an incredulous expression.

I returned to the bedroom, but just as I reached for her pack that was lying on her bed, she had pushed in in front of me. She grabbed the pack before I could react and clutched it to her chest.

'Josie, what are you doing? I just want to check your pack,' I said reaching for it.

She turned her back to me.

'Josie, what the hell's the matter with you?' I reached for it again.

She moved away from me. 'You have the bug already.'

'Look, if there's another one.....'

She cut me off. 'Is this you being paranoid again? Leave it for God's sake.'

I reached for her pack. 'Come on. Give it here?'

'No! She insisted.

'Why won't you give it to me? What's with you anyway?' I'm getting closer to her now.

'What's with you?'

I'm beginning to lose my cool with this girl. 'Give me the pack now or I'll be forced to take it from you.'

That incredulous look again. 'What! Don't be ridiculous.' She started to back away from me now.

I followed her. 'I don't want to have to do this, but if I have to take it by force, you could get hurt.' I'm half bluffing.

She started shouting at me now. 'You're crazy; you know that? You should be locked up!'

'I beg your pardon?' Now I've lost it for sure.

She was about to turn away from me, when I took this opportunity to tackle her. I made a dive at her legs and brought her down onto her bed on her front. She had landed heavily on her pack that was still clutched to her chest. She let out a scream and started to cry. She let go of the pack now and I began pulling out the contents.

'What the hell?' I cried when the strong smell of mom's perfume hit my nostrils. I don't believe this. She's still crying as I rummaged through her things. My hand touched a small cardboard box and I recognised it immediately as mom's perfume.

'Josie, what the hell is this?' I opened the box and.... the bottle cap was broken, and most of the liquid had been soaked up by the box. I was fuming. As she was still lying on her front, I turned her onto her back and sat astride her and pinning her hands above her head on the bed. 'Why Josie? Why didn't you just ask? You had to go and steal it!'

She struggled and fought me. Jesus, she was like a wild animal! In seconds, I found myself being thrown off of her and onto the floor on my back. I gave a loud gasp as it knocked the wind out of me. I guess my self defence lessons were working for her now. I was back on the bed again in a flash, but by the time I got back onto it, she had escaped to the other side of the room towards the door. She was just about to open it when I caught her up. I grasped her arm and tried to pull her with me back to the bed. It's better if we fight on that rather than on the floor. Well I guess she had other ideas. She pushed me backwards and I lost my balance. I'm on the floor on my back again; Josie on top. She's sitting astride me now and started hitting me on the head with her fists. I had to protect my face from the blows, so I grasped both her wrists and in seconds, had rolled her over onto her back, still holding her wrists. She broke free and went for my hair. I felt the clasp go and my hair came down over my face. I grasped her hands and tried to pull them off my hair as it was hurting bad.

I screamed at her to stop, but she only screamed back. 'You bitch! I hate you, I hate you!' She was sobbing and screaming at me.

I shouted, 'Shut up, shut up!'

Then I found myself on my back again with her on top. She started hitting me again with one hand, while the other pulled angrily at my hair. I'd had enough of this now. I grasped her hair and pulled on it tight. She screamed even more loudly, and cursed and swore at me.

I rolled her off me intending to get on top again, but only succeeded in letting her escape. She made another dash for the door, but I was up on my feet in seconds. I caught her around the waist with both arms and refused to let go, then I lifted her off her feet and she started kicking my legs, then one hand went to my hair and began to pull on it hard. I screamed and shouted at her to stop. I turned around, still holding onto her, and took her back to the bed, where I threw her onto her front. She just lay there and cried.

I had an idea. I thought, *'Time for some serious lessons in self defence.'* I went into my pack and found the Scotch tape. I sat astride her on the base of her spine, then drew both her hands round to her back and began to bind them with the tape.

She screamed at me. 'What are you doing!'

I shouted at her. 'You gotta fight me Josie!'

'What!'

I reached under her top and unclipped her bra, then began pulling on it.

She began screaming at me again. 'What are you doing!' she shouted and cried at the same time.

'You have to fight me!' I shouted back.

Once I had her bra free, I rolled it up and, pulling her head back by the hair, stuffed it into her mouth. She began to scream in her throat now and wriggling under me, trying her best to get free, then I wound the Scotch tape round and round her head to keep the bra in place. I pulled her top up over her head, then I turned her onto her back and went straight for her belt buckle. She's screaming in her throat again. I sat astride her again and unzipped her. She tried to kick out but I was sitting on her legs, and that was when I pulled her jeans down.

I was just about to get up off of her and tell her how vulnerable she was now, when she realised her opportunity. She kicked out at me. It caught me between the legs and knocked the wind out of me. The pain was excruciating. I rolled off the bed and landed on my back on the floor clutching myself. As I hit the floor, I could see with peripheral vision, a semi-naked figure roll out of the opposite side of the bed. I heard her struggle with something then she was up on her feet. She just sat on the edge of the bed and cried. Her top was still around her neck; her jeans at her ankles. I got up from my position on the floor and got onto the bed. She moved farther away from me. I went into the secret zipper pocket that I have sown into my jeans at the back and took out the spring-loaded knife that I carry there just in case. I cut her hands free then I started on her face.

She didn't say anything at all to me at this point as I handed her bra to her. She put it on and fixed her clothing.

I stood up and looked down on her. 'You'll have to learn to fight back Josie.'

She stood up and fixed her jeans, then she stared me straight in the eye. I was about to say something to her, when she slapped me hard! Yep, it was hard all right – almost knocked me over – on the right side of my face. I reddened. I think she's mad at me.

With a raised warning finger, she said angrily, 'Don't ever do that to me again or I'll…!' She left the sentence unfinished, then turned on her heel and marched to the door. She turned and gave me a dirty look as she opened the door and disappeared into the corridor.

I sighed and adjusted my clothing, then headed for the bathroom, but just as I was almost there, I heard a voice outside the door say something and in seconds, she was back in the room again. She pushed me aside and went into the bathroom where she slammed the door shut in my face.

'Was it something I said?' I thought, then crossed to the dressing table and began to brush out my hair.

I heard her using the shower. I found my hair clasp on the floor and fixed my ponytail again, then crossed to the bathroom door. I tapped on it. I shouted, 'I'm going down to eat! See you there?'

There was silence from her. If she heard me she wasn't responding.

I shrugged as I said half to myself, 'Oh well, suit yourself.' I went down to the restaurant.

Chapter 17.

I found an empty table easily enough since only about seven out of the twenty or so tables were occupied anyway. I could see a bandstand off to the left as I pulled out a chair to sit down. Were we going to be entertained? I hoped so. Music would be nice to accompany the meal.

I had only just made myself comfortable, when a waiter arrived, but I hadn't heard him approach, and as a consequence, I jumped with my hand at my throat. 'Oh, sorry, I was miles away,' I said reddening and a gave short embarrassed laugh.

He was middle-aged and wore a green velvet jacket and black pants. He asked, 'Would you like a drink?'

I nodded. 'Yes thank you.'

'Wine or….?'

I cut in with, 'Em…, wine. Red please.'

He nodded and retreated back into the building.

I'm thinking Josie won't be needing any fighting skills here, now that we've thrown those jerks off our trail. We can relax and enjoy what's left of our vacation. At the same time, I wanted to get her newly-acquired self defence skills perfected. She may need them in the future.

As I waited for the waiter to return, I could see a couple of guys across the courtyard at the bandstand rigging up microphones and speakers. Just then, the waiter arrived back with the wine. He removed the stopper with a corkscrew and was about to pour it into a glass for me to taste.

I said, shaking my head, 'No, it's OK. I'll take it.' It was from Croatia.

He nodded and left me to study the menu. I filled my glass and took a sip.

Someone began testing the microphone now by hitting it with his hand. It was very loud, and it made me jump. I think we all did. I began to study the menu. Maybe it'll take my mind off recent events. I'm feeling guilty about confronting Josie in the way that I did, but I was so angry with her for taking my perfume! She'll be in a huff for the rest of the day. Probably won't speak to me for days now.

The menu – thank goodness – was printed in English, and German. I guess this hotel would see a lot of German and English-speaking tourists.

What to eat? There's so much here. At the top of the first page; soup or 'supa' as they call it here. 'Jagnjeća Supa' – 'Lamb Broth'. Sounds good to me. I looked around at the other occupied tables but Josie still hadn't appeared. Maybe she's gone to the bar or chatting up some guy. I don't care. Good to have some 'alone time' for once.

Next up on the menu, for the main course; 'Pastrva' - 'Freshwater trout'. My mouth was watering just thinking about it. Now to dessert. I ran my finger down the menu; 'Oris na vareniku' - '*rice pudding*'.

The guys at the bandstand were setting up their instruments now. First out was a keyboard, then a drum kit, double bass and mandolin. Well it looked like a mandolin to me anyway.

The waiter arrived back and took my order. As he was leaving, I looked around again, this time over my left shoulder. Josie was sitting at a table with her back to me on her own. I don't know if she had ordered or not. I wasn't about to join her anyway. She must have seen me sitting here, and will still be in a mood.

I suddenly thought of Bob and wondering where he'd be now. I don't know why I should have thought of him at all. He didn't get to Zagreb after he said he would. Well, maybe he got tied up with his girlfriend.

I looked toward the bandstand and could see an elderly guy dressed in a sparkling grey-blue jacket and matching pants approaching the microphone. Was this the lead singer? Another, dressed in a light-blue jacket and matching pants sat himself at the drum kit, then several others dressed in the same uniform joined them. On a signal from the guy at the microphone, the band started up. It was a slow one, and then the guy at the microphone began to sing. It was such a haunting melody, but I didn't recognise it at all. It reminded me of a Greek number I'd heard somewhere, and maybe it was too. No matter, it was beautiful. The music was loud and some people were dancing I noticed.

The waiter came back with my soup and a small baguette. As I cut into it with my knife, my cellphone rang. I jumped and almost dropped the knife into the soup. That's because I hadn't heard it go off due to the music, but I did feel the silent ring vibrator in my front pocket.

I took out the phone. 'Hello?' I had to cover my other ear.

'Hi Sam, it's me, Bob.'

This time I did drop my knife, but it was onto the tabletop. 'Oh, hi there,' I said brightly. 'Where are you?'

'Belgrade. Where are you?'

'Podgorica.'

'Err… where's that?'

'Montenegro?'

'Right. OK.' He didn't seem too sure where that was either.

'So, you going to see your girlfriend again?' I said teasing.

There was silence for a few seconds, then, 'No, actually I thought we might meet up somewhere. Are you free any time soon?'

I looked across to Josie, or at least to where she ought to have been, then I spotted her dancing with a guy old enough to be her dad. I almost giggled out loud. 'Yeah, I'm free - for now.'

'OK, so what about Josie?'

'What about her?'

'Is she suitably preoccupied? I'd like us to meet alone, if that's OK with you?'

'Oh yeah, you bet. She's preoccupied all right.' I gave a short laugh. 'And sure, I'd like to meet you somewhere Bob, preferably without Josie.'

'Good. Em… you two fall out or something?'

'Yep.' I sighed. I hesitated. 'It was just a silly argument over a bug. It was getting in our hair.'

'You fought over an insect?' he asked disbelievingly.

I sighed again. 'In a manner of speaking. It was in my pack and I just wanted it out of there. Don't like bugs.' I nodded.

'But it's gone now?'

'Yep. Kinda flew off you know?' I almost laughed, but caught myself in time. I suddenly realised that the music had stopped, then I remembered that my soup was getting cold. I started on it again, and holding the phone to my left ear. Yep it was cold, well lukewarm anyway.

People started to clap and cheer. I just had to join them. I put the phone down face up on the table and stood up, clapping loudly. Hey, I just have to get his autograph to add to my collection. I heard Bob say something, but I didn't catch it due to the noise.

I picked the phone up and sat down again. 'Sorry, what did you say?'

'I was asking where you'd like to meet me. Where are you staying?'

I told him the name of the hotel. I started on my soup again and managed to finish it off quickly. Just then the waiter arrived back and took my plate away.

'OK. Just made a note. Well I'll see you later then Sam?'

'Yeah, sure. Just don't wait too long. We'll be moving on soon.'

'Where?'

I shrugged. 'Oh I don't know. Zadar I think. We have to head back to the coast anyway to catch our flight.'

'Of course. Well bye for now.'

'Bye.' I clicked off the phone and pocketed it.

Now my full concentration was on the guy at the microphone. He had just started another number. It too was beautifully sung. Yep, I just have to get my hands on one of his albums.

The waiter arrived back again with my trout. He had brought a side salad too consisting of the usual lettuce, tomato, etc. I could also see coleslaw there. I carefully avoided that. Yuck! I started on the trout. It melted in my mouth.

Later, when I had just finished off my rice pudding, the band broke off for a break after having played at least six more numbers, none of which I knew. I just had to get his autograph. The only problem was that I didn't have my autograph book with me. Well I didn't expect I'd be needing it. What was I expecting him to sign? I'll cross that bridge….. I stood up and waved nervously at the lead singer to get his attention. He spotted me signalling to him. My heart missed a beat; well several actually. As he came across to me, I had a large lump in my throat, then it slowly dissolved. I picked up my napkin. Will he sign this?

Gosh, he was so handsome up close. He was old enough to be my dad. I had a broad smile on my face; so had he. I wasn't sure what to say to him at first, then I went for it.

'Hi. I wondered….,' I swallowed hard; my voice almost gave up completely, 'if I could have your autograph please?' There, I said it. I smiled at myself for being so brave. I added nervously, 'It's for my daughter.' I nodded. I'm a terrible liar. I could feel my ears and face burn.

He said, 'Sure. It's a pleasure. What's her name?' Was he intending to write it on a slip of paper?

'Oh, em….' I hesitated then offered him the napkin to sign. 'I don't have my autograph book with me. It's Sam.' Oops! Did I mess up or what?

He just smiled, then reached into his inside pocket and produced a CD in its jewel case. He opened it and began to write on the cover sleeve. He said, 'To Sam from Oliver Stojanović'.

I can hardly contain my excitement. As he handed it to me I said, 'Thank you. Em…. how much?'

He shook his head. 'It's OK. It's free. I always give my new albums away free to the first person to ask me for my autograph.'

'Oh thank you.' I thought I heard someone at my back. I turned to see Josie standing there. No!

She pushed in in front of me. 'Hi. Could I get your autograph please?' She held a small book out to him to take.

He nodded taking it from her. 'Sure.'

As he signed the book, I shot her a sideways glance. She had a self satisfied look plastered on. I'll knock it off her face. I said, looking him up and down, 'Like your outfit. Very nice.'

He smiled. 'Thanks. Not everyone compliments my outfits. I have several with me.'

'Really? Are they all like this?'

He nodded. 'I'll take you backstage if you like and show them to you.'

My smile just got broader. 'Oh, thank you. That would be cool.'

I heard Josie utter, 'Humph,' then march off.

I smiled to myself. 'Serves you right Josie.'

He said, 'We were just going for refreshments. Care to join me?'

I nodded, 'Sure. Why not?'

He hesitated. 'What's your name by the way?'

I smiled. 'Sam Winter.' Josie will be jealous. Serve her right.

We walked back the hotel and into the bar where he spoke to the bartender. He sat on a stool. I sat next to him.

'What part of the States are you from?' he asked.

'Mendocino, California. It's a very small town. You've probably never heard of it though.' I wrinkled my nose and gave a short laugh.

'What will you have?'

I shrugged. 'Oh, err…. What you having?'

'I only drink beer when I'm on the road.'

I nodded. 'Sure. Beer would be fine. Thank you.'

'Yes, I know your town. I stayed there once on vacation.'

The bartender placed two beers on the bar.

Now he had my full attention. 'Oh really? When was that?' I took a sip of my beer.

'It's a few years ago now. One of the reasons for going there was to visit a second-hand book store on the south side of town. I was…..'

I cut him off, spluttering through my beer. 'That's my dad's shop. There's only one second-hand book store there.'

'Wait a minute.' He thought for a moment. 'I remember you now. You were about…. nine or ten. I was looking for a set of the "Complete works of Dickens" and…..'

'And I found them for you. Gosh, was that really you?'

He cut in with, 'Yes! Then you managed to drop them on the floor as you carried them to the counter.' He laughed. 'It really is a small world isn't it?'

I reddened.

'That was before I was famous of course.' He laughed again. 'I'll take you to my dressing-room now.'

I left my half-finished beer on the bar and followed him through a door on the right. We were just about to push through another door when it suddenly opened, and a twenty-something guy wearing the band's uniform and sporting a very short haircut came out. He was a bit of a hunk.

'This is Paulo my drummer.' He introduced me to him.

I shook his hand.

He just smiled back.

Then it was into the lounge. There were two of the band here. They stood up as we came in. Another couple of hunks. I almost laughed. Can't believe I'm doing this.

He said, 'Velimir, my keyboardist and Damir on double bass and strings.'

I shook their hands too. They both nodded and smiled.

We left the lounge and headed for his room. Oliver had just opened the door, when someone arrived at our backs. We both turned to see a guy built like a mountain and with shaven head standing there. He said something to Oliver and left again.

'That was Dario. He's responsible for security.'

He left the door open as he crossed the room to open a walk-in closet. I followed him there. There, hanging on a rail the entire length of the closet were more identical costumes. They only differed in their colour.

'Gosh, they're beautiful!' I exclaimed. I turned to him. 'How long are you staying in town?'

'I'll be leaving for Croatia tomorrow. Heading back home to Pula.'

'Oh, really? That's where we're headed next week to catch our flight.' My excitement was mounting.

'Well, maybe you would like to go to my concert there? It'll be in the Roman amphitheatre.'

'Oh, that would be so cool! I squealed. 'How long are you there for?' My heart was thumping.

'I'm there for the whole week. It won't cost you anything, and you can bring your friend too.'

'But without a ticket….?' I trailed off wondering.

He patted my arm. 'I'll fix it, don't worry.' He crossed to the door and opened it, then called for someone.

Dario appeared again in the doorway. Oliver mentioned my name and explained something to him in Croatian and he nodded his understanding.

Dario left again and Oliver turned back to me. 'Just turn up at the gate. Dario will be there. He'll remember you. Just tell him your name and that's all you have to do.'

I didn't know what to say except, 'Thank you.' I shook his hand.

He said smiling, 'You're welcome.'

I still clutched the CD that he had given me. I held it up and said smiling, 'I'll frame it. Thanks again for the….' I felt myself begin to sniffle, then I stood up quickly on tiptoes and kissed him on the left cheek.

He said, taking me by the arm, 'Let's get back to the bar.'

As we entered through the door into the bar, the thing that took my attention was Josie standing there chatting up one of the band members. I made straight for my beer that still stood on the bar and downed it in one. It was flat!

I heard Oliver say behind me, 'We're going back outside shortly.'

I turned to him with a smile. 'Oh, OK,' I said absently.

'Enjoy the rest of the evening, and I'll see you at the concert in Pula?'

'Yeah, thanks.'

He went back outside.

I turned my attention to Josie again. She had just finished with the guy she'd been talking to.

Taking her by the arm I said excitedly, 'Some fantastic news Josie!'

She said surprised, 'Eh? What?'

We went outside and made for the outdoor restaurant.

I said, 'Oliver is in concert in Pula next week when we're there. He's invited us to it. Isn't that fantastic?'

I heard her say at my back, 'Cool! How much are the tickets? Where is it being held?' She strolled beside me.

'Nothing. We've just to turn up at the gate of the Roman amphitheatre and they'll let us in. A good ending to our vacation huh?' I sat down at a table; Josie opposite.

'Yeah. Sounds fantastic.' She changed the subject. 'Guess what?' That little cute smile appeared again.

I didn't say anything, then I spotted a waiter approaching. He wanted to know if we wanted refreshments. We asked for beer.

She whispered, 'I've got all of their autographs!' She giggled.

'What?' I couldn't believe my ears.

She nodded giggling again.

I said smugly, 'I've got his autograph too and a free album CD.'

The waiter arrived with our beer.

All she said as she picked up her glass was, 'Humph!'

I smiled and picked mine up too. 'And I got to kiss him on the cheek.'

'He's old enough to be your dad,' she giggled.

I said in a slightly irritated tone, 'Pardon?'

She laughed. 'Did you see his crow's feet?'

Keeping a straight face, and only just managing to prevent myself from spluttering through my drink, I said, 'I'm not in a habit of looking at other people's feet, thank you very much.' Then I couldn't contain myself any longer and spluttered, and laughed.

'*What?*' she spluttered too.

Just before I broke down in a fit of laughter, I said, 'Gosh. How do you think he gets them to fit into those shoes?' I laughed and laughed. She joined in.

She said, rising to her feet, 'Let's go upstairs. We can relax and listen to the music there on the balcony.'

I agreed, but when I tried to stand, I found my head was swimming. Josie spotted me swaying a little and put an arm around my waist. I picked up our glasses with my free hand and we made for our room. Josie opened the doors for us.

When we got in, I made straight for the balcony. There were two reclining chairs here. Just before we entered the building to come upstairs, I had heard the band start to play again. We stood there watching them perform and enjoying the music, then, a tune I thought I recognised. Yep, I did too; it was Yankee Doodle Dandy. I waved to get his attention. Josie joined me. Oliver waved back.

'What a guy,' I said as I finished off my beer.

'So what did you two do back there?' she asked finishing off her drink.

I sat on my lounger. 'Josie, he was in Mendocino when I was about ten. He visited our shop. Isn't that scary?'

She didn't say anything.

'He remembered me dropping the books on the floor that I went to fetch too.'

She sat down. 'Somebody remembering you? Yeah that's scary all right.' She laughed.

I punched her on the thigh. 'Shut up,' I said and laughed.

We listened in silence to a couple more numbers that neither of us recognised, then I felt my eyelids close and that's all I remember until I woke up next morning.

Chapter 18.

I don't know if Josie slept right through the night or not, but she was certainly up and into the shower before I was. I could hear her singing to herself in there. I stripped off my clothes having slept in them last night, and made for the bathroom towel-wrapped.

I was just about to open the bathroom door when it opened suddenly. She said, 'Hey, what do you fancy doing today?'

I pushed past her and and tested the water temperature. 'Tell you when I'm done.'

I heard her close the door.

We had breakfast brought to our room. It's more private that way. It was left on a tray outside the door.

I dressed in my blue jeans and cropped white top; Josie her light-blue cropped top and low-cut white jeans. The white shows off her California tan, oh, and her cute little Celtic tattoo on her lower back.

We sat on the balcony to enjoy our meal. Josie found a tray next the TV and used that on her lap. I used the one that the breakfast arrived on. I put the breakfast on the coffee table between our chairs and poured the coffee into our cups.

'I thought we'd rent a car and explore the south,' I said as I buttered a slice of toast.

She shrugged. 'Sure.'

'May as well see some of this country before we set off for Croatia again. We're due there next week anyway.'

All these international hotels seem to serve up the same breakfast. This one we ordered consisted of bacon, fried egg, sausage, and fried bread. I like it but it wouldn't be my first choice of breakfast back home.

We were well into our meal when my cellphone rang its musical tone. 'Damn,' I said softly.

It was Bob. 'Oh, hi Bob. Thought you were joining us here?'

Josie's chewing on a bacon rasher and looking at me inquisitively.

'I would be, but something came up. Where are you heading next?'

'Renting a car today and exploring around, and I want to get some landscape photos before I go home, then moving back to Croatia. We have to be there next week anyway to catch our flight.'

'What town? Zadar I think you said yesterday?'

I looked at Josie. 'Zadar?'

She nodded as she looked at me over the rim of her cup.

'What about the photos Sam?'

'Em… we've still got them.' I hesitated, then quickly changed the subject. I told him about Oliver and our free concert in Pula.

'Oh you lucky people. How did you manage to pull that one off?' He laughed.

I laughed too. 'I made him an offer he couldn't refuse. What do you think?' I laughed again.

He laughed too. 'Don't tell me; you offered him your body, right?'

I said laughing, 'I beg your pardon? Well of course; wouldn't you?'

'I prefer the females thank you very much.' He laughed again.

'OK Bob,' I said laughing. 'I'll see you in Croatia. Bye.'

'What was that all about?' she said as she poured herself another coffee.

I looked straight ahead. 'He's meeting us in Zadar.' Well maybe not. Maybe his girlfriend will get in the way again.

She said, 'I wouldn't stake my life on it.'

I said seriously, 'You're jealous aren't you? Just because you can't get a guy.'

'We're not here to "get" guys. You said so yourself. Remember the soldiers?'

She stood up and took her tray into the bedroom, placing it beside the TV. I did likewise.

I said as I made my way to the bathroom, 'Yeah, but that was different.'

We left and made our way to an Avis Car Rental office. We came away with a light-blue Mercedes sports convertible. Yep, you guessed it; another manual shift.

As we headed out of the city, we passed the most lovely old buildings, some of which were in ruin. As we were passing an old church, my cellphone went off. I jumped. I don't know why I do that every time. I took it from my front pocket and handed it to Josie.

'Answer it.'

'What?' she asked with that puzzled expression of hers. She took it from me, then with a shocked expression she said, 'It's them.'

Oh God! My heart sank. I took the phone from her. 'What the hell do you want?'

Just then, I heard a clock chime in the church tower. It was a such a beautiful sound.

'So, we've finally caught up with you at last. I know where that church is, so it's only a matter of time before I get my men over there.'

I was silent. I'm trying to formulate a plan in my head, but so far.....

'OK,' he continued, 'this is the plan. You'll meet a roadblock at some point on the road south, then you'll get out and walk towards them where they will meet you halfway. You will have the photos with you.'

I said defiantly, 'Maybe, and then again maybe not.'

'In which case they'll just have to kill you!'

My heart was racing as I shouted, 'Go to hell!' I snapped off the phone. I said to Josie, 'Lets go.'

We took the main route south toward the Albanian border, but of course, we had no intention of going there. We didn't have visas for a start.

Up till now the scenery consisted of mainly flat land with the odd hill here and there, and quite green in places. Sometimes a lake, but no mountains to speak of. Lots of dry scrubby land that was probably the result of erosion over the centuries. You'd think nothing could possibly grow on this rocky limestone, but, surprisingly, even here, there were small shrubs and even some trees growing. In other places such as this particular area we were in now, there were a lot more trees growing, especially along the road ahead of us where it disappeared into them.

Josie spotted something and pointed to it off to our left. 'Stop!'

I couldn't see what she was pointing at. I had to stop the car. 'What is it?'

'Didn't you see the sign?'

'Em... what sign?' I really didn't see it. Well it didn't register with me anyway. My mind was elsewhere.

'Back there. Look!' She pointed to it again.

I had to back up. 'What's it say?' Then I knew when I drew parallel with it. It was a picture of a camera with a slash through it; 'NO PHOTOGRAPHY'!' Oh! I looked across to our left and could see a large lake, or it could have been the sea. On our right, a steep hill with very little vegetation and a few trees.

'You're not thinking of taking photos here are you?' she asked.

'What do you think? It'll only take a minute.' I found a suitable place to park the car on the right and stepped out.

Josie stepped out too and came around to my side. 'Sam, you can't. Suppose someone should come along?'

'I'll just go up there,' I said pointing to the hill, 'and hide behind one of those trees. You can keep lookout. You can do that can't you?'

'You're crazy. We'll be thrown in jail.'

I went to the trunk and opened it. Our packs were in there. I said, 'Josie keep watch.'

She joined me at the rear. 'I still think you're crazy.'

'Josie, you worry too much.'

I opened my pack and took my SLR out. I'm not sure why I felt uneasy, but this was one of those moments when you feel you're being watched. From where? I looked up the hill and I didn't see anything unusual, then across to the lake, again with the same result. I turned around to look behind and still nothing, then, almost simultaneously with Josie's exclamation, I spotted a white Fiat hardtop farther down the road on a bend and partially hidden by trees.

She said, 'Sam there's a white....'

I cut her off. 'I know,' I whispered. 'Get in the car and don't look at it.'

She did without protest.

I had a bad feeling about this. I'm not sure why. I closed the trunk, leaving my camera where it was on top of my pack, then got into the driving seat. Had the car moved since I had first seen it, or was my paranoid mind working overtime? Was it moving now? I couldn't be sure.

I said to Josie, 'What do we do if it is the police? We don't have any excuses.'

'But we didn't take any photos did we, so they can't do anything to us can they?' She didn't sound too confident about it.

'I don't know. You hear stories....' I broke off because I noticed that the car was now moving towards us slowly, and it was on the wrong side of the road – our side!

'What's he doing?' she asked.

'I hope it's not "them",' I said, my heart thumping.

How could that be? We got rid of the bug, so they can't follow us anywhere. I almost laughed out loud when I suddenly had visions of the pigeon landing somewhere inaccessible and them trying to trace it. I'm hoping it visits a police station. Maybe the same one that we'll end up in if we're not careful. The car increased speed now and eventually pulled up alongside us.

I thought with my heart doing a marathon, *'Oh my God. We're in for it now!'*

Josie's face was flushed; God knows how mine looked!

He opened his door and stepped out. He stood about six feet tall, and was about thirty-something with black wavy hair and moustache, and wore black pants and green sports shirt.

My heart was in my mouth and I had a large lump forming in my throat.

He put one hand on the door and said, 'Ah, you're American aren't you?'

Jesus, I couldn't speak. 'How the hell....!'

My thoughts are running wild now. How the hell could he know that? If this was one of 'them', why did he ask that? It has to be the police doesn't it? I'm confused and scared. My heart was thumping hard. I shot Josie a sideways glance. Her face was scarlet and she wasn't happy about this either. Are we going to be arrested? We haven't done anything wrong have we? We've just stopped here and it's all quite innocent. What was the purpose of the sign? No buildings here of any kind, so what were they trying to prevent people from photographing?

He hasn't shown any ID, so what's he playing at? Then he did! He said as he put his hand into his shirt pocket and pulling out a small wallet that he opened and flashed quickly before my eyes, 'Police.'

It was so quick, I only got a brief glimpse of it.

'Oh my God!' I thought quickly. *'What do we do now? Hope he doesn't think of looking in the trunk!'*

My shirt was sticking wetly to me. God, it was hot! I could feel beads of sweat running down the back and front of my shirt.

He began to walk slowly around the front of the car and when he had reached Josie's side he said smiling, 'All the way from America. It's a long way from home, isn't it girls?'

Josie was staring straight ahead. She refused to look at him standing there.

He said, one hand on Josie's door, 'Nice around here isn't it? So peaceful and quiet.' He started walking slowly towards the rear of the car.

Josie's looking at me apprehensively.

He continued, 'Very picturesque don't you think? Just right for pictures.'

He knows something. He suspects something, but he can't prove anything. He had now reached the trunk, then he stopped. I could see him in the rear-view mirror. He was looking down at the trunk. My heart was threatening to leap right out of my chest and make a dash for freedom! He ran his fingers over the paintwork then moved on slowly.

Back on my side again he said, 'Passports please?' His tone was becoming unfriendly.

I said in a croaky voice that was just barely audible, and my heart racing, 'They're in the trunk.'

I was just about to open the door to get out, when he stopped me. He was looking across to Josie who, I noticed, was covering something with her hand at her thigh. I couldn't think what she was doing at first, then I suddenly realised what it was; her camera was fastened there to her jeans' belt, dangling from its wrist strap.

He went around to her side. 'Camera please?'

As she unclipped the strap from her belt, that little cute smile appeared again on her lips. She's up to something; I know it. What the hell's she done? I hope whatever it is, it doesn't get us into any kind of trouble. She handed him the camera and he switched it on.

I'm thinking she didn't have time to take anything, or did she? I wasn't watching what she was doing before we hit that sign. I'm hoping to God that she hasn't done anything stupid. He just stood there looking down on her; studying her. She stared straight ahead but didn't say anything.

After about thirty seconds of thought he said, 'Get out of the car.'

He stood back for her to get out.

She did.

'You have another card somewhere. I want to see it.'

Did he see her take a photo? I hope to God she didn't!

She shook her head. 'Don't have any more.'

He held his hand out to her palm up. 'Card please?' A hesitation, then, 'All of them.'

I got out of the car and went round to where they stood. 'If she says she doesn't have any more then she doesn't.'

'Keep out of this!' He reached around to his back and produced a handgun!

'*Oh my God,'* I thought, my heart thumping hard.

He said to her, 'Put your hands against the car and spread your legs.'

She did.

He put the gun into his waistband at the front of his pants and began to frisk her starting at her ankles.

I said quickly, 'The others will be in her pack in the trunk.'

He didn't respond. He went up and down her legs twice, then his hand went into her back pockets, and her waistband at the back.

She said frantically, 'OK, OK. I'll show you where it is.'

He stood back.

I thought, *Josie. What the hell are you up to?'* We're going to be in deep shit if she's done anything stupid!

'Stand aside,' he said to her.

She did.

He began to feel down the back of the seat cushion. He seemed satisfied that it wasn't there. As he turned to face her, his eyes went directly to her chest. She had a worried look again. He began to search her front pockets now, then her waistband. Still nothing.

He demanded, indicating her chest with the point of his weapon, 'Take it off!' He meant her top.

Josie had just turned a darker shade of scarlet. She hesitated then crossed her arms and pulled off her blue top.

After telling her to turn around for him slowly, he seemed satisfied that she didn't have anything tucked away in her brassiere.

'You can put it on again,' he said. 'We can go to the trunk now.'

The three of us went to the rear of the car, and I opened it.

'Passports please?' He held out his hand.

I opened my pack, having first laid my camera on the floor. He picked it up and switched it on. He won't find anything there because I didn't get the chance to take anything. Whilst his attention was on the camera, I turned to Josie who had her two hands well down into her pack and was doing something there. She winked at me and that cute smile appeared again. She's going to get us arrested yet!

He said, 'OK. Passport?'

I had to go into the zippered pocket where I keep it. Meanwhile Josie was emptying her pack onto the floor of the trunk. He stepped around me and began to rummage through her things, leaving nothing out.

I had found my passport, but I had to stand and watch him attending to her.

She said suddenly, 'Oh shit! Isn't that just....?' She was looking at her camera screen.

'What?' he looked up surprised.

'Battery. Damn! Wish I had more with me, and no way of charging them out here.' She sighed heavily and shook her head in mock defeat.

I thought, *'What are you up to Josie?'*

He just stood there biting his lip, then he said, 'You Americans are very devious. You could be spies for all I know.'

I handed my passport to him. 'What?' I asked disbelievingly.

'You cause trouble wherever you go. You can't be trusted.'

I said sarcastically, 'Gee, I didn't have a choice of birthplace, but hey, I'll try to be careful next time around. Guess I wasn't thinking straight huh? Damn! I'll have to give myself a good mental thrashing....'

He interrupted. 'Passport?' he said to Josie.

She handed it to him. He examined both of them for a few seconds then returned them to us.

He said to Josie, 'You must have other batteries.' He began to search.

Josie found another two lying loose amongst her clothing. She took out the 'dead' ones and 'accidentally' dropped one on the floor. It rolled away from her out of her reach. She had to climb into the trunk to retrieve it. When she came out again, she had two batteries in her hand, but which two? I was confused. *'Oh God I hope.....'*

My thoughts were cut short by Josie putting the 'new' batteries in the camera, then she handed it to him. He turned it on, then demanded another card. She found one after about a minute, and handed it over. He took out the original one and inserted the 'new'. No sooner had he done that, when the camera screen shouted, 'low battery'!

'Thank you God,' I thought with a big mental sigh of relief. Or should that have been, 'Thank you Josie?'

He seemed agitated, but just before he could say anything more, we heard a voice from a police car radio. It was his. He went to answer it.

I said to Josie, 'About time we made ourselves scarce. I've had enough of this.'

She nodded.

I closed the trunk and we both stood there waiting for him to return. I looked at Josie; she was staring at the ground lost in thought.

When he did return less than a minute later, he said, 'You can go now.' He returned to his car and we to ours.

Did he get an order from someone to release us or what? We weren't caring; just relieved to get out of there with our skins intact.

I played Oliver's CD at a high volume. The world should hear this, and if they don't like it, tough! I was in a rebellious mood and didn't care!

As we sped along the highway at close to 80 mph, I put my arm around Josie's shoulders and pulled her close. I said to her – I had to shout over the music, 'Did you take any pictures back there?'

She turned to me, her little cute sexy smile appearing on her lips again, fixed me with her sparkling, vivid blue eyes and just nodded, then she turned away again. Just like that.

I thought, *'Oh my God!'* She could have got us arrested! 'Why did you take them when the sign.....?'

She cut me off. 'That was just before I saw it.'

'And the batteries?' I asked curiously.

She turned back to me, her smile still in place. 'One fresh, one used. The new ones were cooler, but the used ones had been in my hand so they were warm, so I could tell which were which. Simple. One used battery and one new! Just not enough power.'

I nodded. 'OK. What I'd like to know is how he knew we were American before we had even uttered a word?'

'We handed our passports over to the desk clerk at the hotel didn't we?' she suggested. 'The receptionist took a note of the details in there. Maybe they were passed on to the police?'

'Secret Police more like it. I didn't care for his attitude. Anyway, not much we can do about it now. It's over.'

About an hour later, trees, sand and limestone desert was all around us again. A river on our right snaking out of view through the trees, and the road disappearing around a rocky outcrop. I stopped the car here but didn't turn off the ignition. There was no traffic hereabouts anyway. Seemed deserted at first, then I thought I heard something. Could have been a chopper, then I realised that it was and was somewhere close by although I couldn't see it yet. The sound died or faded away.

'What's up?' she asked.

I didn't reply. I was listening out for the chopper. I'm not sure why. Just a feeling I had. They're such noisy things, you think they're much closer than they really are.

I hit the gas and we moved on. My mind was on what that guy had said on the phone earlier, but I was determined not to let it get to me. I have to keep a cool head if we're going to have a confrontation with these bastards.

We had just rounded a right-hand bend in the road when Josie shouted, 'Sam! Look!'

She pointed ahead, and there, sitting astride the highway and completely blocking it, was a small red, four-seater chopper! I stopped the car immediately and tried to think what to do. My mind was in a whirl. It's all happening too quickly for me. I have to calm down and concentrate.

'What are we going to do Sam?' she asked, panic in her voice. 'We don't have any weapons.'

'I do. The knife in my jeans, but we'd have to get up close and personal for it to be effective, and I've no intention of doing that.'

She shrugged. 'So we just sit here and wait for them?'

I nodded. 'Yep,' I replied looking straight ahead.

Just then, a door opened on the side of the aircraft and three male figures dressed in dark suits stepped out. They were all around the same height; 5 – 8. There was a fourth still in the aircraft, presumably the pilot.

'What did they say on the phone?' She unbuckled her belt.

'Put it back Josie.'

She did.

I told her about meeting us halfway and handing over the pictures.

'You going to?'

With a smug look plastered on I said, 'Nope.'

I'm intending to wait till they get about halfway, then hitting the gas hard and knocking them down like skittles on a bowling alley. I voiced this to her.

She said swallowing hard, 'I don't like this Sam.'

I said, 'You think I do?'

The three stooges began to walk up the highway towards us. They were spread out across the road. Neither one of them had made any attempt to draw a weapon. I'm assuming that they're armed. That'll change when they realise what our intentions are, so my plan has to work first time, because we won't get a second crack at this.

The one on our left appeared to have a slight limp and was trailing a little behind his companions. The one on our right was striding ahead. I reckoned he was in charge, so it's just a matter of taking him out first and playing the rest of it by ear. Isn't it?

I said to Josie, 'When we see the whites of their eyes, I'm hitting the gas hard, and when I say "duck", I mean "duck", OK? When I shout roll, you open your door and roll out, snatching up his weapon, then get your ass in here ASAP. Got it?'

Her face was white as a sheet and I thought she was going to throw up. She just nodded and licked her lips.

I didn't know if Josie could handle a weapon or not, so I asked her. 'Ever fired a weapon?'

She nodded. 'Dad took me out when I was 11 and taught me how to use a handgun.' She hesitated. 'I can shoot a bottle at a hundred yards you know!'

My heart was thumping. 'What! That's it? Josie....'

'Yeah. Sorry. Didn't think I'd ever need it. Didn't get much practice either. Mendocino isn't exactly San Francisco.'

I nodded. 'Well, we'll just have to hope we get lucky and they're out of practice too, then we'll be more evenly matched huh?'

She started to sniffle. She pulled a Kleenex from her pocket and dabbed her eyes.

'Not now Josie. You have to keep your nerve. Don't loose your cool and just concentrate, OK?'

She turned. 'I've never killed anyone before Sam.'

'If they start shooting at us, you will.'

They were closer now and still there was no move to draw weapons. They're thinking we're going to be easy meat, but they're in for a surprise. They'll be wondering why we haven't made a move to get out of the car.

I noticed that the chopper's blades were still turning fast, so no doubt they're intending to make a quick departure from the scene once they've dealt with us, or maybe they'll take us off to some hideout and…. I don't want to think about it!

Now they're a little more than halfway to us. They stopped abruptly and the one on the right put his hand inside his jacket.

I thought quickly, *'Oh my God, this is it!'*

My knuckles were white on the wheel as I tensed myself for the action to come. Josie watched me take a deep breath and put the car into third gear, then I hit the gas to the floor. I could hear the tyres screeching and blue smoke billowed around us we shot off down the highway towards our intended goal, and that's when they drew weapons. The one on our right aimed his weapon carefully, but the one in the middle hesitated as if awaiting instructions.

I shouted to Josie to duck; she did! I was doing about 60 by the time I had reached them! There was, I could see, alarm and complete surprise on the faces of those three jerks. I drove directly at my intended victim. He tried to jump backwards out of my path, but I swung the wheel to the right and struck him hard. He flew up into the air and landed heavily, crying out as he hit the deck, and that's when I shouted to Josie to roll. She did and vanished from my view. I swung the wheel to the left, hitting the brake hard. The car's rear swung around and hit the second guy hard. He shouted and fell onto the ground. I brought the car to a sudden halt and shouted for Josie. She didn't answer. The goon with the limp had his weapon out now. I know this because I found it pressed against my right temple. I froze! Damn! This wasn't supposed to happen. Hey, did I mess up again?

He demanded, 'OK, get out of the car now!' He sounded mad. Yep, I think he was too.

I froze again. Would he shoot a woman in the head? Probably. These guys have no manners at all! Just then, I heard a shot ring out very close to my ear. I thought I'd been shot! I also heard a scream and the goon holding the gun dropped it right into my lap. I said surprised, 'Oh, thank you!'

He staggered back clutching his wrist – I guess the slug passed right through it - and disappeared from my view, and that's when Josie suddenly made an appearance by jumping headlong into the passenger seat. I hit the gas hard again and we shot up the road heading for the bend. I could hear the air-craft's engine getting louder. They're going to pursue us, but it'll take them a few minutes to get their injured into the chopper, so this was the moment for us to abandon the car and make for the trees. I have no intention of being pursued by a chopper on the highway. We'd be sitting ducks like this in an open top car.

I could hear the aircraft's engine increase speed now as I rounded the bend. There was good tree cover here off to our left on the side of the hill. We'll head for that. I brought the car to an abrupt halt and shouted to Josie to get out! She had remained in the same position as when she had entered the car; head pointing downwards towards the floor. She got out and came around to my side still clutching the weapon that she had 'borrowed' from the first goon we hit.

'Got spare clips too,' she said grinning at me.

'Nice work Josie,' I said as I got out of the car. Looking up into the trees I said, 'Let's get up there into the trees. We'll split up. Together we're too easy to hit.'

She didn't argue as we made for the wood on the hill. I reached it first.

I shouted, pointing to a thicker clump of trees farther up the hill from this one, 'Get up there Josie and when you hear me fire, shoot at the windshield; not the blades, OK?'

She nodded and ran up the hill to where I had indicated. I was already well hidden in the trees, but I had a clear view of the road. It was then that I heard the sound of the chopper's engines increase in volume. It suddenly appeared, rising over the rocky outcrop that I mentioned earlier and hovered above the car for a few seconds. They were trying to work out where we had got to, then it moved towards our hiding place. Did they see Josie? I could see one of the windows at the front on the passenger side slide open and what looked to me like an AK47, but then I could have been mistaken. I don't know much about guns. No matter; it was pointing down at me, then it opened fire! I threw myself flat on my back and rolled to the right. Just as well too, as several slugs thudded into the ground where I had just been standing. Several more buried themselves in the hillside. I couldn't help wondering, if they didn't want us dead, why were they shooting at us? Well, I'm not about to debate the point. I stood up and took careful aim, holding the weapon tight in both outstretched hands. I couldn't see my target – the pilot – properly because of reflections on the glass, but I pulled the trigger anyway. The windshield cracked and the aircraft wobbled a little. He flew off someways to my left then resumed course, that is, just before I heard a shot ring out from somewhere. I wondered where it had come from, then Josie came to mind, then I realised that it had come from the chopper. That was followed by several more shots. I ducked. Thankfully they all missed, but it was a close call as I could hear the slugs slam into the trees behind my head. Those shots were returned seconds later – five I think - as they echoed from farther up in the trees behind me. Then, I watched as the windshield of the aircraft suddenly disintegrated, then it seemed to wobble and take a nosedive towards Earth. The propeller blades began to snap off now as the aircraft flipped over and debris was flying at high speed in all directions. That's when I ducked further into the trees out of the way. Seconds later, there was the most almighty explosion as the gas tank went up! The bang was deafening and sent pieces of metal high into the air.

'Josie's done it!' I shouted, and danced out of the trees in delight. I looked around for her, and trying to keep out of the way of the fireball that suddenly engulfed some of the nearby vegetation. Then I spotted her running down through the trees above me.

She was totally out of breath by the time she had reached my side. 'We did it!' she shouted as she flung her arms around my neck and cried tears.

As I hugged her tight I said, 'No, you did it! I knew you could do it Josie!' I kissed her on the cheek then pulled away. 'Come on,' I said taking her by the hand and pulling her with me. 'Let's get back to the car.'

'Luckily your plan worked huh?' she said sniffling through a Kleenex from her pocket. 'Hey, did you have a plan "B"?'

I turned and smiled just as we reached the car but didn't say anything.

She sniffled again. 'You….. didn't have a plan "B", right?' she said slowly.

I examined the front of the car for damage. 'Nope.'

'O-K.' She sat herself in the passenger seat.

I noted that there was no damage to the car because the bumpers were made of rubberised plastic. Well at least we can return the car with a clear conscience.

I still held the handgun. I don't like guns and don't carry them at home. When I got back into the car, Josie was playing with hers. I said, 'We'll have to dispose of those.'

'Yeah, but where?'

I thought for a second. 'Remember the lake we passed? We can throw them in there.' I had no sooner uttered those words when I thought I heard the distant sound of a siren. Had someone called the police? A quick change of plan. 'Wipe them clean, then we'll go back up there,' I said pointing up to the trees where we'd just been, 'and throw them into the trees.'

I pulled a Kleenex from my pocket and began to wipe my weapon clean of fingerprints. Josie used the hem of her shirt. The siren was getting louder now, and I quickly realised that it wasn't one that I was hearing but at least two!

Josie opened her door and stepped out. She said desperately, 'Give me that!'

I handed my weapon to her and she broke into a run, heading for the trees and the still-burning chopper; black smoke billowing up into the sky. She threw the handguns as far as she could into the trees then returned to the car. I had the engine started before she even reached it, and once she was in her seat, I hit the gas hard to the floor. We shot off up the road heading back towards Podgorica and the hotel. As we sped through a crossroads, the police and several fire department vehicles were approaching us from the left, then headed off south, the way we had just come.

I turned to Josie with a big sigh. 'God, was that a close one or what?'

She just grinned back.

Chapter 19.

Next morning we left Podgorica around 9 o'clock and headed off to the Croatian border. No incidents this time thank goodness. We stopped off in Dubrovnik for lunch and found the most wonderful family-run restaurant. We sat outside in the sun, it being a very warm day; over 100°F according to my watch. We had left the car with the rental company and found the bus station where we left our packs at the Left Luggage Office.

After scrutinising the menu for what seemed like eternity, Josie handed it to me. As I scanned the first page, she put her hand on my wrist. 'Sam. I'm sorry about the perfume.'

'Oh yeah?' I said facetiously.

'Look. I didn't steal it, I....'

I interrupted as I looked at her over the menu. 'I know you didn't Josie.'

'I borrowed it, then somehow the top broke and it ended up in my pack. You were in the hospital then.'

'It just up and walked did it?' I heard my phone sound it's musical tone. I sighed. *'God. Who is it now?'* I thought with irritation.

It was Bob. 'Are you still in Podgorica?' he asked.

I didn't answer immediately. I settled on my favourite, fried squid. I'll start with a prawn cocktail I think. When I was ready I said, 'Pardon?' I'm winding him up.

'Podgorica? Are you...?'

I interrupted with, 'No.'

He said, sounding a little annoyed, 'So, where are you then?'

'It begins with a "D".' I'm just managing to stifle a giggle.

Josie saw me. She started to giggle too.

'A what? It's noisy here.'

I repeated what I had said.

'A "T" did you say?'

I started giggling too. '"D" as in Dubrovnik?'

'Oh, OK. So where are you now?'

I couldn't stop giggling now.

'Sam? You OK? Sounds as though you've had one too many.' He laughed.

'*Excuse* me?' I giggled again with my hand over the phone.

Josie is practically under the table. Her laughter is way out of control! Other clientèle are turning to look.

The waitress arrived now. She took our orders and departed again.

I heard Bob say, 'So where did you say you were?'

I sighed, 'I didn't. It's Dubrovnik. Having lunch in Restoran Dubrovnik. It's overlooking the harbour.' I added, 'You'd better hurry though. We're moving on as soon as we're done here.'

'Oh? I'll try to get there as soon as possible.'

I thought quickly, '*Not if your girlfriend gets in the way again you won't.*' 'We'll have a look at some of the sights too.'

'Listen Sam. I really want to see you again. I promise I'll be there as soon as I can. I'm on a train at the moment. I did get to Podgorica, but you were gone.'

I thought, '*Really?*' 'OK Bob. I'll see you around.' I snapped off the phone. Then, 'Maybe and maybe not,' I said half to myself. He's not going to be able to reach Dubrovnik any time soon, because there's no rail link to the city. I'm not holding my breath on that one.

The waitress returned with our food. I was quite hungry. I started on it immediately.

Josie leaned across the table to speak to me. 'Sam. That guy Bob? I'd dump him if I were you. He's a loser.'

I didn't say anything. Yep, I was getting tired of his broken promises all right. But at the same time, I really liked him. She's jealous; I know it. Just because she couldn't get a guy.

I noticed the waitress coming back with our next course. My fried squid; Josie's lasagne. I had boiled potatoes, peas and carrots; so had she. We both settled on a fruit trifle for our sweet.

At the end of the meal, I marched off to find the loo. I had just entered a cubicle when I heard my cell go off. I jumped. It sounded so loud in there. I noted that the signal was weak, so I retraced my steps to the restaurant to see if I could get a better one. I'm wondering who this is. Most likely mom wanting to know if we're OK. Unfortunately it wasn't her. I recognised the voice immediately. It was those bastards! It was the same voice again.

'We got news that our helicopter was being shot at.' He coughed. Sounded like a smoker. 'You really do like to live dangerously don't you Miss Winter?'

'You haven't seen me in action yet. Anyway that was Josie. You just don't wanna get in her way either.' I laughed.

'That wasn't a good move, what you did to Milos? He's not happy about it at all.'

'Hey that's real tough man. My heart goes out to him.' I continued, 'Listen you creep. You don't know where we are and we're not about to tell you, so you can go to *hell*!'

Just then, I heard a clock strike twice somewhere in a church nearby.

He was just about to say something when I butted in, 'And we're taking the evidence to the police, and there's nothing you can do about it, OK?' I added for impact, 'We could have done this before, but we just thought we'd let you sweat a little first.' I laughed. 'Bye-ee!' I hung up before he could say anything. It gave a me a whole lot of satisfaction just to say that, even if it wasn't the most intelligent thing to say just then. They can't touch us now.

When I returned to our table, I told Josie about the call. She just laughed. I joined her, then we walked out of there arm-in-arm and a spring in our step, safe in the knowledge that at last we had them beat. We could relax now and enjoy ourselves in this very old city of Dubrovnik, and not have a care in the world.

We headed off to the harbour. A cool breeze accompanied us as we made our way to the quayside. We just stood there looking out to sea, and to all those beautiful islands out there in the water just waiting for us. What I'd give for a swim right now in some secluded cove.

It was fairly crowded with visitors and many were eating ice cream. I turned to Josie who, I think, read my thoughts again. Yep, we just had to find this seller of ice cream, wherever they were. After some searching, Josie pointed out a shop selling candy and ice cream. We both bought a coronet; vanilla with raspberry through it. We started on them immediately then headed off to the harbour again.

We spotted a tall ship someways along the quayside, so we made for that. A large group of onlookers had gathered at the rail. We joined them there. We were all jostling for space at the edge of the quay. Josie was standing behind me taking photos of this magnificent ship when it happened; I was hit in the back by someone walking into me.

I turned quickly thinking it was Josie. 'Josie....!' I stopped myself as I realised that it wasn't her at all.

A young and very good-looking guy about early thirties, with black hair cut short stood there. He must have been about 5 foot 8 anyway. He wore a red t-shirt and white pants.

He said, 'Oh, sorry.' He had an east European accent.

I also realised that a large piece of my ice cream had dropped onto the top of my shirt just under the neckline.

'Oh sugar!' I said half to myself as I fished in my pocket for a Kleenex. I didn't have one.

He said quickly, as he put his hand into his pocket, 'Let me.....' He handed me a light-blue cotton handkerchief.

I just smiled and rapidly dabbed the ice cream, but much of it had already soaked into the fabric. I reddened as I returned his property to him. I said, again half to myself, 'That'll just have to do for now.'

'Sorry,' he apologised again. 'Can I interest you in something?' His hand was reaching into the pocket of his t-shirt as he said it.

'I'm sorry?' I said.

He handed me a small white card. He said, 'My business card. Maybe you would like to stay on the island where I work? It's a health spa resort.'

Josie materialised by my right side now, and my ice cream was wilting. I had to act quickly. As I licked the ice cream, I asked, 'Health spa resort did you say?' My smile just got broader. So did Josie's.

He said, 'Yes. It's quiet and secluded. We have all the amenities for a re-laxed and healthy vacation.'

I thought, *Well, after all we've been through lately, maybe we can relax and wind down now.'*

Josie said looking to him and back to me, 'Sounds like a real cool place to stay.'

He said, 'It's all females at the moment.'

Josie and I exchanged glances. She had a disappointed look as she said, 'What, no guys? How boring.'

I elbowed her in the ribs then nodded and smiled. 'Yeah,' I said brightly. 'Sounds good. OK.' I nodded again. 'Thank you. Could do with a proper rest for once.' I looked at the card; 'Marijan Kovačić' it stated. I'm wondering about the ferry. 'What time does the ferry sail?'

'There isn't one to the island. We get there by powerboat.' He pointed down the quay.

We looked to where he was pointing.

He said, 'We can go there right away if you like?'

We both nodded.

I said, 'Yeah that would be cool. Thank you.' I said, as I took Josie's hand and began walking backwards away from him, 'We'll have to get our packs from the bus station first though.' I had just finished my ice cream. Josie had consumed hers ages ago.

We returned to the bus station and collected our packs, then it was back to Marijan who was waiting for us by the tall ship. We followed him down the quay to his powerboat where he descended a rope ladder to get onto the craft. Unfortunately the ladder wasn't quite long enough to reach the deck and he had to jump down onto it. It was only a couple of feet. He told us to throw our packs down to him, then I followed him down, but just as I had reached the bottom rung, I misjudged. I thought that there was another rung to go yet, but there wasn't. I would have fallen backwards onto the deck, only Marijan caught me in time. I blushed and said, 'Thank you.'

Josie came down without a problem, but just as she was about to step onto the last rung, he lifted her off the ladder. She just smiled back. Her face was flushed, but that could have been due to the heat.

He got into the driving seat and I sat beside him on his left, Josie beside me. He started the engine and we took off at high speed. As the boat bounced up and down over the surface, Josie and I stood up and held on tight to the windshield with one hand. With my other one, I removed my hair clasp as did she and we just let the beautiful cool breeze run through our hair.

I'm wondering which island we were going to, so I asked him.

'You can't see it from here. It's farther out over there to the left!' he shouted over the roar of the engine and pointed.

I nodded.

I heard Josie shout, 'God Sam! It's fantastic!'

'Yippee! Sure is!' I shouted.

Another ten minutes and we were heading for a large island that was mainly covered by trees. As we approached, I thought I could just make out a large building through the trees. A house maybe? Again, the beach that we were approaching was rocky. Sand has to be imported from elsewhere to some tourist beaches.

As we cruised in towards the jetty, Marijan cut the engine and guided the boat in with an expert hand. This time we didn't have to jump onto the quay-side; just step off the boat. Despite this fact, he insisted on helping us down. We nodded our thanks and followed him along a gravel track into the trees. I was right. There was a house here; a mansion by the look of it with two storeys and a balcony at the front. As we made our way to the house, I could hear female voices screaming and laughing and the occasional splash. Yep, some-body was having a good time anyway, and we'd be joining them soon.

This building was constructed using the local stone and had a traditional red tiled roof. We walked up several steps to the door and made our way into a very spacious hallway. A corridor with many rooms branching off lay ahead. That much I could see.

Marijan turned to us. 'We'll get you checked in first.'

He led us to a desk where we signed a visitor's book and that's really all we had to do. He didn't ask for any payment from us. That'll probably come at the end of our stay here. He told us we had free run of the place and we could basically go where we liked. All the doors in the building were marked, like sauna, solarium etc., so we shouldn't have any difficulty finding our way around he said.

He said, 'I'll show you to your room.'

We followed him down a corridor where he stopped and opened a door with a key. Room number three.

As we trooped in, he said, 'It's a double bed. You'll have to share.'

'That's OK,' Josie said brightly.

I thought, *'No it's not, but it seems I'm stuck with it.'* I'm hoping she's left that kitty cat in the hotel, and not tucked away in her backpack.

He crossed the room to a patio door that looked out onto a rocky beach. The view was awesome. Lots of tree cover out there, just right for shading us from the sun. A high wall made from the local limestone on either side of us too. Lots of privacy here. Just what we need.

He opened the door and stepped outside. 'It's completely private, but there's no pool here. That's on the other side of the house.'

I said, 'Yeah, that's OK. We prefer the sea anyway.'

'My boss said you could have this room. Normally reserved for privileged guests.'

I said surprised, 'Oh really? Why did we get it then?'

He shook his head. 'I don't know; he didn't say. No doubt he'll tell you himself later.'

I thought a little confused, *'Privileged? Us? How come? How could he know we were coming?'* I stepped outside to get a better view.

He said, crossing the room again to the door, 'Have fun and make full use of the facilities here. I have to get back to the mainland now.'

'Thank you!' I shouted to his back. 'Josie, it's *beautiful!*' I squealed.

'Sure is. Yeah, we're going to have a fun time here Sam. We need the rest. We deserve it after all we've been through.'

I came back into the room. 'You bet.'

'Can't wait to get into the sea,' she said putting her pack on the bed.

'Yeah, me too.' Then, 'Hey! You're not wearing that…. bikini of yours are you? It's way too skimpy.'

'Yeah, so you said,' she said sounding annoyed. 'Hey! Race you to the beach?'

I nodded, then stepped outside and began to sprint in the direction of the water. I thought I had a head start on her, then a semi-naked figure shot past me stopping only briefly to pull off her panties, then dived headlong into the sea with a big splash!

When I reached the water myself I said, standing with hands on hips, 'Josie, what the hell are you doing?'

She was swimming around in the shallows then she came back to me. 'What's wrong?'

'Josie, this isn't California. You can't just….'

She cut in with, 'What's wrong with you? I like it this way.'

'Maybe so, but you can't do this here. The laws….' I broke off. Oh, what's the point in arguing with her?

'He said it was secluded didn't he?'

'No he didn't,' I said in frustration.

'Yes he did,' she insisted. She pulled herself out of the water and sat on the flat rocks.

'Sorry Josie. He didn't. He said it was private. That's not the same thing.' I looked back to the house. Only the windows of our room could be seen on this side.

'Come in and join me. You'll like it.' At that, she turned and dived, disappearing behind some rocks. I didn't see where she had gone. The water was crystal clear and you could see right to the bottom. I made my way back to the house, picking up her clothes as I went. I dropped them onto the bed and changed into my bikini. I found a couple of towels on a table and returned to the beach with them. Josie got out of the water and I handed her one of the towels.

She wrapped it and sat on a rock beside me. 'You think Bob will be here?' She giggled.

'Josie, he doesn't know we're here.' I said. 'Anyway, I've written him off for good. He's out of my life.' I added with a sigh, 'Not that he was ever in it!'

'I'll get us some drinks,' she said standing up, then went off to fetch them.

I meanwhile, went off for a swim. I dived deep although I kept close to shore. I was soon accompanied by little fish that swam alongside me. Were these the same ones that had bitten our toes earlier? Yep, I think they were too. I thought if I swam faster they wouldn't follow me, but I was wrong. Every move I made, they were there again, getting ever closer until I felt something bite my big toe on my left foot. I turned onto my back as I pulled myself out of the water onto the rocks in a hurry. Damn! That was a sore one! What was it with these guys anyway?

Josie was back now and dressed – if you could call it that – in her bikini. She carried a black plastic tray with our drinks; a cloudy white liquid with ice cubes floating in it. Lemonade?

She sat on a rock beside me. As she sipped her drink, she looked at me curiously over her glass. 'What's up Doc?'

I sighed, 'Oh, nothing, just....' I broke off as I stared into the shallows at the fish that had amassed there and rubbed my toe. Damn, that was sore. Piranha fish came to mind. If I were to fall asleep with my feet in the water, would I waken to find I had no flesh left on them?

She laughed. 'Is that those guys that were biting our toes before?' She sat with her knees drawn up to her chest, making sure that her own feet weren't in the water.

I nodded. 'Yep. Sure looks like it.'

She giggled. 'That one looks like the one that bit my toes. I'd stake my life on it,' she said pointing to one individual.

I laughed. 'Think he's the leader huh?'

She nodded. 'Yep. He's got that real mean look.' She giggled.

I reached for my drink on the tray that she had placed between us. As I raised the glass to my lips I said, 'How do you reckon he found us?' It was lemonade. Cool. Just what I needed.

'It's me he was looking for.' She giggled.

'Yeah, right. Where you get the lemonade?'

'Fridge. It's fully stocked with drink. There's beer and....'

I cut in. 'Food? Any food in it?' I'm feeling hungry. We hadn't eaten since lunchtime.

She shook her head. 'Lemons and limes. For the drinks I reckon. That's it.'

'We'll have to go find something to eat,' I said standing up. 'I feel like a bite.'

'Yeah, OK. I'll stay a while longer,' she said looking up at me smiling. 'Let me know if you find anything.' She sighed and stretched, then lay on her back.

I shrugged. 'Sure,' I said brightly and made my way to the house.

I pulled on my blue jeans and red t-shirt, but left off the sneakers. Out in the corridor I went exploring. Where would the dining room be? Just follow the smell of food I guess. So that's what I did. I couldn't determine what the cooking smells were, but it sure made my hunger pangs ten times worse! I turned right into another corridor. The first room that I came to on the right was marked gym. Double doors here with a small window in each. I pushed the doors but they were locked. I had to stand on tiptoes to see in but it was in darkness.

Next up on the right again was a single door marked massage parlour. Wouldn't mind spending some time in there. I made a mental note of that one. I moved on. The next door on the left said sauna. Yep. We'll spend some time in there too. Haven't used one of those in a while. Where is this damned dining room anyway?

As I turned from the door, I bumped into a young woman around my own age, height, and build, with long blond hair pulled back into a ponytail. She wore a white t-shirt and shorts, and carried a towel in her hand. She looked as though she'd been exercising.

I said quickly, 'Oh! Sorry.'

With a surprised expression she said, 'Ah! Cool! Another English speaker.' Her accent was American.

I turned and laughed. 'Oh, yes.'

'Where are you from?' she asked as she wiped the back of her neck with the towel.

'California.'

'Montana.' She smiled and offered her hand. 'I'm Tess.'

I shook it. 'Sam. Oh, I was looking for the dining room?'

'Just follow the cooking smells.' She laughed.

'Yeah, that's what I've been doing. We haven't eaten since lunchtime.'

'You with somebody?'

I nodded. 'Yeah, Josie. We fly home on Tuesday.'

Her smile had just gone. 'Oh....?' She broke off.

I said, 'How long have you been here?'

'About two years.'

'Really? Wow! That's a long vacation.' I laughed.

'I'm not on vacation. Not now anyway.' She turned and started walking backwards away from me. 'I - I'll talk to you later. Have to go.'

I was just about to say something when she disappeared round the corner. I thought, *Liked it so much she decided to stay?* I shrugged and walked on.

I was surprised that I didn't meet anyone else in my search for the dining room. In a few minutes I found it. I pushed through the double doors and made for the self service counter. I wondered if we'd have to pay for our meals here, so I asked a rather small woman with jet black hair pulled back into a ponytail who stood behind the counter. I was told that meals were included.

'Oh!' I said surprised. 'Thank you.' I turned on my heel and headed back to Josie.

When I got back to the beach, Josie was nowhere to be seen. She's gone for a swim I reckon. I sat down on the rocks and waited for her, then in about fifteen minutes, I saw her swimming towards me. She pulled herself out of the water and sat beside me. She had a smirk plastered on, and I could tell she had found something interesting. Well I thought she had until she told me what it was.

'What you find?' I was massaging the toes of my right foot.

'Oh, nothing really,' she sighed. 'Just a couple having sex on a rock.'

I just stared at her. 'Really? No guys here. You heard what he said?'

She stood up. 'Yeah, I know.'

I stood up too. 'O-K,' I said slowly. 'Whatever rocks your boat I guess,' I said half to myself as I began to walk back to the house.

I heard Josie say at my back, 'You find something then?'

As I went in through the patio door I said, 'Yeah. Found the dining room.'

She went to the bathroom to dry off, then changed into her jeans and blue t-shirt. We headed off to find the dining room.

As we walked down the corridor from our room, I turned to her. 'I met a girl called Tess. She's been here two years. Comes from Montana. Must be one of the staff.'

'I could stay here *forever!*' she exclaimed.

'You don't mean that Josie,' I teased. 'You'd soon get tired of it, and want to get back to your mom.' I smiled and almost laughed as I pushed through the doors of the dining room.

She turned and made a face. We went straight to the self service counter. I reached it first. It's only a snack. Don't need much, just a sandwich. I heard Josie at my back open a glass cabinet.

I turned and said in a low voice, 'What you got there?' She had large piece of strawberry gateau on her plate just oozing dairy cream!

'Eyes off,' she said grinning.

I turned back and reached into a cabinet of wholemeal sandwiches without thinking what I was doing. I usually like to make sure that there isn't anything unpleasant lurking there between the slices.

I was just about to put one onto my plate when Josie said, 'Sam?'

'What?'

She pointed to my sandwich that appeared to be oozing something white. Cream! Yuck! No way! 'Sugar!' I said half to myself.

She heard me and giggled. 'No. Mayonnaise I think.' As she pushed past me to reach the coffee stand, I heard her say, 'You should take cookery lessons.' She giggled again.

I heard myself say, 'Shut up Josie.' I grabbed a couple of wholemeal bread roll sandwiches, but not before lifting the top slice to examine the contents; cold meat – veal I think – tomato, and lettuce. Yep, that'll do nicely.

Josie found us a table by the window.

Chapter 20.

I wasn't exactly thrilled about the prospect of sharing my bed with Josie. I guess I could get used to sleeping without a cover, but if she started tossing and turning… I'm used to sleeping on my own back home and the slightest sound will waken me.

I lay there trying to sleep for what seemed like hours. The patio door was partially open to admit the cool night air. I lay on the right side of the bed with my back to her, and holding tightly onto the cotton sheet that covered us. At this point, I had my share of the bedclothes, but no doubt this wouldn't last, and it didn't! She turned onto her left side and I suddenly found myself un-covered. I was wearing a long t-shirt and panties.

I sat bolt upright. That's it. I've had it! I said in a loud voice, 'Josie!'

She sat up quickly. 'Sam! What is it? What's going on?' She snapped on her bedside lamp.

'What do you think?'

She just stared at me. 'Is this to do with the sheet?'

'You bet it is.' I nodded. I began to pull it back. 'Give it here!' I demanded.

She pulled it too, and now we were engaged in a tug-of-war.

I said frustratedly, 'Look Josie. You've got more than your fair share of it, so….'

She cut me off, 'Grow up why don't you?'

She was just about to pull the sheet back, when I said, 'You grow up. I only want what's mine!'

'OK!' she said as she let go of it. 'There! Satisfied?' She lay down on her left side.

'Yes. Thank you. At last!' I sighed. 'Maybe I can get some sleep now.'

In the morning, after breakfast, which we had in the dining room, we thought we'd go for a swim, since the temperature was around 95 degrees.

Josie said she'd show me where she had found a secluded spot, so we swam out together. The rocks that she had found were on an island that had a good cover of vegetation, mainly trees. It was some distance from shore and certainly was secluded.

We hauled ourselves out of the water and lay in the hot sun for a while. About an hour I think. Then it happened. A loud scream! A woman's voice, and it came from somewhere nearby. Well so much for our seclusion.

Josie was lying on her front when she heard the scream. I had been watching the little fishes in the water; yep, the same ones that 'attacked' us before. She turned onto her back and sat up.

'What....? Did you hear that!' she said in alarm.

'Yeah. Where did it come from?' I said looking around, then I stood up.

A female voice shouted, 'Help, someone, please help!'

'Oh Jesus! Somebody needs help Josie!' I'm in a panic. Where did it come from? We'll have to go look.

Josie said, as she stood up, 'Where the hell do we start looking?'

I said, pointing left into the trees, 'You take the left, I'll take the right.' I had visions of someone in trouble in the water.

We both broke into a run. I reached the opposite shore within minutes but, try as I might, I could see no-one at all; not in the water nor out of it. I ran along the shore searching, then I heard Josie shout my name. I ran as fast as I could in the direction of where I thought her voice had come from. As I drew closer, I could see her sitting astride someone with her back to me so I couldn't see exactly what she was doing. Another woman with blond hair, and wearing a yellow bikini, stood close by watching anxiously, then she put her hands up to cover her face and cried uncontrollably. As I got closer still, Josie was kneeling beside the swimmer. By the time I reached her, she was blowing into the woman's mouth and holding her nose closed with her free hand. This was not a swimmer who had got into trouble; it was a young woman with short blond hair and wearing jeans and a yellow t-shirt! Did she fall overboard from a boat? Why didn't someone come looking for her?

I said as I knelt down beside Josie, 'Sure you know.....?'

She cut me off with, 'I've done this before.'

The other woman got down on her knees beside her friend and held her hand. She couldn't speak for crying.

I could see the woman's chest rise as Josie blew air into her lungs, then fall again as the air was expelled. She repeated these actions over and over again, but it clearly wasn't having any effect, as the woman didn't appear to be responding at all.

I said to her, with my hand on her arm, 'Josie, it's not working. She's gone.'

She wasn't listening to me. She carried on breathing into the woman's mouth, but it was hopeless. I felt for a pulse on the woman's wrist, but there was nothing there, then I remembered something that I had seen done to people to get their hearts beating again. I put one hand flat on her chest where

I supposed her heart would be and began pushing down hard with the other. I was told that you have to be careful how you do this as it can cause damage. Anyway I lost count how many times I did this, and it didn't appear to be having any effect, so I gave up. She'd been in the water too long. There was nothing anyone could do for her. She was gone and that was that. Unfortunately Josie wasn't seeing it that way, as she kept on blowing air into the woman's lungs.

I said in frustration and pulling on her arm, 'Josie, she's gone. There's nothing you or anyone can do for her now!'

She cried, 'Stop it Sam! I know I can do this!' She was crying along with the other woman who was still kneeling by her friend; tears running down both their cheeks. Suddenly she let out a loud cry and stood up shaking her head. 'No! It's not fair! I tried everything and…. maybe….. maybe I didn't try hard enough? It's my fault she's dead…!' She sat on her bottom beside the dead woman.

I cut in, 'It's not your fault. You did your best Josie. She could have been dead before she went into the water.' I'd just realised the implications of what I had just said.

'What?' she asked incredulously and wiped her nose on the back of her hand. 'Murdered?'

I shrugged. 'I don't know. Maybe. Or fell into the sea from a boat?' I suggested.

She said standing up, 'Why didn't someone come looking for her if she fell off a boat? We'd better get back to the island and tell the police.'

The other woman stood up and said, 'You're new here?' She sniffled. Her accent was British.

I said, 'Oh, yes. Just got here yesterday.' I gave a short nervous laugh.'

Josie stood up too and extended her hand to the woman. 'I'm Josie.'

'Susan,' she said, then looked at me smiling.

I said smiling, 'Sam. Pleased to meet you.' I shook her hand too.

'This your friend?' asked Josie looking down at the dead woman.

Susan nodded. I thought she was about to cry again, but she caught herself in time.

'So, how long have you been here?' I asked her.

She shook her head. 'Not sure exactly. About nine months?' She sniffled.

'What type of work do you do?' Josie asked.

'Em….,' she hesitated. 'Oh, this and that.' She gave a short laugh.

I asked curiously, 'What made you come to this island all the way from England?'

Susan smiled nervously, 'A guy made me an offer I couldn't refuse, and I've been here ever since.' She gave a short laugh.

I said laughing too, 'Would that be Marijan Kova……something?' I laughed again.

She shrugged. 'Don't know anyone by that name.'

I shrugged too. 'Oh, well, it doesn't matter.'

'How did you get here?' asked Josie. 'Powerboat?'

She nodded. 'Yeah.' She stepped back a few paces towards the sea. 'Look, I'll have to go. Somebody will be looking for me.'

I shrugged. 'Sure. Yeah, nice meeting you. See you later maybe? Sorry about your friend.'

She gave a small wave then turned and dived into the water.

I turned to Josie. 'What do you make of that?'

'What?'

'She swims over here from the island on her break maybe, then just happens to find her friend in the water.'

Josie shrugged. 'Oh I don't know Sam. Best leave that one to the police.'

Back in our room we changed into our clothes again, then we thought we'd go looking for Susan. Hopefully she'd already alerted someone about the body and the police have been contacted. Josie had sauntered off on her own. Said she was going to the bathroom.

The first person I bumped into – literally - was Tess. She'd been walking backwards out of a room on the right. She turned, 'Oh, sorry,' she apologised.

'Tess, have you seen Susan lately?' I sounded anxious, and I was too.

She saw my look. 'No. Something wrong?'

'Yeah. You bet....' I hesitated. 'Um. Can we talk somewhere in private?'

She nodded. 'Sure.' She took me by the arm and led me down a corridor on the right. 'In here,' she said ushering me through a door. This was her room.

As she closed the door I said, 'Tess, we found a body, or rather Susan did.'

She looked at me unbelievingly. 'You're serious, right?'

I said, 'What? Do you think I'd joke about something like this?'

She just stared at me in disbelief.

Now that I had her full attention I said, 'It's a young woman dressed in jeans and t-shirt. Susan's friend, or one of her friends anyway.'

'Who was it?'

I shrugged. 'Dunno. She didn't say.'

'Where's the body?'

I shrugged again. 'On one of the islands out there. We swam out to the island and lay on the rocks for a while. That's when we heard her screams, then we went to investigate.' I told her about Josie giving her the kiss of life, and me trying to give her a heart massage.

She just stood there, hand at her mouth and in a state of shock.

'I wonder if anyone has contacted the police yet,' I said turning to the door.

She said, 'I don't like the idea of police swarming around here. It's frightening.'

I opened the door and stepped into the corridor. 'Yeah, let's hope it's just a tragic accident.'

As she closed the door behind her, I spotted Josie farther down the corridor. She didn't see me. I shouted to her and waved. She came bouncing down towards us. 'Hi Sam....' She hesitated, looking at Tess and back to me.

'This is Josie,' I said, as I turned to Tess, then to Josie. 'And this is Tess.'

'Oh hi,' Josie said brightly with a big smile as she shook Tess' hand. She turned to me. 'Em.... The police have been called. They'll be here soon.'

'Oh, OK. What did you tell them?'

She shrugged. 'Not entirely sure. I didn't call them. Reception did. It wasn't in English.'

We met him at the reception desk. He introduced himself as Marko Živković, Police Inspector. He towered above me. He must have been all of six feet tall and then some. It was almost intimidating. He wore a brown leather jacket and black pants. I estimated his age to be around 55, and weighing about 200 pounds, with greying hair at the temples and some on top too. He said, 'Can we go somewhere private to talk?'

I shrugged.

The girl behind the desk indicated a room down the hall on the right. We went there. It was a small windowless office, but we had the place to ourselves for now anyway. Josie and I sat on blue reclining swivel armchairs facing a desk; Živković preferred to stand with his hands stuffed into his jacket pockets, then he began to pace the room. I don't like it when someone does that. Makes me nervous.

He stopped his pacing for a second. 'Which of you ladies found the body?'

I said, looking at Josie, 'We didn't. Susan found her.'

'Susan?'

'Yeah,' I said. 'She works here I think. Said she's been here for nine months.'

'And Susan's second name?'

I shrugged.

Josie piped up. 'She's from England.'

We both exchanged glances.

'OK,' he said and resumed his pacing, 'tell me what happened?'

I told him about us swimming out to the island and hearing Susan's screams. He listened carefully as he propped himself against the edge of the desk but made no comment.

'I found Susan trying to pull her friend from the sea,' Josie said. 'She was crying hysterically. I tried to revive her friend with the "kiss of life" that I learned at school, but it didn't work for me.'

'And I had a go at heart massage but I've only ever tried it on a dummy. What can you do? You have to try even if it doesn't work out in the end.' I told him what she was wearing when she was found. 'I thought maybe she'd fallen from a boat, but you'd think someone would come looking for her.' I looked to him for an explanation.

Now I had his full attention. He stood up straight again and began pacing up and down in front of us. 'Fully clothed you say?'

We both nodded.

'So she could have been killed before she hit the water,' he said.

Who said anything about killing?

He added speculatively, 'Or pushed into the sea.' He shrugged. 'Who can say at this stage. We'll go to the place now and you can show me where the body is.'

Josie stood up. 'I know where the island is.'

'Good,' he said. As he crossed to the door he said, 'The police launch is out front.'

We exited the front door and made our way down to the small jetty. I could see another similar police power boat pulling up alongside Živković's with five figures preparing to put on white coveralls.

Minutes later, we were pulling up at the flat rocks where we had lain in the sun before we had heard the screams. We all clambered from the launch.

Živković said, 'Show me where it is.'

Josie led the way and in less than a minute, we had reached the opposite shore. The guys in white were following and carrying boxes. Forensics I guessed.

Josie stopped abruptly when she reached the flat rocks where we had left that poor woman. 'Sam!' she exclaimed with her hand at her mouth.

I looked over her shoulder and gasped, my hand at my mouth too; the body was gone! I was totally speechless. Josie must have got the wrong location surely, but it sure looked like the spot where we left her. We're both looking around but can't believe our eyes. I'm not taking this in properly. *'What the hell's going on here?'* I thought. *'Did someone remove it?'*

Živković saw our shocked expressions. 'What's wrong?'

We both said almost simultaneously, 'She's gone....' I continued with, 'Josie must have got the wrong spot. Yeah that's it. It has to be that.'

Živković shrugged. 'You're sure it was here?' he said, his hands deep in his pants' pockets, then he began to pace up and down. I wish he'd stop doing that.

I nodded. 'Right here, I'm sure of it,' I said pointing down to the ground. I said to Josie, and pointing left, 'You take the left Josie, I'll take the right.'

Well it isn't exactly rocket science is it? The body's either there or it isn't. I walked along the shore and through the trees, with Živković following on behind like a little dog on a lead. Or maybe that should be bloodhound! Several minutes later of fruitless searching and it was obvious that this poor woman's body was missing and we had to admit defeat. Josie came back to us shaking her head.

Živković had something to say about it though. 'So. It seems you two young people have been wasting police time.'

'*What?*' Josie said incredulously.

He gave a signal to his forensic team and they departed.

I said, hands on hips and looking him straight in the eye, 'I beg your pardon? You think we made this up?'

'If you can produce evidence....'

I interrupted him with, 'There's Susan. She'll tell you.' I nodded.

He stood there rubbing his chin in thought then he said, 'OK, let's find Susan then, if she exists.' His tone was almost sarcastic.

As he turned to go, I said, '*What?*' I'm getting really sick of this guy's attitude.

Živković arrived back at the police launch before we did.

As we followed him there, I glanced across at Josie. She had a worried look. I whispered, patting her arm for reassurance, 'Susan will back us up, don't worry.'

Her worried expression remained. She wasn't convinced.

Back at the island we made our way directly to Reception again. He turned to us. 'OK. Take me to Susan.'

I said, 'Yeah. OK. Um..... Where do we start?'

Josie said, 'Try the swimming pool? I know where it is.' She led the way.

'Oh, yeah. OK,' I said to her back as I trotted after her.

The little dog followed on.

I think the swimming pool was on the back of the house, but no matter, we were here to find Susan. She's our witness. We entered through a patio door into the swimming pool area. There were probably about twenty-five females here of differing ages. I scanned the faces, at least the ones that I could see. Some were lying on their fronts soaking up the sun so I couldn't see their faces at all. Several had their faces obscured or hidden by sunshades as they lay on a lounger. I said to Josie who stood on my left, 'See her?'

'No. Where?' she said looking around.

'No, silly. Oh never mind.' I was becoming pissed off. I decided to do a little reconnoitring.

Just before I left her she said, 'I only asked....'

I cut her off sounding annoyed. 'Yeah, OK.'

As I crossed the flagstone floor, the little dog didn't follow me this time, so I took this window of opportunity and picked someone at random. She was wearing a light-blue bikini, and was lying on her front and facing away from me, her head shaded by a cream and blue striped umbrella. Long blond hair flowed down her back.

I didn't want to startle her, so I bent down and said in a low voice, 'Excuse me?'

She jumped and so did I, then turned her head to face me. 'What...?'

'I'm sorry. Didn't mean to.... um, do you know anyone called Susan by any chance?' I straightened up, looking around.

She turned onto her back and sat up. 'Well, sure.' Her accent I couldn't place.

I was about to ask where, when she pointed across the pool. 'There, in the red swimsuit.' A woman in a red, one-piece swimsuit lay on her back on an airbed next the pool.

I thanked her then turned, thinking Josie was nearby, then I spotted her kneeling beside a sun lounger where a young blond woman in a green bikini lay. I trotted over to her.

Josie turned and stood up when she heard me approach. 'Find her?'

The blond woman looked at me over her cool shades.

I smiled at her as I replied to Josie's question. 'Dunno. Maybe.' I pointed across the pool at the red swim-suited girl still lying on her back. 'There, in the red.'

Josie said something to the blond woman that she'd just been talking to, then marched off along the poolside. I followed on. When she reached the woman, she began talking to her. I didn't hear what she said as I was out of earshot, but as I got closer, I heard the woman's reply. Her accent was British. 'Sorry, can't help you. Don't know any other Susans here.'

I looked around the poolside at all the faces; the ones that I could see anyway. *Damn!* I thought in frustration. *Where is she? Where could she be?*

I could see Živković standing across the pool looking very bored, hands thrust into his jacket pockets.

I turned back to Josie. 'Check some of the others Josie.'

She nodded and went off to speak to some people whose faces were not visible to us. When she had completed this task – it took a few minutes, she returned to me shaking her head. 'No luck Sam.'

'Shit,' I said. It was almost a whisper, then I indicated Živković. 'Come on,' I said turning away from her. 'Maybe she works somewhere here.'

She shrugged, and followed on.

Živković seemed agitated. 'What did you find?'

I shook my head. 'She's not here. I'm sure of it, but she might be working in the building.'

Živković just nodded and turned on his heel, leaving through the patio door. We followed him back to Reception.

He turned to us. 'OK,' he said with a sigh. If it turns out later that you've been making all this up, you'll be in serious trouble, OK?' He leaned against the desk.

I nodded as I said, 'Uh-huh. We're not making this up. Why should we?'

He shook his head. 'I don't know. Some people will do anything for money, like selling their story to a newspaper?'

Josie shook her head. 'No. We wouldn't do that. A woman is dead and now she's missing.'

He thought for a moment, then he said, 'I'm going to have a word with the Administrator and see if he can shed any light on the whereabouts of this Susan. Do you have a name for the dead woman?'

We shook our heads.

He shrugged, turned on his heel and walked away from us.

We took ourselves off to the dining room as it was fast approaching noon. We'd had enough! I was thoroughly pissed off. Well, I guess if I were in his shoes, I would have difficultly believing us too. But why would we make up a story about something like this?

I sat opposite Josie close to a window that looked out onto a garden. There were so many trees out there, you couldn't see beyond them, but no doubt the sea was lurking somewhere nearby.

The dining room was deserted. Where was everybody? Maybe they're all on some kind of diet. Well, I smiled to myself, all the more food for us then!

Josie was taking forever to scrutinise the menu. It was printed in English this time! Gosh, things are improving. I pulled the top of it gently towards me and said, 'Josie. For somebody who can eat just about anything, you take....'

She cut me off; her smile gone. 'Hey! I'm not done here!'

I snatched it out of her grasp. 'You are now.'

'Hey!'

She tried to snatch it back but I clutched it to my breast. 'I'll choose for you, *after* I've chosen mine.' I smiled at her over the menu as I ran my finger down the dishes listed there. I chose chicken soup first followed by another favourite of mine, chicken tikka masala.

Her smile was back. 'What am I having?'

I replied, my smile still in place, 'Wait and see.' I rested my arms on the table.

She kicked my ankle.

'*What?*' I snapped.

'Come on!' she said through clenched teeth.

'What? For someone who can eat anything.....'

She cut me off again. 'I'm entitled to know what I'm eating.'

I leaned on my arms and looked into her gorgeous blue eyes. 'You don't like surprises do you?'

'I just like to know what I'm eating, OK?' She was beginning to sound irritated.

I leaned ever closer to her and said almost sarcastically, 'Tell me something; when you come to open your Christmas presents, do you ask your mom what's in them first?'

'No. That's different.'

An overweight woman with greying hair pulled back into a bun, squeezed herself out from behind the counter and approached our table. I picked up the menu and pointed out the soup, then the chicken tikka masala. I held up two fingers. The woman nodded and walked away.

Josie turned away from me towards the window, her smile gone and avoiding my gaze. I wondered what was wrong with her. Was it something I said? I almost giggled out loud. It was only a wind-up for God's sake. Then I was concerned that there was something troubling her. That's because as she turned back to me, I thought I could detect a tear in her eye.

I put my hand on her wrist as it rested on the tabletop. 'Josie?'

She sniffled and licked her lips before answering. 'It's that poor girl that we tried to save...' She broke off, turning again to the window. A tear ran down her left cheek.

I squeezed her wrist just as the overweight woman arrived back with the soup.

Josie's eyes brightened as she watched the plates being placed on the table. Her smile returned as she said, 'Thanks.'

Later, when we had finished our meal, we met Živković, and again it was in Reception. He said, 'I spoke with the Administrator and he says that Susan helps out in the kitchen, so, shall we go there?' He finished off with a smile. That was the first time that I saw him do that.

As we entered the dining room, the overweight woman who had served us earlier, stood behind the self-service counter watching us. She had a smile on her face, and was chuckling to herself as though having just shared a joke with someone. She nodded acknowledgement but otherwise didn't say anything.

'Could I speak with Susan please?' I said.

She looked at me blankly. I thought I'd try Italian. 'Ciao. Potrei parlare per favore a Susanna?' *Hi. Could I please speak to Susan?'*

'L'italiano, sì!' Her smile just broadened. 'Io sarò solamente un secondo.' *'I'll only be a second.'* She turned and disappeared into the kitchen.

Susan came out wiping her hands on a towel. I think she'd been washing dishes. She scanned our faces with a puzzled expression. 'Do I know you?'

I suddenly realised that this was the woman in the red swimsuit that we had spoken to earlier at the poolside. 'Oh, I'm sorry. We spoke to you at the poolside. We thought you were someone else.' This was embarrassing.

Josie said, 'We're looking for someone called Susan that we met earlier only briefly, and now seem to have lost.'

Susan said, 'I've been here a while and I know that there is no other staff member by that name. Maybe she's new, like a visitor?'

I shrugged. I said resignedly, 'Yeah. Maybe you're right.'

Živković said, 'Let's get back to Reception.' He turned and pushed through the door.

I turned to Josie. She shrugged and we headed back to Reception.

Živković turned to us as he reached the desk. 'Well I guess that takes care of that. Case closed. There's nothing to investigate, is there? No body.....' He trailed off. He continued, as he put out his hand for me to shake, 'I'll be off now.'

As I shook his hand, I could feel something pressed into my palm, like a slip of paper? *'What's going on? What's he doing?'* I thought. He's passing me a message, but why? I quickly put both hands into my front pockets. Josie didn't see what I was doing. The girl at the desk was typing on her computer when he shook Josie's hand, then departed.

I said to her as I took her by the arm, 'Let's get back to our room.'

Back in our room, I took the paper out of my pocket slowly. What the hell was it? My heart was racing in anticipation.

Josie sat on the edge of the bed watching me. She saw my expression. 'What's that you got?'

I didn't say anything immediately, then I read it. It had a telephone number and the following words, which I read out to her; 'I believe you when you say you found a body, and about the witness called Susan. See if you can find her, but be careful. Keep in touch.' Signed M Živković. I said, 'Josie, he believes us? He suspects something I think.'

'Maybe they've had problems here before Sam?'

'Like what?' I crossed to the fridge and opened it. I'm looking for a cold drink.

She shrugged. 'I don't know. Maybe something illegal that the police suspected but couldn't prove?'

She had me thinking now. I found a bottle of lemonade. The real thing. Josie handed me a glass from the top of the fridge. I poured her some, then I found a glass for myself.

I said, 'Let's find somewhere to relax and wind down.'

'Sauna?' she suggested.

'Oh yeah. Sure,' I said taking a gulp of my drink. I'd forgotten about the sauna. 'I've been told they're very relaxing. Never tried one though.'

'Well, now we can. We should be making use of all the facilities here Sam. Make the most of our time here. We'll be flying home soon remember?'

As I finished off my drink I said, 'And we've a concert to catch too when we get to Pula.'

'Oh that'll be so *cool*! I can't wait to see him on stage again. What a guy, huh?' She put her empty glass down on the fridge.

'Yeah,' I said dreamily.

Josie took my arm and pulled me to the door. 'Come on. Let's let's do the sauna thing.'

I didn't protest.

We entered into a small office where a young guy dressed in casual green open-necked shirt and black pants was seated behind a desk. He'd been hiding behind a newspaper when we entered. There was no immediate reaction, then he lowered the newspaper just enough to study us briefly. 'Vi želite saunu?'

I hadn't a clue what he said but I smiled and nodded anyway. 'Uh-huh.'

'Svlačionica kroz tu. Imate sat.'

I just shrugged and shook my head then I thought I'd try Italian. 'Italiano?'

He shook his head.

I just smiled at him again and said, 'Thank you.' I trotted after Josie who was already standing by the door. She couldn't wait to get in there.

Inside the dressing room, we stripped off in one of the four changing cubicles on the right then wrapped ourselves in hot towels that were draped over a warm radiator, then it was through the door and into the sauna. Gosh it was warm in there! And that was before the fun even began!

There were wooden benches here around the walls, and heat regulators on the wall just above one of them, so we had full control, and a red emergency button as well just in case. Josie lay stretched out on her front on the bench opposite me, and using her rolled-up towel as an improvised pillow, her head turned to face me. I sat with my left leg drawn up to my chest and the other stretched out. I could see she was lost in thought. 'What you thinking?'

'The body we found? Someone must have found her.'

'Yeah, guess so. I'm wondering what happened to Susan. Maybe we'll find her in the building somewhere. She did seem anxious to get away.'

That night in bed we decided to make the massage parlour our next stop. This should be interesting.

Chapter 21.

After breakfast, we headed for the massage parlour. We arrived outside the door and just stood there staring at it. Oh I felt so *excited*! In fact we both did. Couldn't believe I was doing this for the first time! We both had broad grins plastered on. She giggled; I joined in.

I said excitedly, 'Let's do it!'

She nodded.

I giggled again as I pushed through the door. We stepped into a small office, where a girl with black hair in a ponytail and wearing a white robe sat behind a desk. She looked up smiling as we entered.

I didn't know what to say to her at first, and Josie's giggling didn't help. What I tried to say was, 'We've come for a massage', but my words came out in a splutter of giggles instead. 'Sorry,' I apologised. I cleared my throat nervously and continued, 'We've come for.....'

She cut in with, 'Sign here?' The accent was east European. She pushed a form in front of me on the desk.

Josie and I exchanged glances with our broad smiles intact. I signed on the dotted line, then pushed it back.

Josie whispered to me, 'Is it a guy?' She giggled again.

I whispered back, 'Is what a guy?' I wasn't getting this.

She whispered again, 'You know?'

She thinks the masseur is a guy? How would I know? I shrugged.

Her smile had vanished temporarily as she said, 'Oh, I thought....' She broke off as the girl came round the desk to us. Josie was beside herself with excitement. She giggled again as she looked at me and back to the girl.

'Come this way,' the girl said as she turned away from us.

We followed her to a door on the left of the desk.

She turned and said to Josie, 'You're in the other room. Over there?' She pointed across to the right of the desk.

Josie shrugged and her smile had gone. 'Oh! OK,' she said disappoint-edly. She hesitated then crossed to the door where the girl had indicated then she turned. 'Em....'

The girl said, 'Just knock,' then turned to me. 'In here.'

Just before I followed her through, I looked back at Josie. Her smile was back and the door had just been opened for her. She gave me a little wave before she stepped inside. I returned it.

As we entered the room, I could see a curtained cubicle on the far right; a massage table straight ahead with a black leather mattress stood under a window with closed Venetian blinds. A cart stood close to the table with plastic bottles and stuff on it. I wondered what was in them. The girl told me to un-dress in the cubicle. I'd find a towel in there, she said.

I thought just before I drew the curtain aside, *'Towel?'* To wrap yourself in stupid! My heart was thumping with anticipation. What was it like to get a massage? I had no idea. As I pulled my top off, I wondered if, when I was done here, the 'new' me would walk out of here feeling a new girl and a spring in her step. I sat in the chair provided and kicked off my sneakers and pulled off my socks. Once I had completely undressed, except for the panties of course – I have to keep those on, I placed my clothes neatly on the back of the chair.

I thought of Josie. Would she walk out a 'new' girl too? Not that there's anything wrong with the 'old' one. I almost giggled out loud. Well, maybe a little tweak here, and a little tweak there wouldn't do any harm. There's always room for improvement. I smiled and nodded to myself in agreement.

My thoughts were interrupted by a voice from the other side of the cur-tain. 'Just come out when you're ready madam.'

'OK. Nearly done!' I shouted back.

I took a deep breath, wrapped the towel and pushed through the curtain; the dark green carpeting soft under my feet. I watched her spread a white sheet on the table, and a white cotton pillow at the top end, then I was told to lie on my front and remove the towel. She came around the top of the table and began to apply oil to my shoulders from one of the bottles. As I lay there, my head to one side resting on the pillow, I could smell a lovely fragrance. I couldn't place it. Was it the oil, or was it coming from her? No matter, I was now fully relaxed and I felt *all* my worries just ebbing away. The massage went deep into my neck. *Jesus*, this was good.

'Thank you,' I whispered. 'That feels so good.' With peripheral vision I saw her smile.

After some minutes, she started on my shoulders, then my arms. I'll def-initely do this again sometime. I made a mental note to join a health club when I got home. She turned to the window and opened it a little. A lovely cool breeze wafted across my back. Oh, *God*! This was *oh*-so relaxing. If it wasn't for the massage, I could quite easily drift off to sleep, as I could feel my eye-lids heavy and I was yawning a lot. I wasn't sure how long this session was to last, nor had I any idea how long I had been here, as I had left my watch in the cubicle. But no matter; I was enjoying myself. I hadn't felt this good in ages. The girl went around the table, pulling the cart behind her, and as she did so, I noticed that her feet were bare. No wonder I didn't hear her move across the floor. Now she started on my legs.

I thought she'd finished with my legs and this session over when she announced that she was taking a break. I was to help myself to the wine that stood in an ice bucket on a table against the wall on my left. I watched her move towards the door and heard a soft click as she closed it behind her. I got up and crossed to the ice bucket. After opening the bottle, I poured myself a glassful and brought it and the bottle back to the massage table where I lay down on my front again, the wineglass close to my head. I lay there for a few minutes, then emptied the glass. I really liked the taste of this wine from Croatia, so I sat up briefly and poured more of it, then lay down again. Now it's not a good idea for me to lie down with a glass of wine in my hand, because as sure as hell, I'm going to drift off to sleep. Well, I thought with a big contented sigh, *The girl will waken me if I do, so......'*

I could feel the hot sun on my back as I lay on my front on the sand; my bikini top off, but the bottom part in place. Someone; a muscular male, lay on my right, his face turned towards me. I didn't recognise him, so what was he doing here? Where was I? It seemed to be a beach, because I could hear the breakers rolling in.

I didn't feel comfortable lying beside this stranger. As I turned my head to the left, I appeared to be alone with this guy. Jesus, what was I thinking, sharing this space with a total stranger? He was just too close for comfort! Time to move. I tried to get up, but my limbs didn't respond, and it was then that the stranger opened his eyes and smiled at me. It wasn't friendly. His teeth were shaped like daggers. My heart was racing and I began to panic, then, something strange happened; I felt something on my spine! It felt like a finger, then I was certain that it was a finger! Then it became two fingers, then a hand, then I panicked big-time! I tried to move away, but I still couldn't move my limbs! What was wrong with me? The stranger's mouth opened *too* wide and I could see saliva dripping from his lips! I screamed and.... I woke up! Something traced a line down my spine. It's those fingers again, and it wasn't the masseur this time! Those fingers belonged to a male! My heart was in my mouth as I tried to collect my thoughts and reason this out. Did a male masseur replace the girl who was on her break? If not..... And what was he doing with his fingers?

'Holy shit!' I thought, my heart thumping hard. I said with trembling voice, 'Who the hell....!' I tried to turn my head round to see who was there but he grasped my wrist tightly and pinned my arm to the bed. I cried – some of this was from the pain, 'Let *go* of me!'

Then a familiar voice; Milos? No, it couldn't be. How could he know we were here? *'Oh shit!'* I thought as I realised that this is where the gang was all along, and we'd just walked into a trap.

He said slowly, 'So, here you are at last. I knew our little plan would work. Make you an offer you couldn't refuse and…..' He laughed.

I tried to pull free of his grasp but I couldn't do this properly without turning onto my back and exposing my bare top half! I said angrily, 'So this was all your work?'

'No, not at all. More a team effort, as you might say.' He laughed again and, pulling my arm from the bed, turned me over onto my back, pinning it above my head. I tried to lash out at him with my free hand, but he grabbed that too with his other one. Now both my arms were pinned above my head and I was completely helpless and exposed, in more ways than one! He was just standing there and looking down on me. My chest was heaving after the effort of trying to struggle free, and my heart was thumping hard. I was per-spiring a lot and I could feel the sheet I was lying on was soaked with it.

He said, 'You know, you look even more beaut……'

I cut him off with, 'Shut up!' I turned my face away to the left and refused to look at him. I hated that bastard and he knew it. I was trying my best not to cry, but the tears came anyway.

He let go of my arms now and straightened up. 'You know what I'm here for don't you?'

I didn't reply. With my face still turned away from him, I could see the towel that I had discarded lying by my side. I grabbed it quickly to cover myself, but I don't know why I bothered now. Tears ran down my face and onto the sheet as if it wasn't wet enough already. I was losing control!

He said, arms folded across his chest, 'Look, if you just tell me where it is, I'll take it to my boss and….'

I cut him off; it was almost a whisper. 'I don't know where it is and even if I did I wouldn't tell *you*!' I spat out the last word.

He tut-tutted before saying, 'I thought you'd come to your senses before now, but you chose to do it the hard way.' He thrust his hands into his pants' pockets then continued, 'I'll give you a few days to think about it, and if the answer is still no, then we'll just have to let Boris extract it from you. He's good at it too.'

'Go to *hell*!' I spat out the words. 'How do you know we won't just leave the island?'

'You won't.' He just stood there, hands on hips and a smug look on his face.

'Of course we can. You can't stop us. Marijan will take us back to the main-land.'

'Who?'

'He brought us here in the powerboat. He can take us back,' I insisted.

'Oh. So that's what he calls himself these days.' He laughed.

Jesus,' I thought. *'So he was part of this too?'* I said defiantly, 'We'll find a way to get back.'

'You could try, but I wouldn't attempt it if I were you. Some have already tried to leave, and failed.' He laughed again.

I thought quickly, *'What the hell's he talking about? Others have tried and failed? What happened to them?'* Then, *'Oh God no. The girl we tried to save!'*

I watched him reach for a bottle on the cart and begin to slowly unscrew the top. He bent closer to me, his hand holding the bottle poised as if to pour the contents onto my chest just under my breasts, then he did! I couldn't see where the oil was going due to the towel blocking my view, but I did feel the cool liquid run down slowly and gather around my navel.

He put his hand on my stomach and, with slow circular movements, began to rub the oil into my skin.

'What's he doing? Is he trying to scare me? If he is….,' I thought, beginning to panic big-time, *'he's succeeded!'*

His hand was just above my panties' waistband when he said, 'You will tell your policeman friend that you made a mistake about the body that you found…..'

I swallowed hard; my throat was dry as I felt his hand slip under the waist-band, 'Otherwise…..' He trailed off. At this point his hand had slipped down further, and that's when I grasped it firmly with both hands and attempted to pull it out.

He took it out himself and moved it up towards my chest instead. He poured the oil onto his hand and applied it between my chest and navel. Again the circular movements.

'And you will forget that you ever met that woman on the island…..' His hand moved under the towel between my breasts.

I said in a threatening tone, 'Get you hand off me or….'

He cut me off with, 'Because if you don't….' He pulled the towel off me! I managed to grab the end of it, but he won this tug-of-war and began to wipe his hands on it, then threw it back to me, 'I'll just have to set Boris to work on Josie!'

'No! You leave her out of this!' I was practically screaming at him now.

He said, backing towards the door, 'Remember what I said.'

'Get out of here!' I screamed. As he turned to open the door, I reached up quickly behind my head and grasped the neck of the wine bottle, then threw it as hard as I could towards the door. He already had it open by this time and the bottle smashed harmlessly against the door lintel.

'No! Shit! Shit! Shit!' I broke down. I've lost it. I came here to relax and now look at me.

He escaped through the door, slamming it shut behind him.

I went to the cubicle and dressed quickly. My intention was to get back to Josie. I don't want those bastards getting their hands on her.

Back in the office, the girl was already up from her desk as I entered. She would have heard the breaking glass. She asked concerned, 'Are you OK? The glass? Are you hurt?'

I shook my head with tears in my eyes. 'No I'm not.' I dabbed them with a Kleenex. I sniffled and added quickly, 'Is Josie still in there?' I pointed at the other door as I headed towards it.

She said as she ran after me, 'Oh you can't go in there!' She grasped my arm and began pulling on it.

I pulled away with, 'Sure I can, just watch me.' I tried the handle and hammered on the door at the same time, but it was locked.

She pulled on my arm again. 'I don't think…..' she said, 'It's private!'

I unfastened her fingers from my arm. 'She's my friend for God's sake.'

She retreated back to her desk.

The door opened and a muscular male wearing only a pair of white shorts stood there. He was taller than me too. So what's new? His expression said, 'What do you want?' He wasn't smiling.

I said, trying my best to see into the room over his shoulder for any signs of Josie, 'My friend…..'

He cut in with, 'Your friend is occupied at the moment…..'

I interrupted, 'Excuse me?' Then, 'Josie get dressed and come on!'

He said in an aggressive tone, 'I said, she's occupied…..'

Just then, Josie appeared at the guy's back clutching a towel to her front and a large grin plastered on. 'Hi Sam. Enjoy your massage?' She giggled.

'Josie get your clothes on and let's get out of here.' I was reaching into the back of my jeans for my knife. Now I had it out, but hidden behind my back.

He tried to push the door closed in my face, but I put my foot in it. He said, in a threatening tone, 'Get your foot out of the….'

I interrupted, 'Open the door please? I won't say it again.' I pressed the button on the knife and the blade popped out.

Josie had her hand at her mouth. She was speechless. Then she disappeared from my view. He tried pushing the door against my foot, but my right hand holding the knife came around to the front in a flash. I presented the point at his throat and he stood back quickly; a look of shock on his face. He grasped my knife hand tightly and twisted my wrist. I screamed, then Josie hit him with something. A chair I think. His knees buckled and he dropped where he stood. I put my knife away and removed the key from the door. I helped Josie, now fully dressed, to drag the guy back from the door. I closed the door and locked it then pocketed the key. I'll lose it somewhere. We hugged one another and I shed a tear and sniffled. Was that for Josie or was I just feeling sorry for myself?

She said smiling as she pulled away, 'I enjoyed that.'

I said sarcastically, 'What the massage or hitting him over the head?'

As we left the small office I spotted a large plant in a pot on our right. I dropped the key into it. I turned to Josie. 'Milos was here.'

She stopped in her tracks. '*What? Here?* When?'

I swallowed hard. I had a lump forming. 'He came into the room where I was lying when I was asleep.'

'No,' she said shaking her head. 'What the hell's he doing here?'

'It's them Josie. They're here. Milos threatened us and he knows something about that poor girl we found and Susan too.'

She looked shocked. 'Oh my God, what do we do now?'

'There's something going on here Josie and we've just walked into a trap. Milos is involved in it and someone called Boris and the Boss whoever he is.'

'You think they're staying here too? I thought the guy who took us in the power boat said there were no males here?'

'Yeah he did, but I think he was referring to the clientèle.' I sighed. 'And he's part of this whatever is going on here too.'

'Oh God,' she said with a shocked expression and her hand at her mouth.

I thought I detected a tear. I hugged her and rubbed her back. 'We have to stick together at all times Josie. Don't go wandering off on your own please. I want to know you're safe.'

I didn't know how the hell we were going to get off the island now, but Josie came up with a solution. 'Sam, couldn't we get Bob to help us out?'

I said, not believing my ears, 'Josie, are you mad? Bob? How could he help us?' I threw my hands up in exasperation.

'You got a better idea?'

I took her by the arm and pulled her with me. I intended to go back to our room. We don't want to attract too much attention out here in the corridor.

'What?' she asked as she followed me.

Back in our room I said turning to her, 'Josie, Bob is as good as a......'

She cut in with, 'Hey it was only a suggestion.'

I began to pace the room. We were going to have to steal one of the powerboats. How else were we to get off of this God-damned island. We'd have to get the keys first though. I'll work on that one later.

That evening, there was to be a party at the house. I overheard a conversation between two girls I had passed in the corridor earlier. Guests would be arriving and this could be our opportunity for escape. Plan of action; Josie climbs over the wall and makes her way towards the front of the house where the party is, then sneaks over to the jetty and takes the keys from a boat. Yep, that sounded like a plan, so I voiced my thoughts to her, well some of them anyway.

'*What?*' was her incredulous reaction. See, I knew she'd like it. 'Why me?'

I said softly to her, 'Because, you're intelligent, beautiful, adventurous......'

She interrupted. 'What are you talking about?'

I sighed. 'This way.' I put my arm around her shoulders and led her through the patio doors. As we stepped outside, I said, 'Oh, and you're my best friend too.'

She turned to me and nodded. 'So....?'

'You're the best one for the job, oh and because I said so.' Well that's told her.

Now all we have to do is move the table to the wall and Josie can climb over it. Well that was the plan anyway.

I said, moving to the table, 'Give me a hand with this Josie?' I began pulling the table over towards the wall, but she just stood there with arms folded and with that incredulous look plastered on.

I stopped pulling the table momentarily and said exasperatedly, '*What?*'

'What are you doing?'

'Building a bridge? What does it look like?' Now I had the table against the wall. 'Chair?'

She shrugged.

I sighed again and fetched a chair myself. I placed it beside the table. 'OK get up.' I indicated the table.

Again that incredulous look. 'Up?'

'Josie are you really that dumb? The table girl. Get on the table, OK?'

She shrugged again then climbed onto the chair then the table.

'At last, now, over the wall.'

'Why?' Yep, that incredulous look again.

'Because, if you don't,' I said beginning to loose my cool, 'I'll put you over my knee and spank your little bottom for you.' I almost laughed out loud.

She made a face and turned to the wall then looked over. 'Jeez, it's dark down there.'

'No kidding?'

'So what do I do?'

I thought, *Jesus, here we go.* I got up beside her on the table. With one arm around her shoulders I said, 'See the building?' I pointed to that section of the house that was a mirror image of our side, complete with patio doors.

She nodded.

At this moment everything here was in almost complete darkness. As our eyes slowly adjusted to the dark, shapes of tables and chairs began to form in front of the house. I could just make out the wall on the right of the building that Josie was to climb over to reach the front. I pointed to it. 'See the wall at the side?'

She nodded again.

'You go over it and then you get yourself, somehow, to the jetty and take the keys from one of the boats like I said, OK?'

She turned, frowning. 'That's kinda dangerous isn't it? Suppose....?'

I cut in with, 'Yep sure is, but you'll think of something.'

'But suppose there aren't any keys, what then?'

I ignored her question. 'Put your leg over.'

'But.....' She put her right leg over the wall and hesitated.

I lifted her left leg onto the top of the wall. 'Now go for it girl.'

She hesitated again. 'But....'

I interrupted by pushing her gently towards the chasm that was the darkness below. She screamed a little scream as she fell, then silence. I thought, my heart thumping, *'Hope she's OK!'* I shouted in a whisper into the darkness, 'Josie, you OK down there!'

Silence.

'Jesus, Josie!' I'm panicking now.

A voice replied, 'Yeah sure.' She giggled. 'Just winding you up.'

I breathed a big sigh of relief. 'Josie don't ever do that to me again please.' I left her to it and returned to the house and the party.

Chapter 22.

I thought I'd get as far as I could to the front of the building and maybe even the jetty, so I could find Josie and get the keys from her. When I had reached the lobby, it was already crowded with guests; male and female. The language here was Croatian, and they had obviously come from the mainland. I guessed that some of the women I had seen at the poolside earlier would be here too, so maybe I'd recognise someone. The women wore cocktail dresses and the guys in black suits. I'm looking around for Josie. She shouldn't be too hard to spot though. She'll be the only one wearing jeans and t-shirt. In fact we're going to have to find dresses to wear so we blend in with the crowd. We stand out here like a couple of beacons in a snowstorm.

Being only five feet tall I have trouble finding people in crowds, and Josie is the same height as me so this is gonna be tricky. Try as I might I couldn't see the entrance properly for all the bodies, but I'm working my way towards it. Then, at last, she appeared through the open doorway. She's spotted me too and she's got a wide grin plastered on. I hope she's got the keys with her otherwise we're going to be in a fix.

I saw Josie reach out and pick up a glass of something from somewhere. She sipped it as she approached me smiling.

I smiled back as I whispered, 'Any luck?'

She nodded. 'Uh-huh.'

My spirits rose. 'You're an angel.' I laughed then hesitated. 'Josie we've got to find dresses like those. Don't want to stand out from the crowd, otherwise getting to the jetty later could be tricky.' With that I took her by the arm and guided her away from the crowded lobby.

With a look of curiosity she asked, 'Where are we going?'

'Come on,' I said as I headed for the first corridor, then I stopped and turned to her. 'I've got an idea.' I remembered bumping into Tess earlier. She was around our height and build. Maybe she could lend us a couple of dresses. I voiced my plan to Josie. She sipped her drink and just nodded.

I continued, 'Oh, and shoes too. We'll have to lose those sneakers.'

Josie turned back to the lobby sipping her almost-finished drink. 'So how do we find her amongst this lot?'

Drinks had been placed on a table just behind us. Josie reached out and put back her almost-empty glass, then picked up two more.

My heart leapt into my mouth. I said in alarm, 'No!' I snatched one of the glasses from her grasp spilling some of it then took a sip. Champagne. Cool. 'I want you to have a cool head when we try to.....,' I said lowering my voice just as a tall hunk in a suit passed us by. 'You know?'

Josie's eyes followed him into an adjoining room where many of the guests were now moving.

I tugged on her arm to get her attention. I said in a low voice, 'Josie, are you listening to me?'

She nodded without turning and took a gulp of her drink.

'Josie we're looking for Tess remember? She's about our height and blond....' I broke off as I realised that she wasn't listening to me.

She pointed towards the room where the guests were gathering. 'Look!'

I looked. 'Jesus, it's her!' I whispered as I realised it *was* her, and she was hanging on a guy's arm. He was only slightly taller than she was and dark haired. She was wearing a red cocktail dress that came down just past her knees.

Josie shouted. 'Tess!'

'What you doing?' I whispered my heart thumping. We don't want to attract too much attention here.

Tess stopped in her tracks and turned this way and that trying to identify the source of the shout, then she spotted the two of us standing together. The guy turned too and smiled. Josie had her ubiquitous smile plastered on and my face turning red.

Tess let go of the guy's arm and came across to us. 'Hi. Nice to see you again. Won't you join the party?' She picked up a glass from the table and looked at us both in turn.

I said, or tried to say, 'Yeah, but....'

Tess broke in. 'You're not dressed. You probably feel out of place here.' She nodded.

I said, 'Yeah you bet. Listen, can you do something for us?'

Josie said quickly wrinkling her nose, 'We just need to borrow a couple of dresses from you if that's OK?'

I trod on her foot and gave her a look that would have stopped a mountain lion in its tracks. I whispered, 'Josie!'

Tess broke in again laughing. 'Sure you can, oh, and you'll need shoes too.' She turned away. 'This way.' She put her drink on the table as she passed.

We followed her to her room. Of course I'd been here before. We went in and Tess headed straight for a closet on the left beyond her bed. Josie and I exchanged glances. She still had her smile on and it broadened gradually when Tess brought two satin dresses out on hangers; a blue one and a red one.

My spirits just soared. 'Oh you're an angel.'

A voice at my side said, 'That's the second time you've said that today.' She spluttered through her drink and started giggling.

I turned to her quickly and gave her my stare. I said through clenched teeth, 'Shut *up!*'

Tess laughed and said, 'Any colour suit you? I've got....'

Josie broke in. 'I'll have the blue one thanks.' She nodded and took the dress from her.

I smiled as Tess handed me the red one. 'Thanks,' I said softly, then I remembered the shoes. 'Oh....'

Josie broke in before I could say it, 'Shoes!' She put her glass on the dressing table then bent down quickly, snatching up a pair of light-blue high heeled shoes from the bottom of the closet before I could react.

'*Well the nerve,*' I thought annoyed. 'Josie!' I said through clenched teeth again.

'What's up?' she said brightly and began to strip off her clothes.

'I'll leave you two to it and get back to the party,' Tess said as she made for the door. She turned just as she opened it. 'Have to get back to Tom. He'll be wondering where I am.' She laughed, and disappeared from the room.

I found a nice pair of red heels and within minutes we were ready to return to the party. We left our clothes on Tess' bed then we were off.

Just as I was turning to pull the door closed behind us, I remembered the keys that Josie had taken from the boat. I whispered, 'Josie, the keys.....?'

I broke off as she interrupted me, her glass still in her hand's 'OK.' She walked away heading it seemed, for the room where the party was.

I trotted after her, unsteady in my 'new' heels. That was because my feet didn't quite fit comfortably in them. Even before I had reached the door to the room where guests were mingling, male heads were turning to look at me. I just smiled back and followed Josie. As I entered, she was nowhere to be seen at first, then I spotted her reaching for a full glass of bubbly from a table. I headed straight for her intending to chastise her for consuming too much alcohol, when someone grasped my right arm.

I turned my head......Milos! He had a large grin plastered on but it wasn't friendly. 'Having a pleasant evening?' he asked as he sipped something from a glass.

I pulled my arm out of his grasp. 'Shut up!' I said venomously. I turned away and took Josie by the arm, at the same time guiding her into a corner. 'Josie?' I whispered.

That incredulous look again. '*What!*' She sipped from another full glass then hiccuped.

I whispered, 'Keys? What did you do with them?'

She shrugged, then giggled.

I'm really getting pissed off with her antics now. I grasped her wrist before she could raise the glass again. 'Josie, come on! What did you do with them!' I pleaded.

'Stop it!' she screamed. 'You're treating me like a kid again!'

I screamed back, 'Stop acting like one then!'

Heads turned to look at us now. I'm not caring. She's got to snap out of this. I felt my right arm grasped tightly again. I turned quickly. It was Milos.

He said, 'OK, enough of this. You're causing a scene....'

I cut him off shouting and without turning, 'Let go of my arm!' I made sure that all present heard me.

Heads turned.

He shouted back, 'I said.....!'

I screamed and tried to pull away. 'Let *go* of me!'

A voice from my right with a thick east European accent demanded, 'OK let the lady alone.' A tall middle-aged gentleman with a receding hairline approached us.

I turned then to face Milos.

He turned to the guy and shouted, 'Stay out of this!'

The other guy tried to grasp Milos' arm. 'Come on....!'

Milos cut him short by pushing him viciously in the chest knocking him backwards. He collided with several other male and female guests, most of whom landed on the floor. Women screamed; guys shouted. It was chaos. Someone grabbed Milos from behind. He broke free and turned, throwing a punch at the other man. It made contact and the other one fell backwards onto the floor. Milos was on him in a flash and began to rain blows on him. Several guys tried to restrain him.

I didn't see what happened next as someone grasped my left arm. It was female fingers this time. Thinking it was Josie, I turned quickly to her.

It was Tess. She said, 'Come on. Let's get out of here.' She led the way through the mayhem that the party had turned into.

As we exited the room, I noticed that many of the guests had beat us to it and began mingling again in the lobby. Most wore shocked expressions. Some of the women were crying. Tess and I headed for the far wall; Josie the drinks table. One young guy came out of the room holding a handkerchief to his mouth and made for the toilet.

I turned to Tess. 'Who is this guy Milos anyway?'

Before she could answer, Josie offered her a glass of bubbly. She took it from her with a nod and a smile, but turned away from us, and glancing towards the room where the party had been.

I was curious. 'What's up?'

'Oh, nothing.' She took a gulp of her drink and coughed. It'd gone the wrong way. Without looking at me she asked, 'Milos? Who's that?'

I said, 'Um....the jerk who threw the first punch?'

'Oh,' she said surprised and shrugged. She took another drink and spluttered and coughed. 'Excuse me. I'm going to look for Tom.'

I just shrugged at her back as she walked off in the direction of the party room. I thought with resignation, *Well guess that's the end of that conversation.*

I thought we'd go back to our room and work on the next part of our plan. We have to get to the boat and head for the mainland as soon as possible. I voiced my thoughts to Josie.

She just nodded and sipped her drink.

I snatched the glass out of her hand and put it on the table, spilling some of it in the process. 'Come on.' I took her by the arm and led her to our room. We had just reached it when I thought I heard someone in there. With my heart racing I whispered, 'We've got a visitor.' I just remembered that I'd left the key in my jeans pocket.

'You sure?' she asked.

I didn't answer. Instead, I turned the doorknob slowly and cautiously pushed the door open. There, lying on his back on our bed and apparently asleep, was a thirty-something guy wearing black pants and white shirt and no tie. His coat was lying beside him. 'What the hell?' I whispered as I approached the bed, Josie at my back.

She asked softly, 'What's *he* doing here?'

'That's a good question,' I whispered again.

Something else I remembered; I locked the door when I left earlier, so how the hell did he get in here? Yeah, I've got it! Of course! He's been in Tess' room. Her door wasn't locked and she had the key. I remembered closing it behind me. So the bastard's been into my jeans. What the hell's going on here? I'm trying to think if I had anything else in my pockets that he could have taken. I grabbed his coat and began to search the pockets. I could feel something heavy through the fabric of the jacket. I'm curious. It was in the inside pocket; a gun! *'What the hell....!'* I thought, my heart doing a marathon. I took it out and weighed it in my hand. I wasn't familiar with this weapon, but then that could apply to almost any gun that I came across.

Josie's eyes almost popped right out. 'Sam!' she whispered. She wore a worried expression.

A smile appeared on my lips now. 'Josie,' I said. 'Lose it.' I handed the gun to her.

She smiled as she took it from me and headed for the bathroom. Seconds later she reappeared minus the weapon.

The jerk on the bed hadn't opened his eyes so far, but that was about to change. We'd have to get rid of the guy soon if we're going to make our escape, and now that we had a weapon, well that changed everything.

Chapter 23.

I wasn't sure whether to trust Tess or not. Was she really part of whatever was going on here, or was she just working here?

My thoughts were interrupted by the guy opening his eyes. A smile appeared on his lips now. His speech was slurred as he said, 'Vi ste seksi.'

I thought, *'What the hell's he talking about!'* I said, 'You speak English?' Blank stare.

'Parla italiano?' I asked.

He shook his head, then he sat up slowly.

'Español?' Josie asked.

Again he shook his head.

I turned to her and gave her another of my stares. 'No! They don't do Spanish here Josie.'

She shrugged. 'Yeah OK whatever,' she said and turned away.

He slurred, 'Vi želite pomaziti dijete?'

I said to her, 'Let's get this jerk out of here.'

She turned back to me. 'Why don't we just leave him here. He's too drunk to do anything anyway.'

I was about to disagree with her when the guy flopped back onto the bed. He was asleep the moment his head hit the pillow.

I asked Josie to go fetch our clothes from Tess' room. We'll need them here if we're going to attempt an escape. When Josie had gone, I decided to search the guy's pants' pockets for our room key. I searched his coat just in case I'd missed it, but didn't find anything. Next, I stood by the bed and felt his right thigh with my hand, trying to find the pocket. Well, how else was I to find it? He moaned and grunted but didn't waken. OK, now I've found the pocket. Nothing! I felt around his left thigh but couldn't find the damned *pocket* this time!

'Must be lying on it', I thought irritatedly.

Just then, he opened his eyes a little.

'Shit!' I said softly to myself. I was intending to withdraw my hand quickly, but he grasped my wrist tightly before I could take it back. 'Ah!' I shouted in agony. 'Let go of me you creep!' I yelled.

'Vi ste seksi,' he slurred.

That phrase again. I didn't know what he said, but I'm assuming that the last word is the same as in English, if so..... I heard the door open and turned to see Josie enter clutching our clothing. I felt the guy loosen his grip on my wrist, and I withdrew my arm quickly.

'Hi,' she said brightly. 'I found the key in your pocket.'

I said startled, 'Oh! OK. So he used a master key then?' I said teasing her, 'And what else did you find there?'

Her smile just vanished. 'Beg your pardon?'

I straightened up shaking my head. 'Nothing.'

She said softly, 'He can't stay here. We'll have to get someone to help us get rid of him.'

I noticed the guy's eyes had closed again.

'Yeah,' I replied absently. That was because I was working on a plan, well sort of a plan anyway. I said to her quickly, 'I know a way to get his attention. Just hope it works.'

My plan was to give the impression that there was a fire in the building, and that we'd have to leave by the nearest exit, namely, through the patio doors and outside. Next, get him to go over the wall; the same route that Josie had taken earlier. That'll get him out of our hair for a while. Yep, that sounded like a plan. I voiced my thoughts to her.

'O-K,' she said slowly.

As I crossed the room to where our packs lay, I said, 'Phrasebook and dictionary?'

I threw Josie's pack to her, but she just stood there staring at me inquisitively.

I said, as I rummaged through my pack for one of the language books, 'Look for the word for "fire" or something.'

My hand found a book. It was the dictionary. I'm searching quickly through it now. Josie found the phrasebook, then we both came up with something almost simultaneously! How cool was that? I had found the word for 'emergency'.

She whispered as she quoted from the book, '"Quick! There is a fire in the building!"'

I found my notebook and pen and threw them to her. 'Write it down Josie.'

She did, then, 'What now?'

'Give them here.'

She did. She had written 'Brzo! Tu je požar u zgradi!'

I turned the page and wrote 'hitna'. OK, we were ready to go. I ripped the two sheets from the notebook, but kept all three together. I wrote in my notebook, 'Idi preko zida!' *'over the wall!'*

I said, 'OK, let's do it.' I handed Josie 'her' sheet while I tried to waken him by shaking his arm. His eyes opened. I held 'my' sheet up for him to see. It shouted 'EMERGENCY!' Then Josie held up hers. That's when he freaked out big-time! He stood up quickly from the bed and said something I didn't catch. He was unsteady on his feet, but I pulled him with me to the patio doors anyway, Josie in pursuit. I showed him the final sheet. When he saw what I had written, he got up on the table that we had left there at the wall earlier, then we got up beside him. He lost no time getting over the wall, then he just fell into the blackness below with a thud. Oops!

I laughed, in fact we both started giggling almost simultaneously at how ridiculously easy this was. Maybe too easy. Anyway I wasn't going to worry about it now. We had a weapon. That was good wasn't it? Well it was a start anyway.

Josie went straight to her pack and found her cellphone.

I said, 'What are you doing with that Josie?'

She didn't answer. The shocked look on her face was enough.

'What's wrong?' I said, my heart thumping.

She looked at me as she said, 'No signal!'

My heart sank. Jesus, that's all we need. 'Who were you trying to call?'

'I just thought I'd call home but.....' She trailed off disappointed.

'Josie, Milos threatened me today. They want those photos bad. He's given me a few days to think about it, and if the answer's still no......' I trailed off because I didn't want to have to tell her the truth.

She looked at me curiously. 'What?'

I hugged her close. 'Josie don't go off on your own please. I have to know where you are at all times.'

She pulled away and said concerned, 'Sam what are you talking about?'

I avoided her gaze as I replied, 'We have to stick together....' I trailed off again, then a quick change of subject. 'Oh and he warned us about the woman on the beach. We've to tell Živković that we made a mistake about the body.'

'So it looks like they've killed her, doesn't it?'

I nodded. 'Looks like it Josie. And that Susan we met? Maybe she's met the same fate!'

'Oh my God!' she exclaimed. 'What are we going to do?'

'I've got an idea,' I said as I began pacing the floor. 'We find Tess and find out from her everything she knows.'

She nodded. 'Yeah, OK.' I could tell by her expression that she wasn't happy about this idea. I was right. She said, 'That might not be a good idea Sam. How do we know we can trust her? She could be part of this too?'

I stopped pacing and turned to face her. 'Guess we'll just have to chance it. What other choice do we have?'

She said, turning to the door, 'I'll just go find her.' I nodded, but I wondered if that wasn't such a good idea; Josie going off on her own like that.

She opened the door and was just about to step out into the corridor, when Tess passed by. I shouted in a whisper, 'Tess!' in fact we both did, almost simultaneously. Tess turned with a look of alarm.

Josie shouted, 'Come on!' as she beckoned Tess into the room.

As Tess came forward, Josie grabbed her by the arm and pulled her into the room. Tess just stood there looking at us both in turn; a rather large question mark forming over her head.

I said as Josie closed the door and locked it, 'Tess, what's going on here? Who are these guys? What are they running here?'

'It's a health spa and it's run and owned by the Administrator......'

I cut in. 'His name?'

She shrugged. 'Does it matter?'

Josie said, 'We told you we found a body on one of the islands.'

Tess nodded.

I said, 'When we go back there with the policeman, the body's gone. What's going on?'

She shrugged again. 'I-I don't know......'

Josie interrupted, 'And the woman called Susan who found her can't be found either.'

I said, 'I guess she could be working here and maybe we just haven't seen her yet.'

Tess sat on the edge of the bed. I could see she was in a state of shock.

I said, 'So we've decided the best move is to try to escape before we become victims ourselves.'

She said, looking at us both in turn, 'That's a crazy idea!'

I sat on the bed beside her. 'Tess, Milos threatened me today while I was having a massage.' I told her what he said about not trying to leave the island.

She said, 'All the more reason why you shouldn't....'

I interrupted. 'We've acquired a weapon....'

'*What.....!*'

Josie broke in. 'And I've got the keys to one of the power boats.' She held them up for Tess to see. There was a little plastic ID tag attached.

Tess couldn't believe her ears. 'No...! How!'

I said, 'And you can come with us and be our interpreter too.' I finished up with a smile.

'Em....' She hesitated. 'I-I don't want to leave....' She fidgeted with her necklace.

I broke in. 'How long have you been here now? Two years and you don't want to leave this God-damned place?'

'Well, no! I work here,' she said avoiding my gaze.

'Doing what?' Josie asked.

'This and that.'

'Hmm. Strange. That's what Susan said she did too,' I said. I decided not to pursue the question of her job for now. This next statement wasn't true, but I just wanted to test her out. 'I heard you speaking to someone in Croatian, so you could help us escape from here.' I finished off with a smile.

She turned to me. 'I-I can't...?'

I said, 'Can't or won't?'

Josie sat on her left; her Cheshire cat-like grin plastered on. 'Define "this and that" please?'

Tess turned to her and started to speak. 'Well....'

I interrupted as I made a face at Josie. 'Who *are* all these people anyway?'

She turned back to me. 'Boss likes to entertain his business acquaintances.'

I asked, 'And the women? Wives of those business acquaintances?'

She nodded as she said, 'Mostly. The others; *they're* the entertainment.'

'Oh, O-K,' I said nodding slowly. I wondered what kind of entertainment. Striptease? I almost giggled out loud. And maybe that wasn't so far from the truth.

Josie said, 'When we came back to our room there was a guy sleeping on our bed. He was drunk. That's when we found the gun in his coat pocket.'

'Yeah,' Tess said nodding. 'He'd be looking for a woman to sleep with.'

I thought to myself, *'Well, that solves the entertainment mystery then.'* I said, a little shocked, 'Oh, I see. So, what's with the weapon?'

She said, 'He'll be with Security.' She added, 'Oh, and I don't have much Croatian, sorry.'

Josie said brightly, 'OK cool, um.... about the language I mean.' She laughed.

I smiled, 'Security huh?' I looked at Josie. 'Let's hope they're all as drunk as this jerk. If they are, escaping from here could be a breeze.' I laughed.

Tess said concerned, 'Don't be too sure.'

'How many security guys are there?' I asked. 'I mean, would you know them by sight?'

She shook her head. 'No, sorry.' She stood up from the bed and crossed the room to the patio doors. She stood staring out into the darkness. 'And I don't know how many.'

Josie said, 'Our cellphones don't work here, so we're going to have to use a landline.' She stood up and moved to the door. 'Where's the nearest one? Reception?'

Tess nodded. 'Might not be a good idea to use that though.'

'I want to call a friend,' I said. 'It's someone we met on our trip.'

She looked at me with a troubled expression. 'When were you planning to do this?'

I shrugged. 'Um....soon. Tonight?' I looked to Josie for support. She nodded.

'You'll be taking a chance if you don't want to be seen or overheard.'

'Maybe, but we don't have much choice,' I said as I joined Josie at the door. 'Hey you can keep watch Tess.'

'What? Now?' She crossed the room to join us at the door. 'OK, but we'll have to be very careful. They don't like anyone using the phone at Reception.'

'Tough,' I said as I opened the door.

I was about to step into the corridor when Tess pushed passed me. 'I'll get the phone and bring it back here.'

I said, startled, 'Are you sure it's safe?'

Josie asked, 'A telephone point in here?'

Tess nodded.

I sighed. 'Yeah, remember what the guy said? "This room was for privileged guests"?'

Josie just nodded.

Tess headed for Reception. We stepped back into the room and closed the door. Josie poured some wine for us from the fridge.

As she handed me a glass she said, 'Hope she doesn't get caught.'

'When she returns we'll have to work fast before someone misses it.' I said.

I'm wondering just who the Boss is. Was he at the party too? Of course he was *stupid*! Why invite guests around then hide yourself away. So he'd know who we were by now. We've been walking around in our own clothes for long enough, for heaven's sake!

I'd wanted to phone Bob. I wanted to see him again before we went home, that is, if we ever got off of this island. Maybe by some miracle, he might be able to help, but maybe that's hoping for too much. He never seemed to be around when we needed him. I thought it was worth a try anyway; maybe he could contact the police and....

My thoughts were interrupted by Tess returning. The door opened and she came in clutching the phone, then she went straight to a telephone point beside our bed. She plugged it in and said, 'Just dial the number and....'

I cut her off as I threw my arms around her. 'Oh, you're an angel.'

I could see Josie was about to say something, so I shot her my killing stare. She made a face but said nothing.

I sat on the bed as Tess crossed to the door again. She said, 'I'm going back to Reception to keep guard. I'll make sure nobody asks too many questions. I'll think of something anyway.'

I said, 'OK thanks. Just be careful Tess.'

She disappeared from the room closing the door behind her.

I took my cellphone from my pocket and retrieved Bob's number from the directory, then picked up the receiver and dialled. I waited and waited, then a voice spoke. It wasn't Bob. It was a young woman. 'Pozdrav, tko je govorio?' she said in Croatian.

My heart was racing. 'Do you speak English?'

'Yes.'

I thought quickly, *Thank God for that!* I said relieved, 'Oh, is Bob there?'

'He's having a bath. Can I help you? Who is speaking?'

I hesitated. 'Em.... Sam Winter. Could you pass a message to him please?'

'Yes.'

'Could you,' I said as my hand found the note the policeman had given me, 'please get him to phone this number? Our cellphones don't work here.' I quoted the phone number on there. I don't want those bastards cottoning onto my plan. The line could be bugged for all we know. 'And one other thing. Tell him we're staying on an island off Dubrovnik, and we're having a wonderful time at a health spa, OK?'

'OK, I'll tell him. Is that all?'

'Yeah...yeah that's all thanks.' I hung up.

In the morning after breakfast we made our way to the shore from our room to wait for Tess to pick us up. Josie had given her the keys to the powerboat. We'd swim out to it if necessary. Our clothes would dry on us anyway with the hot sun. We sat together on the rocks listening for the sound of the boat's engine. Well the sound of any boat really, but hoping that it was Tess and not some of the gang out looking for us.

The seconds grew to minutes and I was getting apprehensive about Tess. Had she been apprehended by someone? Josie and I had barely spoken since we sat down. Josie's thoughts were elsewhere anyway, I could tell by her worried expression. I turned to her, about to say something when we heard the sound of a boat's engine starting up. In less than a minute, we could see it approach and my heart leapt in anticipation. Can we do this without getting caught? When Tess had gotten as close to the rocky shore as she dared, we waded out to the boat, but had to swim the last few yards. Tess helped me climb aboard then the two of us helped Josie.

Tess said as she sat herself on the rear next the engine, 'This is as far as I go.'

I said, my heart thumping, 'No! You have to come with us Tess. This could be your only chance for escape.'

'Tess.....! Josie said.

Tess shook her head. 'I have to get back before I'm missed. Someone will be looking for me.' With that, she dropped over the side into the water, then began to make for shore.

We'd have to move fast if we were going to make a clean getaway. I turned, intending to make for the driving seat, but Josie had beat me to it! No, I can't allow her to drive, she'll only slow us down. She doesn't have the experience. Well I don't have any experience either when it comes to high-speed powerboats but at least I've held a driver's licence for longer than she has, so......

She was about to turn the key when I grasped her arm. 'No, Josie. I'll drive.'

She wasn't prepared to listen to me. I could tell by the way she unfastened my fingers from her arm. 'No, it's OK. I can handle it.'

Just then, I heard the sound of a powerboat engine start up and voices shouting from the direction of the house. They're on to us! Somebody must have raised the alarm!

I shouted, 'Josie come on! Let me drive! Hurry!' I grasped her arm again tightly intending to pull her from her seat.

She ignored me and turned the key and at the same time hitting the throttle! The boat shot forward like a bullet throwing me onto my back as it bounced over the surface of the Adriatic. With great difficulty I was able to scramble into the passenger seat and fasten my belt. The roar of the other boat grew louder now. I had been hoping that it had been heading for the mainland and the shouting had no connection with our escape, but I guess that was just wishful thinking on my part. I'm also hoping that Tess wouldn't get into any kind of trouble for helping us escape.

I shouted over the roar of the engine, as I shot a glance over my right shoulder. They were gaining on us fast! 'Josie, they'll be on us in no time!'

The island that we swam to earlier was coming up fast. She shouted, 'Gonna try to lose them!' She's gotta be kidding. Out here? She's crazy!

I shouted, 'Josie are you mad! What are you thinking!'

They were gaining on us fast. Any second now and they'll be up our ass! A voice shouted through a loudhailer. 'Stop now or we'll open fire!'

With peripheral vision, I saw Josie thrust something at me. It was the weapon that we had found in that jerk's pocket. I could have kissed her.

A shot rang out and slammed into something nearby. I jumped. That was just *too* close. Now it's war! I'm furious. Nobody shoots at me; if they do, they can expect full retaliation! I loosened my belt and leaned out over the side. I took careful aim at the driver of the other boat. I wasn't sure how many guys were on there. Aiming is difficult with all this bouncing up and down, and I can't afford to miss. I don't have unlimited ammunition, and they'll have more than one weapon at their disposal. Several more shots, and this time they hit the rear of our boat. They're trying to disable us. I aimed for the driver again and pulled the trigger, once, twice, then the windshield shattered and the craft veered off to the right. His companion I could see, was trying to regain control of the boat, but without too much success. Good! Just the opportunity we needed to buy us some time, and for me to work out a plan of action.

I shouted to Josie as I positioned myself back in my seat. 'Get to the other side of the island and slow right down. I want to get off so I can get a shot at their engines, then you head back to the mainland and get help, OK!'

She shouted back, 'Are you mad!' She grinned back then accelerated.

We shot off towards the head of the island then made a left turn. I'm hoping the jerks in the other boat haven't seen us. Josie slowed right down and close to the rocky shore.

I shouted, 'Now!'

She killed the engine briefly and I took a giant leap onto the flat rocks. I landed awkwardly and lost my footing. I tried grasping a tree branch so as not to lose my balance, but I slipped on something and went down heavily on my front. That sure knocked the wind out of me. Luckily I didn't hit my head on the ground. I heard Josie start the engine again and she headed off towards the mainland as instructed. I picked myself up slowly, making sure I hadn't broken anything, then stepped behind the nearest tree and waited. The other boat appeared now around the headland. They slowed down as they passed my hiding place. Several of them are standing up trying to discover where I am. They would have heard our engines stop then start again and assume that I had got off here. I intend to disable them good then take them out one by one. Well, that was the plan anyway.

Seconds later, they continued on their course slowly, then I quickly took aim at their engines and fired; one, two, three shots and their boat was dead in the water. Smoke billowed from the rear and the first of the guys leapt into the water. It was only waist deep, but it slowed his progress to the shore, just enough for me to put a bullet in his chest. He dropped where he stood. Another three jumped overboard, weapons at the ready, but they're sitting ducks. They have no cover and so it was just a matter of picking them off one by one. Well that is how it should have gone anyway, but one of the guys managed to reach the shore before I could take him out. He had gotten himself behind a tree and began firing at me. He's trying to cover for his two companions. Shots rang out from the other two who were still in the water. They struck the tree above my head. I returned the fire and shot one through the heart. The other one kept firing at me. I kept my head down and inched forward keeping very low. The guy behind the tree poked his head around just enough for me to put a bullet in it. He didn't know what hit him. The last of them was only now getting out of the water. He spotted me aiming at him and opened fire. One of the slugs struck a tree on my left, the other hit me in the left shoulder. I was thrown backwards then I lost my balance and fell on my back. The pain was excruciating! My shoulder was on fire and blood was oozing out of it. I rolled onto my stomach and just lay there gasping for breath. I thought I was going to black out. I could see my adversary crouching low and running to the nearest rocks, then the sound of the cavalry arriving. I could hear the sound of a boat engine approach. So could he because he turned his head towards the sound. He had gotten himself behind a tree and had been aiming at me lying there on the ground, but the sound of the engines distracted him just enough for me to hit him with two in the chest. He dropped to the ground out of sight into the vegetation.

I picked myself up slowly and clutching my shoulder as the sound of the powerboat drew close. I waved to it thinking it was Josie returning for me, then I felt my head begin to swim and my knees buckled. I blacked out before I hit the ground. That's all I remember.

Chapter 24.

As soon as I came to, it hit my nostrils; that acrid smell of cigar smoke. I hate it. My arm had been bandaged where the slug had hit me. It was still hurting bad. I was in what appeared to be an office, and tied to a computer swivel chair. My ankles were tied together and the legs of the chair; my hands were behind my back and a single rope had been wound around my middle and the chair back. I could get out of this one if left alone here, because I had my knife in the back of my jeans and could reach it easily enough, only I was sharing the room with someone, and they were at my back. I could tell it was a male because he coughed several times, then continued to draw on his cigar without saying anything.

I'm wondering what's happened to Josie. Did she get away safely or did they catch her too? If she was, she should be in this room with me. Unless....! I didn't want to think about that. Would she tell them where the pictures were? I hope they don't hurt her. I'm hoping maybe she's somewhere in the building or hiding out somewhere on this island. If she's come to any harm, God knows what I'm going to tell her parents if I ever make it out of here in one piece.

I heard a door open at my back and someone came in closing it behind them. They came round to stand in front of me. He was a big guy, built like a mountain and standing about six feet tall. His head was completely shaven, but his round red face was badly in need of one. It was impossible to guess his age. He just stood there looking down on me with a silly grin plastered on. He's awaiting instructions from his boss before he starts on me.

The guy behind me said in a husky voice, 'You're probably wondering where your young friend has gone?' He coughed.

I thought, my heart leaping, *So she didn't get away after all!* I kept quiet. I'm working on a plan. If they think I've fallen out with Josie..... I said, staring at the floor, 'I don't give a *shit* about her!' I put as much venom into it as I could muster.

'Oh? Well that's not what she said about you.'

I said nothing.

'She said you and she were the best of friends.' Cough.

I said, 'She was speaking in the past tense.'

He coughed just before he asked, 'Your shoulder still hurting? You were lucky it was only a graze.'

I kept quiet.

The goon standing in front of me nodded. He'd just taken an instruction from his boss. He struck me hard on my sore shoulder and I cried out, then he hit me again; harder this time! The blow knocked my chair over and I landed on my right side. Tears were filling my eyes. This was from the pain. I gritted my teeth and tried hard not to show any emotion. He picked me up again making sure that it was by my shoulders to cause me maximum pain. I screamed out briefly and my head slumped forward. My t-shirt was soaking with perspiration and sweat was stinging my eyes. I was feeling sick and my shoulder was on fire too. I couldn't stop thinking about Josie and what was happening to *her*. She was a strong and determined girl. I was sure that she would take care of the photos and come up with a plan to throw them off the scent. She's not about to hand over the photos to anyone except maybe the police. She'll find a way. I know she will.

The guy behind me said, 'OK, are you ready to tell me where you've hidden the pictures?'

I said through the pain, 'I don't know,' I gasped, 'where they are. *She's* got them!' I shouted the last few words.

Maybe she's already told them, but if I know Josie, it won't be where she says they are. I just hope she doesn't do anything stupid though. Why do I keep *saying* that?

The goon standing in front of me hit me again, this time it was on the left side of my face with the palm of his hand.

'Ah!' I screamed.

He hit me again, harder this time, but on the right side of my face. I could taste blood now. Again I cried out! The pain was excruciating. The chair teetered on two wheels and almost toppled over before quickly righting itself again.

The guy behind me said, 'Come on Miss Winter, you know better than that.' I heard a lighter snap. 'The pain will only get worse if you don't tell us where they are. It's up to you.' He coughed.

I shouted, 'Go to *hell!*' I gasped again before screaming, 'I've already told you! She's got them!'

'As you wish,' he said.

He gave an instruction in Croatian to my torturer who nodded in response, then walked across the room to my left and returned with a vicious-looking knife.

My heart leapt into my mouth. *'What the hell now!'* I thought, my heart thumping hard.

He pulled my t-shirt out at the front and above the rope at my middle, then sliced it from the hem to the neckline! Next step's the bra! Thoughts such as, *'I'm in deep shit now; I can't tell them what I don't know, and how the hell do I get out of this one!'* were racing through my mind just then. I couldn't believe this was happening. My torturer hooked two fingers under the piece of fabric that held the cups of my bra together and inserted the knife there.

'Shit! I thought. 'No!' I screamed. He's trying to scare me, and this time he's succeeded.

A broad grin appeared across his face now. But just as the knife moved slowly upwards, there was a knock on the door. The knife was lowered. Thank God! The guy behind me answered it. There was a brief exchange of words in Croatian, and my torturer threw his knife onto a table off to my left. I breathed a big sigh of relief but didn't say anything.

I heard the door close again. The guy behind me said, 'Well it seems your friend has told us where to find the pictures.'

I breathed another sigh of relief on hearing this. I'm wondering what she's told them. I'm also hoping that they didn't have to resort to torture to get it. She might even be..... I can't go there. I have to stay calm. Think positively. Take a deep breath and let it out *very* slowly. I did.

The guy behind me said, 'You're going for a boat ride now, or rather Boris here will take you and your friend.....'

I cut him off as I shouted, 'What! You've got your damned photos! What more do you want!'

'You were warned not to try to escape but you chose not to listen.' He coughed. 'Oh, *and* you managed to kill a lot of my men. Now *that* wasn't nice.'

'And you're next on my hit list!' I screamed. 'I'll take you all out one by one!' I'm losing control. Tears are forming, but I have to keep my nerve. I've got my knife. It'll be OK. Yeah. Jesus, what have I got us into.

'You're not going to do *anything* my dear except go for a dip. I know you like the sea.' He laughed.

Boris came round to my back and blindfolded me, then he pushed the chair forward and I was wheeled from the room. Minutes later we were in our room and I was placed before the patio doors. I know this because he removed the blindfold. Then he left the room again.

'What the hell's he playing at! Why remove it?' My thoughts were interrupted by someone entering the room.

I turned to see Josie tied in a similar way to a computer chair. She was placed beside me. She was wearing a blindfold too, and was crying and her t-shirt had been cut just like mine. Her bra was on her lap but her breasts were still covered by the t-shirt so I couldn't see what they had done to her, if anything. Her chin was on her chest. I just wanted to hug her but of course it was impossible. I'll kill them all if I ever get out of this!

I said, a large lump forming in my throat, 'Josie, I'm here.'

'Sam!' She broke down. She's lost it! Now she can't stop.

I said, trying to console her, 'Josie it's going to be OK.' I don't know why the hell I said *that*. Of course it *isn't* OK. We're about to die. Drown in the sea for God's sake!

She just whimpered and cried. I tried to stay calm, but I could feel the tears forming, then one of them rolled down my left cheek and I could taste it's saltiness. Plenty more salt where we're going! I felt my chair being lifted now and I was pushed through the patio doors towards the sea and set down on the rocks at the water's edge. Josie was placed beside me. She was still whimpering.

I whispered, 'What did they do to you?'

She didn't answer immediately.

Someone put my blindfold back on.

She said through tears, 'They used a cigarette lighter....' She could barely get the words out.

I didn't hear the rest as the sound of a power boat starting up drowned her voice. I could hear it getting louder as it approached from the left. In seconds it was only a few yards from where we sat. I felt myself being suddenly lifted and carried once more. I guessed at this point that two of the gang were lifting me across to the boat because I could feel my feet in the water, then I was placed in the boat. The engine was started and we sped off at high speed. I'm not sure where Josie was at this point, as the roar of the engines would drown any sounds from her.

In less than a minute the engine was cut and I could hear Josie crying, in fact she was hysterical. She let out a loud scream, then her voice was cut off by a loud splash.

'*Oh my God!*' I thought, my mind in a whirl. '*They've actually thrown her overboard! Jesus, it's my turn now!*'

It was too. I felt myself being lifted by two guys one second, and the next I was hitting the water with a loud splash. I took a deep breath just before my head went under the water. Josie can hold her breath longer than I can. She demonstrated that earlier in the vacation, but will she be able to hold it long enough for me to reach her!

'*Christ, here we go! Where will I land on the bottom? How deep is it? Will I be able to reach my knife in time? Where's Josie?*' Those thoughts were racing through my brain. I heard the power boat engine start and it sped off, presumably back to the island.

I'm still blindfolded. First things first. I felt the chair hit bottom then it toppled backwards. Damn! I was lying on my back now. This was going to make it difficult for me to reach my knife! I've no idea where Josie is. They threw her over the opposite side, so she could be anywhere. I've lost my bearings completely. My hands are tied together but my left is not so tight. I'm trying to free it now with the help of my right, but I can only use the tips of my fingers for this. At last, in what seemed like eternity, my left hand was free. I breathed a big mental sigh of relief. Now my hand was sliding down the back of my jeans and I found the secret zippered pocket. My lungs are beginning to hurt and I don't know how long I can hold my breath for. I unzipped and drew the knife out. I pressed the button on the handle and the blade sprung out. I lost no time in slicing through the rope on my right hand. It only took seconds. The blade is very sharp and has no difficulty cutting through most types of rope.

Next came the blindfold. I'm looking around for Josie but I can't see her. Jesus! Now my legs and I'm free at last! I'm heading for the surface now. My lungs can't take any more; they're bursting for the lack of air! I gasped as my head appeared above the surface, then I took a deep breath and dived again.

Where the hell is she! I dived right to the bottom, then I spotted her. She'd been behind me all the time! Why didn't I see her? Her chair was up-right, but there was no sign of life! She looked like a rag doll just sitting there with her head slumped forward on her chest; now then bobbing up and down with the whim of the currents. Was she unconscious? I lost no time on reaching her, then I got to work on her ropes immediately. First her hands, now her legs. She still didn't show any signs of life! *Jesus,* am I too late!

My mind shouted at her, *'No! You can't die on me Josie! You just can't!'*

I was too late and she was dead, and that was that! No, it can't be! Now I had her free of the chair, but I didn't want to waste any more time with her rope, so it was straight back up to the surface with the rope still tied around her middle. Getting her to the surface was like swimming in treacle. It seemed to be taking forever. Then, at last we made it. As her head came out of the water, she gave a loud gasp and coughed and spluttered. I thought she was going to choke to death!

'Josie, we're safe now! We're safe.' For now anyway but I'm not expecting that to last.

We just clung to each other and cried, then after a few seconds she coughed, cleared her throat and said, 'What's our next move?'

I shrugged. 'Dunno. I'll think of something in a minute.'

I was looking towards the main island where the house was. The island that we had swum to earlier was about a quarter mile behind me. I'm thinking we'd swim back to the main island and retrieve our packs, that is, if they're still where we'd left them in our room. I voiced my plan to Josie. She nodded.

I said, 'These bastards think we're dead, and we've got to keep it that way. That means keeping a low profile and at the same time finding a weapon that we can use.'

'OK, let's go,' she said. She didn't wait for me but started swimming away from me.

I followed on.

Chapter 25.

Back at the island we got ourselves behind some rocks just before we climbed out of the water. It was only knee deep here. I suggested to Josie that she tie her t-shirt into a makeshift bra as it was useless anyway. She pulled it off and folded it several times then I tied it for her at the back. OK, that'll have to do for now. We stepped out of the sea and approached the building with caution. There were no windows on this side of the house save the patio doors and they were closed. I'm hoping they're not locked. We have no cover here if we have to hide, so there's no turning back now. We have no weapons to defend ourselves bar my knife. I wondered, if others had been allocated our room since we had gone, how they would react to us trying to enter this way. But my biggest concern was meeting one of the gang here.

We made it to the doors without incident. Well, Josie reached them first. She had pulled them open before I could stop her, then she disappeared inside. There was silence for a few seconds. My heart leapt into my mouth. If there's anyone in there that we'd rather not meet.....! There was. Well, not in the *room* exactly. As I stepped through the patio doors, Josie was clutching her pack to her chest and pointing to the bathroom without saying a word. I wondered at first what she meant, then I heard water running. Someone was having a piss at least that's how it sounded to me!

She whispered, 'What do we *do*?'

I had a quick look around the room then I had a plan. I whispered back, 'You get out there.' I pointed to the patio doors. 'But keep the doors open. I want to distract him.' Assuming it is one of them and not one of the female staff.

Josie did as instructed whilst I hid behind an armchair in the far corner and facing the bathroom. The patio doors are on my left, and when the guy crosses the room to close them, or goes to investigate, I come at him with something heavy. Well, that *was* the plan anyway.

So, there I was, crouching behind the chair and Josie standing just outside the patio doors. I heard the toilet being flushed then water at the sink. Seconds later the door opened and he came out. I could see him from my hiding position. It wasn't Milos and it wasn't Boris, and he was too young to be the Boss. He wore black pants and a green sweatshirt. I held my breath and prayed that he'd come over to where we were, but he stopped at my pack that was lying on the floor and then hesitated. He's probably wondering what's happened to Josie's pack. He's spotted the open patio doors and comes over. He's got a weapon stuck in the waistband of his pants at the back. This could be our ticket out of here. My spirits just soared. Josie's standing just outside with a big grin plastered on; her pack beside her.

I thought, *'Jesus, what's she up to?'*

He's wondering too. He hesitated for a second and that's when I made my move. Well, what I intended to do was come at him from behind with the heavy vase from the coffee table and bring it down on the back of his head, but, as I snatched it up quickly, I tripped on the leg of the armchair. He heard it and spun on his heal to face me. I dropped the vase quickly and straightened up to face him. He had a look of shock on his face. He said something in Croatian, I think, then Josie went into action. She hit him with something heavy and he dropped where he stood.

I gave her a big hug and said, 'Oh you're an angel.' I could see Josie was about to say something, so I said, teasing, 'Don't even *think* about it.'

She made a face, then, 'Look what I've found.' She held the weapon up for me to see.

I snatched it out of her grasp. 'Thank *you*. I saw it first.'

'But.....' she protested.

I cut in. 'Find a cord and tie him, then we'll put him in there.' I indicated the bathroom.

She pulled the electrical cord from a table lamp and began to tie his hands. I pulled his shoe laces out and tied his feet, then between us we dragged him to the bathroom and left him in the tub. I had a wash at the sink as did she. Back in the room, I changed into my cream-coloured jeans and light-blue t-shirt. I felt a new girl already. Josie wore her short white t-shirt and her only other pair of cream-coloured jeans.

I said, as I picked the gun from the bed where I had dropped it, 'I wonder if he has any more clips.....' I broke off as Josie held two of them up for me to see. 'Oh! OK,' I said startled. 'Give them here.' She did. I pocketed them. I said thoughtfully, 'Have to find *you* a weapon somehow because we're going to have to tackle those bastards sooner or later.'

'Sam, how do we get out of here without being seen?' she said with an anxious look. 'We can't just walk out the door can we? We'll be spotted immediately.'

She had a point. OK, plan of action. I voiced my plan to her. We go over the wall like Josie did the other night, but it's going to have to be quick. Find a window of opportunity and go for it. It'll have to work first time; no second chances here. I'm hoping that Bob *did* contact the police, and that they're on their way now, but we can't just sit here and wait and see, because if he didn't....

'OK let's move,' I said as I put on my pack.

We made our way outside, my gun in my waistband at the back and hidden by my backpack. The table was against the wall where we had left it, thank goodness. She was up there first, then she gave me a hand. She was over the wall first too before I could stop her! Too late now. She had dropped down onto the ground below before I could warn her that I had spotted a male emerge through the patio doors on this side. He hesitated then turned on his heel and dashed back inside. He appeared to be middle-aged and balding on top. He wore a bright yellow Hawaiian shirt and white pants.

I shouted to Josie, 'Did you see that!'

'No, what!'

I jumped down beside her. 'That guy....' I pointed to the house.

'What guy?'

'Jesus!' I said under my breath.

I pulled her with me across the yard to a round table with four chairs. I pulled the table over onto its side to give us some cover because I suspected that we were going to be shot at. He re-emerged with a handgun. He doesn't know that we're armed and I'm not about to tell him. We want to be able to leave here unobserved. Yeah, right. We'll see.

He said as he approached us crouching there behind the table, 'Come out. We go see boss now.'

'No way,' I said softly to no-one in particular and stayed put.

Josie stood up quickly with her hands up.

I whispered, 'What the hell are you *doing*!'

But it was too late; she was already stepping out from behind the table. Is this part of some plan? If not..... I had no choice but to stand up too. She stopped in her tracks and waited for me, then as I came forward to join her, she put her arm around my waist. I'm curious. What the hell's she doing? I felt her hand remove the weapon and with peripheral vision, watched her put it into her own waistband.

'Oh God,' I thought. *'Here we go.'*

He walked ahead but every now and then, he turned to point the gun at us. Once in the house, he crossed to the door then turned to us.

He said, 'OK, we go see boss now.'

He turned away again briefly to the door and had only just put his hand on the door handle, when Josie made her move! She pulled her weapon out in a flash and pointed it at him. My jaw dropped. This girl is full of surprises. I handed her a cushion off of a chair to use as a silencer just in case.

She said, 'Don't even *think* about it. Drop your weapon and don't turn round.'

But he *did* turn and know doubt thought that he'd catch her out, but Josie was quicker. Just as he raised the gun towards her, she pulled the trigger; once, twice in the chest. He dropped where he stood.

I threw my arms around her. 'God you're an angel!' I said. 'You've done it again.'

She said as she pulled away, 'I don't like killing people Sam. This is going to hit me later if we ever get out of here alive.'

'Yeah, maybe,' I said absently. That's because I was working on a plan. I took the guy's gun and found several spare clips in his pockets. As I straightened up I said, 'Josie, time to kick ass. We've had enough trouble with these people already. I think it's time for some revenge huh?'

She nodded, but I could tell that she wasn't too comfortable with that idea. Yep, I was right too. She said, 'We're only two against God knows how many others.'

I said, 'Yeah I know, but we do know Milos and I've met Boris. God I'd know guy anywhere.'

'Yeah, just like you knew Bob huh? Remember, in the restaurant?'

'Shut up Josie,' I said annoyed. I turned my attention to the guy on the floor. 'Help me get him into the bathroom.'

So between us, we dragged him into the bathroom and dumped him in the tub again.

She said, her smile returning, 'Do we work as a team or what!' She gave a short laugh.

I said, crossing to the bedroom door, 'Yep we sure do.'

I opened it cautiously and peeked round it. No-one around. The coast is clear. I was almost through the door when Josie tapped my shoulder.

'Sam?' she whispered.

'Not now Josie,' I snapped.

'Sam!' she insisted.

I turned to her quickly. 'This had better be good.'

'Wouldn't it be better to stick to our original plan?' She sounded anxious.

I stepped back into the room and closed the door. '*Excuse* me? *Our* plan?'

She said, 'I'm scared and just want to get back home in one piece.'

'You don't think I do?' I added as I began pacing the floor, 'Hey who do you think got us into this in the first place?'

She said incredulously, '*What*! *I* got us into this?'

'OK let's see; I get this frantic phone call from you suggesting that we go away together on a vacation to Europe……'

She broke in. 'Frantic….?'

I said, crossing to the patio doors, 'Come on. We don't have time to argue over trivial things.'

'But….'

She trailed off as I interrupted with, 'You coming?' I laughed.

Outside we headed for the wall at the side of the building that Josie had climbed over last night, then, if we're quick enough, we'd get ourselves to a power boat at the jetty. But knowing our luck we'd pick one that was low on gas, or had no keys in the ignition. Personally I'm not really caring *how* we get one. I'll quite happily beg, steal *or* borrow, or maybe even hijack! I'll do *anything* just to get off this island!

This wall was a piece of cake to climb. It was about nine feet high and made of the local grey-white limestone slabs, so plenty of footholds. Yep, this should be a breeze. Josie was up there first but I managed to catch her ankle before she reached the top. We have to make sure the coast is clear first. No mistakes.

She looked down and whispered, '*What?*'

I smiled back. 'Wait for me?' I climbed.

When I got to the top, I put my head over and surveyed the scene before us. We had a good view of the entrance; a guy slouched close to the doorway smoking; two women sitting laughing at something. I turned my attention to the jetty now. There were three power boats tied up there. Two were facing towards us so we couldn't see if they had keys in them or not, but he third was facing away from us and had a guy in it, and by the looks of it, was waiting for someone. He kept looking around and fidgeting with the keys that he held. He was about fifty-something, about 170 pounds and balding on top. Our taxi? My spirits just soared.

I turned to Josie with a grin and whispered, 'See what I see? Don't run, just walk down to the jetty and casually climb aboard, OK?'

'Yep.' Then she was over the wall and jumping onto the ground below. I followed.

We strolled down to the jetty. Josie kept looking around nervously. When we reached our 'taxi', we climbed aboard in a hurry. That's because the guy at the controls had been facing away from us, but as we stepped aboard, he must have heard us and turned. He looked startled. We obviously weren't who he'd expected.

I dropped my pack on the floor and pulled my weapon out. I pointed it at him. 'Drive!' I said.

Josie poked me in the ribs to get my attention. She said quickly, 'Sam, that guy on the door has just gone inside in a hurry. We'd better move!'

I got into the passenger seat and poked my weapon into the guy's ribs to emphasise the fact that I meant business. He got the message and put the key into the ignition. In seconds we were heading off at high speed. I indicated to the guy that he should head straight for the mainland ASAP! He nodded his understanding.

We hadn't gotten far when we heard the sound of an engine start. I turned to the left and said to Josie, 'Keep an eye out for that boat. Tell me if they....'

I didn't get a chance to say anything more, as the guy beside me elbowed me savagely in the face! I cried out from the pain and could feel blood. I think I cut my lip, then he grabbed my right wrist in an attempt to wrench the weapon from my grasp.

Josie had seen what happened. She hit him hard on the left side of his face with her weapon several times, and each time he cried out.

I almost let go of the weapon, but Josie's attempts to disable the guy before he snapped my wrist, appeared to be having some effect because he loosened his grip slightly. That's when I broke free and began hitting him in the face too. There was a lot of blood running down his face now, then Josie I think, couldn't take any more.

She screamed, 'Let go of her or I'll shoot you dead!' She pressed her weapon into his shoulder.

The guy probably thought she was bluffing because he chose to ignore her threats, and that's when she pulled the trigger. He screamed and grasped his shoulder with his right hand. I began to hit him on his blooded shoulder with all my strength.

Josie shouted, 'There's a boat coming up fast Sam!'

I shouted at the guy, 'Get out of the seat or I'll shoot you!'

He did, and retreated to the rear of the craft. I didn't see what happened next as I was too preoccupied with getting myself into the driving seat, then we shot off in the direction of the mainland. The next thing I heard was a loud bang from the rear as a firearm was discharged. I turned quickly as I was concerned for Josie's safety, then I realised that it was she who had fired the shot. The guy was lying on his back on the deck with a hole in his chest.

'What happened!' I shouted over the roar of the engine.

'He pulled a gun on me! I didn't have a choice!'

Now we have another weapon and more ammunition. Something told me we were going to need it. I took the gun from her and stuffed it into my waistband at the front beside the other one.

It was just as Josie got herself into the passenger seat and fastened her belt, that I thought I heard another boat's engine start. That didn't mean anything in itself, but I was sure hoping that this wasn't backup for the one already on our tail. Any time now and they'd be firing at us. They'd want to make sure we never reach the mainland.

I wasn't familiar with the instrument panel here, but if the 'clock' down on the right-hand corner was what I thought it was, we were low on fuel! That's all we needed. I'm formulating a plan in my head. We're low on gas so reaching the mainland at this speed just isn't gonna happen, so, I plan to turn around and ram them. I voiced my intentions to Josie, and, yep, you guessed it; she wasn't happy about this.

Bullets began to whiz over our heads now. I began to zigzag erratically to avoid them. It caused our craft to bounce alarmingly over the surface. Just as well we were strapped in.

I shouted, 'Josie we don't have a choice about this! We're low on fuel so we're gonna run out soon!' It's not rocket science is it?

I could tell by her expression that she still wasn't happy about it. I shouted, 'Just before we hit, we jump overboard OK!' Well that was my plan anyway.

'You're crazy! They'll just run us down with the second boat!'

I shook my head. 'No! When we hit the water, we dive then come up again and take them by surprise!' I nodded, satisfied that I had explained myself fully.

'Yeah, right!' She still thinks I'm crazy, I can't think why. 'How do you propose to do that!'

'Josie you ask too many questions! You'll know what to do when the time comes!'

She didn't say anything. She's till not entirely convinced. I can't say I blamed her. If I was in her shoes, I'm not sure I would feel at ease either, considering our present predicament.

A bullet just hit our windshield and shattered it. Damn! Now that was just *too* close! Lucky I'm still zigzagging. Now it's war. I'm *very* angry, and that means only one thing; revenge! Oh God, am I going to enjoy this! Time to put my plan to the test. I swung the wheel fully counter-clockwise and the craft made a sudden left turn. In seconds, we were heading straight for the nearest of our adversaries. This is going to have to be quick, because I just had a sudden change of plan. I want to shoot at them rather than ram them, but Josie will have to drive.

'Josie, take over the wheel!'

'Pardon!'

I'm beginning to lose my cool now. 'Josie come on! Take over the driving!'

I vacated the driving seat and she took my place, albeit, reluctantly, then she cut the engine.

'What the hell Josie!' I said in alarm as I grasped her arm. 'Why are you stopped!'

She just grinned back.

'*Oh Jesus! Another of her plans,*' I thought quickly.

She got herself up and onto the front of the craft and lay flat on her stomach and took aim at the other boat which had also now cut its engines. They were only just within shooting range. They probably think they have the advantage because we only have handguns, but they're in for a surprise. I noted that there were four figures in the other boat.

She said laughing, 'Think they're going to surrender!'

'Nope,' I replied as I removed both my guns and took careful aim. 'They're not taking any prisoners either and neither am I!'

I heard her say, 'She's serious!'

'You bet!' I shouted back.

Several shots from an AK47 or something, whizzed over my head, then they turned their attention on Josie. More shots but this time they struck our boat close to the front. Any higher and Josie would have taken one in the head. She removed herself rapidly from her position and slid down beside me. More shots from the AK47 and this time they were clearly meant for me. I know this because I'd just taken one in the right shoulder. It threw me backwards onto the floor. I clutched my shoulder tightly and gritted my teeth against the searing pain. Josie grabbed the weapon out of my right hand and began to shoot at the gunman who had just shot me. She went into action with both guns blazing. One, two, three, four, five, six bullets fired off in quick succession. Three of them hit their target! He went down with two slugs in the chest and the other shattering his jaw. I could have kissed her.

She turned to me. 'Hey, you see that!' she shouted triumphantly. 'Am I good or what!'

'Yeah! Keep your head down or you'll get it blown off! These guys mean business!'

As she ducked her head she said, 'No kidding!'

Another of the guys picked up the AK47 and took over where his comrade had left off. He began to fire indiscriminately at our craft. Bullets thudded at random into the side of the boat then over our heads. After several seconds of this, there was a brief pause as he stopped to reload another magazine. That's when Josie returned the fire with just two shots. They struck their intended target and he was dead before he hit the deck.

Just then, I heard a sweet sound; that of a police siren. I glanced to the rear of the boat and could see a series of flashing red and blue lights speeding our way.

'Ah, the cavalry's arrived at last!' I shouted in triumph. I could make out three police launches.

Josie's attention had been on the enemy until I made that last remark. She changed her position on the floor and turned to me quickly, and that's when she made her mistake.

I heard a shot very close by then she cried, 'Sam I think I've been hit!'

Now my attention was fully focussed on her. 'No, Josie where!'

She was clutching her left side at the waist. I could see blood oozing from between her fingers.

I pulled off my t-shirt. I said, 'Press this into the wound. Have to get you to a hospital.'

A police power boat pulled up alongside us now on our right, at the same time I was suddenly aware that the firing had stopped. Not only that; the second boat that had been pursuing us had gone. Where had they got to? Back to the house? When I looked around, I saw that the two guys in the other boat were standing up now with their hands above their heads. Another police power boat moved in to make the arrests. I recognised Živkoviæ immediately. As he stepped aboard, I spotted Bob in the power boat with two helmeted policemen dressed in what looked to me like riot gear and carrying semi-automatic weapons. I guess Bob and I had spotted each other at the same time. There was a big smile across his face.

Živkoviæ said to me as he looked around the boat quickly, 'Well I see you two have been busy.' Then he spotted Josie sitting there. 'What's wrong.....?'

I cut him off. 'She's been shot.'

Josie looked up. 'I don't think it's anything serious. I'll live.'

The policeman bent down to examine her wound.

I said with determination, 'Josie, you're going to the hospital even if I have to drag you there myself.'

Meanwhile, Bob had stepped aboard. I threw my arms around his neck and kissed him lightly on the left cheek then pulled away again.

He looked a little puzzled at first. 'Is that it?'

'Uh-huh.' I nodded and smiled.

'Sam I thought we....'

I interrupted. 'Bob, you're nice and sweet and everything but there's nothing doing between us. Let's just keep it as friends huh?'

'But....' he pleaded.

'Listen, I need someone who I can rely on to be there for me. Know what I mean?'

He was silent.

'You were never where you promised to be, and constantly followed around by your girlfriend or pen pal or....'

He cut in. 'She's *not* a girlfriend.....' he insisted.

I sighed and shrugged, 'Yeah, whatever.'

I suddenly realised that Živkoviæ was talking to Josie. She had just finished explaining something to him, but I didn't catch what it was. He nodded and stood up.

I said to him, 'You gonna let the bad guys get away then?' I smiled.

He looked puzzled. 'What do you mean?'

'Didn't you see that boat that was following us?'

'That boat that turned around and left in a hurry you mean?'

I nodded. 'They'll be back at the house I'll bet.'

'It's possible,' he said looking across to the island. 'Or they could be fleeing the country. Anyway you should head back to the mainland now with your friend. She needs a hospital.'

I nodded, then I suddenly remembered we were low on gas. We'd never make it. I mentioned this to him. He suggested that the three of us; me, Josie and Bob return on the police power boat with the two uniformed officers to the mainland. We all thanked Živkoviæ and said our goodbyes. Živkoviæ took our weapons. We won't be needing them now he said, then we climbed aboard the police launch. Well now at least we were on the start of our journey home. Josie can see a doctor and Bob and I can say our goodbyes properly.

Chapter 26.

We all sat strapped in together there on the rear seat; me in the middle with Josie on my left and Bob on my right. I let my mind wander since there was no conversation from those two. I was thinking about how the concert in Pula might go, and looking forward to hearing Oliver's awesome voice again. I had just about started thinking about what I would tell mom and dad when I got home, when my thoughts were interrupted by the police radio making an announcement.

The policeman in the passenger seat turned to us shouting, 'We have just received a report about one of our helicopters being shot at from a power boat with three men aboard! We are going to have to respond because we are closer! Hopefully it won't take too long!'

'Oh my God,' I said to no-one in particular. 'Here we go.' I turned to Josie, remembering her wound. 'You OK?'

'Yeah,' she replied nodding. She was still holding my t-shirt against her side.

'Don't look OK.'

She looked into my eyes smiling. 'I'll be fine, really.' She winced.

We veered off sharply to the left then the policeman in the passenger seat said, 'We've got a distress signal here. We can track them.'

Bob gave a short laugh as he looked at me smiling. 'Do you normally go around in your underwear?'

'I beg your pardon?' I said sounding annoyed. 'As it happens, I was trying to help Josie, OK?' I wasn't smiling.

We began to slow down, and I just realised that we had now located the helicopter, but it wasn't flying. It was in the sea and going down fast. Nearby was a power boat facing away from us with several figures aboard. It was impossible to make out from this distance just how many people were on there. As we drew near, I could just make out two figures in the sea swimming away from the aircraft as it was about to disappear under the water. One of the figures in the boat stood up and machine-gunned the men in the water. He looked suspiciously like Milos.

We all gave a collective gasp of horror, then the policeman in the passenger seat pulled a microphone from under the dash and spoke into it. His voice boomed out across the water. I don't know what he said. The language was Croatian. There was no response from the other boat at first then the weapon was turned on us. Our windshield was sprayed with a volley of bullets and disintegrated. The two policemen didn't stand a chance. Our boat was heading straight for the other craft. Any second now and we'd hit the rear of the other boat. We had to get the driver out of his seat fast! Keeping as low as I could, I dashed forward. Bullets started hammering into the front of our vessel. Josie screamed. Bob tried to hold me back but I shook his hand off of my arm. I tried pulling the poor guy out of the seat, but he was too heavy for me. Bob came forward now and helped me drag him from the seat. By this time our boat was slowing, so Bob jumped into the driving seat. He hit the throttle and we struck the other boat with a resounding crash. I was hoping that we'd destroyed their engines but I guess that would have been asking for too much. I heard a volley of bullets discharge and I guessed the guy with the machine gun was taken off guard. With any luck he's just shot his companions. Bob just continued driving.

There was no point returning to the island because, although we could see islands from here, we couldn't decide which one we had come from, so we headed for the mainland instead. Hopefully the crash would buy us some time. As I looked back at their boat, they still hadn't recovered from the collision, and in no time, we had left them well behind.

The two policemen were well-armed. Between them they had two semi-automatic weapons, two handguns and lots of ammo. They wore bullet-proof vests but in this case, the shots that killed them hit them in the face or neck. Between us, Josie and I stripped the policemen of their vests, helmets and weapons. We laid their bodies on the floor on either side of the boat; just somewhere to put them.

I suspected - well it was a just a hunch - that there were more weapons aboard. They were simply hidden from our view. I voiced this thought to Josie. She looked around the craft as she sat on the bench seat at the rear, then looked up grinning.

'What?' I asked puzzled.

She patted the seat.

'In there?'

She nodded.

I didn't believe it at first, but it was worth a try, so together we removed the bench seat, and.... Jesus! There were enough weapons and ammunition here to start World War III! A rocket launcher with four rockets; tear gas canisters; two assault rifles with scopes. I could go on and on. Let's hope we don't get hit on the rear or this lot will go up like a 4ᵗʰ of July fireworks display with us in the middle.

Josie asked grinning, 'You thinking what I'm thinking?'

I hope not. 'No, what?'

'When I get home, I'm having one of *those* in my trunk.' She pointed to the rocket launcher and giggled.

As I lifted the weapon from its cradle I said laughing, 'Yep, this could give a whole new meaning to the term "road rage".'

She laughed again. 'If the guy behind gets too close, just *blow* him away!'

'You would too, wouldn't you?'

My attention was on the seat back because I had just spotted a hole there. I still held the rocket launcher. It had a 'spike' protruding from the bottom that I reckoned might just fit into this hole. I was right. I fitted the launcher into the hole. OK, we're ready to take on just about anything our adversaries care to throw at us. Well, almost anything.

I don't know why I even thought of it right now, but I suddenly remembered about Josie and the pictures. What did she tell these guys, so I confronted her with it.

'Bob's got them,' she said just like that!

'*What*! *Why*!' I don't believe this girl.

She looked towards Bob there in the driving seat. 'I just thought it would be better if *he* took them to the police.'

'But you didn't think to tell me about it, huh?'

She shook her head.

'And what did you tell those dickheads back there?'

'That you had them?' She smiled.

'*What*?' I said incredulously. 'No wonder that guy was going through our packs. Josie that wasn't a smart thing to do.'

'What did *you* tell them?'

'That you had them?' I laughed. 'So what *did* Bob do with them?'

'You'd better ask him.....' She broke off suddenly and pointed back towards the stern. 'Look!' she said anxiously.

Now my attention was firmly focussed on the object of her concern. We were being followed *and* at speed! Still some distance away but gaining on us fast were our adversaries. We required a clear plan of action and it was going to have to be quick!

Time to discover who these guys really are. I picked up one of the assault rifles and, taking up a crouched position, put the stock to my shoulder and looked through the scope. I suspected that one of the figures in the other boat *was* Milos, but the other two?

'What can you see?' Josie asked.

I didn't say anything at first because I was trying to find the focussing thingy on the scope. Now if this boat would just stop bouncing up and down I'll be able to examine this properly. Then I spotted a switch on the scope. I pushed it and put my eye to the eyepiece and.... it jumped into focus! Autofocus! Cool!

Josie put her hand on my arm. 'Can I see?'

Without taking my eye from the scope I shouted, 'Go tell Bob we need more speed!'

She did.

They were gaining on us fast. Any time now and they... A bullet whizzed over my head. I'm thinking, *Damn, that was close! Too close!'*

I turned my attention to the subject in hand once more. Through the scope I could see Milos. He's armed with something and it's not a handgun. The driver is Boris. I'd know that bastard anywhere. I hope I get to tackle him myself and make him suffer for what he did to me. The third one I can't see properly. He's hidden behind the driving seat. I'm guessing he's the boss. Can't get a clear shot of any of them for all this bouncing up and down.

Bob is zigzagging now, trying to avoid their bullets. Several shots slam into the rear of our boat. I'm guessing that the hull is armour plated otherwise we'd be sunk by now, we've been hit so many times especially at the front. The bench seat is still off and I'm using it for cover by standing it vertically. It's also shielding Bob's back.

I told Josie that I was going to join Bob and that she was to fire at will. I got myself into the passenger seat and pulled the mike from under the dash. I'm calling for assistance if I only get the damned radio to work. Maybe there was a distress beacon on here. Maybe we were already being tracked. Wouldn't Živkoviæ come looking for us anyway? We hadn't reported back to him and we were supposed to be going to the assistance of the helicopter.

Bob zagged to the left, or was that zigged? No matter; he was doing a good job here. I wondered why I hadn't heard any shots from the other boat, then Josie answered that one for me.

She shouted, 'Sam, I think they've run out of ammunition in that machine gun!'

'Might be a trick! Keep your head down Josie!' I shouted back.

If it *was* true that they had run out of ammo, they'd be resorting to handguns now.

Bob asked without looking at me, 'What are you planning?'

'Calling for help?' I'm looking at the digital readout on the radio and wondering if this is the frequency that we should on. Best keep it where it is. But what do I say?

'You know how to work it? You don't speak Croatian.....!'

I broke in. 'Bob, you worry too much! I can handle it!' I spotted a button on the mike and stabbed at it. I shouted frantically in Italian, 'Per favore c'aiuti! Noi richiediamo assistenza!' *'Please help us! We require assistance!'*

'What did you say!' he shouted.

I turned to him with a grin. 'Trust me! I know what I'm doing!' I didn't. I'm just playing this one by ear.

Just as Bob started to say something, the firing started again. Something hit us on the rear. I heard Josie return it, then, at last, a voice from the radio!

'Hello?' It was Živkoviæ. 'Why didn't you just use English!'

I said startled, 'Beg your pardon?' Oh shit! Why didn't I think of that? It's all this stress. Yeah that's it!

He said, 'Sit tight, we're on our way!'

'*What*!' I shouted. 'We're being shot at here!'

He said, 'Find the rocket launcher. It's......'

I cut him off with, 'Hey, been there, done that!' I laughed.

'Sorry!'

'Nothing.....!'

'You know how to use it?'

'Um.... well not really had a chance to....'

I was cut short by a loud bang behind me. That wasn't a gunshot! What the hell's going on? I turned to see Josie with the rocket launcher and smoke billowing from it! She's just fired a rocket, but where did it go? As far as I could see, our adversaries were still very much alive and gaining on us. I shouted, 'Josie, what are you doing! We've only three rockets left!'

I crept out from behind my seat and hunkered down beside her.

'Oh, hi!' is all she said. Then, 'It's OK. I'll get the hang of it.'

She reached out to grab another rocket when I stopped her. 'No way Josie! Stop it! We don't have time to "get the hang of it" for God's sake!'

She pushed me away. I lost my balance and fell over onto my left side!

Before I could recover she said, 'I'll fix them. You'll see!' She shouted as she grabbed another rocket.

I screamed, 'We don't have time for target practice Josie. Come on!'

She had the missile in place before I could stop her.

I made an attempt to grab her left arm, but instead I struck her on her wound. She screamed and grabbed the rocket launcher for support, but I guess her hand made contact with the trigger. It had been pointing straight up into the sky. There was a loud bang and the rocket flew heavenwards!

'Shit Josie! What have you done!'

I watched it soar and.... No! It had disappeared out of sight! Well I lost it. What, in a cloudless sky? Then I spotted it, as it was on it's way down again and heading, it seemed for us!

I dived towards the front and Bob sitting there. 'Go left!' I shouted at him.

'What!'

I looked up. It's going to hit us for sure! I shouted quickly, 'No! Go right!'

'What's going on.....!' he shouted back.

I didn't reply. Instead I grabbed the steering wheel and turned it quickly to the right. The craft made a sudden sharp turn and I fell across Bob's lap. The missile hit the water harmlessly only yards off the starboard side. Jesus!

'Back in a tick,' I said as I removed myself from Bob.

I heard him say, 'What's going on Sam!'

I returned to Josie. Bob was still zigzagging. Bullets still thudding into our stern but thankfully it seemed, harmlessly. Josie's just about to fire another rocket! Not if I can help it. We've only two left! I pulled the launcher over out of her grasp. It landed on the floor between us.

'Hey! What you doing!'

'Josie, you've got plenty of ammunition to use. The rifle?'

I picked the other rifle from its rack and made sure it was loaded and ready for use, then looked through the sights. I'm on the left side of the vertical seat back, she the right. We've both got our eyes at the sights now. With all this zigzagging and bouncing, I wasn't sure how I was going to hit anything at all, but it was necessary if we wanted to avoid being hit by their bullets. One of them just slammed into our stern and another hit the seat back. They'll be trying to conserve their ammo.

I said as I picked up the two policeman's helmets, 'Ever used one of those before!' I was referring to the rifle.

She took her eye from the finder to look at me. 'Pardon!'

I put one of the helmets on her head. 'The rifle!'

'Oh, cool,' she said in response to the helmet.

I asked quickly as I put the other helmet on my own head, 'Well have you!'

She put her right eye to the scope once more and said as cool as you like, 'Nope.'

I sighed. 'Jesus,' I whispered.

'How we going to hit anything with all this bouncing around!' She added, 'My scope's all fuzzy!'

'Switch on the side! It's autofocus!' I shouted.

'Hey, how cool is that!' she said putting her eye to the scope once more.

'Don't shoot to kill Josie! Not unless there's no other choice! Aim for the arm, or a leg if you can find one!'

She giggled.

I said, 'Got a plan!'

She turned with a look of curiosity.

I shouted to Bob to go dead slow. Thankfully he heard me this time and slowed right down, in fact he was almost stopped. Now they're gaining on us for sure. We have just seconds left to hit them and hopefully disable them.

I shouted to Josie, 'You take Milos, I'll take Boris! Shoot after three, OK!' My finger was on the trigger and my sights fixed on Boris' right shoulder. I'm going to hurt him like he hurt me. Yes, revenge is sweet! 'One, two, three!' Our shots hit their intended targets simultaneously. Boris clutched his shoulder with his other hand just as the craft spun out of control and veered off suddenly to our right.

'Yes!' we both shouted in unison.

I could see blue and red flashing lights now approaching fast. 'Here comes the cavalry at long last!' I said still keeping my head down.

The other craft turned right around and headed away from us and the approaching lights.

'Shit, they're getting away!' I shouted.

Before I could stop her, Josie had picked up the rocket launcher.

'No Josie! We don't want to kill them!'

I tried grabbing the weapon from her but she managed to discharge it anyway. She didn't have time to aim properly but at least this time it was pointing in their direction. It struck their stern with a thwunk! sound. Someone shouted a warning and all three figures on board jumped for their lives into the water, then the gas tank went up in a fireball; debris flying everywhere.

We both stood up and hugged each other tight, then, 'Ah!' She cried clutching her side.

I drew back apologising. I forgot. And that's when the cops arrived on the scene, too late as usual. I felt my own wound hurting too. My left shoulder was OK now but the right was hurting bad. We both started laughing when we saw these three jerks flounder in the water. We're not about to rescue them; that's the police's job.

Živković arrived now alongside us, while the other boat dragged the scum from the sea. He said, 'Well you've been busy again.' He smiled.

We both had broad grins plastered on. 'See you left the women to do all the cleaning up huh?' I laughed.

I heard Bob's voice behind say, 'Hey I played a part too remember.' He laughed.

I turned on my heal to face him and poked him in the chest. 'The guy sits in the chair while the women do all the work?'

Before he could reply, I kissed him full on the lips and just held on to him tight, then I felt my shoulder hurt again. I winced. He spotted it.

'Sam are you OK?' Then, 'Hey you've been shot!'

I nodded and a tear ran down my left cheek. Josie's standing there looking bored. She's jealous, I know it. Just because she couldn't get a guy.

Živković drove us back to the mainland and we were taken to a local hospital to have our wounds attended to. Josie's weren't serious and neither were mine thank God. As we emerged from the examination room, my two shoulders bandaged, Boris and Milos were sitting there with two armed guards and with long faces, their hands handcuffed in front of them, and their legs in shackles. They'll have even longer *prison* sentences ahead of them. I reckoned I had a score to settle with Boris though, and this would be my only opportunity to do it. There was no sign of the Boss anywhere.

As the two were standing up ready to go into the room, Milos ahead, I went up to him. 'Well you won't be needing the photos now will you.' I laughed in his face. 'I told you I would never give them to you!'

He just scowled back and looked away again. Then I approached Boris, but instead of speaking to him, I waited until he shuffled in the direction of the room, then I made my move. I tripped him up and he fell onto his right side, and yep, you guessed right; his damaged shoulder. He cried out and I thought I could see tears in his eyes as one of the policemen tried to restrain me. Just as well too because if I had my way, I'd have kicked him when he was down and the end result would not have been pretty.

I shouted, 'That's for hurting me!'

They picked him up and he was taken through the door.

Before we left for Pula that evening – yes Bob too. He wanted to go to the concert with us - Živkoviæ thanked us for bringing those thugs to justice, and wished us a safe and pleasant journey home. And I would be writing to Tomislav's mom later to tell her of the good news. I got my revenge at last. Well I said I would didn't I?

We caught an overnight bus to Pula because of the long nine hour journey. We stayed at a large hotel in the town just across the road from the Roman amphitheatre. We turned up at the gate that same night, and told the guy Dario our names as instructed and he let us in. Bob had to pay though. As we looked around for a suitable seat, someone took me by the arm and led me down close to the front row seats. Josie materialised on my left; Bob was nowhere to be seen. I kept looking around to see if I could spot him, but with no luck. Josie pulled on my arm, trying to get my attention. I turned to see Bob who had just arrived at our backs.

Oliver appeared now on the massive stage and stood before the microphone. The entire stage was beautifully lit up with multi-coloured lighting. The instruments had already been set up, and the band members assembled, then, after a signal from Oliver, they started to play. Then we all stood up and cheered, then we just swayed with the music. I think they were his own compositions as I hadn't heard any of them before, but they all had a typical Croatian melody and sung in that language. We thoroughly enjoyed ourselves that night. He's such an awesome singer and musician.

Before we went for our flight, the three of us had a meal at a restaurant in the airport. Bob just wanted say his goodbyes properly. He wasn't due to leave the country till later on in the week. We promised to write each other and keep in touch. There's nothing doing between us, just friends.

As far as Josie and I are concerned, we are planning our return trip to Croatia already, hopefully without the trauma and dangers that we experienced this time.

Gosh, I could do with a break after all that!

The End